Where Time Begins

Where Time Begins

A Novel

Sasha Paulsen

SHE WRITES PRESS

Published 2022
Printed in the United States of America
Print ISBN: 978-1-64742-413-8
E-ISBN: 978-1-64742-414-5
Library of Congress Control Number: 2021925157

For information, address:
She Writes Press
1569 Solano Ave #546
Berkeley, CA 94707

She Writes Press is a division of SparkPoint Studio, LLC.

"It is not down on any map; true places never are."
Herman Melville, *Moby Dick*

For Winneky and Rich, who thought of his name

# Foreword

You might ask me: Why am I writing this story when it happened so long ago and the world is so different now? Is it? You might ask, are any of these people still alive? Do these places still exist? I don't know the answers to many questions. My job is to ask them, listen to answers, and try to figure out if they are true or not. I do know that the impulse to share a story is strongest when we are in the dark and waiting for the light to return. Remarkably, yes, we are all still alive. Maybe it comes from finding an island where time begins.

—Shelley Ilillouette

1

There is an island in the Kingdom of Tonga that has risen above the surface of the ocean twice, and twice has sunk back beneath it. I know there are several explanations for why it did this, but here is the one I like: it changed its mind.

I was trying to figure out where the Kingdom of Tonga was when I read about this island in a yellowed newspaper cutting that had been stuck inside an old travel guide. There was no photo—the island must have been in a sinking stage at the time—but I could imagine it, a small new world, working its way to the surface, looking around at all that water, and wondering what to do next. Maybe it saw another island filled with noisy things, scurrying about, digging holes, and chopping down trees. It got worried: Were they contagious? When these busy creatures spied the new island, they hopped on a canoe and began speeding toward it. The island ducked out of sight. Then, however, it had a serious talk with itself about the importance of trying to live in the real world. It tried again and sank again.

I identified quite a bit with this island when I first read about it. Possibly, the reason I went to the Kingdom of Tonga was that island.

Choice really is the enemy of commitment. My brother David said that; he always has something to say. When he was an idealist, he used to quote Thoreau and say we had to wish to know an entire heaven and an entire earth, but now he is a congressman, and so he and Thoreau have parted ways on what constitutes an entire heaven and earth.

David is also big on the importance of living in the real world, but whenever he tells me to make an effort, I have to wonder how many people would buy his definition of real. It is odd to think that there must have been a time when you didn't have to wonder if you were living in the real world or just a confused imitation. When you didn't have to go searching for it like a Holy Grail, or examine each bit of your life and ask, is this real or not? When you couldn't help but live in the real world because that was all there was. Now, you can treat the world around you like an annoying mosquito. Repellents are available, some of which work better than others. You can design the world you prefer with or without news, rules, gods, or devils. Or you can hop a plane and fly away. You can sink back beneath the ocean. It's all your choice. Or is it?

It was in David's office that the Tonga business began. His main district office is in Santa Rosa, but he has satellites, including one in Vallejo, which is run by Penny and Gail, who think he is the greatest thing since the hot air balloon; still they always panic when he comes to town. This was why Penny called me on a Monday morning. David was arriving with only twenty-four hours' notice. They had scheduled him for meetings from ten till one and two till three but had nothing for him to do between one and two. Did I have any ideas? Also, Penny had an appointment with the mayor, and if Gail drove David, there would be no one in the office. She was too polite to say they knew I wouldn't be doing anything. She just wondered if I could come up and answer the phones.

In the old days, David used to be able to think of what to do from one till two all by himself and could even drive himself there, but I said maybe they could put him in a story hour at the library. But I also said OK. I borrowed Jesse Goldensohn's Volkswagen and headed north from San Francisco.

The Vallejo office is a no-frills cubbyhole that barely fits two desks, an American flag, and all the government brochures with useful information advising you to avoid the calamity of rabies and always wash your vegetables. On the wall is a photo of David, boy wonder and political Mozart, surrounded by The People. The sun is glowing off his golden head, his tie is straight, and even if he isn't wearing a jacket, he has one slung over his shoulder. It was the most acceptable picture anyone had taken of him at that point on account of the coat and tie. Still, it didn't please Dick, the latest hired genius who was reworking David's image with the goal of upgrading him to the Senate. Dick said the problem with the photo was that David looked undemocratically tall, young, and handsome alongside The People, who were all dumpy and peasant-like in comparison. Dick has a poll that shows a man does not like to vote for someone who is taller than he is. David is not really that tall, but I said maybe he could be amputated at the knees, and I believe Dick put the idea on his list of Viable Alternatives, which he is constantly revising.

Dick's other objection to the photo is that you can see David's eyes. No one can do anything about them, and it's not just that it would be preferable if they were blue, instead of brown, to go with his golden hair. His eyes have a gleam that no one has been able to extinguish. One glance at David's eyes and you know he is looking for trouble. You can envision, at his back, hordes of ancestors fleeing one political disaster or another. If it were not my intention to write the story of what happened when I accidentally went to Tonga, I could have filled this book with tales of predecessors who were burned in Spain, poisoned in Italy, beheaded in France, exterminated in Russia, and run out of Mexico. David, you might say, is fundamentally a repository for a collection of genes that have barely escaped being shot, hanged, stabbed, smothered, or in some other way put a period to. This might explain his predilection for meddling and his odd choice of work, but at least he had a job, something I could not say of myself.

I settled down at Penny's desk with a cup of coffee. No phones were ringing, so I put in a call to the Department of Health and Human Services.

"This is Congressman Ililouette's office," I said. "I'm calling for a constituent who would like to know if there is any help for the overly intelligent unemployed."

"Oh my," said the woman at the other end of the line. "Let me check." They always have to be polite if it is a congressional call.

"She would also like to know if she could be put in jail if she can't pay her bills."

"Oh, that would be Justice—well, of course not. Whom does she owe?"

"Everyone."

Another line began to ring. I put the woman on hold.

"Hello," said the new voice. "I am calling for my sister who is in the Kingdom of Tonga."

"Would you hold a minute?" I asked. The light for the HHS woman had gone out, and I must have pushed another wrong button for the Tonga caller, because her light disappeared too. I hate those phones.

Things began to get lively. A man wanted to know if David would chain himself to a rock to protest something, and I put this on a list of things he could do from one till two. Then I took three calls from people who were mad at the president, and only one believed it was still Nixon.

I said, "You know he resigned. A year ago. August 8, 1974."

"That's what you think."

"Yes. It is."

"How do you know?"

"It was in the newspapers."

"Newspapers print anything. How do you know he isn't still in the basement?"

He hung up before I could bring up another article I'd read pointing out that the chief threat to a democracy is voters.

Next I talked to fourteen women, all asking if it were true that David would be in town. I said I hadn't heard anything, a necessary precaution since the time an enthusiastic volunteer gave out his schedule and a dozen women showed up to discuss civic works with him. David had to climb out the back window to escape.

"Where is David?" Lally Packhorst, also known as the Bismarck, never gives her name, as she believes everyone should recognize her by her bellow. She is another reason an island might sink, if she sailed near it.

"No one knows."

"Is that Shelley?"

"Who?"

"Goodness, who let you answer David's phones? Shelley is David's little sister."

"Is that the one they keep in an attic?"

"Of course not! She is—well, she doesn't have her brother's looks or brains, of course, but she is a cute little thing. Who are you?"

"David's pet parakeet."

"The DC office said he is in Vallejo today. I can't think why—"

"He drove himself. Accidentally landed in his district."

"Tell him to call me."

"May I have your name and number, please?"

I knew this would make her nuts. She hung up.

Next, a woman called to report that her son, a Marine, was about to be murdered by his own unit and had to sleep with knives strapped to his ankles for protection. She believed it had to do with his secret undercover work. "He is just the all-American boy," she said. You never know what might be true; I called the Marine liaison, who promised to check it out.

"Hello," the next caller said, "I am calling for my sister who is in the Kingdom of Tonga."

Then all the lights went on, and I lost her again. Health and Human Services was calling to apologize because I'd hung up on them. Another caller wanted to know if it was illegal to raise his rent. "Probably not," I said. "There's no rent control."

"Then what's the point of wage and price guidelines?"

"No one knows. But—"

"I don't know why you can't tell me. I pay your salary with my taxes, and I want to know if this means I can raise the price of anything as much as I want."

"Yes, you can, but it doesn't mean anyone would buy it. Why don't I ask someone in Washington to—"

"I'd like to talk to someone who knows something," he huffed, and I was sorry I hadn't hit a wrong button for him too. "Here I am calling my congressman and you are just fogging."

"That's interesting," I said. "Not too many people use fog as a verb, but technically I believe it's correct."

He hung up. I started a new list of Lost a Vote and called the library. "This is Congressman Ilillouette's office. Do you know where the Kingdom of Tonga is? Is it in Africa?"

"Oh my," the librarian replied. "I will have to check with my supervisor. May I ask her to call you back?"

"Certainly."

I recognized the next soft, melancholy voice. Adam checks in regularly with Penny and Gail to let them know he is standing on the San Andreas fault line. He had a traumatic experience as a flight controller in the Air Force, when he saw two blips collide on his screen; for ten minutes he thought it was his fault. It turned out to be only a technical screwup and no planes were anywhere around, but he's never been the same since. He was discharged from the Air Force but can't get disability benefits. The Air Force's position is that they don't doubt Adam is cuckoo, but he has not proved it was their fault. They have a list of about eight thousand things Adam is supposed to do, including getting a letter from God testifying that he went crazy in the Air Force. Penny and Gail are working on it. I found his file and told him they were about halfway there. He said OK; things were quiet on the fault that day.

"This is Marlene Foster-Thomas, head librarian," the next caller announced. "I am returning a call to Congressman Ilillouette."

"Oh."

"Or is it only you?"

"It's only me."

She talked to me anyway. "It took some research to find the Kingdom of Tonga," she reported. "Because of its position, it is often cut off maps or lost in the crease of books. The Kingdom of Tonga is in the South Pacific."

I had the buttons pretty well under control by the time the Marines called back. You may have noticed that one of the impressive things about a congressional office is that everyone calls back. It's probably why I let Penny and Gail talk me into answering their phones, just to know that somewhere in the world, someone is getting called back.

"I have checked out the case for you," reported a man who identified himself as a colonel-general-admiral or something equally grand. "I am sorry to have to tell you that the young man in question may not be one-hundred-percent Marine. In fact, he is a young man who, when he should use tact, uses his fists."

Apparently, the all-American boy had a tendency to start fights with anyone who stood within three feet of him for any reason. Also he read novels, which gave him a confused notion of reality, the man said. "And that is not the Marine way. I am sorry if he gave you a different impression, but allow me to assure you that if he had been participating in covert intelligence activities related to apprehending purveyors of illegal substances, he would have been strenuously protected, guarded, and shielded."

I could have listened to this guy piffle all day, but another line lit up, and so I only said I was glad to know that the other one-hundred-percent Marines were out there using tact instead of their fists. He laughed. He had to; Congress votes on his budget.

"Hello." The caller spoke rapidly. "I am calling for my sister who is in the Kingdom of Tonga. I don't know why she wanted me to call Congressman Ilillouette and why she thought he would help her, but she has always been eccentric. She is an artist, and she married a Frenchman. She would like the congressman to find her a companion."

"To live in the South Pacific?"

The woman was impressed. "Most people think Tonga is in Africa. I apologize for taking up your time, but I did tell her I would do it, although I was surprised that she would call from half a world away and insist I call a congressman instead of Ann's Household Agency."

"It's all right. Last week, a man called because he needed a recipe for potato salad."

"I know Congressman Ilillouette is one of the good ones, but I don't know why he would know who could help Bette look for a lost island. I'm sure it's one of her legends. She collects them."

"And she married a Frenchman too."

"You understand. She will pay all the travel expenses. Actually, I will, and she will pay me back, I hope."

Another line began to ring, but I ignored it until she said I could put her on hold. It was a call from someone in Elko, Nevada, who had a party of aliens ready to land on Earth. They would solve all of the problems in the world, but they were too polite to land without an invitation. Would the congressman oblige? I put this on the Viable Alternatives list and then went back to the woman with a sister in the Kingdom of Tonga.

"To tell you the truth," I said, "the congressman might not be the best person to find her a companion; his specialty is radical judges and useless bureaucrats. But, as a suggestion I might make if, for instance, we were standing in the street, he does have a sister who might be able to recommend someone. She might even be interested in the job herself."

"Wouldn't she be too busy?"

"No."

"What an excellent idea."

I agreed and gave her my home telephone number.

The fog was rolling in thick and cold by the time Penny and Gail returned. They said everything had worked out, including one till two. David had bought them lunch at Lady Jane's Soul Food. They just love David.

They had driven him back to Santa Rosa and returned with three boxes of things Dick was throwing out because they were unsuitable to David's new image: a plaque with a large, dead, gilded fish presented to him by the North Bay Fishermen; the brass sheep with a clock in its stomach from the Future Farmers of America; the congressional seal Mrs. Biagini had made from painted seashells after David's staff found her lost Social Security check; and the thirty-two drawings of octopuses sent to him by the third graders at the Hook's Bay Elementary School after he visited their class to talk about What the Government Does. Dick had also banished David's collection of mermaid statues and all the photos of Gabriella Asher.

The largest photo was of David and Gabby driving down Highway 1. David was wearing the weird hat Gabby had crocheted for him from rainbow yarn; when it stretched out of shape, he'd bunched up the extra in a rubber band and kept wearing it. It was the car David was driving as much as the hat that had upset Dick. David had bought his Alfa Romeo with the money he made from publishing his senior honors thesis about the future of the world—was there one or not. He was crazy about that car; he kept it his first year in Congress. He used to take it out at night and drive fast down Highway 1. When he had to go somewhere in public, he rented a Chevy. It's gone now.

Dick had also chucked out the photo of David and Gabby on a sailboat, which the staff called "Apollo and Aphrodite in Hawaii." The problem with this one, in addition to its being a photo of David with a woman who is not his wife, is that if you look closely, you might notice that Apollo has bright red toenails. After David got elected to Congress, Gabby painted them so he wouldn't forget her when he went to DC. The toenails almost killed Dick; he couldn't believe that the picture had sat on David's desk, and he'd still been reelected twice.

"Even this one went." Gail held up a tiny, framed photo that David had snapped of Gabby dancing ahead of him on a path on a mountain above the ocean. You could see only the back of her, but you could tell from the way she held her arms and head that she was dancing. Gabby was always dancing.

"Of course, Dick is right; he shouldn't keep pictures of her on his desk." Penny sighed, sadly, as if Gabby had died and not just gone the way of the Alpha. "I wonder how she is."

"I wonder where she is," Gail said.

"Is anything left in the office?" I asked.

Penny showed me the new official photo. It was David with a group of ranchers, looking serious about cows. He was leaning over to pat a cow, so he looked as short as everyone else, and the photographer had caught him with the sun in his eyes.

"Awful, isn't it?" Gail asked. "But we told him not to worry about his things. We'll put them in Penny's garage. Except the clock. We needed a clock."

"And the seashell seal," Penny added. "It really is patriotic. I know it made him happy. He wanted us to stay because he is taking the Santa Rosa staff out to dinner because no one murdered Dick today, but we said no, we needed to let you go home. But you should go, Shelley! David said he hoped to see you sometime. Well, he said he should put you on his payroll."

They both laughed when I agreed. But I said no, I wouldn't go to dinner because if Dick had his way, I'd end up in a box in Penny's garage too. They laughed again and said I was just the all-American girl. They always say that. It always kills me.

2

An hour later I was back in San Francisco, and by evening I'd found a parking place near Jesse Goldensohn's flat. A man on the sidewalk was wearing a sandwich board announcing a special on being reborn. "The Dark Ages are over!" he called. "The Age of Aquarius is finally nigh!"

"How nigh?" I asked. It's true that people were recycling paper to save the trees and making whole wheat bread without preservatives, and if you couldn't eat it, you could use it as a doorstop. Also, I was pretty sure that Nixon was no longer president. But by this year, 1975, the Age of Aquarius had been a long time coming.

He offered me his discount for the unemployed, but I said I could probably do it myself with a snorkel in a bathtub, and I ducked into Mother Earth's Produce to end the conversation. I was wondering what it would be like to be half a world away, and I must have been squeezing the pineapples because all of a sudden Mother Earth herself was frowning at me. I apologized.

"Oh no," she replied instantly. "Please, feel free. It's so important to feel the energy of the things you buy. Let me show you how I do it. I pick up something in each hand and I feel its energy. And I can tell which is the right one for me."

She demonstrated by feeling the energy of two tomatoes, although it looked like squeezing to me. "Try it."

She put two lemons in my hands, and I felt their energy. "Wow," I said. "I think the left one is a nuke."

"The worst part is she believed me," I told Jesse as I returned his car keys. "I'll bet she wouldn't have any problems getting her VA benefits."

"Have you had dinner?"

Considering my larder and the prospect of one more peanut butter sandwich, I followed Jesse into his flat, which resembles a used bookstore, every wall covered with books. He is a great cook and also a poet; his pasta is as poetical as his sonnets. While the water boiled for linguine, I watched him concoct a sauce of herbs, garlic, and olive oil. We didn't have to talk.

I've known Jesse ever since the time David tried to take a bus into Oakland, looking for a girl he was crazy about. He was sixteen. He got lost, but Jesse rescued him. I don't know if they ever found the girl, but David brought Jesse home. Jesse had never been to the ocean. Sometimes I think I could pass David in the street, and I might not recognize him until he shook my hand and asked me for my support, but Jesse is the same as he was that first day he came to my grandfather's house above the sea: short, slight, and the color of a Hershey's chocolate bar. I was nine and I had never met someone who was such a beautiful color. I couldn't resist nibbling his finger a little, to see what he tasted like. David almost strangled me, but Jesse said it was OK. I almost fell in love with Jesse, when I believed in things like that.

He opened a bottle of wine, added some to his sauce, and poured two glasses. "Any good news?"

"The Dark Ages might be over. I am not sure, however."

"Did you talk to David?"

"No."

"He might have an idea for you."

"And we know how well it worked out the last time he had an idea."

"One disaster doesn't mean you should give up."

I wasn't sure which one disaster he meant, although it was probably my sole job interview, which had turned out to be with a man who thought David should be tarred and feathered.

"It's OK, Jesse. I've decided I'm going to be a posthumous writer."

"Then you have to write something, besides letters to the editor for David's constituents."

"Some of them were good."

"Masterpieces of fiction."

"No, they are all true. And each person liked their letter. Even Crazy Dick liked them. He has a list of people who will sign letters if I write them. I just don't know if I can do it."

"Is your conscience finally catching up with you?"

"No, it's just that my brain is frozen. There's nothing left in it. No passion, no sense of adventure, no wonder, except when I wonder what's going to happen to me. No hope, no spirit, no food—"

He drained the pasta and was tossing it with the sauce. He served up two plates and grated cheese over them. I was momentarily distracted from my list.

"You could get married," he said.

I gagged. "Why?"

"Most women want to get married."

"Yeah, and you're the expert on women."

"Isn't Jackson coming back soon?"

"I don't know."

"Hasn't he written to you?"

"What kind of herbs are these?"

"He's coming to San Francisco, isn't he?"

"So what?"

"I wouldn't mind seeing him."

"He's not your type."

"That's too bad. Those blue eyes. All those muscles. I bet he'll look good after all that time in the mountains."

"Unless he froze his nose off." I gave myself another serving of pasta.

"Too bad he is in love with a redheaded woman with big brown eyes."

"I don't know what difference that makes."

"Shelley, don't be an ass. It's the only thing that does make a difference, but it's up to him to explain it. He just had to work up his nerve by climbing Mount Everest first."

"It's not Everest. It's a little weird mountain called Gunga Din or something like that. Besides, there are always avalanches."

"You really are scared to death of him, aren't you?" Jesse laughed, although I didn't see what was so funny.

"I just don't want to see him right now, that's all. But come to think of it, I might marry you." I didn't really mean it, but I knew it would make him pipe down about Jackson. "If I ate your cooking every day, I might be able to think of something to write. And your being gay wouldn't be a problem. Gay men are the only ones you can have intelligent conversations with. I can live without sex. I might be the only person in California who can, but I can."

Jesse frowned. Sex, really, is the only thing he is touchy about. "You must be missing your cat. That's always when you propose."

This is a sensitive subject for me, and so we ate in silence until I remembered the Kingdom of Tonga. Jesse had never heard of it either, but he found, among his books, a travel guide to the South Pacific. Tonga got two pages titled "Where Time Begins."

3

My neighbor was waiting at my door. We shared the top floor of a Victorian that had been cut up into flats, the smallest of which were the two stuffed in the attic. Toby followed me into my half, as was his habit. He had run away from a privileged upbringing in Connecticut, although he had not entirely succeeded in leaving his childhood behind.

"Damn," he said. "I really miss your cat. Do you know what I miss? The way he used to sit by the door and take a swing at me whenever I walked in."

While I folded my bed up into the wall, which made room to unfold a table and chair, Toby sat down on the floor. The room did not have such things as a kitchen or a bathroom—these were down one floor—but it did have a fireplace with a screen. He put this between us.

"I have to control myself," he said. "So, what do you think of my hair?" He had shaved it in clumps so that it resembled the surface of the moon.

"It's great."

"But I can't decide whether to go orange or purple. Or red. Then we could match. Did I ever tell you I'm crazy about redheads?"

"Yes."

"I went out once with someone as old as you. No, even older. She was twenty-four. Did I tell you about her?"

"Yes."

"Oh. Well, I didn't tell you I almost got arrested last night."

"What for?"

"Drunk driving. They had to let me go, though."

"Why? Weren't you drunk?"

"Oh hell, yes, but I wasn't driving, only sitting. They can't arrest you for drunk sitting. And I had fifteen joints and a gram of coke on me, and they never found it. I hid it in my underwear. I was going to save some of it for you, but I didn't. Sorry."

I said it was all right he hadn't saved me any of the cocaine he had stored in his underwear. I tried cocaine once, but it only made me feel the same way I felt when I accidentally walked into a door frame nose first.

"Oh yeah, I got your mail." He pulled a battered envelope out of his pocket. "It's from Nepal. I think it's from that guy. Would you like me to read it?"

"No."

"Shall I toss it?"

"No."

"Do you want to get drunk? Loaded? Loose?"

The phone began to ring. "Oh, my God, it's him," Toby gasped. "He's back." He collapsed backward, screen and all, knocking the phone onto the floor. I recognized the voice of the woman, faintly warbling hello.

When I hung up, I told him it was only a woman wondering if I might be interested in a job in the Kingdom of Tonga, South Pacific.

"Oh wow, Paradise! I'll go with you." First, however, he had to go out for his nightly carousing.

When he was gone, I picked up the envelope he had dropped. It was blue airmail paper with a cluster of green and burgundy stamps and Jackson's unmistakable writing.

Climbing in the Himalayas had been the dream of Jackson's life, ever since he knew they existed. He'd finally gotten a chance when Gavin Chandler invited him to join an expedition. Gavin is twenty years older than Jackson and taught him most of what he knows about mountaineering—what mountains haven't taught him, anyway. Gavin had gone on expeditions to Everest twice and had nearly died twice. Before he tried a third time, he wanted to climb a different mountain. It was only twenty-seven thousand feet high, but no one had climbed it yet.

He was going during the brief window in autumn. Jackson had come to see me to discuss it; he knew if anyone would agree it was a good idea to take time off from med school to climb a mountain, it would be me. He was something of a wreck, skinny, pale, and nervous. I was not in much better shape, however, as I had just arrived in DC to stay with David and his wife. I am not much good at civilization, although Jackson is worse.

I'd not heard from him since they landed in Kathmandu. He'd written a long, funny letter about monkeys at the airport and the people on whom his life would depend when they were halfway up the mountain. It was a trifle mushy, but I knew that was just in case he fell into a crevasse. Now, he'd written another letter, but it was thin. I held the envelope up to the light, but I couldn't make out any words. I put it down and opened the guide to the South Pacific. Folded inside it was a faded newspaper clipping about the disappearing island.

Tonga was described as an archipelago of one hundred and seventy islands, give or take one. On the map, it looked like a broken string of pearls, scattered over five hundred miles, from north to south. Because they were the country closest to the international dateline, the Tongan king had decided this was where time began, and apparently no one had argued with him. No one had told him that time is only a convenient illusion we paste over the surface of things; time can't begin any more than it can be recaptured. I probably would not try to explain this either to someone who weighed more than four hundred pounds.

The night wind was blowing hard against the window, rattling it, rustling the trees. I used to think that the wind was a mysterious thing that had the power to break through walls and set anything free. On nights like this, my cat would disappear out the window and I would run after him. He would wait and spring out at me from behind a hedge, and we would roam together down the streets until it didn't seem like we were in a city at all, but a vast, wild, enchanted place filled with mystery and possibilities. Life took on a shimmering quality in such a wind, of something to be caught and held and let go to fly again. Jackson and his mountains were part of this world; so were Jesse's silver-spun words and David's dauntless old ideals. They had been things of magic for me, but they were lost now, and even their ghosts were beyond recall. It was only a cold, empty wind blowing this night, and I decided to go to the kingdom.

4

The Peace Corps had been singing for two days. They knew one Tongan song and the soundtrack from *The Wizard of Oz*. They had sung these from San Francisco to Honolulu, from Honolulu to Pago Pago, and from Pago Pago to Neiafu, Vava'u, in the Kingdom of Tonga, even though on the last leg of the flight we were traveling upside down through a hurricane on a fluttering gnat of an airplane.

I often wish I'd studied physics so I wouldn't have to wonder why a plane doesn't blow apart at times like this or why a metal tube can fly at all, under any circumstances. This day I worried even more, due to the cheerful oblivion of the lunatics around me. An average person would have left off singing as we dipped and rolled through the sky, but I understand that the Peace Corps is where they send incurable optimists and enthusiasts for life. They kept on singing.

We began to dive at a speed that caused the singers to hit a few odd notes. My brain thawed rapidly during this descent, uncovering various items that had frozen there, chiefly a reverence for life. I rediscovered it with faint joy, the way you might find a trash can lid that got buried in snow during a long winter. Like a reprieve, an island appeared.

I called it an island hopefully because it could also have been a whale covered with coconut trees. We bounced over their tops, and when we ran out of land, we careened upward. The Peace Corps faltered in their song. The pilot came on the intercom: "Sorry about that missed approach!" he chortled. "You might have felt those winds! I'm going to try again, but if I don't make it this time, we'll have to return to Pago before we run out of gas!"

Again we zoomed downward, upside down. I might have fainted because the next thing I knew we had landed.

The airport was a single cement block room that quickly emptied as the Peace Corps nuts were borne away in the back of a truck, singing in the storm. The only person left was the customs agent, a man wearing a blue wraparound skirt with his shirt and tie. He smiled at me, and I smiled back. Until this moment I'd been so concerned with landing myself here, I'd not thought about where I was going. Or what I was doing.

I had met the woman whose sister wanted a companion. I said I could leave right away; my rent was due. She gave me a ticket and two hundred dollars, and said she would let Bette Omont know I was on my way. I offered to pay Jesse back the money he'd loaned me, but he said to wait. He gave me a sack of books, Maugham, Stevenson, *The Tempest*, and *A Guide to the Wildlife of the South Pacific*. He drove me to the airport and kissed me goodbye. When I thought about changing my mind, he shoved me in the right direction. Sometimes I think that when you almost fall in love, you never really fall out of it.

On the plane I reread Jesse's guidebook. I was going to Neiafu, the main town on the Vava'u islands, the northernmost in the kingdom, considered the most lush and beautiful. Most of the Tongan population, including the royal family, lived on Tongatapu, in the south where the capital, Nuku'alofa, was located. Between Vava'u and Tongatapu, a third group of islands, the Hai'pai group, was mostly uninhabited.

Now I was here, alone, and no one might speak English. I could see nothing but rain, and the sun was setting.

"You are lost?" the agent asked, still smiling.

Some of the racket in my brain calmed down. "I am waiting for someone to meet me. Bette Omont."

"Oh, this is too bad."

"It is? Why?"

"Because she is not here. And there is her island." He pointed at shadowy trees, blowing about wildly.

"Island? She lives on an island?"

"We all live on islands," he observed. "But she lives on a very small one, and if you try to go there now—flip!—you will die. Perhaps you would like to go to a hotel."

This seemed a preferable alternative to flipping and dying, and soon I was in a canvas-covered Jeep taxi, bouncing along a crushed coral road through a green landscape, rendered blurry by the storm. The driver said for hotels I had my choice of the fancy Port of Refuge or the *fales*, huts by the sea. I opted for the fales.

We stopped amidst a cluster of thatched-roof cottages, scattered like mushrooms in a garden of many-colored flowers and towering coconut trees. I couldn't see the ocean, but I could feel it on the wind. A woman wearing a long black dress took my suitcase from the driver as they chatted in cheerful, incomprehensible Tongan. I gave the driver some money. They laughed heartily and he gave most of it back. We all shook hands and he drove away. I followed the woman to a hut framed by red hibiscus blossoms. "Your fale," she said, and she disappeared into the rain.

It was one room with a window, walls, a light, and a bed, yet the familiarity of these items only emphasized their strangeness. The window had no glass, the light was a solitary dangling bulb, and the walls were covered with rough brown cloth painted with black geometric designs and stick figures. The bed was covered with the same cloth.

The world outside was dark, rain was drumming on the tin roof, and the coconut trees were swaying like giant wands with feathered star tips. I sat down on the bed. Sometimes you start something and then you have to go through with it before you can get out, like the time Jackson and I went into the World Famous Cave of Horror and Wonder at the Napa County Fair even though signs warned us that once in, there was no turning back. Just inside the dark, hot tent, we came face-to-face with a one-eyed monster who had a hatchet in his head and blood dripping down his face. "Get out of my cave," he growled. We ran. We lost each other, our money, and most of our wits before we got out of that place. We never knew if there had been any wonders.

This reminded me that Jackson's letter, still unopened, was in my pocket. I took it out. It was addressed to "Miss Shelley Ilillouette." I traced the letters the way I used to when he wrote to me after he'd been sent away to school in England. I thought his handwriting was extremely elegant, and I'd imitated it in my letters back to him. He had been miserable then, homesick and sad, but now he slipped in and out of foreign places as easily as the wind, and I was the coward who couldn't even look at my own thoughts, let alone his.

"I had to do something," I said to the envelope. "You might be in San Francisco by now. You might have come to see me. You might have said something like, 'How are you?' So, here I am, and I have to go through with it. Otherwise, I'll just be in more debt for one plane ticket, one taxi, one hotel, and three bags of M&Ms with peanuts." I eat M&Ms when I get anxious; I had finished them all before I got to Hawaii.

I heard a polite cough. A young Tongan woman was standing outside the glassless window. I didn't know how long she had been there, but apparently she hadn't wanted to interrupt while I talked to my letter. She carried in a tray, set it down, smiled, and left. It dawned on me there might be advantages in being where no one spoke English.

On the tray was a pot of tea, buttered toast, a cup, a knife, two clamshells holding sugar and jam, and one yellow hibiscus blossom. Jackson, being one-half Brit, tends to view tea as a cure-all, at least for half of him. He has other cure-alls for the half that isn't British, but I won't go into that now. I poured tea, added sugar from the clamshell, stirred it with the knife, and wondered if I'd feel better or worse if I read his letter. Finally, I put it back in my suitcase and opened the notebook I'd brought. It was filled with blank pages and likely to remain so.

The rain was lightening up and I stepped outside. The air was warm and so heavy it seemed you could catch it and hold it in your hand. The path we'd followed to my fale went on to a wooden shelter where a family of pigs was rooting in the mud. Chickens were wandering among them. A goat was bleating and trying to eat the rope that tied it to a tree. A woman, dressed in black with a coarse woven mat tied around her waist, was stripping the edges of long, thin leaves with a machete. It was a peregrine landscape that could have turned any other I'd known into shadows, had it not been for the Peace Corps volunteers who filled the other fales around me. "Oh, God, we are in Paradise!" they were exclaiming. "Now I don't have to worry about going to Heaven!" and "Toto, we're not in Kansas anymore!"

5

In the morning, it was raining again. I was watching coconut trees blow sideways when the same smiling girl who'd brought tea the night before appeared at the window.

"*Malo e lelei*," she said. This is the Tongan greeting. I had read in my guidebook that it means "thank you for living." Tongans might vary it and say thank you for cooking or sweeping or anything else you might be doing, but she said thank you for living and added, "I have brought you a *palangi* breakfast."

I opened the door, and she came inside, studying me with a curiosity that matched my own. I wondered what she saw. Like *taxi* and *hotel*, the word *woman* is manifest in quite a few forms. She was built like a rugby player, but she moved like a dancer, in a long pink calico dress. She had a round, glowing face, and she wore purple flowers in her waist-length hair. In comparison to her, I felt like a shipwrecked wooden figurehead that had lost its paint, its arms, and its ears. "I am Lebeca," she said.

"Shelley Ililiouette."

"Seli," she repeated. In Tongan you can't put two consonants together, and this is how I became Seli.

"You speak English?" I asked, trying to remember what I'd been saying to my letter the night before.

"Of course! I did not wish to disturb you last night when you were praying, but now I shall tell you that I am the best at speaking English, and so you can ask me, oh, questions and anything like that." As she talked, she was uncovering the tray that held tea and flowers, half of a papaya, and a plate of spaghetti on toast.

"What is palangi?" I asked.

She laughed in a rippling way. "Do you not know yourself?"

Palangi, she explained, means cloud-burster, which is what Tongans thought the first white visitors were, owing to the fact that they had come sailing through the clouds on their large boats. It's too bad, really, that Tongans didn't have a word for tourist at the time. Cloud-burster has a magical clout that a mere tourist can't equal. Possibly, then, these visitors would not have been seen as such superior creatures, and Tongans would not have accepted so reverently all the bits of Western ways that landed with them. I figured this out later; at the time I just ate my spaghetti on toast.

"It's quiet," I said. "What happened to the Peace Corps? Did you chloroform them?"

"Oh, it is very sad, but they only came here for one night. Today, they go to stay with Tongan families." She described them for me: who did what, who had bathed, and who did not wear underwear. I thought she had the makings of a fine journalist, but actually I was being introduced to the coconut wireless, an intelligence network that could humble the CIA. I wondered if part of her mission was to fill in a few missing facts on me. She asked me where I'd come from and if California was close to Kansas. When I asked where the shower was, she nodded approvingly.

"Do you know Mrs. Omont?" I asked.

"Oh." Her voice became guarded. "Sometimes."

"I hope she wears underwear."

"This I do not know, but she does not go to church. It is why she has ghosts."

"She does?"

Lebeca nodded.

"I am going to work for her, you know."

"Yes, and I am so sorry."

"Because of the ghosts?"

"No, because she is not here."

"Where is she?"

Lebeca shrugged. "Palangis are like little bugs that always must be hopping about."

"She lives on her own island?"

"A small one, not so far from here. Kalavite will take you in his boat. He is the brother of Moses, who brought you here. But you cannot go today, of course. It storms."

"I know. Flip, I die."

After breakfast, I set out to find the post office to send a telegram telling Mrs. Omont's sister I was here, but Mrs. Omont was not. I followed the crushed coral road through a patchwork of houses, eclectic creations of wood, tin, and coconut fronds. Everywhere were flowers, yellow, red, lavender, and pink. I also saw curious designs in the ground made of round brown stones, all surprisingly uniform. I passed a great many chickens, squawking beneath shelters, and pigs wandering happily in the rain. About every four feet was a church.

"Hello, palangi," children called. "Hello, hello." When I asked where the post office was, they laughed and ran away, but one called back that I'd find it around the corner from the church. Since I had nothing else to do, I figured I had time to turn all the corners near churches, but around my first corner, I found, instead, a mountain.

By Himalayan standards, it wasn't much of a mountain, more of a bump whose top had been sliced off, neat as a cucumber, but on those Kansas-flat islands anything that ripples the horizon is a mountain.

"Oh, you are lost!" Lebeca sprinted up, carrying an umbrella.

"No," I said, "I'm going to the post office around the corner from the church."

"Why did you not tell me, so I could go with you? Now, you are alone and lost, but I have found you. We will go."

We walked on together, Lebeca diligently holding her umbrella over my head. We visited three churches and Burns Phillips, the Tongan Macy's. Next we went to her grandmother's house where a half-dozen women were sitting beneath shelters in the garden, pounding on logs with wooden paddles. They were making tapa cloth, Lebeca explained; this was the brown fabric that lined the walls of my fale.

Lebeca introduced me, from which I gleaned that my job in Tonga was to bring Mrs. Omont to church and that I was not afraid of ghosts. Lebeca's grandmother brought me a light snack of tea, pineapple cake, jelly roll, papayas, bananas, and tomatoes. She wanted to open a can of spaghetti for me, but I said I preferred bananas, although I had to eat four before she believed me.

A woman put a yellow hibiscus blossom in my hair, and everyone clapped; another gave me a pair of woven slippers with purple straw pompoms on the toes. Lebeca's grandmother gave me her teacup because I said it was pretty. She also wanted me to take her goat because I'd admired it too, but I had to turn it down because I didn't think I could take a goat to Mrs. Omont's island; then everyone cried because I would be leaving.

Only one woman did not join in the ruckus. She sat apart, bent over her work, painting in black on a brown square of tapa cloth.

"She is Mafi," Lebeca whispered. "Many women paint tapa cloth, but Mafi is an artist. Come. Look."

We went closer. Mafi looked up. Her face had none of the round-ness, the affable openness of the others. Her bones were nearly break-ing through her skin, and her eyes were so deep set they would have been hidden if they had not been so large. They fixed on me as if she were observing the state of my heart, lungs, and liver, as well as the tangle inside my head. Jackson has the same look sometimes, although I've never really worried that he can read my thoughts. He has enough trouble figuring them out if I explain them.

I did not know about Mafi's illness then. I only noticed that in this group, she was like a spindly sapling in an orchard of blooming peach trees. Her faded black gown hung about her thin frame, and her hands had the substance of spiderwebs, more delicate than the border she was finishing around her painting of a mountain that rose from a stormy sea. Peering out from a cave in the mountain was a woman with long, wild hair. In the sea below her was an octopus that could have been the woman's sister.

"It's beautiful," I said.

She bent her head. "Bette Omont is my friend," she murmured. Her voice was polished but halting, as if she would rather paint than talk. "Perhaps, you will walk with me."

Despite her fragile appearance, Lebeca and I had to sprint to keep up with her as we left the garden. "You have come to visit Bette?" she asked.

"Not exactly. She asked her sister to hire a companion."

"Companion? Can you purchase a friend in America?" She smiled, but it was a flicker, a candle's flame in the wind, gone in an instant.

"Do you know where she is?"

"No, perhaps the answer is at *Ile Perdue*—"

"A lost island?"

Mafi halted. Far down the road, a solitary figure was approaching us. "It is my husband coming for me," she said. "I will go now, but perhaps you will come to my house tomorrow for tea." She hurried off.

"Mafi has lived much with palangis," Lebeca said, as if this explained a multitude of oddities. "Now we will go to the post office, Seli."

"Are you sure? Isn't there any place else we should visit first? How about the hospital?"

"Do you wish this?" she asked.

"No! No, I will live without visiting a hospital."

Only then did we get to the post office. Three cousins joined us there. Lebeca cautioned me not to be embarrassed if they watched while I wrote my telegram to my *mafu*. "Sweetheart," she translated, and they all broke into a chorus of "Love Me Tender."

"But I don't have a mafu."

Lebeca's eyes widened. Evidently, this was as calamitous as my being lost. I changed the subject. "Where do we find the guy who could take me to Mrs. Omont's island?"

"Perhaps we must find you a mafu instead," Lebeca offered, and everyone giggled, except me. The palangi in line in front of us turned around. He was young; he had more acne than beard. His hair was scraggly and faintly red, as if it had been stained with unripe tomatoes. In his dark suit and tie, he resembled an overheated, nervous, pink rabbit.

"Pardon me," he whispered, "did you say you are going to Mrs. Omont's island?"

Clearly he was not on the coconut wireless. "I am trying to."

"May I escort you?"

"Do you have a boat?"

"No, but God will provide one."

"He will?"

"God provides everything if you are doing His work."

"No kidding? Well, Paradise is His district, after all."

An umbrella poked me in the back. It belonged to a woman swathed in white plastic rain gear, spattered with mud. I could only see her eyes, narrow but fiery. "God," she said in ominous tones, "does not look kindly on flippant remarks about His kingdom."

She turned her stern look to the young man, who flinched, as if he had been caught in an unnatural act, like clapping at the wrong time at the symphony or talking sensibly to the press. "And you, young man, should know better."

He withered, and I wondered, know better than what? I've never figured out how people who cast down these judgments have gotten up to their lofty place to begin with. It's like David's political geniuses who are so sure they have figured everything out and believe that by manipulating the details—the color of his socks and the part of his hair—they can create the big picture. They don't work for him; they take possession of him until I think they believe he sprang full-grown out of their heads. I've watched them sweat and fidget when he deviates from their prepared texts or tarries too long to talk to someone of no consequence. While I doubt that anyone would argue that he's not a necessary part of the show—like the microphone, there's always a hullabaloo if he is not around when it begins—would he exist without them?

As for the woman in vinyl, her candidate, apparently, was God. I was sure she could tell anyone where He stood on any issue and would have no qualms about making Him change out of His favorite tie, if it was a giant salmon painted by a woman who was not

His wife. The kid, on the other hand, was the enthusiastic volunteer who got to pass out flyers and, if he was lucky, shake the hand of the candidate's sister. All in all, it might explain why God made such infrequent public appearances these days and preferred to hide out in the celestial Camp David.

"Where is this lost island?" I asked Lebeca.

"You must ask Mafi. It is very wonderful that she wishes you to come to tea. Mafi is of a noble family."

"Well," I said, "I'm a shirt-tail relative of Lucretia Borgia, myself, through my great-grandfather, Father Orsi, who was famous for stealing the horse of the only Protestant in his village." This was true, even if I was only saying it for the benefit of God's advance team, who appeared to be eavesdropping even as they were discussing why the kid should know better than to wish to go to Mrs. Omont's island.

6

"Is there a trail up the mountain?" I asked Lebeca as we returned to the fales.

"The mountain?"

"Well, the half-mountain. I'd like to climb it. Just to think."

"To think? But it rains, Seli, and you will be alone. Now, I must work, but perhaps tomorrow we will go with you, Salote and Tupou and I, to climb a mountain. To think."

I said OK, and when we parted, I set out on the crushed coral road that led away from the town into the dense green landscape called the bush. There, the mountain disappeared. I don't know how mountains can do this, but they can. Herzog even lost Annapurna on his way to climb it. I was wondering where this one could have got to when a man appeared, strolling leisurely in the rain. He resembled a sturdy, silver-topped tree wearing a green shirt, a brown wraparound skirt and a mat tied around his waist. He bowed and offered me his umbrella.

"Thanks," I said, "but I don't mind a little rain."

"But then I have no gift for you."

"I don't have one for you either," I pointed out, and since he spoke English, I asked if he knew where the mountain was.

He laughed. "If you must lose something, it is best that it be as large as a mountain. If you follow this road, what is lost will be found, as your saints say."

"They are not my saints."

"Nor are they mine. Indeed, I prefer to think that the saint of lost things may have borrowed a trick from Mali, who would take things from humans for the pleasure of watching them search."

"Who is Mali?"

"Not is; he only was. We have your God now, who is not nearly so amusing."

"He's not my God either."

"Ah."

I noticed that we were walking back toward the town, and he was holding his umbrella over my head. Although he seemed to know who I was and why I was in Tonga, he did not expect any prescience on my part. He introduced himself. His name was Fresh Air.

"Tongans often show their respect for Western ways by giving a child an English word for a name," he explained. These names were sometimes chosen haphazardly and often from the labels of Western goods; he had only narrowly escaped being named Franco-American. When I asked where he had learned such perfect English, he told me he had been sent to England to study. "But the string that holds my heart to this island is too short. It pulled me home. Ah, here we are."

We were standing in front of a large, cement block house, painted sky blue and surrounded by flowers. A path to it was made of the ubiquitous round brown stones. Lebeca hurried up to us. "It is good that you found her!"

Fresh Air bowed. "We were thinking, Seli, perhaps you would prefer to stay with Foeata until Mrs. Omont returns."

"Foeata is very friendly, very funny, and fat," Lebeca said. "She is rich and almost royal. She loves American Peace Corps, and she cooks good palangi food. You will not be lonely."

"She invites you," Fresh Air added. "She is waiting for you."

Foeata was large. She nearly filled the doorway of her house, and in her red hibiscus print gown, she gave the impression of a mountain in full bloom. And she was friendly. She greeted me by throwing her arms around me and tossing me in the air like a pizza.

"My daughter!" she cried. "Oh, my daughter!" When I landed, she patted me on the back, which caused me to stagger a little. "You are weak! You are thin! You are ill?" I was trying to put my internal organs back in place.

"This is very kind of you," I said, a greeting sadly anemic in comparison. "I can't seem to get out to Mrs. Omont's island."

She put up her hand imperiously. "First, you must eat and rest. Then we will talk." She ushered me into her dining room. Fresh Air and Lebeca were gone.

Foeata's house was built like a honeycomb with rooms going in all directions from this room, which had a long table and chairs made of dark, polished wood. A matching sideboard held a collection of china, carnival glass, and one Tupperware tub. On the wall were framed photos of John and Robert Kennedy, Queen Elizabeth II, and the Tongan King Tupou IV, a handsome and regal-looking man. I didn't know if Lebeca had meant Foeata was related to the king, but she certainly resembled him, not only in size but in majestic bearing. She returned with tea, three boiled eggs, a loaf of bread, Marmite, strawberry jam, a papaya, three bananas, and a dish of pudding. She told me to eat everything. I did. Something about her brought to mind the ancient Tongans who had stewed palangis. I'd probably have eaten the dish if she'd told me to.

"Do you know if there are any legends about that flat-topped mountain?" I asked when I had eaten my pudding.

"No," she replied solemnly, "there are no legends."

"But I think my job is to help Mrs. Omont collect legends."

"Then you have no job!" This amused her more than it did me, and she declared I must rest so that I would be able to laugh better. She showed me to my room, painted butter yellow and furnished with a mahogany bedroom set. The four-poster bed was draped with a mosquito net canopy, and a dressing table had a flowered skirt that matched the bedspread and curtains. A ruby glass hurricane lamp sat on a bedside table. My suitcase sat beside it.

"I brought this furniture from New Zealand to make a room for palangis," Foeata explained. "It is like your home?"

"No." Instantly, she looked worried. "I've never had anything as beautiful as this," I told her. "I've been living in one room where the bed and table and chair all fold out of the walls. They didn't all fit at once, so I had to fold up the bed before I could unfold the table and chair."

She laughed, although there was no evidence she believed me. "You make good jokes, Seli!" She took apart the bed to show me sheets and pillowcases embroidered with dragons. She untied the mosquito net and doused the room with enough bug spray to kill anyone who wasn't a native of Los Angeles. She told me to rest and not worry; she would take care of anyone who tried to look in my window to see her new palangi. She left.

I opened my suitcase. Whoever had packed it had put my letter from Jackson carefully on the top. I set it next to the ruby glass lamp, opened a window, climbed under the mosquito net, leaned against the dragons, and waited for time to begin.

7

"Seli, Seli, Seli, Seli." I woke up with a start and tangled with my mosquito net. "Seli, Seli, Seli." I opened the door and found Foeata about to begin another chorus. "I have fixed you a little supper, Seli."

We toured the house on the way to the dining room, viewing the parlor, the bathroom, and the kitchen, the outer walls of which were made of screen. She showed me her hot water system, which her late husband had invented: A network of pipes went from the wood-burning stove to a water drum and then to a stall. With the exception of the Port of Refuge Hotel, she had the only hot showers on the island. She invited me to try it, and so I showered while she stood outside and asked if it was hot.

"Yes, indeed."

"As hot as in America?"

"Absolutely. Hotter."

When I emerged from the shower, she tied a red-flowered, sheet-like skirt over my jeans and put yellow flowers in my hair. She was laughing, and I, having forgot the part about Foeata being funny as well as fat and friendly, followed her to the dining room with no idea she might be cooking up a good joke. I admired her electric frying pan and coffee pot as she pointed them out. Then, with the same pride of possession, she presented a blond man who only looked small because he was standing next to her. She giggled and skittered into the kitchen.

"Hello," he stammered. "I mean, malo e lelei."

"What?"

"You speak English? Oh, of course you do. Well, shall we sit down? Do you know why the table is only set for two? Where does everyone else eat?"

"I don't know."

"Oh, that's right, you've only just arrived too. Did you know I'm staying here? Skip Robinson. Peace Corps."

"Ah." I waited for him to start singing.

"And damn—pardon me—wow, I really lucked out in my home stay. Hot showers. Not that there's anything wrong with cold showers. They're just cold. But this is the greatest place I've ever been to. Now I don't have to worry about going to Heaven." I must have flinched. "Sorry! I forgot you are probably religious. Are you Wesleyan?"

"Huh? Who? Me? What?"

Foeata returned, carrying two plates. She hung her head, but her grin, the size of a wedge of watermelon, was still visible.

"I have been so bad," she sighed, "but how can I help it? I can't keep my mouth closed. I need fresh air. And so, when the new American Peace Corps doctor, who will stay in my house, asked me where I had learned to speak such nice English, I had to tell him that once I was married to an American who took me away to America. But I was too homesick for my island. I came back but I left my daughter, and this very day, she has come home to me."

"She has?" I asked.

Foeata roared and clapped me on the back. I hung on to the chair so I wouldn't fly across the room. "My daughter! I had her when I was, oh, seventy-six; now I am thirty-seven. I am so sorry." She chuckled without remorse. "He does not know what to think. But I had no daughter. Three sons, no daughter. Now, I have a daughter and one more son, and for them I have cooked a palangi dinner."

"I believed it," Skip mumbled as we sat down. "I thought you were her daughter. I figured you got your red hair from your father. It's hard to know what to believe. . . ." His voice trailed off. In front of us, a plate was piled high with pancakes and a platter of spaghetti crowned with a curry of corned beef. There was a loaf of white bread for each of us.

"When you're not in Kansas anymore," I said.

We ate alone. The Tongans, we learned, would eat after us, in the kitchen. Once a cloud-burster, always a cloud-burster; this is the first thing a palangi trying to learn Tongan ways is taught. Although Foeata would not eat with us, she did sit at the table to chaperone. At intervals, someone would pass through the room, going to the kitchen to borrow a pineapple or a few bananas, pausing to observe the three of us as we discussed the health of the American president and the price of butter in the United States. Foeata asked if my American parents would mind if she had adopted me.

"I doubt it," I said. "They're dead."

Her eyes filled with tears. "But if you have adopted me," I pointed out, "I'm not an orphan anymore." This restored her spirits, and she went to get dessert.

Skip groaned, stretched, and patted me on the shoulder. "You're good at this. Culturally sensitive without even going through the Peace Corps training."

I moved away, but he kept his hand on my chair. He resembled an amiable sheepdog, and I suspected that his outlook on life had a canine simplicity. "Damn," I could hear him telling a patient. "It's terminal!"

"Would you like to go to a kung fu movie?" he asked.

"No."

"How about the Vava'u Club? Do you like to dance?"

"No."

"Drink?"

"No."

"Well, then we could go to the Mormon social and not dance and not drink."

"Thanks, but I don't have to worry about going to Heaven on account of this being Paradise."

"What are you doing here?"

Foeata reentered the room with another platter. "For my palangi children, a palangi dessert," she announced.

I believe it had been created with the idea that if one thing is good, then eight are better. A pineapple pie was covered with two layers of cake, a meringue, and chocolate pudding. Over this she had sprinkled chopped Jell-O and canned fruits. "Oh," she said as she set it down in front of us. "I forgot the *ici kelemi*."

"Ice cream," Skip translated, looking culturally sensitive but doubtful. I could tell that he hadn't been to many political dinners in his life.

"And for you, Seli," Foeata continued, "a message from Kalavite. He went to Mrs. Omont's island, as you wished him to do, but she is not there. This we knew, for she flew away many days ago. Moses drove her to the airport. So, she is gone, you do not have to leave, and we can all be happy. Now, eat a little more."

8

Foeata was not nearly as baffled as I about why a woman would hire me and then leave before I had arrived. Evidently, she viewed it as only one of a dozen peculiar things a palangi would do before breakfast. She had other things on her mind, I learned the following morning.

She sat down with me in the dining room, telling me not to mind the people outside the window. Palangis were generally better entertainment than radios, and they were waiting to see if I would eat an egg. Most Tongans couldn't bring themselves to eat eggs, she said, but they got a bang out of watching palangis do it. She had boiled three for me, all arranged with a papaya, a loaf of bread, and instant coffee. I ate an egg and was wondering if I should bow or wave when Foeata remarked, "So sorry you missed, this morning, the nice Peace Corps doctor, Sikipi."

"Oh well. Foeata, do you know Mrs. Omont?"

Foeata blinked and her brows furrowed.

"I expected her to be here," I added. "Because she hired me."

Her frown deepened. I hoped there was nothing wrong with my outfit. According to my guidebook, Tongans had taken missionary teachings so seriously it was advisable to hide all evidence of owning elbows or legs if you were a woman; this was why Foeata had wrapped the *lava-lava* over my jeans. Rather than wear it again, this morning I'd put on a dress. It wasn't great looking, but it was the only one I owned. The used-clothes store had rejected it when I'd sold my other things. The dress had looked good in a catalog, but it was on a model who was probably six feet tall. Also, in the photo it was pine green, but it had turned out to be a dismal shade of dead seaweed. It was sleeveless, so I'd put on a shirt to cover my elbows. It was brown, printed with cows and cactuses. Jackson's grandmother had sent it to him, it being her idea of what to wear in America. It shrank when he washed it, so he'd given it to me. Aside from issues of taste or fashion, I didn't think the outfit was offensive; still, Foeata was studying me with concern, especially my feet. My shoes were unfortunate, being chartreuse running shoes with aqua stripes. I'd bought them on sale. The guidebook hadn't mentioned anything about shoes.

"He is a nice man," she remarked. "Not tall, but smart."

"Who?"

The inevitable result of putting a man and a woman under one roof on a tropical island is so unquestioned only a person as jaded as myself could have missed it. Courteously, Foeata observed there were several reasons why I was wandering around the world with no mafu: I had no mother, I probably had tuberculosis, and there was the problem of my feet. The mother was taken care of, and the tuberculosis soon would be, but the feet remained a challenge.

"My feet?" Until then, my small feet had been my only point of vanity. I never knew, until Foeata told me, that a man searching for a wife would look for fine big feet, a sign not only of beauty but of a good breeder. Still, she reflected, a mother such as herself could offset even so great a defect as my feet.

"And," she continued happily, "if you marry Dr. Sikipi, you would not have to worry where is Mrs. Omont. You would not have to go to her island. You hear the wind? It returns."

On cue, the wind howled, and I had to admit that this was the best argument for marriage I'd heard so far in my life.

"But perhaps," she mused with a harrowing smile, "there is already someone you love, and he is far away."

"No. There isn't."

"Ah. Then you must rest and eat, Seli, and when you are fat, you will fall in love."

There was no telling where this conversation would have gone if a group of people had not appeared at the kitchen door. Foeata spoke to them in Tongan and turned to me.

"They are here to take you for your visit."

"To Mrs. Omont's?" I asked. The wind was roaring now, and it occurred to me that I might rather get in a cart to ride to the guillotine than into a small boat on the ocean in a storm, but then I remembered that Mafi had invited me to her house. This, most likely, was my royal escort.

We set out. We viewed various landmarks on our way, including a warehouse full of bread. We stopped in front of a forbidding, gray cement building. No one had to tell me it was a hospital. I was in a hospital once, and everyone around me had died; this left me sure that if I ever entered another one, I'd leave worse off, if not dead altogether. Climbing the steps of the hospital was no place to explain this.

We went in. Sick people were lying on shelves behind the admissions desk. It smelled like a hospital. I began to feel clammy in the head. A man came forward to greet us. He apologized because he could not speak much English, and I apologized because I could speak no Tongan, except for *malo e lelei*, and *ici kelemi*. After I had shaken hands with everyone, including the people on the shelves, he indicated I should follow him, and he laughed when I asked if the *tabu* sign in the hallway meant we should keep out. We visited the surgery, the supply rooms, and every patient's room. I shook hands with everyone who wasn't unconscious, but I didn't faint until I read the English on Mr. Helu's chart.

9

That afternoon Skip Robinson knocked on my window. "I hear you've picked up a case of leprosy," he said. "How does Foeata, who doesn't have 'full' in her vocabulary, know 'leprosy'?"

"I told her."

"Would you mind coming outside so I can take a look? I can't come into your room without violating rule two of decorum."

As I came into the garden, he asked, "Why were you touring the hospital, anyway?"

"I don't know."

"I wonder if they asked for me and this was another good joke Foeata couldn't resist."

"Either that or they figure one palangi is as good a doctor as another."

This he ignored. He was examining my hands. "Can you bend your fingers?"

"They're stiff," I said. "But it's the bumps—"

He nodded. "I'd say you either have a hysterical reaction to shaking the hand of a man you thought was a leper—or heat rash."

"Heat rash?"

"Do you think I'd be holding hands with you if I thought it was leprosy?" Giggles came from behind Foeata's hedge. He dropped my hands. "Damn," he said. "Oh damn."

He started to walk, and I went along out of curiosity. It had been a while since anyone had called me hysterical and then proceeded to show signs of the disease himself.

"It might offend someone from California, but they have behavior codes here," he said as we passed goats and chickens on the crushed coral road. "It's sort of a missionary-inspired Polynesian Victorianism, but if you want to fit in, you'd do well to acknowledge it. The first rule is that women shouldn't have arms and legs and men shouldn't have chests. It's why women have to wear skirts to swim, and men can be arrested for appearing in public without a shirt. Rule two is men don't go into women's bedrooms until after the wedding, and men and women never touch each other in public. Maybe you can if you're married; I can't remember. Rule three is women don't go places alone. Would you like some ice cream?"

"Is it all right with the code?"

"I knew you'd find it offensive."

We stopped at John's Takeaway, a red and yellow hut that served ice cream and hamburgers. The ice cream came in plastic cups, served with forks.

"There are exceptions to the rules," Skip continued. "For instance, men can hold hands with men and women with women. It's a missionary oversight that drives the Mormons crazy. Also, men can dress as women; if a family wanted a girl and got a boy, they sometimes dress him as a girl, and he'll keep it up until he gets married. *Fakalaities*, they call them. *Faka* is the prefix meaning 'in the manner of.' And here's another odd thing: No one is doing it now because I'm with you, but several times, when I've been alone, women have whistled at me. Last night, I went to a movie, and when they put the lights out, someone started tickling me and pinching me and rubbing my neck during the romantic parts. It was kind of weird. Not too bad, however."

"What would have happened if you'd tickled back?"

"The Pan Am award."

"The what?"

"A ticket home. As the director says, you might as well go home for all the good you'd be."

"Do you wonder why you did this?" I asked him.

"Why? No."

"Do you remember Kennedy announcing the Peace Corps?"

He blinked. "Do you?"

"Not exactly. Maybe."

"How old are you?"

"Extremely old. How old are you?"

"Thirty-one."

"I plan to be a posthumous writer by then."

"Hey, maybe that's what he meant." Skip was watching ice cream drip from the tines of his fork. "The Peace Corps director, when he welcomed us, said this was a way of looking back to what life in the United States was like in another time. I couldn't figure it out. Goats, grass shacks, missionaries, women dancing sitting down so you won't notice that they have legs. Maybe he just meant it was looking back to when there were ideals. I don't know about that, of course." He coughed. "I did have reservations about coming here. I thought I might develop a tumor if I had to go two years without ice cream. But there's ice cream all over. There, I've bared my soul to you. What about you? What brings you here?"

"I'm going to be a companion to Mrs. Omont if I find her."

"I've heard about her. She's the local palangi eccentric. An artist. Her husband was normal, however. A doctor."

"There's normal for you. Was? Is he dead?"

"He died thirty years ago. He and his wife came to these islands
before World War II. He practiced for ten years in the Big Nuke, the
capital in the south. He was well liked, I'm told. They moved north
to help develop medical services here, and the government let them
build a house on their own island. Then he died."

"What did he die of?" I asked. "Overeating?"

"I don't know. Something fatal. So, what does a companion do?"

"I think she wants to find legends, something about a lost island."

"That'll drive the missionaries crazy. They've nearly done away
with legends."

As he talked, a man walked by, swinging a machete. He was
wearing a wraparound skirt, a hibiscus print shirt, and earrings. His
face was decorated with bits of white paper, the gummed edges from
sheets of postage stamps, which were all the rage. Women, wearing
long black dresses and carrying baskets and parasols, walked amidst
wandering pigs, goats, and chickens. The Peace Corps director had
said it was a way of looking back, but to what? I had to admit Skip
had a point there.

10

When we returned to Foeata's, women were doing needlework in the kitchen. Laughter, not unlike applause, rippled around the room, and they poured me a cup of tea. Men appeared, inviting Skip to join them for a drink in another room. Foeata gave me a piece of cloth, a string, and a needle, and while I tried to thread the needle, I was thinking if I never found Mrs. Omont, I might run for the Tongan Congress, so effectively was I mingling with The People. There I was, discussing how sad it was that Anni was in love with Lopeti, but her parents had said no when he came to ask for a kava party; and how curious it was that Lebeca had loved Kalavite for so long with no results until now, when she was admiring the new Peace Corps volunteers; and then—I was the last to figure it out because most of the significant words were in Tongan—I was agreeing what a fine thing it was that I was going to marry the Peace Corps doctor. It caught me in the middle of a gracious smile when I had damn nearly threaded the needle. About this time Skip emerged from the other room looking panicky, but this might have been because he had been drinking kava, a drink whose main effect on palangis is to cause a condition known as *fakaleilei*. *Faka*, you will recall, means "in the manner of" and *leilei* is the verb "to run."

Foeata jumped up and hugged him so enthusiastically he was four

49

inches taller when she released him. The men called to him to hurry back to drink more kava. I was amused until I heard Foeata tell him not to worry, the ladies were going to take me with them to choir practice.

Skip was struck with providential inspiration. "Gee, Shelley," he said, "I guess this means we can't go dancing."

Foeata reflected. "No," she decided, "dance."

"Admit it," Skip said as we walked toward the Port of Refuge Hotel, accompanied by a cluster of chaperones, dogs, and goats. "It was a great idea." It was rumored, he added, that Tongan men could sit up all night drinking kava, and I had to agree if I had a choice between going to a hospital and going dancing, I'd probably choose to dance. *Sotto voce*, he asked me if I knew we were engaged. "It might not be a bad thing," he mused. "It might save me from being pinched."

The hotel's dance floor was decorated in the authentic South Pacific style with tapa-covered walls and giant, glowering wooden statues. Four musicians wearing blue hibiscus print shirts were playing on a stage beneath a thatched roof. The room deviated, however, from any Tiki Room in Texas or New Jersey in that the southern wall was no wall at all. It was open to a starlit view of the Neiafu harbor, of clouds parting over coconut trees, of dark distant islands in glittering water. This was, so to speak, the real thing.

"Dance?" Skip asked, and as we walked onto the dance floor, a memory came into my head like a bat through a window that has been left open at night. It's quite mortifying, but still, I am trying to tell the truth, or as much of the truth as is possible for someone who has worked in politics. It was when I was sixteen and a social failure, a consequence of being homely, odd, and a trifle uppity. Jackson, at school in England, had five hundred girlfriends and had been reduced to anemia, owing to his overactive sex life, according to his letters. I used to try to imagine what it would be like to go out on a date with Jesse Goldensohn, who, as far as I could tell, never went out on dates either, but that's as far as I got. This is the terrible thing about love: Even if you don't know what it is, as soon as someone tells you it exists, you can't help wishing for it.

Then one weekend, teachers took a group of the smart social misfits to visit UC Santa Cruz. We stayed in a hotel by the beach, next to a place called the Coconut Grove where you could pay a dollar and dance. Since no one knew us, we made up fake identities; I decided I'd be dumb for one night to see what it was like. I said my name was Josephine and I was a pompom girl. I danced every dance. At midnight, the Coconut Grove closed, and back in the hotel, I worried about whether it was the real world or not, but my roommate said, what did it matter, if you were dancing?

I never told anyone about that night; in fact, I might have blocked it out of my mind altogether until this evening when I wondered what my sixteen-year-old self would have thought if she could see me now, dancing in the platonic ideal for Coconut Groves with the doctor to whom I'd recently become engaged.

Just then Skip stepped on my foot. He didn't notice. He was staring at a woman who was the type to gape at, goggle-eyed. She was tiny, svelte, and shiny, like a beetle with waist-length black hair. She was wearing a short, tight, purple satin dress with red rhinestone buttons. Her toenails and fingernails were scarlet, and so were her glittery, spike-heeled sandals. Her fingernails were as long as her fingers. She was surrounded by a flock of men who did not appear to be bothered by the fact that her feet were too small for her to qualify as a real beauty.

I didn't think she was Tongan. Aside from her bare elbows, something about her said palangi. "If it isn't Dr. Robinson," she murmured. "Are you surprised to see me? I've been waiting for you." She fluttered her eyelashes, as long as broom straws. Not a beetle, I thought, a scorpion or maybe a black widow. I once read a paper about black widows that said the female beckons a male to his doom by lying on her back and waving her legs at him. He is hypnotized, and then he dies.

"Would you go?" I asked Jackson.

"Probably," he said. Life force is so weird.

She took Skip's arm and shot me a brief, venomous look; this was something that had never happened to me, not even the night I acted dumb. She appeared to be establishing a claim to my fiancé, which I, coward that I am, was not inclined to contest.

Skip, however, did not look so much hypnotized as walloped by a baseball bat. The woman was digging the pointy tips of her nails into his arm, which appeared to be afflicting his speech center. "This is Lily—Lily—" he stammered. "Lily, this is—ah—uh—"

"Shelley Ilillouette," I said.

"Lily Omont."

"Omont?"

She spelled it.

"Are you related to Bette Omont?"

"Why do you want to know?"

"I'm looking for her. She hired me."

"Hired you? Why?"

"I don't know exactly."

"I thought she was losing her mind, what she has of it."

"Do you know where she is?" I asked. "Kalavite said she is gone."

Lily shrugged. "Maybe she is dead. Then I shall be rich. Aren't you going to ask me to dance, Dr. Robinson?"

Skip was absorbed into the group around her, and it closed like a castle gangplank, leaving me on the other side of the moat. I was heading to the exit when a man tapped me on the shoulder. "Dance?" he asked.

He was big, bronzed, and wrinkled with intense, bright blue eyes under a profusion of white hair. His shirt had leaping frogs on it. I said I'd dance. He danced well; that is, he knew how to. He moved like a sailor used to keeping his balance in high winds. He could even talk and dance at the same time. His name was Joe Storey. He was from Australia.

"What's your name?" he asked.

"Josephine."

"Tourist or Peace Corps?"

"I've just come home to live with my mother, who is Tongan."

He squinted down at me. "Well, you've got the Tongan eyes."

"Who are you?"

"A sailor passing through. I've done so for years. I like these islands. You won't find better people anywhere. The Friendly Islands, Cook called them. How did you like the States?"

"It was all right, but it wasn't home."

"I like the Yanks, myself."

"They're rather goofy politically."

"I don't know about that. I was around for World War II. The Yanks saved my country."

It was so odd to hear something good about us I was stumped for a reply. He said, "So, who's the beauty who just walked off with your boyfriend?"

"Lily Omont."

He whistled. "So that's Lily. That explains a few things."

What it explained I didn't learn, because the danced ended, and for the second time that night, I lost my partner to Lily. As Joe Storey waded into her throng, I left the dance floor by way of the missing wall.

The world spread before me, dark silver water and a darker sky. There was no moon, just a glittering spread of stars and drifting thunderheads. Palm trees framed the shadowy views of the island and distant ones beyond it. I was knocking on a coconut tree to be sure it was real when a man materialized beside me. He was small for a Tongan, nimble and elfish, with spiky black hair. He wore the fashionable white bits of paper decorating his cheeks and a paper clip dangling from one ear. "Hello," he said. "I am Kalavite. You do not know me."

"But I do. You went out to Mrs. Omont's island in the storm. You're either brave or crazy."

"No." He grinned. "Just like my name. Most strong. My father, he is a *fie fe cow*, and he wished for me a most powerful name. Do you agree?"

"Cavity? I guess so. They eat teeth."

"No! It is what holds us here instead of flying up to the sky."

"Gravity?"

"Most strong."

"What is a fie fe cow?" I asked. "A farmer? I haven't seen any cows."

He laughed. A fie fe cow, he explained, was a minister. I could see his father's cows all around me. "But," he continued, "I have to say something most important. If you come out here and stand alone and look so *faka ofa ofa*—so beautiful—and I see you, I might think something. I might say something. You see?"

"See what?"

"I might say something like 'oooh-la-la.' I might think you were not like a Tongan girl." He glanced at the dance floor and Lily.

"Is she really Mrs. Omont's daughter?"

"Not always. Many years ago, someone gave Lily to Dr. Omont, who had no children. Lily is one-half palangi, and so it was better that she lived with them. Mrs. Omont sent her to school in America. Now she is back, but we do not know why."

"Do you know Mrs. Omont?"

"Yes, of course, but she has her own little boat, and so she has no need of me." He shrugged. "Now, we will go inside."

Just then the clouds parted, revealing the half-mountain. "Do you know why it is flat?" I asked.

"Oh yes. Because the Devil stole the top."

"Is that a legend?"

"No, it is the truth of what happened. Many Tongans saw it."

"Do you know any stories about a lost island?"

"No. There are no stories."

"Why not?"

"Because," he said, "the gods are all dead. This is also true, and this is how it happened: There was a child who was ill. His mother took him to a wise man in the bush, and he said, 'I will cure this child because that is my knowledge, but it makes me sad because when he grows up, he will cause the death of the gods.' And the wise man cured the child, who grew up and became king. And when the palangis came through the clouds, he took their ways, and the old ways became tabu, and so the gods had to die."

Abruptly, Gravity frowned and returned to the dance floor. He propped himself against a scowling wooden statue, watching Lebeca, who was dancing with Skip. At the entrance, I saw the missionary kid from the post office, motionless as another statue. He was staring at Lily, who was at the bar batting her broomsticks at Joe Storey.

I left, walking down the coral road alone. Overhead were more stars than I'd ever seen except maybe on a moonless night in the mountains. Looking up at the sky, I tripped over a rock, and this is how I noticed the egg plant; that is what I named it because each of its long green spikes was crowned with a single, perfectly egg-shaped white flower.

"Hoo-ha, fiancée!" Skip sprinted up out of the dark. "Why'd you leave?"

"I figured the engagement is over."

"Oh, yeah, wow, what a woman, the kind my mother warned me about. She's driving every man on the island nuts, even that poor missionary kid. Well, she dropped me for a white-haired yachtie who reeks of gin and money. So, why are we standing here?"

"I'm just looking at this plant."

"What plant?"

11

Foeata was in her kitchen when we arrived. She escorted me to my bedroom, and I was wondering if it would violate any rules if I went back out to brush my teeth when I heard a commotion arrive. Peering out, I saw a crowd gathered around Skip. They carried him away. Foeata left too. It seemed like a good time to brush my teeth.

The house was empty and silent, except for the wind rattling the screen wall in the kitchen. I made myself a cup of tea and sat down to work on threading a needle. On the other side of the screen, I saw the flash of a silver paper clip. It was Gravity. I got up to open the door for him.

"Oh no," he said. "You cannot open it. Foeata locked you in so you will be safe while they look for Mafi."

"Mafi!" I thumped my head. "I forgot! Why are they looking for her?"

"Tonight, she got out."

"Got out?"

"At night, if her husband does not lock the door, Mafi gets out and she runs. The *tevolos*, the devils, make her run. Tonight, Pulu forgot to lock the door, and she ran. It is sad for her but more sad for me."

He sat down in the dirt; tears ran down his face. "I will tell you,

Seli, in Tonga, we have many dogs. Ugly dogs, and people do not love their ugly dogs, but I love my dog. Where I go, he goes. When I walk, he walks; when I fish, he fishes. But tonight, when I came home, I found my dog. My brother said a truck drove very fast past our house, and my dog—he is dead."

"I am sorry," I said. "Once, I had a cat."

"And you loved him, and he loved you?"

"He was my best friend."

"He died?"

I nodded.

"And this broke your heart?"

"He was all I had."

We sat in silence on either side of the wall until he got up, bowed, and walked away. I went back to my needle but to no comfortable thoughts. What happens when people break through your sky and leave you to catch the pieces? When your gods die and the devil sneaks in and steals your only mountain? Are all lost things gone forever or merely wandering in the night, like a woman who has escaped through a door that someone forgot to lock?

It was much later when Foeata returned, accompanied by Gravity, Moses, and another brother who, I am sorry to say, was called Ever-Ready. Gravity brought me a pair of woven bracelets, a bottle of Tongan oil, and a huge pot of stew because we were now friends. Foeata heated up her frying pan and began cooking pancakes. When I asked what time it was, she gave me a look that indicated this was irrelevant. She was worrying that this meal was too meager when Skip arrived. He looked weary, and she insisted he eat before he talked. Gravity dished up his stew, which we ate with the pancakes. Skip and I ate first; then the others joined in.

"This is good stew," Skip said. "It must be real Tongan food." The others nodded. "I like it. Is it—let me see—it's not *ika*, fish. It must be *pulu*? Beef?"

"*Icai*," Gravity said. "No, it is *koli*."

We met a few minutes later at the wash basin, brushing our teeth. "We won't die," Skip said in a strangled voice, "just because we ate a stew made from his dog."

"We might."

"Why didn't you ask what it was?"

"I got stuck on *huacow*."

"On what?"

"Huacow. Milk. Foeata brought in a bottle of milk and said, 'Huacow,' and I asked, 'Who has a cow?' and everyone laughed so I stopped talking."

"People from California are so damned touchy." Skip looked back to the kitchen, where everyone was still eating. "I wonder when they sleep."

"Did you find Mafi?" I asked.

"No. They found her boat, adrift and empty. There was no sign of her anywhere. It looks like she drowned."

12

Outside, a man was digging a pit to roast the Sunday pig, and Foeata was making packets of lamb and clams in coconut cream wrapped in taro leaves to bury along with the pig in the underground oven. I saw a basket of shellfish go by my window, and another filled with pineapples, mangoes, and papayas. Even the Mormons singing across the street seemed to be joyfully anticipating the feast. It was possible, however, that I was going to miss it because of the spider on my mosquito net.

It was there when I woke up, and it hadn't moved, this creature the size of a dinner plate, with its millions of eyes all focused on me. Unless it had recently eaten its way through the wall, I had already spent two nights in the room with it. The delicate crunching sounds I had thought were cockroaches walking might have been the spider, feasting on the bones of the last palangi resident. Or maybe the spider had just been waiting for Foeata to fatten me up before activating its digestive poisons. I tried telling myself that spiders have their place in the world and if there were no spiders there would be too many flies, and flies would overtake the world and be worse than Republicans. Still, I couldn't persuade myself to move.

"Seli?" Foeata opened the door, and when she saw the spider, she gave the net a shake that sent the creature flying. She had brought me a Sunday dress to wear. It was a purple Mother Hubbard, floor-length, long-sleeved, and it included a few extra yards of fabric around the middle in case I grew during the day. She also gave me a grass skirt made of braided strips of pandana leaves. Women wore them or grass mats, *ta'ovalas*, tied over their Mother Hubbards.

"It is a sign of respect," Foeata said.

"Respect for what?" I asked, but she did not have time to answer because Skip had emerged from his room, clad in a red and white lava-lava and, God forbid, no shirt. Foeata rushed him into the shower, however, before I could run amok.

I dressed and went into the garden. The sunlight was sparkling off a profusion of red, pink, and purple flowers, but thoughts about Mafi kept creeping into my head like the silent spider. How could anyone be dead on this bright morning? Skip came outside in a blue wraparound skirt, which he wore with a white shirt with a button-down collar, a tie printed with whales, a grass ta'ovala tied around his waist, and flip-flops. He lacked only a paper clip to be a complete Tongan.

"Hey," he said, "you look almost female."

"Thanks. So do you."

"Watch it." He readjusted his mat. "Do you think this will keep my skirt from falling off? I've never worn a skirt before. Have you ever lost one? Well, it may be worth it to wear something expandable today. I understand that on Sundays we feast, in comparison to what we've been doing the rest of the time."

Foeata joined us, smiling. "Now we can go to church," she announced. It was the first time I'd ever understood Paradise Lost.

"Stop gagging," Skip admonished as we walked to the blue and white Wesleyan Methodist Church. "If you can eat dog stew, you can go to church."

"I can't," I said. "I went to church once, and it gave me more scars than the Cuban missile crisis."

"Just listen to the singing. It's supposed to be great."

"I can't."

"Why not?"

"I'm Jewish."

"Really?"

"No," I admitted. "But Jackson's grandmother might be, and I've often wished I were." We were at the entrance. I paused, trying to work up a faint or a fit, but I couldn't. We went in.

The church was full of men in skirts and women in Mother Hubbards, and everyone was wearing their grass mats. I saw other Peace Corps volunteers sitting with their families, but a minister escorted us up to the front of the church. We were not going to sit with The People but in a roped-off section for fie fe cows and other big shots. Foeata looked pleased, but I saw sweat forming on Skip's forehead. I could tell he didn't know if we'd be married before we got out.

"I was thinking about Mafi," I told him. "Jackson had a patient who had epilepsy and sometimes she ran when she had seizures. She was a nun. They called her the running nun."

"Who's Jackson?"

"The tevolos took Mafi," Foeata said firmly, and the singing began.

It was quite nice singing, but it stopped too soon, and the fie fe cow came to the podium to speak. He was a palangi, the Reverend Ron L. Ogg, a freelance minister who traveled between Polynesian islands on his yacht. In hushed tones, Foeata explained that it was a great honor when he visited their church; his wife was descended from the original cloud-bursters. This woman was sitting in the front row, wearing a navy-blue polyester dress and a hat sprouting red, white, and blue pompoms. She was the one who had poked me with her umbrella at the post office.

Ogg was tall and shaped like a potato. His head was bald and lumpy, and his face was red and sweating. I didn't know why anyone would want to go to Paradise with him, but that is what he invited everyone to do: to go with him to the real thing, as compared to their shabby imitation. He included a few lines in Tongan, which he read from a paper. I got the gist of it because every other word was *tevolo*. Foeata listened intently, looking worried. I wondered why she would take him seriously. I wouldn't have believed him if he said his vegetables were organic or his company's wastes weren't toxic, so I didn't see why anyone should believe him when he came around peddling Paradise.

Still, all the talk about devils reminded me of the other time I went to church, an experience even more harrowing than when Jackson and I went as spies to a Republican Round-up for David's opponent.

When we were kids, David and I lived with our grandfather, Antonio, in his grand, old place on the north coast of California. He called it the House of Lost Things. Jackson and his mother, Hannah, lived with us too, because she had left his father and had nowhere to go. My mother's two somewhat eccentric Russian aunts also lived at the House of Lost Things. They were somewhat useless for practical life, so Hannah looked after things such as dinner and bills. We were all quite happy until David got a yen to go to school. The nearest one was St. Joseph's, and Jackson and I ended up there too. It was quite a hair-raising place, full of statues of men nailed to crosses or with their chest torn open and their heart falling out and women squashing snakes with their feet. David, always a quick study in survival, figured out the cast of characters, God and so forth. He became quite religious, for a time, and even thought about being a priest until a girl showed him where she had written his name on her thigh with indelible ink, and there went the priesthood.

Jackson and I did not fare so well, and the worst part was when we went to Mass. It was like a haunted house, spooky and full of strange smells, shadows, and wobbling candles. When people started mumbling, "He died for us," I went looking for David to see if he knew who had died, but I found Jackson first and sat down with him to be more comfortable. The kid next to him said, "Jackson has a girlfriend," and I said no, and Jackson said maybe, and Father Shea paused in his chants and fixed an awful stare on me. That day, he came into the lunchroom. "Do you know what happens to girls who talk at Mass?" he roared. "The Devil takes them to Hell for All Eternity. He is coming for Shelley Ilillouette."

I knew my life was over, especially after David explained what the Devil, Hell, and Eternity were. Jackson said he'd go to Hell too; it was only justice, and it couldn't be worse than school. All the same, we built a devil catcher, but only David fell in it and broke his arm. It was quite a relief when Hannah moved Jackson and me to Hook's Bay Elementary School, where no one talked about devils. David went to boarding school and ended up believing in politics instead of God. I forgot about the Devil, more or less, although one time, I asked Jesse Goldensohn what he thought about it. He thought the Devil was only a scarecrow that kept people from exploring the dark side of the world, where they might find powers of their own instead of praying to God for miracles. This is all somewhat extraneous now, except I remembered it as I sat in the church listening to Ogg. Had the Devil come for Mafi? What had she done? Had she talked?

When the service was finally over, the resident minister hurried up to announce that we were summoned to drink tea with the great Ogg himself.

"Why?" I asked.

"I do not know," the minister whispered. "But the Reverend Ogg has asked this."

Foeata said she had to go check on her pig.

"Come on, Foeata," Skip said. "Don't be a chicken."

"But I do not have the courage to meet great men," she insisted. "And it is a very large pig." Relieved to be spared the honor of shaking the hand of the man who would save her soul, she headed to the door.

I followed her. "It's just Skip they want to meet," I explained as she stopped and fixed a stern eye on me. I went to the missionaries' tea party.

13

In a back room of the church, the Reverend Ogg shook hands with Skip and me while smiling at the air. "Good work you are doing," he boomed, although we were standing six inches from him. "Great work. God's work."

This was the sum of his speech, for he had caught sight of his reflection in a window, and he began rearranging his strands of hair. If I hadn't been used to politicians, I might have concluded he'd been saving souls in the sun too long.

"It was a pleasure," I said, since Skip was bereft of conversation. "Well, goodbye."

Mrs. Ogg was blocking the exit, however, inspecting the back of her dress. "Mud," she grumbled. "There is too much mud on this island." She looked up at me, and I had a feeling I was not much of an improvement on the mud, but for Skip, she pasted on a smile. "So nice of you to come to greet my husband, but he is a busy man, and we are expecting guests." She had an interesting way of talking, as if she were simultaneously sucking a lemon.

The reverend said, "Eh?"

"Dr. Robinson should be here any minute," she said, clearly used to putting back the screws in his head that regularly fell out. Still, her conversation seemed to enter Ogg's ear and exit the other, unobstructed.

Skip cleared his throat. Mrs. Ogg looked at him again, and her gaze lingered on his skirt. "You are not—you couldn't be—"

I don't know what offended Skip more, the intimation that he was not himself or that he could not be. He adjusted his mat. "I am Dr. Robinson." Mrs. Ogg frowned at me. I don't know why. Skip added, "Peace Corps."

Her jaw dropped, but she caught it midway to the floor and whacked it back in place. Really, she was sharp as a shark's tooth. "You are going to run the hospital?"

"Oh hell no," he said. "I'm a surgeon, not an administrator."

"Why on earth would a doctor join the Peace Corps?"

He grinned. "To escape my past. Isn't that why everyone comes to the South Pacific? In my case, however, my past is regret—regret—"

What caused him to fumble, just when he was doing so well, was Lily Omont, who strolled into the room. She was wearing the same purple dress she had worn the night before, but the allure she had exuded was subdued. Maybe it was because she had covered her elbows with a black shawl or maybe she was seen best by the light of flickering torches. Still, Reverend Ogg gaped at her happily, and Skip flushed so bright red I expected to see smoke come out of his ears.

"You needn't run away," she said to him. "I'm looking for Reverend Ogg."

"Eh?" Ogg bobbed to order. "Hello, my dear! What a pleasure to see you! Fine work you are doing. God's work."

Lily's eyelashes fluttered. "I have more questions for you."

"Wonderful! Only too happy!" He was interrupted by the clatter of teacups. Mrs. Ogg, arranging her tea tray, looked like she had just swallowed a spoonful of salt. "Be a nurse, I always say. Fine profession for a woman."

Lily continued, "I met your friend Joe Storey last night."

"Joe?" Ogg echoed. "Did that SOB finally get here?" Mrs. Ogg fixed him with a stare that could turn a man into a turnip, and he mumbled, "Don't worry, my dear. Only Joe."

"He was so kind." Lily smiled. "He is going to help me with my story."

"Are you writing a story?" I asked, for the silence was profound. "What about?"

"About a child, abandoned at birth, then rescued. Then, her rescuer was murdered."

"That is nice," Mrs. Ogg cut her off emphatically, as with a cleaver, "but we have only recently come to these islands. We know no stories. And we are not friends with Joe Storey. Now, please excuse us. My husband is a busy man."

Ogg smiled with an unclouded expression. "He's busy waiting for Dr. Robinson to arrive," I told Lily.

"That's too bad," she said. "I waited a long time last night for Dr. Robinson, but he never showed up."

"There was an emergency," Skip mumbled.

"So I've heard," Mrs. Ogg said. "I hope it was not serious. Cream or lemon, doctor?"

"Lemon, please. It was fatal. A drowning."

Outside the window I noticed Lebeca waving at me. I opened the door. "Come in," I said.

She shook her head. "Foeata said to find you here. Here is a gift for you. From Mafi." She shoved a roll of tapa cloth tied with a red ribbon into my hands. Then she was gone.

"Love giving gifts, these Tongans," Ogg said. "Generous people. What's theirs is yours. Takes me back—"

"Yes, but she's the one who died," Skip said.

"Mafi?" Lily asked. "Dead?"

"Are you sure?" Mrs. Ogg asked and offended Skip again.

"It's a requirement to graduate from medical school," I said. "You have to get it right three out of five times: Dead or alive?"

"Wouldn't mind some of that tea, Mother," Ogg said, and a thought must have bit him, like a stray dog. "Mafi? Wasn't she the one married to that wild fellow who came to see us when I was in my bath? Never understood what he wanted."

As he fumbled along, trying to assemble a thought without the benefit of tools or instructions, Mrs. Ogg handed him his tea, but I'd only have drunk it if a taster had tried it first.She turned her gargoyle look on me. "Who are you?"

"Me?"

Lily said, "She is the half-wit my faux mother hired to look for stories. Like mine—"Mrs. Ogg's eyes were rolling like billiard balls that had got a good whack, and Skip jumped to catch her as she keeled over. She clung to him for a second before she stiffened up. "How silly of me," she exclaimed. "It is this dreadful heat. I must go." Skip stayed with her as she hobbled to the door. Ogg trailed after them.

"That was odd," I said to Lily, for we were the only two left at the tea party. "Not the oddest event I've ever gone to, but odd enough."

"Liar."

"No, it's true."

"Why do people lie? Do they think everyone is as stupid as they are?"

"In some circles it becomes a sort of habit."

"In yours perhaps, but really now, this is God's. Oh lord," Lily groaned as the missionary kid popped up like a rabbit outside the window.

"Lily!" he called rapturously. He sprang into the room, fell on his knees, and clutched at hers, causing her to spill her tea on his head.

"Let go of me." Her voice was weary, as if she had said this a million times before.

"But I love you." He tried to kiss her knees. "I would do anything for you."

"Then go away." She jerked herself backward, but the kid held on.

"Sorry to interrupt." Skip had come back into the room, and he stepped around them. "Mrs. Ogg forgot her bag."

"Skip!" There was something like pain in Lily's voice, but he had walked away. She booted the kid with her pointy-toed shoe. "Get out of here!" she cried. He rose, looking like he'd been stabbed through the heart and not just doused with tea and kicked.

"You're in love with him," he whispered.

"Get out!" She threw a teacup at him, and he ran. Lily smashed two more cups against the wall. "I hate this. God, I hate this."

"I know," I said. "So do I."

She remembered me with a glance, and her face tightened until it was blank, drained of all emotion. I wondered if you could really take feelings and chuck them out with the trash.

"It's just what I get for lingering too long in the house of God," she said. "Men: a biological necessity, an utter absurdity. Have you ever met one who wasn't like all the rest in the world?"

"Yes. One. No, two. No—"

"Never mind. I just hope you're not counting Skip Robinson among them." She picked up a cookie from a platter, bit it, and grimaced. "These are disgusting. The reverend's wife must have made them herself with a minimum amount of sinful sugar."

I wasn't sure why she was talking to me, but you have to ask questions when you can. "Do you really think Mrs. Omont is dead?"

"That was just wishful thinking. Of course she isn't dead. Of course it would be Mafi who died. I have always wondered how long

Mafi would last. One day, the world may become a tolerable place for strong women, but never for gifted ones. And, God, Mafi was gifted. Do you know, she was eleven when her running fits began, and the missionaries convinced her family that it was the work of the Devil. When Dr. Omont came to Neiafu, her family was keeping her locked in a room, and she was drawing on a dirt floor with sticks. They believed the Devil made her draw too. Dr. Omont persuaded her parents to let her live with Bette and him. He saved her life. As he did mine, apparently. I've always wondered why. So Mafi has finally killed herself. It's too bad. Or is it? Why did she send you a gift?"

"I don't know. She invited me to tea, but I forgot to go."

"True Tongan style. Send the rude palangi a gift. Now, it's a message from beyond the grave."

"This story about the abandoned child, is it your own?"

"Do you believe everything anyone tells you?"

"No, but—"

"And why on earth would you care?"

"'We know what we are, but not what we may be.' And so forth."

She stared. "What does an idiot like you know of Shakespeare?"

I ignored this. "Is that why you came back to Tonga, to find out?"

"No. I came back to marry Skip. That will ruin your plans, won't it?"

"Not really."

"You can have him if you want him."

"But I don't."

"I almost believe you, although I never trust anything a woman says about a man. In those circles, everyone lies." She broke off as Joe Storey ambled past the window. Next thing I knew, we had caught up with Storey. I was there because she had dragged me. Joe looked surprised but not elated.

"Thank you for your hospitality last night." Lily's voice was soft as a powderpuff.

"No need for thanks."

"It's a lovely room."

He surveyed her with a look so cold I was glad to be the shadow and not the object. "Stay as long as you like."

"Come and see me."

"I'm going fishing. I doubt that's your idea of sport. G'day." He tipped his hat and walked on. Lily stared after him, like a cat considering its strategy, but at least she retracted her claws from my arm.

Back at Foeata's, I put Mafi's tapa cloth, still rolled up and unexamined, on top of my empty notebook next to Jackson's unread letter. It was time for Foeata's feast.

14

For the first time, Tongans and palangis ate together, sitting on long mats of tapa cloth and coconut fronds spread outside. Fresh Air and the others joined us to eat roast pig, lamb, clams, and fish baked in coconut cream. There was ufi, taro root, tomatoes, mangoes, papayas, pineapples, watermelon, white bread, and a token palangi dish of crepes filled with corned beef. For drink, we had pitchers of orangeade.

I was thinking there was quite a bit to be said for Sundays when Foeata announced that Sunday was by no means over. Yet to come was afternoon church, Sunday school, and evening church. She hoped Skip and I could teach Bible stories at Sunday school.

"I don't know any," I began, although in a pinch I probably could have told the tale of Noah's ark. Skip was more effective. He stood up, opened his mouth, and fainted. This left Foeata torn between worrying because I knew no Bible stories and because the new Peace Corps doctor had just dropped dead.

"I've never done anything like that in my life," Skip said an hour later. He was in his bed, where Foeata had put him.

"It was a good time to start," I said. "Should I bring in your tea or throw it from the door?"

"Come in."

"If I do, who gets the Pan Am award?"

"You do." He grinned and sat up. He added sweetened condensed huacow to his tea, sipped it, and lay back down. "Where's Foeata?"

"Afternoon church."

"How did you get out of going? Did you tell her your leprosy is acting up?"

"No. I think Foeata realized you can't give palangis too large a dose of God or food at once, so she told me to rest and digest it all. Apparently, if you are half dead, it's all right to leave us alone. And I promised to make you tea if you revived."

"So you're OK?"

"Yes, as long as I don't have to teach Sunday school."

"Good—good. Sit down, Shelley."

I sat down, curious to see what was making him look so pensive. "Do you think it's odd, Mafi giving me a gift?" I asked.

"Why? No, the Rev is right. Tongans love giving gifts. And it's not like she was dead when she sent it to you. What's it a picture of?"

"I don't know. I haven't looked at it yet. How well do you know Lily?"

"Why do you want to talk about Lily? Don't let her worry you. She's a little intense, but she just has these delusions, like a kid who decides she was stolen as a child and these ordinary Joes, her parents, are fakes. She thinks she's the lost queen of Moribunda so she should be treated that way. And she seems to have notions about me, well, us. Hell, I don't know. I'm not a shrink." He drained his teacup and gave me a raised eyebrow look that indicated his brain had gone off on a detour. He murmured, "There's something to be said for repression, isn't there?"

"There is? What?"

"It makes things exciting."

"It does?"

"Come on, when was the last time it was a major accomplishment for someone to get you into his bedroom?"

"It always is."

He laughed as if I'd said something witty, not something true. He touched the edge of my grass skirt. "This is really nice. It's too bad you have to wear the dress with it." His eyes were taking on a glaze that could have been the vapors returning.

"Are you going to faint again?"

"Maybe. We could be Adam and Eve, you know."

"Huh?"

"One man, one woman, Paradise."

Now that I'm writing this down, I've noticed there are times when I wouldn't mind fiddling with the truth of what happened. For example, here I might rather fade out, substitute drumbeats for the Mormon chorus singing in the background, and let you imagine what transpired beneath the mosquito net. But I feel obliged to tell the truth. It's a late-bloomed thing, but I have come to the conclusion that there is a fundamental truth to the universe. I don't have a notion of what it is, but I feel like I should at least respect its glimmerings. All of this is to say that when Skip reached up and rubbed my neck, I jumped. I couldn't have done better for a spider. The tea tray went flying through the air, and the next thing I knew, I was on my way up the half-mountain.

15

The top of the mountain turned out to be an overgrown web of vines and trees that was a breeding ground for the kind of spider that had visited my room. They dangled silently in gargantuan webs all around me. Primeval giants, they could have been companions to the dinosaurs; no doubt, they had been around when time began.

I sat down on a log. Every way I looked, I could see the ocean, which gave me an idea of just how small our island was. The distant islands were even more inconsequential, like bubbles liable to disappear any minute.

A spider the size of a man's hand crept toward me. "All things considered," I admitted, "I'd rather be here with you than at tea with the Oggs or under a mosquito net with an amorous palangi. But I'm not the person you're looking for. He is probably in San Francisco by now. If you catch the next flight out, you could meet him. You could have dinner with him and discuss whether or not you have a future."

The spider stopped walking. It was probably gagging.

"It's not what Jackson wrote," I said, not that I knew what Jackson had written. I was fairly sure that, even at high altitude, Jackson wouldn't write dumb things like that. He suffers from occasional romantic fits and lapses into masculine obscurity, but only once in our lives did he ever say we had to talk, the same way you would also say you had to go get a rabies treatment. He had called in the middle of the night from England, and we were talking fairly well until he said he thought we needed to talk, and then neither of us said anything for the next ten minutes. Finally, he said maybe we should wait until he came to San Francisco.

"He wouldn't do it again," I told the spider. "And not with you. He'd like you. You'd like him. One time, a spider spun a web above his bed, and he talked to her. She laid her egg sack, and he watched over it till the spiderlings hatched. He told them he'd known their mother."

Clouds closed overhead and rain began falling, warm and heavy. It's probably a function of growing up in California, but I tend to think of rainstorms as gifts that arrive after long dry spells. Gifts can be strange things, however. David's old girlfriend Gabby was always making clever, crafty gifts. One year, she made baskets out of baked, varnished bread dough. She sent one to an elderly couple on the East Coast, but it broke in the mail, and they wrote back thanking her for the lovely toffee. She never knew if they'd tried to eat it, but it worried her a little.

I had a feeling that Western culture had fallen onto these islands in the same way, like a questionable gift that shattered on impact. The people had dutifully collected all the pieces they could find to reconstruct it without directions. Or maybe that's just what all of life is: an unbidden and unexpected gift, and you must wonder why someone has given you this thing, and what you are supposed to do with it. What if you never opened it but left it in a box on a shelf?

What was this place, anyway, these islands full of gifts? It wasn't a place I'd ever sought consciously, although now that I thought of it, Jackson and I were always looking for an island when we were kids. We looked for everything: ghosts, dragons, sharks, criminals, buried

treasure, trouble. Mostly we just found trouble. Jackson always
wanted to find an island. One time, we stole David's sailboat and
made it out to a rock that was an island during high tide. We weren't
the least bit worried when it began to shrink. We were only upset
that we were rescued before we found any pirates' treasure. David
threatened us with life imprisonment in the attic if we tried it again.
We did, of course. We just didn't get caught again. Jackson and I were
pretty good at being kids together, just lousy at being grown-up.

But here I was on an island, a real one that was so curious a mix-
ture of visible and invisible, of pieces lost and found, that if I were
going to hide away some ancient magic until the world was ready for
it again, I'd choose such a place as this. I've never told anyone, but
I've always wanted to believe that magic is afoot in the world.

The rain stopped and the sun set, and I was still on the half-mountain as the color began to drain from the sky. I don't know why
things you can think about in daylight, in a philosophical way, take
on a whole new aspect at night. Ghosts, bank balances, nuclear
wars, brown violin spiders, they all step out of a theoretical mode
to become something lurking at the edges of perception. Of course,
in this vine-cloaked web, the spiders were real, and it was no small
comfort that they were not poisonous. I found a palm tree branch
and waved it in front of me as a spider-finder as I started back down
the mountain.

It should be a law of physics that you can get down from a place
the same way you got up to it, but several times in my life I've found
that this isn't always the case, and this was one of them. The trail I
followed ended; I was waving my spider-finder over a cliff. I back-
tracked and began descending in circles on what might have been a
path, although not the one I'd followed before. I came to a gate. Dusk
had given way to darkness, but I could see shadowy banners and

fringed scarves, garlands of flowers, and decorative arrangements of the round brown stones on mounds of sand, all in the same telltale coffin shapes.

There's nothing like a graveyard to set the mind thinking about infinity, and I don't know anything that's worse than infinity. No beginning and no end; I've never been able to imagine it without feeling spiders crawling on my spine. The reason I've never studied physics, and therefore don't know why airplanes can fly, is that everywhere you look in physics, you come to infinity. It's the great tarantula of the universe.

Still, I reasoned that if I went through the graveyard, I might come out somewhere near to town. I opened the gate. The place was silent, and I knew this was because anyone else who was there would be dead. Promptly, my brain started worrying about what would happen after the end of time. I heard a sound like a footstep and got the chilly feeling that something was watching me. In the mountains, it would only be a deer or a bear making notes for Human Studies: Odd Things They Do in Nature, but I'd read that in Tonga there were no wild animals left, except for bugs and fruit bats. I brandished my spider-finder and whacked something that shrieked and ran away. I followed the sound; anything that shrieked and ran was my kind of creature. I tripped and landed on my knees at the edge of a gaping hole. It was a newly dug grave, waiting to be filled. From across it, a face was staring at me. Cold, bony fingers took hold of my hair and pulled it straight up into the air. Dimly, I recognized the eyes.

"Lily?" It was more of a squeak than a word. By way of answer, something whizzed through the air and sliced off the top of my palm branch, as neat as cucumber.

I covered the distance from the grave to Foeata's in about three minutes navigating on instinct, something I'm always amazed to find

I have. As I skidded into the parlor, the world came back into focus. Sitting on a ruby velvet love seat were Lily and Skip.

There are people who can do anything and not mess up their hair, and Lily must have been one of them, for if she had lately been running around graveyards, throwing machetes, she showed no signs of it. While I sagged against the door, mud-spattered, panting, and clutching my beheaded spider-finder, Lily was unruffled. Her eyelashes weren't even disarranged. She was holding a plate and offering bites of bread and bananas to Skip, who looked well, or as well as a besotted man can look. They must have patched up the differences that had been plaguing them earlier in the day. Lily's opinion of men appeared improved, and Skip did not seem worried that his nurse might have delusions she was the lost queen of Moribunda; you could have buttered all the bread in Tonga with him. All in all, they made a much better Adam and Eve.

"Shelley! Hello!" Skip sprang to his feet, and Lily shot me a look that did not make me doubt that she had just chucked a machete at me. "Would you like some tea?" he asked. "I'll go make it."

Lily pulled him back with not much more than a look. "Save your strength," she murmured. This reduced him to near idiocy, and he sat down.

"I was in the cemetery," I said, not that anyone had asked.

"How enthralling," Lily said. "Still looking for Mrs. Omont?" Suddenly, she flinched. She flicked Skip with her fingertips. "Maybe you should make more tea, darling." When he was out of the room, she mumbled, "Where is the bathroom?" I pointed. When she returned a few minutes later, her face was damp, as if she'd thrown water on it.

"Are you sick?" I asked.

"Talk about something else."

"OK. I've been thinking maybe I could help you."

"You? How?"

"Well, we're somewhat alike."

She looked so appalled I dropped the thought. "I need something to do. Are you trying to find out who your parents were? You'd be surprised what you can learn, even from a government agency."

She laughed. "I know who my mother was. A peasant who got screwed by a palangi and gave me away. Good. I'm glad. But I wouldn't mind getting a little of what Bette Omont got from my palangi father."

"What?"

"Money."

"Really?"

"Bette Omont lives on her own private island like a minor queen. How does she afford this, the widow of an obscure doctor on these lost islands? I wonder if I could get as much as she was paid for keeping secrets." She smiled. "Do you still want to help me, Shelley Ilillouette?"

"At least you're honest."

"You're a real romantic, aren't you?"

"Me?"

"It's kind of a disease. Do you believe that all we need is love?"

Skip returned, and like a Chinese face-changer, she had a whole new mask, sweet and smiling. "Kettle's on," he announced.

"Such a clever boy," Lily purred, and Skip beamed as if he had invented fire. Still, I detected a trace of nerves—or maybe it was sense—in the randy Dr. Robinson.

"Join us, Shelley," he said. "Please."

He sat down on a chair, leaving me the space next to Lily, although I would rather have sat next to a cobra. Lily said, "I think Shelley should go to Nuku'alofa."

This, I recalled, was the capital of Tonga, on a southern island.
"Why?"

"Bette Omont was there a week or so ago."

"Really?"

"You'll find her lost island there. If you hurry, you might catch the night flight." She slithered over onto Skip and entwined herself around him. "And we can go to my own private island." She shot me a look that was peculiar in its triumph, since there had been no contest. "So long, Shelley."

As I went to my room, I thought of my cat and the way he used to curl around my neck on cold nights. Then I apologized to my cat. A wind was rising, fluttering the curtains in my room. I looked out the window, but I couldn't see anything, not a goat or a chicken or even a curious passerby.

It can hit you all at once, the loneliness of a night. I kept thinking about Mafi running in the dark, and I wondered what happened when you fell into deep water. When did you stop thinking? Did you know when you died? I thought about the Devil, turned real again. Why had Mafi wanted to talk to me? Had the Devil been after her? I thought about Lily turning Skip into a warm pudding, and I wondered why I had thought she and I were alike.

I decided I would look at Mafi's tapa cloth, and that's when I realized it was gone. So was Jackson's letter, although the empty notebook was still on the nightstand. It's nuts how relieved I was when I saw his letter on the floor, but I didn't find the tapa cloth anywhere.

I finally got into bed, but in the dark, I could feel spiders crawling beneath the sheets. I turned the light back on and took the bed apart. There were no spiders, but I left the light on. Maybe I'd been saving Jackson's letter for such a night, when ghosts were rising up and rustling the bushes outside my window, a night when, as much as I wanted to sleep, I didn't want to be in the dark. I opened his letter and read it, and then I was lonelier than I'd ever been in my life.

16

I had just sat down to my morning loaf when Skip emerged from his room. He made a turn in midair and exited with a crash through the kitchen screen door. Foeata, pouring tea, frowned. "It is too bad about Dr. Sikipi."

"He'll be OK, Foeata. He probably just overreacted to eating more at one meal than he usually eats in a month. He'll live."

"And so he will be a good husband. So some people on this island know." She sat down. "Seli, I must tell you about Lily. She is not like a Tongan girl. She should not come looking for Sikipi, but she did. And she makes the big eyes at him like a cow and flutters like a fruit bat. This is not good."

I fortified myself with bread and jam before I said, "I think she likes him. I think he likes her." Foeata sighed, probably because she could not bring herself to call a palangi Peace Corps doctor loopy. "It's all right, Foeata. Love may be a joke no one else can resist, but I'm not very good at it."

She nodded. "Because you had no mother, and your feet did not grow. It was very sad when your mother died."

"I guess so."

"You would know more of love."

I wondered how much she would believe of any story I could tell her. The morning light was sparkling off the red flowers on her green dress, and her dark hair curled like a halo around her face, cherubic, round, and merry-eyed. It made me think of a Christmas tree topped with a slightly roguish angel, yet she was no hapless tree to be chopped down for a sacrifice. Her feet—now there were feet—were such substantial roots I doubted a hurricane could move her.

"She was very beautiful," Foeata prompted.

"Yes. She was. My brother looks like her."

"Not you?"

"No, not at all."

"But you are also very nice to see. Your hair is such a color—wild but nice, like you. A man will love such a red. But you must let it fall, not tie it in knots and stick it with pins." Having demolished my hairdo, she turned to my seaweed dress. "We will go to the market, and I will sew a dress for you. Your mother did this?"

"No."

"But she was clever."

"I don't know. She died a long time ago. Foeata, why do you have short hair when all the other Tongan women have long hair?"

"Oh," she chuckled, "I did not like having so much that is heavy on my head. My husband is dead. It is not a problem to please him. I cut it off. It is so nice. My head can dance."

"When did he die?"

"Oh, it is ten years, something like that."

"Why haven't you found another husband?"

She grinned. "Now I am too big for a man. Perhaps I should sit on him and—poof!—he would be gone. And I have my children, fine big boys, and so I do not need a man for this."

"Where are they?"

"One is in Nuku'alofa, and one is in New Zealand. The other I gave to my sister because she had no children. This is the Tongan way."

"The same way someone gave Lily away?"

"Lily was one-half palangi, and so it was right that the mother gave her to Dr. Omont and that she should go to America to live."

"Does anyone know who her parents were?"

"Perhaps Dr. Omont, but he is dead."

"Is this the first time she has come back to Tonga?"

"It is nicer, Seli, to speak of love than of Lily."

"Lily seems to know quite a lot about love."

"Perhaps you are telling me your heart will not break if Sikipi loves this woman."

"Yes, something like that."

"Ah. It was a nice letter he wrote to you, your mafu?"

It's fairly rare when David or I can't talk, but sometimes it happens, as it did then, when a mouthful of bread lodged in my throat.

"A nice letter," Foeata answered herself. "For, of course, I must see it each day and wonder, who is this man and why does she not read his letter? Now you have read it." She smiled, satisfied.

"Jackson wrote it when he was sleeping on ice. His brain wasn't working very well."

"A nice name, Jackison."

"He's just a friend, Foeata. I've known him all my life."

"And when you grew up, you fell in love?"

"No."

"He does not love you?" She looked so offended I couldn't help but be touched.

"It was mostly my fault. We didn't know how to do it."

"How?" she echoed, looking baffled.

"We messed up pretty badly." I accidentally spread Marmite instead of jam on a piece of bread, took a bite, and almost croaked.

"I do not understand 'messed up,' Seli."

"Most people don't, especially when they do."

"You quarreled?"

"It doesn't matter now. All I want is to write stories."

"But you must have a heart to tell stories, Seli. Like Jesus. He told very nice stories."

"Yeah, but by some accounts he came from an extremely creative family."

She chuckled. "The Devil will hear you say these things!"

"I don't care." I was feeling somewhat invincible, possibly because I'd eaten a whole loaf of bread. "I don't believe the Devil exists, Foeata."

"This is too bad, because he does."

I was about to ask her how she could be so sure when Mrs. Ogg came steaming up to the kitchen door. "It is a great honor," Foeata said doubtfully.

"I cannot come in," Mrs. Ogg replied, although no one had invited her. "I wish to speak to Miss—Sally, is it?"

I waved, curious to see if she would holler her business from the doorway. "How is God this morning?"

"I do not have much time. But I have come here as a fellow white woman—"

It was interesting how she stabbed each word with a pin as she spoke. "Fellow? Really?"

Laughter rippled from invisible sources outside. "Perhaps we might walk," she murmured.

"I haven't finished my tea. Would you like to join us?"

She came inside, looking around uneasily. I don't know what she thought might happen to her. Foeata went to the stove, ostensibly to get more tea, but I knew that nothing would persuade her to rejoin us. I can't say I blamed her. Mrs. Ogg perched on the edge of the chair, as if she would have the minimum atoms in her derriere in contact with it. Three people were watching us through the window.

"I must tell you," she said in a hushed voice, "the Tongans are not the same as you and I."

"Yes, but then you and I are not the same as you and I."

"I feel a responsibility to enlighten you as to some deceptive native practices that could cause you no end of problems. The Peace Corps are fond of portraying Tongans as a warm, generous people. This is because if you admire something, a Tongan will often give it to you. But he will then feel that if he admires something of yours, you should give it to him. And if you do not, he will simply help himself to it. If caught, he will admit it and insist he's committed no crime, so I must warn you against accepting gifts from Tongans, since they are not gifts at all."

"It's a good thing I didn't take the goat."

"I beg your pardon?"

"Of course, if I had taken it, I'd have had a goat for someone to admire."

"It would more likely be your radio or television."

"But I don't have either one. In fact, there may be nothing about me to admire."

"This gift that native woman gave you—"

"But she's hardly likely to turn up asking for televisions, since she is dead."

"I wonder if I might see it. I am interested in purchasing it."

"I wouldn't mind seeing it myself, but I seem to have lost it."

"Lost it? How?"

"I have no idea."

"Things do not just vanish."

"No, but we do lose them."

Excited voices interrupted us. Lebeca and Foeata, in the kitchen, were talking in high-speed Tongan. "Seli," Foeata called, "Lebeca has seen the ghost of Mafi!" Lebeca nodded, her eyes enormous.

"Ghost?" Mrs. Ogg repeated. "That is ridiculous. The woman is dead."

"That's the usual prerequisite to being a ghost," I pointed out, but Mrs. Ogg ignored me.

"You know that ghosts do not exist," she said sternly to Lebeca. "And you know what God does to liars."

"Seli believes in ghosts," Lebeca whispered.

"I do," I said, "and in bugbears and malt-worms too." I was thinking I'd also believe in God if He would, at that moment, goose Mrs. Ogg with a lightning bolt. For a moment, I thought He might have, although it was really only the sight of the Australian yachtie Joe Storey that had discomposed her. He sauntered up to the kitchen door.

"Morning, ma'am," he said to Foeata. "Connie! What are you doing here, darling? Up to your good works? Hullo, Josephine. I ran into your good friend Lily Omont this morning, and she said you want to go to Nuku'alofa. I'm sailing south this morning if you'd like a ride."

"No!" Foeata exclaimed, and Mrs. Ogg was looking equally shocked.

"She will certainly remove all doubts about her morals if she gets on a boat with you," Mrs. Ogg said. Joe looked more amused than offended, but Foeata stiffened and raised her frying pan until she resembled the Statue of Liberty. Mrs. Ogg must have realized that Foeata could flatten her like a fly. She was silent.

"Thanks," I said to Joe, "but Foeata and I are going shopping."

"Another time, then. Come on, Connie, I know Ron is raring to be off. He thinks he can beat me there."

He led her away. Foeata sank into a chair, fanning herself with her pan. "I could not permit it." She might have been explaining things to God. In a moment she had brightened again. "So, we will go to shopping, Seli!"

We set off for Burns Philips.

"Tell me about the ghost," I said to Lebeca.

"Perhaps I did not see anything."

"And perhaps you did. Did you happen to look at Mafi's tapa cloth?"

Lebeca shook her head. "No. Because it was only left at the fales with this note: 'Please give to Seli from Mafi.' I thought, it is a message from a dead woman and not for me."

"Er, yes. That's it. And now I've lost it."

"It will come back," Foeata said. "It was only borrowed."

Shopping with a mother was a new experience for me. Foeata made the shopkeeper pull down every bolt of fabric from the shelf above the canned corned beef, condensed milk, and toothpaste. She vetoed my choice of lime green printed with octopuses and squids; she favored the white satin. When I said it looked like a wedding gown, Lebeca giggled and Foeata smiled. We compromised on a lavender fabric printed with violets and forget-me-nots. She also requested white cotton for a nightgown. When I said I didn't need one, she ignored me. She had been alarmed to discover that my only sleeping garment was Jackson's cast-off T-shirt.

Just then, Gravity bounded up to announce that, it being a fine day, he could take me to Mrs. Omont's island. Foeata and Lebeca switched to Tongan as I left with him. I recognized only one of the fading stream of words: "Jackison."

17

Gravity did not keep his boat at the Neiafu harbor, but in a secret cove protected by steep cliffs that extended into the sea. He had discovered this hidden place as a boy, he said, and he kept his boat there because he could sail away unnoticed whenever he wished. We followed a narrow path through the bush, but when we came to the ocean, his boat was gone.

Gravity was thunderstruck. Where could it be? Who would take it without telling him? It was true he left the key in it so he always knew where it was, but he would lend his boat to anyone who needed it. Why would anyone take it without asking him?

"I must find it," he said, staring at the empty place and all the sea beyond. "But where?"

He set off back to town, but I stayed behind. I had not been so near the ocean for a long time. I climbed up to the top of a rocky promontory, which formed the western wall of Gravity's cove. It was slow going because of the damned dress, but when I reached it, I scanned the horizon. I saw a lot of water, but no boat. On the other side of this cliff was a patch of pristine white sand scattered with seashells. I slid down to have a closer look. They were whole and perfect, and I was collecting a few shells when I heard a laugh.

"Palangis cannot resist collecting anything." The man watching me was a palangi too, a short, plump, bald, red-faced one who resembled a lobster wearing Bermuda shorts and sunglasses and carrying a lumpy burlap bag. He introduced himself: Gil Tarkington, a marine biologist. He wandered through the South Pacific but mostly lived in Tonga where life was inexpensive. He lived in a hut that looked like it had been constructed from ship-wrecks, and beyond this was his research station, a collection of tanks, to which he was headed as he explained that, supported by occasional grants and selling seashells to tourists, he was writing a book about the mating habits of deadly sea creatures. The topic had been inspired by a question that fascinated him as a teenager: How could animals full of deadly poison do the deed without kill-ing each other?

"I suppose it's the sort of thing you think about when you are a teenaged male," I said.

"You've never wondered about it?"

"No, although I wonder how other species, like humans, mate without killing each other."

He plucked a handful of fish from his burlap bag. "Ready for lunch, darling?" he asked, dropping them into a tank filled with sand and rocks. A lump of sand moved; a fish vanished. Whereas Tarkington was merely odd-looking, the creature in the sand was downright ugly: a skulking, wart-covered lump of slime and algae with splayed fins, two bulbous eyes, and a ridge of spines along its back. "Know what it is?" he asked.

"No, but it looks like a senator I met once. A Republican, of course."

"It's a stonefish."

"Deadly?"

"Oh my yes, but you can't say it doesn't warn you off with its looks. If you see it. Sometimes it buries itself in the sand. You only feel it when you step on it. It injects its poison through those spines, and they're tough enough to pierce rubber soles."

"Then what happens?"

"You suffer excruciating pain, and unless someone has an anti-venin handy, you die."

The stonefish, he explained, was a member of a category of deadly sea creatures known as stingers. These ranged from sea urchins and sea stars to a sea wasp that could kill a bather who brushed against it in less time than it would take to stagger out of the sea. Other categories included biters, like sharks and sea snakes, and poisoners, like the puffer fish, which only killed you if you ate the wrong part.

"Who funds you, the CIA?"

He laughed, but he didn't deny it.

"So you're going to study his mating habits?" I had to admit it would be more appealing than studying the mating habits of a senator on either side of the aisle.

"There's a male in there somewhere."

"How do you know you have a male and a female? How do you find out?"

"Very carefully." He chuckled. "The male is a lot smaller."

In another glass tank, a rock moved. It swirled through the water and came to the glass. It was an octopus, who, as I watched it, changed from a spotted stone color to deep red.

"Hello, my lovely," Tarkington said. "Am I ignoring you? This is Dolores, a prima donna."

He lifted the covering on the tank, dropped a few limp fish in her tank, and closed it again. Dolores, ignoring the fish, pressed against the glass, her arms swirling, her eyes fixed on me. It is quite an experience to be studied by an octopus.

"Is she deadly?"

"Not to humans."

"Is that her mate?" I pointed to the corner where Dolores had been disguised as a rock.

"No, that's a rock. I don't have a male for her, which might be just as well. She'll mate once and starve, caring for her eggs. Then she'll die. She's pretty interested in you."

I watched her undulating tentacles. Was she waving hello or telling me something important and waiting for my slow-witted reply? I'd never had a conversation with an octopus and was somewhat out of my depth.

"Want to meet her?"

He shoved aside the tank cover, and Dolores floated upward. Her color changed again to green, like my dress, and while I watched her, mesmerized, she shot out one arm and grasped my hand. Its suction cups fastened onto my skin, oddly gentle. It was weird but not nearly as hair-raising as shaking hands with Richard Nixon, which I once had to do. Another tentacle slithered up my arm, tugging a little, then a third. I might have gone headfirst into the tank if Tarkington had not said, "OK, Dolores, have a fish."

He detached her and put the lid back on her tank. He weighted it down with rocks. "They're escape artists, octopuses," he said. I watched her move each fish along her arm until it disappeared. Who are you, I wondered; what are you saying? The octopus turned back to the glass as if she'd heard me.

"Where did you find her?" I asked.

"Oh, I didn't. My neighbor, Pulu, did." He pointed up through the trees. "He lives up there. A strange guy, but he brings me things when he catches them, and he lets me run electricity from his generators to keep these tanks going."

"How long will you keep her?"

He shrugged. "That's the same thing his wife, Mafi, was always asking."

"Mafi?"

"Kind of an oddball, but nice. She didn't like him catching things for me, but she looked after them when I traveled. I was surprised when she drowned. She always struck me as a kind of sea creature herself. Dolores liked her, didn't you?" he asked the octopus. "Both of you always trying to escape."

"Was she? Mafi, I mean."

"She kept her boat here so her husband wouldn't know when she was going to see her friend, the batty old artist who lives on her own island."

"Mrs. Omont?"

"Do you know her?"

"I've come to Tonga to work for her. It's where Gravity was going to take me." I told him about Gravity's boat, but he hadn't seen anyone sail off in it.

"Hey, I don't suppose you could get me a date with Lily Omont?" he asked.

"You've met her?"

"She stopped here looking for Pulu's house. She was interested in my fish. She liked the stonefish best. Wanted to know all about him. How deadly he was, how long it took to die. How painful it was. Not a woman to get on the wrong side of."

I said goodbye to him and Dolores; I hoped she understood. I went on along the path up the cliff to the house where Mafi had lived.

The land had been cleared around a small, square, beige bungalow, which looked like it had blown in on a tornado from any suburb, USA. It only needed a station wagon and a swing set, one of those metal ones that flip over if you push the swing too hard. Against its lush background of hibiscus flowers and coconut trees, the house looked as uncomfortable as a missionary sweltering in a black suit. I went closer, and through a window I could see a matched set of a gold tweed sofa and two armchairs. Ruffled gold lampshades sat on matching end tables, Early American style. A framed print of a bridge covered in snow hung above the sofa. A breakfast nook had a table and four chairs made of chrome and gray marbled plastic. On the table was an orange plastic napkin holder, salt and pepper shakers shaped like turkeys, and a little metal tree that held four matching orange coffee mugs.

There was a time when David had wanted a house like this instead of my grandfather's crazy house that perched like a lone hawk above the sea. "I just want to be normal," he had said, but he couldn't explain what normal was.

As I studied the house, the front door flung open, and a man barreled out. Mafi might have had strange taste in houses, but her preference in men ran to golden perfection, rippling muscles, curling black hair, and eyes that flashed like lightning.

"Who are you?" Pulu demanded. "What are you doing here?"

"I'm looking for Gravity's boat." My wits are never strong when someone brandishes weapons in my direction, even if it's only an umbrella, a wimpy plastic one at that.

"In my house?"

"Oh, well—"

"Get out of here."

I ran, zigzagging along a path until I was out of breath. I glanced back. He wasn't behind me, so I stopped. I didn't know where I was, but it was a trail, and I figured if I followed it, I'd end up somewhere, maybe even before dark. The trees and bush grew denser, the path narrower, the silence deeper. I came out on a cliff above the sea.

This is something I have wondered about: Is it possible for time and space to dissolve like disappearing walls? Can you be in one place and time, and somewhere else in the future or past, all in one moment? I had been thinking lately about my grandfather's house, and just then I might have stepped through a portal, an invisible door in time. I was standing on a lush green cliff above the calm blue sea surrounding the Kingdom of Tonga in the South Pacific, but I was also on the barren, rugged rocks of the wild Northern California coast. The gentle lapping of waves became the thunderous pounding of breakers, and the hot sunlight turned into a mist, like the gray fog that wrapped around my grandfather's House of Lost Things most of the time. Antonio and the house are both gone now, but for an instant, I could see it clinging to a cliff, and I felt the wind that had never stopped blowing. I heard children, laughing and calling to each other. Then the air cleared, and I saw Fresh Air coming toward me.

"You honor my house," he said.

His house was made of four posts and a roof, nearly hidden by blooming red and yellow hibiscus flowers, banana trees, and feathery palms. The walls were mats that rolled up and tied beneath the roof. He could unroll them if he ever needed walls, Fresh Air told me, but most often he did not. He invited me inside, although we were still outside with the view and the sound of the sea.

We sat on mats, and he cracked two coconuts together to split them. He handed me a half to drink from and carved pieces of meat from the other half. "You have been having adventures," he remarked.

I recounted them. "Why did Pulu build such a strange house?" I said. "Yours looks like it grew here, but it's hard to imagine Mafi living in that other one."

Fresh Air nodded. "It was both Pulu's good luck and misfortune that when he was a young man, he worked for a palangi in Nuku'alofa.

He learned English, and also, he learned to admire Western ways. I believe Mafi might have been happier in a poor old place such as this, but he wished for a Western house for her."

"So he could lock her up? You can't lock a door if you don't have one."

"Love can be"—Fresh Air munched on his coconut as he searched for a word—"a clumsy thing. Pulu, a good sailor, good fisherman, can still—" He shrugged.

"Mess up?"

"Yes. Mess up."

We munched our coconut, and finally I said, "I met an octopus today."

"They are wise creatures," Gravity said. "Some believe that the octopus, so unlike any other sea creature, is the last creature surviving from the wreck of an ancient world. She slipped through a crack in time."

"And now she is caught in our primitive world?"

He cracked another coconut. "This reminds me of a story. A man was sailing from Vava'u to his home on Tongatapu when a storm arose. The wind and waves destroyed his boat. He knew he would die, but he saw an octopus. 'Save me,' he cried, 'and I will give you a reward.' She caught him in her arms and brought him to an island. And when he was safely ashore, he built a fire and cooked and ate the octopus. 'It is only a devil fish,' he said, for that is what many have called the octopus, 'and I am so hungry.'

"When the sea was calm again, he thought, now, how shall I get off this island? He could have made a new boat, but he was a lazy fellow, and he stood on the shore and cried, 'Help me.'

"Another octopus came to the shore, and the man said, 'Take me to Tongatapu, and I will give you a great reward.' So this octopus carried him all the way to Tongatapu, and when he got there, he killed the octopus and took it home to his wife for dinner. 'After all,' he said to himself, 'it is only a devil fish, and I am a man.'

"Not long after, the man went out on a fishing boat, and when they pulled up their nets they had caught, among the fish, a giant octopus. 'Let me go free,' the octopus said, 'and I will give you a great reward. Beneath us deep in the sea lies a pearl, so rare and beautiful it is a pearl for a queen. Let me go, and I will bring it to you.'

"The man threw the octopus back into the sea. It disappeared but, a few minutes later, returned to the surface, holding out a pearl that glowed like the moon. Ah, the man thought, I shall be a rich man. But when he reached for it, he found himself once more in the embrace of an octopus. 'Unlike you, I have kept my promise,' said the octopus, 'but I am so very hungry, and you, sir, are the devil.' And that was the end of the man. A legend," Fresh Air concluded.

18

That night, Skip had a dinner date with Lily; he announced this with the uncertain air of one who knew he might be dessert. Foeata went to choir practice, and I went to my room. I was about to open my still-empty notebook when I noticed that the shells I had collected were rearranging themselves on my dressing table. I caught one as it plunged over the edge. A tiny crab peered out. "I'm sorry," I said. "I didn't know you were in there."

It seemed unjust that they would perish only because they hadn't been able to flee from an acquisitive palangi, so I borrowed Foeata's flashlight to take them home. The dark was coming on swiftly as I headed back to the beach. Tarkington's hut was dark, and the bush was still, except for the flutterings in the trees, night birds or fruit bats. I released my captives and was about to leave when I heard a clattering on the rocks above me and a coconut bounced off my head. The missionary kid tumbled down the cliff. He was panting; his jacket was torn, and his tie was askew. When he saw me, he shrieked and scurried up the trail, fast as a lizard. I didn't see the Devil or even a Peace Corps volunteer chasing him.

Feeling a trifle woozy, I sat down to wait till the racket in my brain subsided, but presently I realized that most of the noise was coming from Dolores's tank. She was trying to shove the lid off her cage. As

I went closer, she turned the color of moonlight. She opened like an umbrella and floated to the glass, twirling her arms, looking at me.

Even when I haven't just been hit on the head by a coconut, I have trouble distinguishing between what is naturally odd about life, which is to say most of life, and what is not, and this becomes more complicated when you've put yourself into a world where you eat ice cream with a fork and are not supposed to have legs, but if you want to know an entire heaven and earth, how picky can you be? All of this is to explain why I was fairly sure Dolores was saying, "Let me out." I took off the lid, and one of her arms slithered around mine.

"Hello," I said. "Is it true that you're the vestige of a vanished world? Is there hope, do you think, for this one?" Another arm wrapped around mine, and she looked at me with her curious octopus eyes. "Have you ever read Masefield?" I asked. "He wrote, 'I must down to the seas again,' which is interesting because either he used 'down' as a verb or—"

Dolores snatched the flashlight. I carried her to the water's edge, hoping she would let go of me before she went into it. She did, and before she vanished, she dropped Foeata's flashlight.

"Thanks," I said. "Well, goodbye." I climbed back up the cliff watching for a glimpse of her in the dark sea. Instead, I saw Gravity's boat.

As I returned to Foeata's, I realized that I had not thought about Jackson in the last half hour. This was encouraging because in San Francisco I'd thought about him at least once a minute, which is how often he once told me that the average man thinks about sex. When I asked him what they thought about the rest of the time, he said probably food. Of course, if I hadn't thought about him in San Francisco, I'd have had to think about other things like how I was going to survive and what I was going to do if I did. Here, where

I was so continually full, the future seemed a comfortable enough thing to contemplate, and the hourly dose of drama—stolen boats, ghosts, caterwauling missionaries, the passionate kissing of knees and throwing of teacups, conversations with octopuses—was enough to make my own romance, or lack thereof, seem a thing of minor consequence.

I wondered if, in the void created by not thinking about Jackson, my brain might come up with a story to write. An idea flitted around my head, blinking off and on like a firefly, deciding whether or not to land. I saw the faint outlines of a face. Was it a character? It vanished. I was at the edge of town, looking at a person sitting on a tree stump. Mrs. Ogg.

"Oh, hello," she said. Her faintly dazed air made me wonder if she too had recently been brained by a coconut. She had lost her hat, and her hair was askew.

"Are you all right?" I asked.

"I was sitting. Just sitting. But there was a stonefish."

An unfortunate image emerged, but I could not persuade Mrs. Ogg to budge from her stump, so I sprinted to the hospital for help. I was surprised to find Skip in the lobby, but I didn't have time to ask why he was there. When I told him Mrs. Ogg might have sat on a stonefish, he rushed off to find her. I trailed behind and listened with admiration as, despite detours to topics such as God, the Devil, and so forth, Skip ascertained that no part of her anatomy had encountered a stonefish. Her head, however, must have suffered some kind of jolt. "Who?" she asked when Skip asked where the Rev was.

"Your husband, ma'am."

"One wonders how God makes marriages, sometimes."

"Mrs. Ogg," I said, "weren't you and Rev. Ogg sailing this morning south to Nuku'alofa?"

"He left. He—left."

She said nothing else. Skip and the entourage escorted her to the Port of Refuge Hotel, where Ever-Ready got her a room. I was on my way to Foeata's when Skip caught up with me.

"What were you doing out in the bush at night alone?" he demanded.

"What happened to your date?" He seemed entirely too irritable for anyone who had spent any quality time with Lily.

"She stood me up."

"That's odd. She seemed pretty interested in you, and I don't think she was just overcome by being in Paradise."

"Not many women are." The conversation died for a bit. "I'm sorry about yesterday," he added.

"Sometimes I wonder what it would be like to be normal," I said, but keep in mind I'd just been brained by a coconut. "To be able to say, yes, here we are beneath the mosquito net in the South Pacific, and see what happens next. But my brain always interferes. It starts wondering what if you are a lunatic with wives stashed in refrigerators or what if you are my long-lost cousin or what if I catch an incurable disease and lose my mind and have to give up writing before I've ever started because of a few minutes when I thought I was in Paradise. Or—"

"You really think about all that?" He was clearly impressed. "No wonder you want to write. Now, I'm curious: Have you ever actually made it into bed with anyone? Or am I being too crude? Should I ask if you've ever been in love?"

"Never mind."

"Ah. Was it this Jackson?"

"No."

"Come on, tell me about him."

"No."

"Foeata says you're devoted to each other."

"Foeata has the soul of a reporter."

"He's a doc?"

"A med student, sort of."

"Sort of?"

"He took a break to climb mountains."

Skip laughed, and I did not like the idea that he was sniggering at Jackson, so I changed the subject to his own love life, which was not hard to do. He described the one hundred and seven times he had been in love. Each affair had had a fine simplicity and the life span of a virtual particle, which, you may not know, dies before it exists or something like that. Physicists thought of it. In Skip's world, people fell into bed and out of it the way people used to fall in and out of love, I guess.

"I wonder what it would be like to be you for one night," I said, "just to see what it's like not to think."

"We could probably arrange this," he offered, and, all of a sudden, I felt a spasm so sharp I had to stop walking. He groaned. "Oh, Jesus Christ, I've done it again."

"No, it's not you."

"Yes, this is evident."

"I think it was the coconut."

19

Skip diagnosed either a mild concussion or a severe aversion to discussing love and sex. Foeata insisted I spend the following day resting in bed and eating. I didn't mind. Ensconced against the embroidered dragons, in a hiatus during which no one made me tour hospitals or drink tea with missionaries or get engaged, I began to feel comfortable with life. It was entirely possible that the coconut had knocked a hole in my head that could be filled in by a story. It would require, however, a character, and one of the things that has always stymied me is this problem: I've never been able to improve upon Oblomov. In this extremely great novel by Goncharov, his character, Oblomov, goes to bed when life gets to be too much for him and doesn't get up again. I was trying to imagine a better hero than Oblomov when Skip knocked on my door and came in, followed closely by Foeata. He looked nice and doctor-like in his tie and white coat, but the overall impression was marred by the paperback book in his pocket titled *Where There Is No Doctor.*

I said, "In politics, there are people whose job is to pluck things like that off the boss before he goes out in public and undermines The People's confidence in him."

"Your head seems to be fine," he retorted. "How's the heart?" He counted my pulse. "There you are, Foeata. Normal. Sad but true. I can't even make it flutter."

"She must eat more." Foeata hurried off.

"Skip," I asked, "could you do me a favor?"

"Hey, maybe I counted wrong."

"If I want to stay in bed, would you say it's necessary?"

"I could be persuaded."

"I need to work. 'Who is the hero of *Paradise Lost*?'"

"Huh?"

"It's a quote my brother likes. Lord Byron asked the question. He answered it too. 'The Devil, of course.'"

"You want to stay in bed with the Devil? Crushed again."

"Did you see Mrs. Ogg this morning?"

"I stopped by the hotel, but she'd already left. She flew south to catch up with the Rev. I wonder how he slipped his leash."

"He was racing Joe Storey. He might have wanted to lighten his load. Maybe her dizzy spell was caused by thinking about what he might be up to."

"Shelley, I am truly fascinated by your mind."

Foeata returned carrying a tray filled with tea, bread, Jell-O, eggs, jelly roll, and spaghetti sandwiches. When I said I might not be able to eat it all, she burst into tears.

"Foeata," Skip said, "she's really all right."

"She just has to stay in bed for two weeks," I prompted.

"She does not."

I lay back on my dragon pillow and closed my eyes.

"I will light candles so Jesus will take care of her," Foeata said.

"You're preempted, Skip," I said.

"Good. Let Jesus explain why you need to stay in bed," Skip replied.

"Foeata, I might have a character," I said. She looked worried, but she might have confused it with a concussion, so I explained. She became interested.

"Is he handsome?" she asked.

"No, not excessively, anyway. I think he has red hair. He's feeling battered by life, which means he's been through a relationship, the way you might also have been through a brick wall. He's studying physics to see if there might be any truth to the rumor that there's a plan to the universe. He has never been near a medical school."

"You understand, Foeata," Skip interrupted, "this is a creature of her imagination, this man she'd spend two weeks in bed with."

"But where there is a character, a story often follows," I pointed out. Foeata smiled. I think she saw herself as a grandmother, and she led the doc away.

That afternoon, Foeata brought in the mail. A telegram from the sister of Mrs. Omont read: "Odd but quite like Bette. Will wire additional funds."

There was also a handwritten note: "If you will have the compassion of a Christian, you will hear my side." It was unsigned, but I made a wild guess at the author, which was confirmed when I saw the anxious face of the missionary kid at my window. I went to meet him in the garden. Rule two, you know.

He looked unwell. He clutched his head as if he were trying to squeeze words out of his brain. He opened and shut his mouth, but nothing came out. I can't say I didn't know the sensation, but still I felt like a many-headed man-eater. Finally, he whispered, "I've been praying you will have mercy on me."

"Did you throw the coconut at me?"

"No! No. I should begin at the beginning. Do you mind?"

"Not at all."

"I did it because I was in love! I was tempted and I gave in, but I will never do it again!"

"Do you know," I said, "it's a literary problem, figuring out where the beginning is. Physicists think about it too, but their beginnings can lead you close to infinity. Maybe you should start at the end. What did you do?"

"I fell in love with Lily! She is so sweet, so kind, so good—"

"What is your name?" I had learned in David's office that you can get the most raving looney to calm down by asking a fairly easy question.

"Albert."

"And you came to tell me that you fell in love with Lily?"

"No. I came to tell you what I did because I fell in love with Lily—but I can't! I can only ask you to forgive me."

"OK." He was motionless, except for his eyes, darting about, I worried, from visions of devils.

"Where did you meet Lily?" I doubted it was at church; he had, I was sure, quite a few forbidden territories.

His face flushed bright red. "You meet everyone on an island."

"And you did something for her?"

"I would do anything for her! Would he?"

"Who?"

"That doctor! What does he have that I don't?"

Rather than answer this, I asked, "What did you do?"

"I am so sorry! I am!"

"I believe you. But what does it have to do with me? You didn't bump Mrs. Omont off, did you?" His expression disintegrated into one so wretched I wondered if this could explain everything, but the image of him croaking someone at Lily's behest faded before reality. Lily seemed a practical person, and if she wanted to get rid of someone, I doubted she'd choose Albert to do it. "It's just an object of ongoing concern for me," I said. "She hired me, but I haven't a notion of where she is. Do you know where Lily is?"

"No! She wanted to go to Mrs. Omont's island, but she couldn't find her boat. But she's gone!"

"You didn't, by any chance, take Gravity's boat yesterday, did you?"

"No! I wouldn't!"

"But Lily would?"

"I don't know." His voice sank. "She asked me: Who has a boat? I told her to ask Kalavite. Then I heard his boat was gone. I went to the cove. I waited. I thought about God and how I had failed. I prayed for a sign that I could have another chance."

"Did you see her bring it back?"

"I didn't see anyone! No one at all! Do you believe me?"

"I haven't told anyone I saw you, if that's what you mean."

"Thank you," he whispered.

"Just go and sin no more."

As he left the garden, the daily storm broke overhead, and I thought about David's office in Santa Rosa. In his early zeal to serve The People, David rented a place next to the Social Security and Internal Revenue offices and just below a mental health clinic, without realizing that dealing with either of those first two places would leave most folks too deranged to climb the stairs for emergency psychological aid, so they staggered into his office. He'd been there about three weeks when I noticed he had a little less conviction when he told me I had to wish to know an entire heaven and earth. Albert wasn't unlike the people who came to David's office when they'd been driven half-crazy by life. They each unrolled a tale of woe, but almost always left out a few pertinent facts. I just couldn't figure out what the kid was leaving out.

The next morning, Foeata made me get up. She announced that a miracle had happened, and I was well. I didn't think it was Christmas or any other significant day, but I had a feeling I was going to church again. She brought me the dress she'd made from the violet fabric. It was high-necked, long-sleeved, floor-length, and made me look like everybody's Victorian. When I pointed this out, Foeata said it was not so bad a thing to be shaped this way, and it might even provide a distraction from my feet. As long as I did not appear to have legs or elbows, I was proper. She gave me a bar of perfumed soap to wash my hair and a vat of Tongan oil to rub on my skin. She wouldn't let me braid my hair but said to let it fall free. She fixed a hibiscus blossom in it.

We went into the garden. She told me to sit down and look nice while she made coconut cream. First, she whacked the coconut on a post to split it. With a flick of her wrist, she grated the insides on a metal claw fixed to a bench. She squeezed the juice out of the meat with her hand. This was the cream.

"Perhaps you would like to try it." She gave me a coconut and went inside.

I hit the coconut on the stick but didn't make a dent in it. I was jumping up and down, trying to hit the coconut hard enough to crack it, when I heard Albert calling from the other side of the passionflower hedge. "Shelley? May I see you? Foeata says no, but I must." He peered around the gate, stopped, and stared as if he'd seen the Devil himself above my shoulders.

"What's up? God on your back again?"

"It is not God." He was pulling on his tie so hard I was afraid he might strangle himself.

"But man? Here we agree."

"You have such courage, such fire."

I dropped my coconut, and it rolled under the bushes. He stepped in front of me as I went to retrieve it.

"You are so beautiful!"

I heard a faint, but distinct, sniggering from the other side of the hedge. Foeata burst from the house frowning like a director whose scene has gone awry.

"You are a good boy," she told Albert, "but go away."

He scurried off. Foeata went back inside. The sniggering had turned to outright laughter. The gate opened. I half expected to find it was God or the Devil getting their kicks for the day. But it was Jackson.

20

Jackson was at school in England from the time he was eleven until he was seventeen, and what he mainly seems to have learned there, besides an aversion to Brussels sprouts, is the art of saying something no matter how bizarre a situation might be. That's why, as I stood clutching my coconut, staggered, thunderstruck, and dumb, he said, "Oh, hello," as if he often turned up on the other side of passionflower hedges in the Kingdom of Tonga. "How are you?"

I went back to trying to crack the coconut while I took an inventory of my brain to see if I could find a reply there, but the region was barren and desolate; a tornado had passed through it and blown everything in its path over the rainbow.

"What are you doing?" he asked.

"Cracking a coconut."

"Do you need help?" He took the coconut. He had to hit it three times before it split. He handed the pieces back to me.

Foeata's immense sigh penetrated my daze. She stood in her doorway, frowning to indicate my behavior was feeble-minded, weak-hearted, and all-around inadequate. Although she would not have needed to know extraneous details like who he was and what he was doing there to welcome him, this clearly was not the case. She stepped forward, flung open her arms, and exclaimed magnificently, "Jackison!"

She bore him off to the house. She reappeared to beckon to me. "I haven't grated the coconut yet," I said.

Drawing herself up to her full height, she assumed her most no-nonsense, my-ancestors-ate-your-ancestors attitude. I knew if I didn't go willingly I'd make an undignified entrance being hauled in by my hair. I stood up and tried to make my knees work. Foeata broke into a huge grin. "Seli, he is so handsome."

Jackson's self-possession is often a short-lived thing, and he clearly had depleted it in saying, "Hello, how are you?" and cracking the coconut. Sitting at the dining room table, he was staring, mutely transfixed, at an array of eggs, jam rolls, papayas, bread, spaghetti, corned beef curry, pancakes, pineapples, and bananas. Five Tongans were watching him through the window. Several more came through the dining room to borrow eggs while outside children sang "Love Me Tender."

Foeata thumped me on the head, and I sat down. She sat down between us, so I could see only fragments of Jackson, his hands, his knees, his feet. "This is so kind of you," he said to her. He was sounding like a Brit, which meant all of his wits were scrambling. "I've never seen so much food."

"Not in America?"

"Maybe in a market."

Foeata beamed. I knew he was being adopted and would probably be her favorite. "You must eat. You are too thin, too pale. Seli is my daughter and so she has my heart; still, a man might wish to beat her with a pandana bush, if she is too interesting and he is too weak." I don't know what Jackson found so amusing in this, but he leaned around Foeata to grin at me and ate his spaghetti on toast.

Foeata made conversation. This was a good thing because if Jackson had knocked the coconut on my head three times, I would

not have been more discombobulated. While Foeata asked about the
health of his parents and of the Queen of England, I studied his left
hand. It looked real, more tanned and calloused than I remembered.
He had five fingers. I was glad he had not lost any in the Himalayas.
Maybe if I touched him and he didn't vanish in a cloud of smoke, I
might believe I wasn't hallucinating, but I couldn't bring myself to do
it. Just then, Foeata gave me a nudge, which all but landed me on the
floor. She was encouraging me to say something.

"I got hit on the head by a coconut," I said. "Yesterday; no, the day
before." Then, I gave myself up to empathy for Albert.

Foeata sighed. "You stay at the fales by the sea, Jackison? It is nice?"

"Yes. It's quite nice."

"But, of course, the showers are cold."

"Well, yes."

"Perhaps you must stay here. I have one more room, not too close
to Seli, and I have hot showers."

"Really?" Crazed mountaineer that he is, Jackson has a weakness
for hot showers and soft beds.

"You would like to try it?"

He didn't know she meant immediately, but she carried him off.
While he showered, Foeata stood outside the stall, discussing the hot
water situation in California and England, and I decided to head up
the half-mountain to see if my brain would work better at a higher
altitude. Foeata collared me at the door.

"Seli, you must not be so much like a chicken who runs away when
the wind blows."

"How did you know he was coming here?"

"Ah, perhaps he arrived so late last night, and Moses drove him to
the fales, and when he said he had come to see Seli at Mrs. Omont's,
Moses could tell him you were at my house. Moses told me this, and

today he brought Jackison here, and it is good that you are looking so fine and beautiful and almost fat."

"Do you know why he is here?"

She patted my head. "You have a very nice brain, and so you must use it, if you will not use your heart. Oh, my girl, I am so happy for you."

When Jackson emerged from the shower, his hair was wet and wavy. When we were kids, I thought his dark hair was beautiful, like Snow White, which had offended him greatly. Remembering this, however, knocked me out of my stupor. I might have even thought of something to say, like hello, but Foeata directed him past me and into her living room, where a group of Tongan men had assembled. Fresh Air was heading the delegation.

"They have come to welcome you," he told Jackson, "and to hear about your mountains."

I wondered what Jackson would do. He is rather shy, and he hardly ever talks about mountains, especially to strangers. It's just something he does, seeking out high places whenever he can. He goes into a decline, like an unwatered plant, if he doesn't see a mountain every so often, if he can't get himself up to where he is unlikely to see anyone else except an eagle or a mountain goat. Exactly what he finds there, the freedom, the wilderness, or just the view, he has never really said. The place within him that matches these wild places lies close to his heart, and that region, I have learned, is as well guarded as any mountain peak. His Brit training resurfaced, however, and he said to Fresh Air, "I should have to speak English."

"This is fine. They will understand."

Jackson sat down next to Fresh Air, rubbed the back of his neck, and started to talk. Hearing his voice was a little like listening to the first rain after a long drought. I have always liked his voice. I suppose he is handsome enough, although he's not like David. He doesn't walk around under the golden light of a superman; you could pass Jackson on a street and not fall down in a hormonal fit. He is the sum of too many odd parts that make him more interesting than beautiful. His Danish grandfather married a Roma woman; his other grandmother, from the south of France, insists she is Arab, Jew, and Provençal. She married a Welshman who, I think, gave Jackson the music in his voice. He is almost as odd a concoction as David and I. We, all of us, are the product of people accidentally crossing paths in a world growing smaller. But there he was, Jackson, wearing his old jeans and a faded blue plaid shirt, explaining, with enthusiasm overtaking reserve, to the inhabitants of a South Pacific coral atoll what it was like to try to get oneself up to the roof of the world.

21

When Jackson finished talking, Foeata announced he must rest and escorted him to a bedroom. I went into the garden. I had left off trying to think of something to say to him since it wasn't clear I'd ever have to. I glanced at his window, in case I had imagined him. He was sitting on a bed reading a book.

"Seli!" Foeata came outside, laughing. "You are like a Tongan now! How can Jackison rest if you stand at his window?"

A minute later, Jackson came into the garden. "I can't sleep during the day," he told Foeata.

She nodded. "And Seli would not stop watching you."

I occupied myself with studying the interior structure of a hibiscus blossom. I accidentally pulled out its insides and was trying to stick it back together when Skip shuffled up in his flip-flops. Gravity and Lebeca, all delight and curiosity, were with him.

Skip said, "You're looking fetching today, Shelley. What's the occasion? Are we getting married at last?"

Foeata made introductions with a dark and threatening dignity. Skip clutched his heart. "No! Not The Jackison?"

"Of course it is the Jackison," Gravity said. "We told you this, Sikipi, and so not to say something that will make Seli's face go as red as her hair, for she has yearned for him so much."

Lebeca added shyly that she had already met Jackson at the fales, and for one minute I wished I were a beautiful Tongan who could make Jackson smile as he did at her. It was quite unnerving to hear myself think this.

"So what brings you to Tonga?" Skip asked Jackson.

I said, "He had an attack of brain-damaging hypothermia in the Himalayas and got on the wrong airplane, like the man who went to Auckland instead of Oakland."

"Seli." Foeata looked stern, briefly; then brightening, she announced it was time for supper. While we'd been talking, women had spread mats on the ground and covered them with enough food to feed China. Jackson stopped smiling at Lebeca.

"Shell," he murmured, "what if I'm still full?"

"Then you only have to eat half of everything before we join in. You're the guest of honor. Save room for dessert."

He pulled my hair, and my flower fell to the ground. He picked it up and tried to fix it back in place, but he did this awkwardly, and it drooped over my ear. When I reached up to adjust it, my fingers bumped his. It felt like I'd touched a live wire that addled my brain, but I managed to sit down and not fall down. Jackson, taking the place next to me, narrowly missed being sat on by Foeata, who paused, smiled, and did not even pick him up and move him to a more respectful distance. Instead, she towered over him like Mount Everest.

"I will make my speech," she said. "Jackison, we welcome you to Tonga, these quiet islands where palangis may rest, grow fat, and fall in love." While she provided blood-curdling examples of her success as a matchmaker, I ate an entire a loaf of bread, and Jackson, previously full, ate a plateful of everything. Foeata beamed approvingly.

Gravity stood up next. "I am most happy to welcome you to Tonga because truly we have many worries with Seli."

"What do you mean?" I asked.

"Always, she is one place when she should be another."

"Yes, I know," Jackson said.

"Yes!" Gravity continued, "First, we hear that she has come here to work for Mrs. Omont, but Mrs. Omont is not here. Seli wishes to go to Mrs. Omont's island, but when I go to the fales to take her there, Lebeca says no, she is at Foeata's, and Foeata tells me, no, she has gone to hospital."

"Hospital?" Jackson glanced at me.

"A tour," I mumbled.

"And when I go to hospital, they say no, she has gone home, very ill with leprosy."

"Heat rash," Skip corrected.

"I come to Foeata's again, but she says, no, Seli has gone dancing with the new Peace Corps doctor."

"Dancing?" Jackson again. Foeata folded her hands and looked altogether pleased.

"But," Gravity said, "at the Port of Refuge she is not dancing but standing outside alone while Sikipi is with Lily."

"Lily is Mrs. Omont's adopted daughter," I said. "No one knows who her biological parents were. My guess is Catherine the Great and Genghis Khan."

Lebeca explained, "Lily is very beautiful but very bad and hot for many men."

Skip interrupted peevishly, possibly because of the slights to his inamorata: "Lebeca, do you know where Lily went?"

"She told Ever-Ready she would go to Nuku'alofa."

Jackson was silently mouthing, "Ever-Ready?"

"Gravity's brother," I told him. "He works at the Port of Refuge."

"Lily went to Nuku'alofa?" Skip interrupted. "But we had a date."

"I am sorry to tell you this, Sikipi," Gravity said, "because we know you have great lust for this woman, but Lily is not so very nice."

"And she was busy stealing Gravity's boat on Monday," I added.

Even Gravity looked astonished. "Why do you say this?"

I thought of Albert strangling himself. "Because."

"It was only borrowed," Foeata said. "It came back."

"She couldn't have stolen it," Skip objected, either because he thought I was accusing Lily unjustly or because I was suggesting she had stood him up for a more enthralling enterprise.

"Maybe she sailed south with Reverend Ogg," I said. "Maybe it's why he left Mrs. Ogg behind. They are big-shot palangi missionaries, Jackson. She came here Monday because she wanted to buy a piece of painted tapa cloth that an artist named Mafi sent me just before she disappeared."

"She drowned," Skip said.

"The same night the truck killed my dog," Gravity added sadly.

"But Gravity kindly stewed his dog for us," I said.

"Dog?" Jackson glanced at his curry.

"Tasty, isn't it?"

"Shelley, for shame," Skip said. "Don't worry, Jackson. Dog is not used for curries, only cat."

"But this is beef from New Zealand," Lebeca said, and Jackson smiled at her again.

"Mafi was like your running nun, Jackson," I said. "She ran when she had seizures. This night she ran away, but they never found her, just her boat."

"Then how do you know she drowned?" Jackson asked Skip, and for that moment, I was immensely fond of Jackson.

"The tevolos took her," Foeata said firmly.

"She invited me to her house, and I thought I was going there, but I ended up touring the hospital. Mafi left me a gift, a painting on tapa, and Lebeca brought it to me after church."

"Church?" Jackson asked. "Who was at church?"

"Everyone," Foeata said happily.

Jackson looked down at his place, organized his face, and looked up again. "What was it a painting of?"

"I don't know," I said. "I lost it before I looked at it. It seemed like a gift from a dead hand, and so I thought I'd look at it after the Sunday feast, but then Skip ate so much he fainted."

"It was my first feast," Skip explained; Jackson nodded understandingly.

Gravity picked up the narrative. "And so Foeata says to me, perhaps another time Sikipi and Seli will teach at Sunday school; today, they will rest. She asks, will I watch the house, and very soon I see Seli running fast, like the wind."

"You were there?" Skip asked, with evidence of collywobbles.

"And I see Lily coming to the house. Where is Seli? It grows dark. I must find her."

"Was that you in the graveyard?" I asked. Everyone looked at me. "I didn't go there on purpose."

"No," Lebeca said. "It was I."

"You?" Gravity asked. "You went there at night? Alone?"

"Yes, because Salote said Sikipi tried to kiss Seli—"

"Sikipi!" Foeata exclaimed, and Skip blushed red as a tomato.

"Oh, but Seli was not like an American movie," Lebeca said. "She ran away so fast, and I knew she would go up the mountain to think. I did not want you to be alone, Seli, so I went by the path through the cemetery, but I was hit on the head by a tree."

"That might have been my spider-finder."

Jackson chortled.

"Just wait," I said. "The spiders here probably ate the dinosaurs."

"And you fought them off with a tree?"

"A palm frond. I was on the mountain when it turned dark. Spiders had been dangling everywhere, but I couldn't see them, so I waved it in front of me. I followed a path that ended in the graveyard. I am sorry I hit you, Lebeca. When you shrieked and ran, I tried to follow you, but I fell in an empty grave. I saw a face, and then a machete came flying through the air and hit the spider-finder."

"I saw the face too," she whispered. "I thought it was—"

She stopped. I said it for her: "Mafi's ghost."

Lebeca nodded. "Mrs. Ogg says I did not see it. But what else could it be?"

"Well, I thought it was Lily. But when I got back here—and I ran pretty fast on account of the machete—she was here, and I couldn't quite figure out how she could have been running around graveyards, shrieking and throwing machetes. Also, my tapa cloth was gone." The silence was profound. "I think it's all connected."

"What is?" Jackson asked.

"Everything."

"That's a bold observation."

"There are mysteries," I said. "Think about it. Mrs. Omont hires me, sort of. She disappears. Mafi said she'd like to talk to me. She vanishes into the ocean. Lily was researching a story that sounded like *Winter's Tale* set in the South Pacific, but she said it was hers. She thinks Dr. Omont was murdered because he saved her. She said she wouldn't mind getting what Mrs. Omont got, money."

There was a moment of gratifying silence before Skip cleared his throat. "Lily may be a bit intense, but her pastimes are hardly murder and blackmail. Or literary research. Besides, Lebeca said she went to Nuku'alofa."

"Where she told me to go."

"She just wanted you to get out of here to anywhere."

"Me? Why?"

"Because, well—because."

"Because it was said you would marry Sikipi," Lebeca said, "and Lily was so very angry. Ever-Ready heard her."

Gravity nodded. "If she had thrown the machete at you, she would not have cut off only the head of the spider-finder."

Skip said to Jackson, "Our engagement was a misunderstanding, owing to the fact that I looked at Shelley's leprosy in public."

"But it saved him from being pinched," I added.

"I'll tell you about this later," Skip said to Jackson, "but in the meantime, you should avoid being alone in dark places."

"Yes, you are so handsome," Foeata agreed. "And, of course, you must not worry if we thought it was a fine thing for Seli to marry Sikipi. We did not like to see her so alone and sad, with no mafu."

To change the subject, I said, "But why was I shanghaied to the hospital if not to be stopped from meeting Mafi?"

"Oh," Lebeca said, "but you asked for this. Do you not remember? When you were lost and I found you so we could go to the post office, you said should we not also see the hospital? It was too late this day, but we thought if she wishes this—"

Jackson was laughing openly now. So was Skip.

"Well," I said, "someone explain what Lebeca and I saw in the graveyard."

"I cannot think it was Mafi," Foeata mused, "for she was a good woman and would not throw a machete at you."

"What they saw, Foeata," Skip said, "were creatures of Shelley's imagination."

"They are old friends of mine," Jackson said.

"So how were the Himalayas?"

"Somewhat quiet, actually. We just climbed a mountain."

"Yes, I can see why you'd have to look up Ilillouette here, for a little excitement, after such a dull time of it."

"Yes," Lebeca said, "it is so nice that when Jackison learns these things he must fly here."

"What?" Jackson asked. "No, not at all. I didn't—I just—I just wanted—well—"

"You wanted to see Seli," Foeata prompted. "This is not so bad."

Jackson was silenced. Fresh Air, who had been listening with the air of a presiding judge, rose. "Jackison, we welcome you. Weary from your travels, you can rest here, where you are already on top of the mountain. There, it was cold; here, it will be warm. There, it was much work to survive; here—" He paused, I suspect, to rewrite his speech.

"Perhaps, if you come to these islands from America, you can say, this is the way life is, a piece here, a piece there, and no reason they should fit together, but I prefer to think that you can still draw a line from yesterday to today and tomorrow. Seli has said there are mysteries. This, I like. You laugh because she wishes to make a story of this. But why not? There are not so many stories in the world: We tell them again and again. Stories of love and power and death, but they are all mysteries.

"Mafi sent a gift to Seli. Now someone has borrowed it, and we do not know why. Perhaps Mafi wished to tell Seli something, but we do not know what. This is a mystery. Mafi was a shy and gentle artist. I do not think death changes one so much that she would throw machetes, so we do not know what Seli and Lebeca saw, and this is a mystery.

"Mrs. Omont, we do not know well. She is different from us. She lives alone, and when she wishes to no longer be alone, she hires someone from far away to be her friend. She is here, then gone, and if Seli had not asked where is she, perhaps we would not have thought of it. A mystery. And Kalavite's boat: Did it sail away and back by itself? Another mystery. And Lily. A beautiful woman, what does she wish for? Is it love? Or did she too run, to not be caught by man or god? Here is the greatest of all mystery. For these many things, I will say to you, you must go to the island of Mrs. Omont."

He sat down. Neither Skip nor Jackson said anything snitty, and in less time than it would take Congress to decide on what day it was, we agreed that in the morning, barring any new storms, we would go to Mrs. Omont's island.

"Now," Foeata announced, "everyone must go dance. This is good for the heart. But first, dessert."

I watched Jackson's face as she brought it out. This time she hadn't forgotten the ici kelemi.

22

"What country, friends, is this?" I said. It's my alternative to wishing to know an entire heaven and earth. Shakespeare, like David, always has something to say.

Jackson nodded and glanced back at the parade of chaperones, dogs, chickens, goat, and pigs following us along the crushed coral road to the Port of Refuge Hotel. He is thirteen months older than I am, and when we were nine and ten, this was significant; even at eighteen, he was inclined to tell me how the world worked. If, in the last few years, his confidence had wavered, I still was not prepared for him to be so quiet. Of course, I wasn't prepared for him at all, in any form; still, it did seem this side of peculiar that, as he must have known where he was going, he would seem so bewildered to have landed here. He said nothing, but kept alternating his studies of the road with glances at the Milky Way.

When we reached the Port of Refuge, the band in hibiscus shirts was playing, people were dancing around the wooden statues, and the fourth wall was open to the vista of trees and the sea. A crescent moon, waxing, was visible among the stars. The band began "Love Me Tender," which I was beginning to think was the Tongan national anthem. Skip asked Lebeca to dance, and Gravity, frowning, went to the bar.

"Would you like to dance?" Jackson asked this so formally he might only have been taking a survey. We had done quite a lot of things in our past, but we had never danced. While I considered this, he took my arm, and we were on the dance floor.

Here is the nutty thing: A few days earlier, I had danced in this room like a normal person, but when Jackson put his arm around me, with a form so proper no Tongan mother could have objected, I promptly fell into a deranged fit. I could only keep my knees from sliding into my ankles by locking them into place, which meant I couldn't move, let alone dance. He halted too, and there we were, rooted to the floor as if an ancient spell was turning us into coconut trees. He bent his head down near mine. "Do you want to get out of here?"

I nodded. We headed toward the open wall and the high cliff overlooking the harbor. I sat down on a rock and thought about blowing away to Tahiti. Jackson stayed standing.

"Shall we walk?" he asked. He offered me his hand, looking doubtful; I suppose he didn't know if this would send me into another dysfunctional plight. I didn't know myself if I could hold hands with him and walk at the same time. I managed it, but my brain collapsed into a weird, mute state, and I didn't know if I would ever find any words in my head or if this would be a permanent affliction, in which case it might be better to go back inside and not dance on the dance floor. I wondered what another woman would have done in my situation, Catherine the Great, for example, or Lily. I didn't think that not being able to talk would have hampered them. But even as my brain hopped about like a panicky flea on hot sand, I noticed Jackson wasn't doing much better himself. He was examining my hand as if he were trying to decipher a message written in ink that had faded a long time ago.

"Did you know the king said time begins here?" I asked.

"Did he? Why?"

"Because it's near the international dateline. But I like it, the idea of islands where time begins."

"Do you? It's not too close to infinity?"

"I hadn't thought of that."

"Sorry—I didn't mean to—it's—well, that's interesting. My grandmother used to talk about an island in time. She'd light candles on Friday night and again on Saturday night, and she said this set apart those hours as an island in time. One candle said guard, and one said remember. I used to ask her, 'Guard what? Remember what?'"

"How is she?"

"Fine. Well, she broke her leg chasing a goat, but she was better as soon as they let her leave the hospital to go home. I went to see her before we left for Nepal. She asked about you. She likes you. I suppose it's because you are so much alike, although you don't really look like her. You're taller—well, not that much taller. And your eyes are brown but hers are blue. Her hair is brown; well, it's white now."

He stopped talking, although I hadn't minded listening to him compare me to his ninety-year-old grandmother and tell me I had brown eyes. We had come to the crushed coral road. He stopped. "Can we leave? Or would you rather go back inside and not dance?"

"I can dance, Jackson. Just not with you." He said nothing, and even the coconut trees were silent. "I wonder what would have happened if we had gone there as strangers. Of course, you might not have noticed me, or even if you had, you might not have asked me to dance."

"That's true." I was sorry that he agreed so readily. "If we were strangers, I'd never have come here at all. I'm only here because of you."

My brain went out altogether, with a sputter, like a burnt-out light bulb. Although I managed to move when he started walking again, but I didn't know if this was like a chicken who can still run when its head has been cut off.

Jackson broke the silence. "What else does the king say?"

"I don't know. That is, that's all I know. He seems fairly nice, however, for a king."

"Good. That's—good."

Another pause. "There's the mountain, Jackson."

"Where?"

"Over there. The Devil stole the top. Otherwise, it would look more like a mountain, but it's the only one there is."

"Is that where you ran to from Mr. Public Service?"

"You would have too."

"Absolutely." He smiled. "It's too bad if you've only got one mountain, that the Devil should steal half of it."

"Yes, I'd never thought of him as a Republican before."

From politics, Jane Austen has observed, it is an easy step to silence, and so we went back to walking but not talking. We came to the egg plant.

"Interesting, isn't it?" I asked as he examined it. "The flowers are so perfectly egg-shaped."

"That's because they're eggs."

"What?"

"Look: they're empty eggshells." He lifted one off a stalk. It was an eggshell. "It is a clever idea, like planting the beer bottles upside down."

"Who does that?" I asked.

"They do here, all over. Those round brown stones that make patterns in gardens. They're beer bottles."

"Oh."

"You didn't think there was an abundance of perfectly uniform rocks, did you?"

"Anything could be possible when you're not in Kansas anymore."

He squinted up at the Milky Way. "I don't think we ever were in Kansas, Shell."

It was one of those rare moments when two people comprehend the same thing, and when I looked up at all the glitter of the stars, a strange, wild Paradise fit overtook me, and I kissed him. I believe I surprised him, although he didn't react as badly as I did the first time he ever kissed me, an episode entirely too mortifying to recount. My knees gave way, and I sat down in the middle of the crushed coral road.

"Shelley?" I knew he was on the ground too because his voice was near my ear. "Look at me, will you?"

"No."

"How can I kiss you, if you won't?"

"I don't know. You'll have to figure it out."

"Jesus, is that a Tongan spider?"

I leapt to my feet. He got up more slowly because he was laughing, so greatly had he entertained himself.

"Just wait, Jackson, until you see a spider that's as big as your head."

"Hush." He put his arms around me. He had never kissed me like this before, laughing at the same time. "This is better, isn't it? God, this is better. I was afraid I was going to talk about my grandmother all night."

"At least you could think of something to say."

"I know. It worries me when you're quiet."

"I didn't expect to see you come wandering out of the bush."

"If I'd told you I was coming, you'd have gone somewhere else."

He started to walk, but he kept his arm around me. I tried to put my arm around him; it kept leaping off. Finally he plastered it against his side and stuck it in place with his hand. "It's OK," he murmured. "If I understand this code correctly, you will only be a scorned and ruined woman; I'm the one who gets beheaded."

I laughed, and the dense, rich covering of stars overhead quivered. I finally understood how people had seen pictures of water bearers and flying horses and lions in the stars. I saw all kinds of things: birds, dragons, a great glimmering ship. The ship drifted down from the sky, picked us up, and carried us along. For the first time in a while, I wasn't worried about life. I wasn't worried about what I'd said or should say or hadn't said. I didn't even think about what would happen next. Out at sea, a solitary light was flickering, bobbing in the peaceful waters, and we glided along on our own private craft. I didn't know where we were going, but this didn't worry me either. I understand that these balmy spells in relationships sometimes last longer than ten minutes.

23

In the garden at the fales, the air was warm and filled with perfume. We meandered along the dark, flowery paths until Jackson stopped at a door. Here, the smooth-sailing ship ran aground or maybe it hit an iceberg. It began to dissolve, part by part, sails, sides, and rudders.

He went in. I stayed in the doorway. A trick of the light cast a weird, chiaroscuro spell over the room, illuminating the black drawings on the tapa cloth walls, the stick figures and spider webs. Jackson's backpack was on the bed, and his anorak on the chair. I knew his pack was green and his anorak blue, but everything was only dark and light.

A woman walked past the glassless window. She smiled at us, but Jackson didn't see her. He was gathering up scattered clothes and stuffing them into his pack. He tossed the pack onto the floor. Our magical boat had not vanished; I'd just fallen off it, although Jackson was still cruising along, in the dark.

"I brought you something," he said. A bag of M&Ms with peanuts flew through the air. It was reassuring to know that Jackson wasn't altogether clueless. He came back to the door, where I stood clutching the M&Ms. He held out a small box covered in embroidered silk. "It's from Nepal."

"Thank you."

"Will you open it?"

I might have done this if he had not, just then, put his hand on my neck. Although he didn't say anything dumb about Adam and Eve, I still had to wonder if all medical students took a class in Neck Rubbing 101 and if Jackson was now like Skip, insofar as all men are like all men, and, therefore, who was he? He was being serious about kissing while I floundered, like someone whose head keeps going under deep water, even though his grip on my arm felt like one he would use holding a rope when he is dangling in the air over nothing.

I twisted the bag of M&Ms until it ripped open. Jackson dropped the box as candy rattled over the floor, and a pig scrambled past me. It began snuffling up M&Ms. Three kids ran in too, chasing the pig, who skittered to shelter under Jackson's bed. They abandoned their pursuit to collect the candy. One kid held out M&Ms to the pig, who ventured out from the bed. With a great ruckus, they captured the pig and departed. Jackson closed his eyes and leaned his head against the wall. I think the pig had knocked him off the imaginary boat too, and it had sailed on to Papeete.

"Jackson, do you remember that guy who got to the top of Mount Everest and then fell into a crevasse?"

"Who?"

"I can't remember his name. But it was too bad."

He lifted his head and looked at me as if he were trying to see through cement. His face was a jumble of things I understood, and more that I did not. He is one part Jackson, graduate of the David Ilillouette School for Dazzling Women, and one part Jackson who might rather discuss mountaineering catastrophes, and often he gets tangled somewhere between the two.

"Shelley." His voice was gentle, which made me even more nervous, and I stared at his shirt buttons until I saw thirteen dozen of them. "What is it?"

"Nothing! It's just—I don't know what you want. Or why you came here. I don't know what's going on."

"Why don't you tell me?"

"Well, I think Lily has probably murdered Mrs. Omont."

"Shelley—"

"It makes sense. You haven't met Lily, but she would make a great black widow spider. You should have seen the way she wrapped Skip in webs—"

"Shelley! I don't care. All right, you asked me, so I'll tell you what I want. I want you to come inside so that we can shut the door. I want you to stay with me tonight. I want—I want you to leave with me tomorrow."

"But I can't leave. I have a job."

"This is not a job."

"Oh, but it has to be." I had not meant to say this. I backed up, probably to escape from myself, and smacked directly into the door frame. I heard a crack; it was my head. Through a blur of stars and rockets, I saw several women. I heard them chattering and chickens clucking and myself saying I was all right. I felt a hand on my elbow. The voices faded. Jackson and I were alone, walking toward the ocean. The tide was out. The brackish air had turned misty. I sat down on the rock sea wall and rubbed the collection of bumps I was acquiring on my head. The next one might break it open altogether.

Jackson stayed standing. He picked up a stone and threw it. He threw thirteen rocks before he sat down. The only sound was the ocean, until he said, "Why didn't you tell me things were so bad for you?"

"They weren't."

"I think they were."

"No. Every day David gets fifty calls from people who are worse off."

"I don't care about them. I care about you. I thought we were friends again, Shelley. I thought maybe you liked me again; maybe you even trusted me—"

"I do."

"No. Because all of a sudden everything changed. When I called you, it was like talking to a stranger. 'How are you?' 'Fine.' 'What are you doing?' 'Not much.' 'Will you come to see me before we leave?' 'No.' 'What if I come to California?' Nothing. I'd hang up feeling sick. I didn't know what I'd done."

"Nothing. You hadn't done anything."

"But I didn't know that. All those nights in the mountains, I didn't have anything to do except think. That's why I decided to go see you whether you wanted me to or not. That's when I wrote—did you get my letter?"

I nodded.

"Did you read it?"

"Yes. Well, the day before yesterday I did."

He threw a few more rocks. "I guess it's better than if you'd read it first and then left the country. When I got to San Francisco, your strange neighbor said you'd gone to Paradise, so I called David and he only said, 'I wonder where she is.' I finally had to ask Jesse Goldensohn, and he implied I was a complete ass for not knowing anything. I was glad you'd left DC. I was worried you liked it—working for that politician, that is, not living with the Lamprey."

He meant David's weird wife. "It wasn't that bad," I said. "Well, it was, but I didn't see her much. She was always off getting her face redone. David was usually gone too. I think it's how they stay married."

"I figured you'd quit because your cat wasn't happy there—" He chuckled, then stopped. He'd been there when Shakespeare peed in the Lamprey's designer shoes. "I didn't know he died, Shelley. I'm sorry. He was a great cat."

It was my turn to say something, but I didn't.

"Why did you quit?"

"I didn't. Pollard fired me."

"No."

"Yes. I just didn't tell David because he's already worried that I am a failure at life."

"But why—"

"I talked. To a reporter."

"Oh."

"It was Mike Harris from the *Chronicle*. David likes him. He talks to him all the time. Mike was in DC, and I ran into him in the hallway. He asked were we getting any calls about HR 15, lobbying disclosure, and I said not so many as HR 33, about Social Security. He said, 'Really?' And I said yes; I knew because I was keeping track of phone calls. He said how many, and I told him five hundred and seventy-three against and two for it. It was senior citizens; they care about things. Mike put the numbers in a story and Pollard went through the roof. I said it was true, but he said it was only true when he decided it was true. He said I belonged on the dark side, with journalists. Then he voted for it, and he told the press the numbers I'd given Mike were wrong. I felt like I'd been working for a Republican."

"I don't know why you think there's any difference."

"There is. David doesn't think he gets to decide what's the truth. And he doesn't lie."

Jackson rolled his eyes.

"He doesn't. If Mike had asked him—David might not have known the exact answer, but he would have asked someone to find out. And if that many people were against it, he would have paid attention. But he was on a fact-finding trip to Iceland. They gave me severance pay, which got me back to San Francisco. But I couldn't find a job because I don't know anything except politics, and every listing had five hundred applicants, who all had experience. I got one interview to be a waitress, but the man asked why I'd left my last job, and I told him, and that was that. Then my car stopped on the Bay Bridge during rush hour." Jackson was looking agitated, so I decided to leave out the part about wondering if it was better to be run down by a crazed driver or go ahead and jump.

"And then Shakespeare got sick?" he asked. "What was it?"

"I can't talk about it."

"Why not?"

"I will cry, and it will upset you."

"It won't upset me. Well, not as much as it will upset you. Besides, I'm already upset. I didn't know any of this."

"It's not your problem. It's just me. I'm not very good at living."

"Don't—say that."

"But it's true. I'm not like you or David or Jesse. You are all something, and I'm not anything. I don't think I ever will be. I don't think there's a place for me in the world."

"Come on, Shelley, I'm the one who dropped out of med school."

"You did?"

"I don't think they'll take me back."

"Maybe you don't want to be a doctor. You don't have to be. You can just be yourself. That's a good thing."

"Why didn't you tell me anything?"

"What difference would it have made?"

I hadn't meant to offend him, but I had. He started throwing more rocks. "At least you could have borrowed money for the vet bills from me instead of Goldensohn."

"He wasn't going to tell anyone."

"He didn't. I just guessed. After I saw David—"

"How did you manage that?"

"I drove him to have dinner with that newspaper editor who is always insisting that David only hires women. David thought everything was fine. I told him that for all we knew you'd sold yourself to white slave traders."

"What?"

"Shelley, Jesse was the only one who had a notion of what you were doing, and that was as clear as fog. 'What's she going to do?' 'Look for a lost island.' 'Who hired her?' 'Some woman gave her a plane ticket.' 'Where to?' 'Tonga.' 'Where?' Even David agreed that it sounded weird. So he bought me a plane ticket."

"Well, now that you know I'm not captured by white slave traders, you can go home."

"I'm not going until you go."

"I can't go until I figure out what's going on."

"Nothing's going on, Shelley. You've just spent too much time with Goldensohn. Talk about spiders. He just sits in his room and spins out stories."

"He likes you. He thinks you have great muscles and beautiful eyes."

Jackson snorted.

"There is this woman who hired me. I owe her something. And I have to stay long enough to pay Jesse back."

"No, you don't."

"Why?"

"It's no big deal."

"You paid him?"

"I had some extra money because David bought the plane ticket. And Jesse doesn't have much, ass that he is."

"Then I have to pay you back."

The last rock he threw might have landed on New Zealand. I didn't hear it splash. "I knew it would make you mad. Good. I'm glad. Because you did it again, Shelley. You were in trouble and you needed help and you didn't tell me, again. You let me take off for the mountains without saying a word, again, without giving me one chance to do anything. Again."

A light flashed from another boat, moving silently through the water, returning to Neiafu, but not for us. We didn't say anything as we walked back to Foeata's. He left me at the gate. I was still standing there when Skip ambled up.

"What happened to Galahad?"

"Don't you have anything to do?"

"Wasn't he the one who was always looking for the Holy Grail? And he had to abstain from earthly pleasures, or he wouldn't find it, so he invented *coitus interruptus*. Drive Jackson nuts, do you?"

"Why do you say that?"

"We saw him beating his head on a coconut tree. But don't worry. Gravity took him to the Vava'u Club. It should make him forget you for at least an hour. Ah, love." He punched my arm. "When Lily comes back from the Big Nuke, let's go on a double date, shall we?"

24

Skip joined Gravity and Jackson at the Vava'u Club that night, and they all passed out later at Gravity's. The next morning at breakfast, Skip was looking raggedy, but Gravity was chirping like a new bird in spring.

"By the way," Skip said, "Jackson asked us to tell you and Foeata goodbye. He had to catch an early plane."

Foeata's face nearly fell off her head. I don't know what mine did. "Sikipi!" Gravity protested. "You have truly too much hot air from the north." Jackson, he said, had only gone to his fale to change.

"It was a joke I couldn't resist," Skip protested as Foeata whacked him on the head with a spoon. "You nearly did lose him last night, Shelley. He got pinched more times than I did."

Just then Jackson arrived, looking poorly. He accepted a cup of coffee from Foeata but declined food, saying he'd already eaten breakfast at the fales.

"But it was not enough," Foeata said, giving me a nudge. "Seli will get you more."

I decided no, Seli would not, particularly if he was going to say hello to Skip, Gravity, Foeata, two chickens, and a goat, and then nod somewhere in my direction. In the interest of cultural differences, however, I offered him half of my loaf of bread.

"Gee, aren't you going to butter it?" Skip asked.

"I do not know about you," Gravity said, "but I would not give a knife to a woman whose eyes flash like fire."

Foeata, however, persisted. "Seli, there are some very good papayas."

"I think," Skip said, "we'd better be going."

"Yes!" Gravity said, "We go to the island to solve Seli's mystery! Like Judy Bolton, yes?"

I accidentally glanced at Jackson, who looked up at the ceiling, leaving it to me to explain to Foeata that Judy Bolton was the heroine of dozens of mystery stories, which in my youth I had loved. Not only did Judy live in a crime-ridden section of rural Pennsylvania populated by thieves, blackmailers, and fake fortune-tellers, but also she had red hair like me.

"We'll be back for dinner, criminals in tow," Skip added, "unless we get trapped on the lost island from which they don't return."

"Myself, I shall seek the ghost of the machete," Gravity declared.

"But, Gravity, supernatural evidence complicates the neat solution."

Gravity nodded. "And it does not solve the greatest mystery of all."

"Do you mean, why women are so difficult?" Skip asked, and everyone laughed but me. Foeata wondered aloud if she should come along to chaperone, but she discarded the idea on the grounds that she might sink the boat.

We departed. As the Jolly Old Boys' Club led the way into the bush, Jackson joined in and they expanded their theme, making it clear that they were undertaking this trip only as a manly exercise in indulging female whims. The unreliability of women was no need for alarm but provided, as women often do, a good excuse for pleasurable sport, in this case, a boating excursion. In telling Skip and Gravity about Judy Bolton, Jackson apparently had omitted mentioning that he had read the books, too, and memorized the Most Wanted posters at the post office, and he had identified as many criminals as I had in Hook's Bay, population one hundred and fifty-seven. As they enthralled themselves with their observations on the rocky maze that is the female mind, as compared to the neatly paved roads that characterize their own, I decided that if Jackson had come to Tonga to be weird, so be it.

It was the kind of day that can't make up its mind if it's going to be sunny or stormy. As we came to Gravity's cove, the sun went behind a cloud and a wind stirred the water into choppy, white-capped waves. Gravity scampered up to an immaculate little red and white boat.

I have not mentioned yet that among the many things in life that make me nervous is water that is over my head. I forget this until I have to get in it or, as in this case, into a small boat heading out to a restless sea. Skip and Jackson climbed aboard. Gravity offered me his hand to follow. I said, "I think I'll stay here."

They all stared at me, and Jackson got back out of the boat. He stood over me, squinting down, his head tilted to one side and his thumbs hooked in the loops of his jeans. Jesse James couldn't have done it better. "You don't want to go?"

"No."

"Why not?"

"No reason."

He looked up at the sky, and this was when he noticed the rocks I'd climbed a few days earlier. "Gravity," he called, "can we see Mrs. Omont's island from up there?"

"Oh yes! Perhaps."

"Want to go up?" Jackson asked me. "You can do it, can't you?"

I reached the top first, lava-lava and all, although he wasn't too far behind when he realized I was beating him. "This is very most wonderful," Gravity called. "Sikipi, we shall try it too?"

"No, thanks," Skip said. "I'm not a lizard."

I walked to the edge of the cliff. Jackson followed me, and he stared down uneasily at the ragged rocks. I don't know why. He has climbed the face of Half Dome, which is higher. He mumbled, "I'm sorry."

"About what?"

"I don't know, but whichever thing I did that upset you, I apologize. And I hope you won't knock me off the cliff if I didn't say that right."

I had been closer to kicking him in the shins, but I considered this idea too.

He stumbled on, "I didn't mean to—last night—I wanted—I didn't want—I don't know—"

"Are you OK?" He is not usually this inarticulate; also, he was a bit gray around the gills.

"I'm fine," he snapped. "I'm just trying to apologize for offending your touchy female sensibilities so you'll get in the boat. All right?"

I offered to shake hands. He rolled his eyes but took my hand. His felt hot, but I didn't ask if he was sick, not that I'd accuse him of having touchy male sensibilities. As unknown as the ocean might be, it doesn't compare to a man; not one thing in it could be stranger, not even those creepy ghost fish that never see the light.

"Shelley, can we—" He stopped. We had both seen it, something wedged against the rocks in the water. It looked like a log festooned in lavender seaweed.

"What do you think that is?" I asked.

"I don't know. I'll go see. Skip," he shouted, "can you climb up here?"

"Not before Friday. Why?"

"Then will you come around the rocks in the boat? There's something strange in the water, on this side. Shelley, stay here."

He swung himself down the cliff. I waited a minute before I followed. He had reached the water's edge when Skip and Gravity coasted around the promontory in the boat. Skip jumped out and waded toward Jackson. "Jesus, what is it?"

"I don't know."

"A big fish?"

"Possibly."

"Weird. It looks like—"

"I know."

"But it could be a fish."

Gravity brought his boat closer to the thing as Skip and Jackson, from a distance, discussed whether it could be a fish.

"It could be a dead fish," Skip said.

"It isn't moving."

"It probably is dead, then."

Gravity prodded the lump with a stick, and it rolled over.

"Oh Jesus Christ." Skip reeled away and began to vomit into the sea.

"We must go back to Neiafu," Gravity said. "It is fastest in the boat."

"Someone should stay here," Skip mumbled. "Someone should go get—Jesus, I almost said someone should go get a doctor."

"You go," Jackson said. "I'll stay here."

"Thanks," Skip mumbled. He jumped into the boat, and they sped away. Jackson came out of the water. I knew he was going to be sick, because whenever anyone around him throws up, he generally does too. I'd always wondered how he would manage in medical school on account of this. I stayed back because the only thing he hates more than other people throwing up is himself throwing up. I waited till he was resting his head against the rocks before I touched his back.

He went straight up into the air, and even after he recognized me, he couldn't speak for a few seconds.

"Sorry," I said.

"Shelley!" He had never hollered at me before, and I was only two inches away from him. "Get out of here! Go away!"

25

The flight to Nuku'alofa was mostly empty, and it wasn't until we were airborne that it dawned on me that other people might have checked the weather conditions and decided to stay on the ground that day. What we flew through did not quite qualify as a cyclone, but it may only have missed the mark by a mile or two per hour in windspeed. We flew mostly upside down but also sideways and backward, lurching and spinning. Three passengers fainted, one went into convulsions, and the flight steward hid in the bathroom until we tumbled out of the sky and hobbled down the runway on Tongatapu.

The airport was crowded. From the air, the island had resembled a medium-sized green pancake decorated with wildly swaying palm trees, and I guessed everyone was leaving before the sea level rose more than a foot and shrank the size of the island by fifty percent. The thundering downpour made this a possibility, but given the choice between getting back on a plane or having to climb a coconut tree, I opted for the latter. I took a taxi to Sela's Guest House, which Ever-Ready had recommended. Sela showed me to a neat, plain room where I wrung myself out while I listened to howling winds and rain.

I had not come to Nuku'alofa because Jackson had said to go away, although I had left the beach rather than brain him with a rock.

Back in Neiafu, I stopped by the Port of Refuge Hotel to see if Lily was back. I was thinking maybe we could have tea or whiskey and reopen our discussion about men, not that I was going to try to figure Jackson out; life is short, and a project such as this would not have left me time to tie my shoes.

Lily wasn't there. I remembered she had told me to go to Nuku'alofa; maybe she had taken her own advice. Ever-Ready booked me on the next flight, and Moses drove me to the airport.

And here I was. Where this was remained unclear because these islands were most often lost in the crease of maps. I'd been hired for an obscure job by a woman who was nowhere to be found. I'd been given a gift that might have been a message from another woman who had been lost in the night in the ocean. I was looking for a third one who liked me as much as she would like a broken fingernail. I wanted to tell her we had found a body in the sea, which, in the opinion of one doctor and one part-time med student, was probably dead.

I don't know why I thought Lily might be interested. No doubt she lost interest in bodies that were dead. I wondered what Lily would do with Jackson but decided that this was a poor choice of words, as she would probably do way too much. For the same reason, I made myself stop wondering what Jackson would make of Lily. I decided instead to think about a story I might write, but any potential character had bailed out of my head on the flight south.

I was relieved when Sela appeared to invite me to tea. She was a rather reserved woman, which is to say, she did not interrogate me, adopt me, or try to marry me off on the way to the tea room. I felt anonymous, like a guest at a hotel. I should have known better, but I was enjoying the feeling that no one knew who I was and also didn't care. I sat down with two other guests. They were Danish students studying the Tonga Trench, a seven-mile-deep ditch off Tongatapu,

which, they said, is the second deepest place on earth. People regularly disappeared into it and so had the generator from Apollo 13.
No sunlight reached its depths; no one knew what might live there,
but these guys had a theory it was inhabited by giant squids because
an eighty-five-foot tentacle had recently washed up on the shore of
Tongatapu. I admitted I was only really looking for Lily and her lost
island. They had heard of Lily, and the notion of locating her was
even more tantalizing than finding a giant squid in the Tonga Trench.
They rushed off to find their maps. Sela poured more tea.

"Perhaps," she said, "you are looking for Ile Perdue. It is not so far
from here."

In all honesty, it didn't derange me to discover that I could take a
taxi or walk to this lost island. Ile Perdue was a gift shop, the brain-
child of a Peace Corps volunteer, run by a cooperative of Tongan
women to sell their crafts. The students, however, were crestfallen
to have no reason to sail over a treacherous trench to seek a disappearing island, once more illustrating the difference between men
and women without which there would be no reason to write stories.
I said I would introduce them to Lily if I found her, but I never saw
them again.

Ile Perdue was near the harbor where women and Peace Corps
volunteers sold baskets to tourists when cruise ships docked. The tiny
shop was filled with woven mats, baskets, jewelry made from pandana leaves and seashells, and bowls made from polished coconut
shells. Large tapa cloth hangings lined the walls. Smaller ones were
stacked on tables. The room was silent except for a ticking clock. The
only other person in it was a gray-haired Tongan woman who was
making a handbag out of a coconut shell.

I examined the painted tapa cloths. Most of them were geometric designs, some simple, some more elaborate, but one was entirely

different. A sliver of a moon and a star hung over a mountain covered with pine trees that rose up out of the sea; near the mountain, two travelers sat in a boat, facing each other, and below them was an octopus. I knew this artist.

"Does Mafi put an octopus in every painting?" I asked.

"She believes they are creatures of much wisdom."

I had enough money to buy it, especially if I didn't go back to Neiafu. While the woman wrapped up Mafi's painting, I asked, "Do you know a woman named Lily Omont?" She looked uncomfortable, and I assumed this meant yes. "I am looking for her."

She thrust the parcel at me and ran out of the room. I heard excited voices, and another woman appeared. "May I help you?" she asked with an air of caution.

"Lily Omont told me to come here. Have you seen her?"

The second woman also ran away. Moments later, an adolescent girl entered. She was wearing a blue plaid school uniform, and her black braided hair was tied with blue ribbons. "Excuse me very much," she said. "But if you will please wait, we will find our Peace Corps volunteer who will speak to you."

"Thanks." Casting about for something inoffensive to add, I asked, "Why is the store called Ile Perdue? Tonga was never a French territory, was it?"

"Oh no. Tonga has never belonged to anyone. This is our problem, for if we had been a colony and had had to win our freedom, perhaps we would not be so poor today. But our Peace Corps volunteer said to look ahead. She said, how could we not know the things we make are wonderful, she who comes from a world where you have everything. She said, you will see, we will make this shop, and palangis, who cannot make anything, will buy your things. She is right. Those who come on boats pay so much for so little."

"But the name?"

"It comes from a painting that was made by a palangi woman. It tells the story of an island she once had but lost."

She handed me a postcard from a revolving stand. It was a wash of blues, shade upon shade, the way mountains appear in a vista from a summit. Ghostly, stormy, and wild, the swirl of clouds and water glimmered with light, and a jagged blue mountain rose from the sea and vanished into a blurry mist. The caption read "*Ile Perdue*, Bette Omont. 1947." I'd finally found my boss.

"This is the woman I'm looking for," I said. "I thought Lily might be able to help."

The girl's ribbons bobbed as she nodded. "Yes, and do not worry that the ladies are old and afraid of ghosts. They did not understand that you do not know she is dead."

"Dead? Mrs. Omont?"

"Oh no. Lily. But, of course, you could not know, for it was only this morning that they found her in the water in Vava'u."

26

I returned to Sela's and fell on my bed, but my thoughts loomed over me like a reflection from a mirror you'd rather not see. I know we all live with the possibility of discovering that any familiar food causes cancer or high cholesterol, that anyone may turn out to be cuckoo on account of their childhood, or that any formerly enjoyable experience has been proven to be toxic or in some other way life-threatening. I had fallen into the habit of imagining the worst possibilities as a kind of ritual protection against them really happening, like looking under your bed to make sure there are no lurking loonies, something I had to do nightly in San Francisco before I could sleep. But even then, as my life had begun to resemble something that had been put through a shredder, I would read in the newspaper about calamities that had befallen others, which made my own seem of little consequence compared with people who had been in the wrong place at the wrong time and so had been shot, robbed, run over, or irradiated. Most likely they were trusting souls who never checked under their beds. Lately life had been surpassing my grimmest expectations. It was akin to checking your closet and finding not a minor devil but Satan himself.

Lily was dead. A dead body is hard to ignore. You can't say go away, don't bother me. Even a politician can't pretend it's something else, no matter what words they come up with as alternatives to "dead": nonfunctioning constituent for whom viability is not a viable option. Even the military can't, although I'm sure they'd try their best.

A knock at the door made me jump, but it was only Sela, bringing a pot of tea. "I am so sorry," she said. "I thought you knew about Lily, but Foeata said perhaps not."

"Foeata?"

"She was most worried."

"You've talked to Foeata?"

"She telephoned from the post office, of course, after Ever-Ready gave her your message that you had gone."

"How do you know Foeata?"

"Everyone knows Foeata."

"Did she say anything else?"

Sela gave me a shy smile, and I said never mind. Assuming she knew everything, I asked, "Do you know Mrs. Omont?"

"Of course. She stays here when she comes to Nuku'alofa."

"Have you seen her lately?"

"Two weeks ago. She came to meet Lily."

"She did? Did Lily stay here too?"

"Oh no. I am not grand enough for Lily. She stayed at the International Dateline Hotel."

"But you met her?"

Sela nodded dolefully.

"What did you think of her?"

"She is dead," Sela said, as if this were the kindest thing she could think of. She glanced upward.

"I have a notion that God doesn't really zap people for telling the truth. Maybe He even knows what it is."

She smiled. "Foeata said you are not afraid of God or the Devil, but only of people."

"I can live without people, that's all. I am, however, a little worried about Mrs. Omont."

"Yes, the last time she was here, I worried also."

"Why?"

"Always before, she was a happy person, laughing, talking, making jokes. This time she was quiet. She said to me she had come to meet Lily, but she did not know why Lily had come back after so many years away. Lily did not love these islands. When Bette returned from meeting Lily, she was nervous, like she had seen a snake. I gave her tea, but still she looked old and frightened. She packed to leave. 'You return to Neiafu?' I asked. 'Oh,' she said, 'I wish there was a place where no one would find me.' She left, and Lily came looking for her, asking 'Where is she? Where is she?' She was angry that I did not know. Oh, I think our Peace Corps volunteer is here. Excuse me—"

I heard another voice: "They just want me to explain that they hadn't meant to offend her. They were only startled because she was asking if they had seen a ghost—"

The speaker came into view, a palangi wearing a long yellow dress and purple flowers in her hair. When she saw me, she dropped her basket.

"Holy shit," she said, "Shelley Ilillouette."

27

Gabby Asher had cut her hair, and my first thought, identifiable as such, was that David would be sorry. Her hair used to be waist-length, dark and glossy. David was so crazy about it you'd have thought he'd grown it himself.

I still recognized her, even though I hadn't seen her since she and David split up and she disappeared from San Francisco. I had liked Gabby, once I got over hating her. She wasn't really as nitwitted as you might have thought she was if you had the misfortune to meet her in David's presence. When she was anywhere near him, her brain disintegrated into fluffy little marshmallows, the kind that are dyed pink and green, but David was worse. When he was with Gabby, he would have been hard-pressed to spell his name, and this was before he ran for Congress and could have someone do it for him. It gave me an altogether dim impression of love. She was nice to me, however. She had to be since I was David's sister, and she loved David's toothbrush, his socks, and any pencil he used. Being perfect, she overlooked the fact that I hated her, and eventually we became friends. When she left the city without a word, I was sorry, but I figured she knew where to find us, if she wanted to. I wasn't surprised that she didn't.

Now, here she was, in the Kingdom of Tonga, gaping at me, thunderstruck, but I was comparatively unfazed. Of course, she had not just flown upside down through a storm after finding a dead body and fighting with Jackson. "Hello," I said. "How are you?"

We went to the bar at the International Dateline Hotel and ordered gin gimlets. They came with paper parasols in them.

"Peace Corps," I said. "It fits. Sherlock Holmes would have figured this out weeks ago."

"Figured what out? What are you doing here?"

"Looking for a woman named Bette Omont. Did you tell her to call David?"

"Why would I do that?"

"She called David because she wanted a companion."

Gabby took a slug of her drink. "I can think of worse companions for a tropical island. What did he do, send you here to check it out for him?"

"I took the job."

"You?"

"I really needed one."

Gabby shook her head. "I wondered when the real world would catch up with me. There's probably an appropriate quote from Plato, but I don't know what it is."

"It's more Shakespeare's situation," I said, only a little alarmed that she would consider me part of anyone's real world. "'By accident most strange, bountiful Fortune, now my dear lady, hath brought to this shore' And so on."

"Right, the guy you like almost as well as Jackson." She twinkled her eyes at me. "Why are you scowling? Haven't you two made up yet?"

"No. And we never will. He told me to go away."

"So you came to Tonga?"

"No, to Nuku'alofa."

"Is he in Neiafu, too? Did he come with you?"

"No, and I didn't invite him either. He just turned up. He thought I'd sold myself to white slave traders."

"You two are so cute, just like Romeo and Juliet."

"Right. There's cute for you."

She finished her drink and ordered another round. "Well, tell me about things, Shelley. I mean it. Go ahead. Tell me everything."

I described what had happened since I arrived in Tonga.

"Good lord," she said in a gratifying way.

"Do you think it's weird? There's more."

"Yes, of course it's weird. The Tongans will be too polite to say it's weird and just think it's more palangi ways, but it's weird. What else?"

I told her about the Old Boys' Club.

"Men." She dismissed them with a wave of her paper parasol. "Just yesterday, I had some supplies to take out into the bush, and another volunteer said he'd put them in his backpack. I said it wouldn't all fit, but he insisted it would, and he squeezed and stuffed and smashed everything and broke the zipper, but he made it fit. And if you put men in groups, their collective IQ drops, inversely proportional to the size of the group. Instances come to mind." I knew she was thinking of Congress, but neither of us said it. "Poor Jackson."

"Why? Because he can't help that he was born a man?"

"He's so in love with you."

I decided to overlook the fact that she viewed this as a reason to feel sorry for him. "The longer I live, Gabby, the more I think Jesse Goldensohn is the only rational man in the world."

"Dear, dear Jesse. How is he?"

"The same."

"Good. I don't want him ever to change. I've thought about writing to him, but I was afraid if I did, then—what was it David used to say about how when you try to isolate one thing in the world, you discover it's attached to everything else?"

"John Muir said that, actually."

"Tell me the rest. I have a new rule not to get distracted from important things by men."

"That's about all, except for finding Lily."

We drank in silence until Gabby said, "I never met her, but she sounded like the type to, well, to—"

"To bury other people."

"D'you know, Shelley, I've known Bette for almost two years, and I never knew she had an adopted daughter. She always tells me when she's coming to Nuku'alofa because she brings things for the shop. But this last time I only knew she was here by accident when I walked into the bar here, and there she was. She did look a bit uncomfortable, but I just wondered how she'd gotten a date with Joe Storey."

Going back to the notion of looking in the closet for lunatic axe-murderers, I'd always suspected that if I ever found one, my reaction would be to shut the door and pretend I hadn't opened it.

Gabby was eyeing my second drink, and so I gave it to her. She went on: "Bette didn't say anything about meeting Lily or hiring a companion or calling David. Why would she do that?"

"She didn't. She called her sister, who called his office."

"I did tell Bette about David one night when I stayed on her island. It's such a damned romantic place. We drank a bottle of wine, and Bette showed me a portrait she'd done of her husband. Armand. He was a funny-looking little guy, but for her he was all that's wonderful. She met him in the south of France, and they adored each other until the day he died. Bette said, 'Not a day goes by that I don't think of him.' I told her about the time David and I ran away to Paris. She said, 'Ah, Paris, that's the place to fall in love.'"

Gabby's eyes filled with tears in that nerve-racking way that used to upset David more than any poll anyone ever took about anything. I asked, "How do you know Joe Storey?"

"He's hard to miss. Have you met him?"

"He asked me to dance at the Port of Refuge."

"He just exudes manliness, doesn't he? 'Here I am, take me or leave me, but it might be fun if you take me.' Maybe by the time a man is seventy, he has it together. I've never gone to bed with a man who's seventy, but it could be nice: safe and warm and not, well, not—" She shook her head like she was knocking thoughts out of it. "I don't want to remember, Shelley."

"OK. Do you know anything about Storey?"

"He sails around in a yacht as big as Japan, and he's awfully good-looking."

"Where'd he get his money?"

"He owns things. Most of Australia, I think."

"I suppose he could murder someone, if he wanted to. Lily thought Mrs. Omont was blackmailing her real parents. She wanted some of the money."

Gabby choked. "Bette? A blackmailer? And Joe's more of a publish-and-be-damned sort, anyway. Unless he has to protect a secret from his past. Love—"

"The Queen of Moribunda."

"Who?"

I said, "It doesn't have to do with love, you know."

"What else is there?"

"Money, power, the evening news. Maybe he has political aspirations."

She frowned. "He spends a lot of time wandering around Tonga for someone who has political aspirations."

"Maybe he wants to be the first democratically elected president of Tonga. Maybe he's plotting the revolution."

"Tongans are awfully fond of their king."

"A flaw."

"If Bette was blackmailing someone, why would she call David?"

"Because if I wanted to obfuscate any issue beyond all sense, I'd call a congressman."

"Oh, Lord," Gabby groaned suddenly, "speaking of odd."

The Reverend Ron Ogg was approaching with all the enthusiasm of a dog who has found his duck. "Hello!" he boomed. "Isn't this fine! Mother is busy doing her good works, and here I am without a thing to do."

We were spared the need to make a reply by Mother herself, who bustled in after him. Her condition had improved from the last time I'd seen her when I thought she had sat on a stonefish. Her hair was tidy, her sweater set spotless, and her smile was so cordial I wondered if her good works entailed working with ether.

"Why, hello, Miss Asher," she said. Her bright aspect faded somewhat when she saw me. "And—oh, my goodness—you. Whatever are you doing here?"

"We are drinking, Mrs. Ogg," Gabby replied. "Shelley has found a dead body. Someone she knew. Is it a strange, small world or what? Would you like a drink?"

"Thank you, but, of course, we do not drink." Mrs. Ogg turned her gaze to me, as if she could not resist viewing a person whose actions were continually in such dubious taste. "Whom do you know?"

"Lily Omont."

A faint twitch, like a rabbit, suggested she remembered the name, although she only said, "How do you know?"

"How do I know what? I probably don't, really."

"They found her in the sea," Gabby added.

"She drowned?"

I said, "I expect they won't know until they do an autopsy."

"An autopsy?" Mrs. Ogg asked. "In Vava'u? How many autopsies do they do on dead bodies in Vava'u?"

"I don't know, but I hope they are all on dead bodies."

"What?" The Rev woke up. "Lily Omont? Nice little lady. Friendly. Needed a ride."

Mrs. Ogg, briefly silenced by some crochets in her head, sprang back to attention. "Miss Omont was far more interested in sailing with Joe Storey."

"Can't think why you'd say that, Mother. Why—"

"Ronald! We must be going." Mrs. Ogg rose, and I had an impression she was going to drag the Rev off by his ears if he didn't get up too. "Good evening, Miss Asher, Miss Illywit." They departed.

"Why do I have the feeling that in another life she was a politician?" Gabby asked.

"I have the feeling that in this life she is a politician, but from the wrong party, of course."

Gabby's glass was empty again. She called for another round. "I'm not really a lush," she said. "Peace Corps has been fun, interesting, and rather healing, but I haven't had a good romance. I haven't even had a good date. I had gotten used to a zero social life filled with good works, and in you walk. All my past rising up to stare at me."

"Is it that bad?"

"Yes. No. Probably."

"Why did you go away where no one could find you?"

"I thought everyone knew why."

No one did really, except maybe David. But after he married Pamela the Lamprey, he kept calling Jesse, asking if he'd heard from

Gabby, if he knew where she was. Jesse said even if he knew, he doubted he'd tell David.

David asked Gabby to marry him about five minutes after they met, probably in his favorite place in San Francisco, the City Lights bookstore anarchy section. He had just turned twenty-five, old enough to run for Congress so he could end a war, preserve the Republic, and save the wild rivers of California. They decided they would get married after he won the election, which he did. They were planning an April wedding when my grandfather died.

Antonio had scarpered out of Mexico during the Revolution of 1910, but he insisted he never minded losing his land, money, haciendas, and cows because none of this had ever really been his to begin with. But he never quite learned to live in another world where he wasn't the guy who owned it all. For us, he was a jolly scallywag who gave us a home when no one else wanted us, and I never worried as much as David about how many of his wild stories were true. After Antonio died, David managed to pay the debts, but he couldn't save the house. I wanted to leave school to help, but David said no. He was sleeping on a couch in his office in DC, calling me every day to see if I was OK. That's how he is, or how he used to be, until he and Gabby broke up and he married the Lamprey.

"She came to see me, you know," Gabby said.

"The Lamprey?"

"Who?"

"David's wife. I didn't think of it; Jackson did. It's a rather disgusting fish. I said it was unfair to the fish."

She chuckled. "I love Jackson. I'll take him if you don't want him. No, it wasn't Pamela who came to see me. It was that woman who said if she were forty years younger and a hundred pounds lighter, she'd give David a run for his money."

"Oh, her."

"What do you and Jackson call her?"

"The Bismarck."

"I thought Lally liked me. I knew Pamela hated me. I loved that. When I met her, I saw the way she looked at David, and I thought, you may be rich and thin and beautiful and think you can buy anything, but you don't have David because he's not for sale." Gabby shrugged.

"Why did the Bismarck come to see you?"

"To tell me I was polluting the shades of Pemberley."

"Huh?"

Gabby gave a perfect imitation of Lally, a foghorn with a mouthful of marbles. "David is a prince. He has the looks, the charm—"

"The mad, exiled relatives, the empty pockets—" I'd heard this speech before.

"She said, 'What can you do for him?' I said, 'I love him.' She said, 'Love is for peasants who don't have anything else.' Then she said, 'Frankly, what he needs is an all-American girl. Not that I am prejudiced, of course, but really, a Chinese Jew? A penniless kindergarten teacher?' I am not sure which she thought was worse."

"David didn't know. He would have killed her."

"Maybe."

"Yes! Remember when she told him that it was nice that he had an African American friend, but couldn't he find one who wasn't homosexual?"

"Oh yes." Gabby finished another gimlet. "And her prince got that look your dear little aunts said reminded them of Uncle Vladimir, who chopped someone's head open with an axe."

"You know Lally wanted David to marry her dopey niece, Dippy, Flippy, whatever her name was. She was an ordeal. I had to sit next to her at a dinner once, and she just stared at David until I finally asked if he had his shirt on inside out. She said no, this was how Jackie Kennedy had gazed adoringly at President Kennedy and she was practicing. She said, 'You must know him. What does he like?' I said for starters he liked women who have brains, and this worried her because, of course, she didn't have enough brains to stuff an olive. I told David, and a few nights later we were having dinner with Bismarck and the Ordeal, and she was trying to be intelligent. David picked up an olive and grinned—" I stopped because Gabby was starting to look sad. "Are you Chinese?" I asked.

"My mother was Cambodian."

"Oh. I always thought you were Greek because Jesse called you Aphrodite. I knew you liked Buddhism because of the time David went meditating with you." Of course, he'd also gone tap dancing with her. "Mostly, I just thought you were a weirdo. That was when I hated you."

"Yes, I remember that."

"So what did Lally want you to do, rob a bank?"

"She wanted me to give him up. She said, 'He's tearing himself to pieces and it's all your fault.' There was truth in that. I knew how bad things were. I did want to get married anyway, but I wanted to go through everything with him. Well, and get rid of all the women fluttering around him. She said, 'If you love him, set him free. If he wants you more than anything else, he'll come after you.' So I did. And three months later, he married Pamela."

"She didn't see that coming," I said. "One day, it will be the shock of Lally Packhorst's life to find out that you and Jesse are the all-Americans."

Gabby picked up her parasol, spun it, and watched it twirl. "I never thought it would happen, Shelley, not to David and me. I just wanted to go where no one would ever find me. So, here I am in the

Kingdom of Tonga, wondering if it's third world or fourth world, all because David Ilillouette crossed my path—"

We were quiet then because we both knew that no one could have made David do something he didn't want to do.

"Shall we blow this place?" she asked, and she winced. It's what David says. "What is it called, Shelley, everything coming apart?"

"Entropy."

"Ah, yes. Entropy. Physics as metaphor for life. If all the nuclei of all the atoms in the world were touching, the world would be the size of a basketball. Which means there is a great lot of nothing in the universe."

Back at the guesthouse, Sela was waiting for us. Lebeca had called from the post office to say that Jackson was ill and dying, and everyone knew it was from remorse for having told me to go away.

"It's more likely Lily's doing," I told Gabby. "You remember how poorly he does around dead bodies."

Sela said, "A palangi will fly tonight on a special plane to Neiafu to take care of the body of Lily, and there is one place for you, Seli."

I hesitated. Gabby kicked me. "Don't be an ass, Shelley. Go to him. I'll come to Neiafu as soon as I can."

Sela summoned a Jeep taxi to go to the airport. Gabby walked with me to the door, where she lingered, polishing the handle. "How is he?"

"Who? Oh, fine, I guess."

"Is he happy?"

"Who knows?"

She nodded and turned away. I went on to the airport and joined the other Tongans who were catching a free ride north on the plane that Joe Storey had chartered.

28

Foeata was in her kitchen, making tea. "Ah, Seli," she sighed, "it is good you are here."

"Where is Jackson?"

She rolled her eyes toward heaven.

"He's dead?"

"No, but he has such pain." She put her hand on her heart.

"He had a heart attack?"

She poured tea. "When he and Sikipi came from hospital, I could not say who looked more terrible. Jackison asked, 'Where is Seli?' When I said, 'She is gone,' I think his heart did break. He could not eat, and when he tried to drink tea, his hand was shaking. He said he would go to his fale, but he could not stand."

This sounded worse than an overreaction to a dead body, but I didn't flatter myself it was on my account. She said Skip had given him something for a fever and told Foeata to let him sleep and not to worry. Skip had gone for a walk and had been gone for many hours.

"But how can I not worry, Seli, when he does not sleep but turns and turns?" She wiped her eyes. "I must go back to him."

"OK."

I followed her, but she blocked the doorway to his room. "Oh no.

You cannot. I, an old woman, thirty-seven years old, will sit with him. But I will tell him you have returned, and this will rest his heart."

"Foeata, do you know Gabby Asher?"

"My first Peace Corps volunteer! You met her?"

"I didn't need to. I've known her for years."

"No, Seli! Yes?"

"She was in love with my brother, once."

Curiosity warred with duty on Foeata's face. She glanced into the bedroom to be sure Jackson would live five more minutes; then she returned to the kitchen and poured more tea.

"Did he love her?" she prompted.

"I think she's the only woman he's ever really loved." I told her about them. It's kind of a romantic story, but of course, I didn't have to make it up.

She shook her head. "I know this must be true because you tell it to me, but I do not understand."

"No one did."

"Did I not tell Mafi this, that Gabby has a pain so deep of which she will not speak? But why, Seli, if a man loves a woman and she loves him and she is kind and beautiful and would be a good mother to his children, why would he break her heart? Why is it so hard to be happy in America?"

"I don't know, but while you figure it out, I'll go see Jackson."

She smiled, not without satisfaction. "Perhaps for one minute, or you will not sleep tonight, thinking of love."

We went into the hot, dark bedroom. Jackson was tangled in his sheets beneath the mosquito net. I opened the window, and the room filled with the sound of wind and rain.

"Shelley?" His voice was drowsy. "How did you get here? It's so far away. It's so cold."

I sat down beside him and patted his head, which seemed more useful than asking him where he was. "God, you're warm," he mumbled. "I love you, Shelley. I love your legs."

The door closed. "Now you've done it," I said. "Foeata's probably gone to get the fie fe cow."

Jackson raised his head. "Where'd you go?"

"Nuku'alofa."

"Why?"

"You said go away."

"But I didn't mean that far. I just didn't want you to see that body." He shivered, but I doubted he was just trying to convey how awful a dead body looked. "Sorry."

"Is there anything I can do?"

"This." He wrapped around me as if I were a pillow embroidered with dragons. "Just this."

When he was a kid, he used to have nightmares. I never had nightmares; it was what I saw when I was awake that bothered me. Even after the Devil had been vanquished, I'd see monsters in the dark: slimy, glowing, orange and red creatures that lit up as soon as I turned out the light. It's a funny thing about monsters: How can you tell a kid they're not real, if she can see them? Real doesn't mean a whole lot, under those circumstances.

Jackson, David, and I had shared the attic in the House of Lost Things. It was the warmest place. Jackson's mom, Hannah, fixed it up with insulation and yellow paint. When David moved downstairs to a room of his own, she divided the attic exactly in half with bookshelves, but whenever the monsters showed up, I would sleep in Jackson's half. He didn't mind.

Hannah and Jackson lived with us until she got sick and had to go to a sanitarium. Jackson's father sent him to school in England.

Jackson didn't want to go. We hid but we got found. Then he was so still and quiet I thought we should take him to hospital. Antonio said that wouldn't help because what he had was a broken heart. I tried to imagine what a broken heart was: If your heart broke, did your blood spurt all over, and then did you die? Jackson left, and David went away to school too, and then I was pretty sure I knew what a broken heart was.

How strange it is that a memory, hidden away in your head, can rise up unbidden, yet with a clarity so precise it renders time or space inconsequential. I could see it all, etched by a diamond, years later, half a world away, in an unlit room filled with the scent of flowers and rain and the sound of wind in coconut trees. It was a moment at the edge of peace; still, as I listened to him breathing, a panicky feeling began to grow inside my head: This would end; everything would. Jackson would die, and I would die, and I might never find him again in the dark void of infinity. These thoughts loomed up like orange-headed monsters, gibbering at me from the other side of the mosquito net. Once I start, I can't stop. I could only lean my head against his and wish that the part of his brain that didn't worry about infinity could seep inside mine.

Skip knocked and came in. "It looks like he is doing better. I can't imagine why."

"What's wrong with him?"

"He's just picked up a bug. Of course, considering where he's been, it could be Dengue fever, malaria, cholera, typhoid—hell, it could be the plague. But most likely, he'll be OK. Unless it's the plague." Skip drew up a chair. "So you like this guy, Shelley."

"Why do you say that?"

"Just a wild guess."

"How are you?"

"Me? Fine."

"I'm sorry about Lily."

"Are you?" His face assumed a stony look, and I made my own wild guess that Lily had never bugged him as much as she had by dying.

"I'm sorry for anyone who dies. Do you know what happened?"

"She drowned."

"But what was she doing?"

"How would I know? I just asked her to have dinner with me. Apparently she decided she'd rather go swimming. Hell, it's not like people don't die all the time."

"Did you know her before you came here?"

"I'd met her in Chicago."

He clenched his fist the same way David does. David used to pound on desks and walls when he was upset, but when he broke his knuckle over civil rights, the aide who drove him to the emergency room accidentally shut his hand in the car door. This cured him of clobbering walls, but he started clenching his fist. Anyway, Skip was sitting there, clenching and unclenching his fist.

"But you don't know why she came here?"

"I have no idea, and that's the truth. But it wasn't for anything as straightforward as finding her real father and blackmailing him."

"How do you know?"

"Shelley, she was playing you. It was her favorite pastime. She could peg anyone in a minute; she knew just what buttons to push. She didn't think there were rules, at least not any that applied to her, and if she decided she wanted to go for a midnight swim, even though she didn't know how to swim, she'd do it."

"Did you see her on Monday?"

"No. It doesn't make much difference now, does it?" He sanded the rough edges off his voice. "Well, sweetie, I'm beat. I'm going to bed. You don't have to sit here all night. He'll be OK, and Foeata won't sleep till you're out of his room, since she has almost as many hang-ups as you do."

"What hang-ups?"

"Shelley, my darling, you remind me of my Aunt Martha who'd never sit in a chair that a man had sat in recently. It's OK. It's refreshing, even if it's a damned shame. So Galahad loves you only for your interesting mind, does he? I don't know—he's looking awfully comfortable for a sick man."

After Skip left, Jackson sat up and scowled at the door. He moved over and threw the bedcovers over me. He was muttering.

"What?" I asked. "What are you saying?"

"You're the one who always says doctors make natural murderers."

"You don't think—"

"No. She drowned."

"Then why did you say that?"

"Why don't you lie down?"

Now here's the nuts thing. Probably at that minute there was nothing I wanted in the world as much as to lie down beside him and pull the covers over our heads and see if the rest of the world would go away. But I just sat there.

"What do you think she was doing, Jackson? You don't go swimming at night alone if you can't swim."

"Dammit." He closed his eyes, shaking again. "Sorry, what were you saying?"

"Maybe we should talk about something else if this makes you swoon."

"Watch it, sweetie. Ouch—why did you hit me? Why didn't you get mad when he called you sweetie?"

"Why didn't you tell me you were sick, you big, dumb ninnyhammer?"

He did his best imitation of a mule.

"Jackson, Gabby Asher is here."

"Here?"

"In Nuku'alofa. In Peace Corps. She knows Mrs. Omont. Gabby told her about David. It gets curiouser and curiouser, doesn't it?" He didn't answer because he was clenching his teeth. "Isn't it easier just to have a fit and get it over with?"

"No, this is worse than being eighteen. 'Oh, Shelley, I'm suffering. My back hurts. I think I have a fever. I'm so dizzy I can't see. I'll faint if you won't kiss me. I'll have a heart attack and die if you won't take off your dress.' How did you ever stand me?" He rambled on; then he groaned. "Christ, what have I been saying?"

"Nothing you've never said before."

"I'm sorry if I was offensive."

"It's all right."

"No. We'll have to talk. What about? Infinity? Now there's a subject that has no beginning and no end. Think about it."

I didn't because I was remembering when he'd first come back to California after being away at school. He had all the worldly experience of someone who'd spent seven years in an English boys' school, but I, who had lived my entire seventeen years at the House of Lost Things, was awestruck by the tall, hairy-legged, deep-voiced stranger who could explain things like Gabby and David's excessive goopiness.

"Jackson, do you know what was wrong with the buttons on Gabby's shirt? Maybe David should run for a role in The Princess and the Pea *instead of Congress."*

"Actually, he was just trying to get her to unbutton it."

"He was? When you were driving him to make a speech? How do you know?"

"I—just know."

"But Gabby didn't know."

"Yes, she did."

"Are you sure?"

"Yes."

"Why?"

"Because she did it."

"She did? How do you know?"

"I accidentally looked in the rearview mirror."

"How do you suppose she knew?"

"Sometimes people just do, when you're—you know—"

"A sex maniac? Do you think she is?"

"Probably not as much as David is."

"Do you ever wonder, Jackson, what it would be like to be obsessed with sex?"

"Let's talk about something else, shall we?"

Mostly to make him pipe down about infinity, I lay down, although not too close, and infinity went on to bother someone else. This must be why people are so goofy about sex, if it can, for ten seconds, override thoughts of the past, the future, and the endless void of time. He said a few more things, but never mind what. I didn't mind, but I did feel sorry for Lily because she was dead.

"Shelley?" Albert, the missionary, was outside the window. "Are you there? Shelley, have you heard about Lily?"

"Yes."

"I have to tell someone: I did it."

"Did what?"

"I killed her."

"You did?"

"I prayed to God to take away my temptation, and she died."

"I don't think that would hold up in court."

"In God's it would."

Jackson got up off the bed and looked out the window. "She drowned," he said.

"Then I did it."

"Drowned her?"

"No, but I knew what she was doing. Isn't that as bad?"

"No."

Skip's voice came from another window. "Albert, the guy is sick. You have to let him sleep. Go home. Do you want something to help you sleep?"

"It is all right, Sikipi." Gravity's voice came from farther away. "I will help him."

Jackson stayed at the window after Albert left. "When somebody talks, this whole island is listening."

Foeata opened the door. "Jackison, it is so fine of you to stand here while Seli sleeps, but you must rest. So I will take Seli now to her room."

29

In the morning, Skip came down with Jackson's symptoms, and dropping the idea that it might be the plague from Kathmandu, he diagnosed flu from California and took to bed. I asked Foeata if I could take Jackson his tea.

"Oh no. This I must do. Palangi men, they get well so fast. But you do not eat, Seli. You are ill too?"

"No, I just had a strange dream last night."

She sat down and poured tea. "Tell me."

"I dreamt I was by the ocean, and I saw a body all tangled up in the arms of an octopus. It was Jackson. It was just dumb, of course."

"Oh no, Seli, this was a big dream."

At this point, the subject of my dream appeared, pale and unshaven, his hair rumpled. When he saw us, he flinched. When I asked how he was feeling, he muttered something that might have been yes, no, or go to the devil and escaped into the shower. Although we realized this meant he was better, I saw in Foeata's face an unchristian wish to clobber him with a frying pan. She digressed to a lecture on "Men Are Strange Creatures but God Made Them Too," part one of an endless study.

"Maybe I want him to drop dead," I admitted.

"No, Seli, no! To die, it is to become something new, this is all. And you love him. Did I not know this when I saw that you carried his letter about like a pearl from the sea?" I heard the door of the shower stall open. I began to cough to see if I could distract her, but it would have been easier to stopper a volcano. "Every day, did I not see the letter always in a different place? I thought, she picks it up and holds it, yet she does not read it. How is it that Seli, so brave to come all alone to Tonga, cannot read this letter? And I see that Sikipi—not big, but a good man—he looks at Seli and she does not care. When he must make love to her—it is bad, but it is a man—then Seli reads the letter. So I understand, she loves—"

"Foeata, do you think the tevolos took Lily too?"

"No," Foeata said firmly, "she drowned."

"Why? Because she couldn't swim?"

"Oh, many Tongans cannot swim. Myself, I sink. It is why we have boats. But Lily hated the sea, and this is hard, if you live on an island. The sea makes you small, like love—"

"Do you know what will happen to her?"

"It's a problem. Is she American? Is she Tongan? But now the rich palangi from Australia is here to say where she belongs."

"I wonder why."

Foeata said something to the effect that the mysteries of people come in layers, with fossils buried in stripes of rock. "But we will speak of nice things. Seli, I think you must marry Jackison, and I will make for you a dress, so nice—"

I went to the post office to send a telegram to Jesse. I knew he'd want to know about Gabby. I kept walking but I couldn't move fast enough to leave all the ghosts behind. They dragged along with me, mute and heavy-footed, clanking their chains. I wondered if Lily would be pleased to know she'd sent Skip to bed and a gold-plated yachtie was making her arrangements. I didn't know why I should feel bad that Lily was dead. I'd probably liked her better than she had liked me, but since she hadn't liked me at all, it might not be that much. Maybe I just wanted to know what had happened so she'd go away. I went to the hospital because that was where they'd taken her. I was standing outside, sweating and feeling weak in the head, when a shadow fell over me, a dapper one in a white linen suit and Panama hat.

"Josephine," Joe Storey said, "join me for lunch."

Ever-Ready looked startled when we walked into the Port of Refuge, and I might have looked startled myself when Joe asked him to send lobster salads and a bottle of Champagne to his room. "Do you mind?" he asked. "I like my privacy. I usually eat on board the *Eel*."

He had a suite, decorated in coconut tree fabrics and paintings of yachts, designed to remind you that you were in the South Pacific, in case you neglected to look out the window. Recalling Gabby's musings, I had to admit Joe Storey was attractive in a lump-of-gold way, but that's as far as I could get on account of my own speculations, mostly about why he'd had to get to Neiafu so fast he'd left his *Eel* behind.

There was a knock at the door, and two people wheeled in a tray with an ice bucket. They began to set the table leisurely; Joe told them not to bother. He opened the Champagne and handed me a glass. "How's your mother?" he asked.

"My mother? She's dead—" I paused. He grinned.

"It's best to keep your stories straight on an island, Miss Ililouette. I understand you flew north with me last night." He spoke so conversationally it was almost possible to overlook the fact that he was watching me the same way my cat used to observe a mouse before he pounced and bit its head off. "What were you doing in Nuku'alofa?"

"Drinking with Gabby Asher and the Oggs. Well, she and I were drinking. The Oggs don't drink."

"Who said that?"

"Mrs. Ogg. Of course, she also said they don't know you."

"Connie only speaks the truth. She doesn't know me." Still smiling, he sipped his Champagne.

"How did you meet the Oggs?"

"You don't think I met them in church? I served with Ron during the war. We came to Tonga on a holiday. It was the first time I'd ever been here. He had relatives he was supposed to look up. Missionaries."

"Is that how he and Mrs. Ogg met? I'd wondered—"

"You are not the only one. No, they didn't fall in love. Ron was a wild guy from a wealthy old family in Mississippi. I gather his family didn't know what to do with him when he got back home, so they recruited Connie to keep him in line. How she got Ron to God still baffles me."

"And God too, no doubt. Why do you care about Lily?"

"Who said that I do?"

"The coconut wireless."

"My only interest is in seeing Lily Omont below ground as soon as possible."

At another knock on the door, three people came in, one carrying salads, one carrying bread, and one a feather duster.

"Everything is just fine, thank you," Joe said. When they had departed, he said to me, "Do you just play with your Champagne, or do you ever drink it?"

"I'm cautious. The one time my brother drank too much Champagne, he agreed to run for Congress."

He laughed, and I was sorry I suspected him of dark deeds. He had great taste in shirts. This day, his shirt had flying fish on it.

"So, why do you care about Lily?" he asked.

"It's always too bad when someone dies."

"Is it?"

"Yes, because you never know what would have happened. My brother says there's no such thing as what would have happened. Still, I wonder: Did she just vanish with a heartbeat?"

"Doesn't everything?"

"I don't know. But a friend wrote to me that—if you love someone, love doesn't disappear if you're separated, so in effect you've created something that transcends time and space—" I took a drink of wine before I told him everything Jackson had written.

More staff arrived, this time bringing an arrangement of fruit and flowers and a vacuum cleaner. I was surprised to hear Storey address them in Tongan. "I just asked them to do the housekeeping later," he explained. "Go on: Time and space?"

"Do you like physics?"

"It comes in handy."

For the first time in a day, I thought about the story I hadn't written, and I decided that the hero, insofar as there was one, would be a physicist. "What do you think of entropy?" I asked.

He was laughing again. "How the hell did you become friends with Lily Omont?"

"Friends?"

"She told me you're a good friend who is always, sadly, falling in love with her lovers, like that young doc who chased her here. Did you follow him?"

"I only met him on Friday. The day before I met Lily. I came here to work for Bette Omont, if I can ever find her."

This appeared to knock some of the salty seasoning off him, and he drained his glass. "You came here to work for Bette? Doing what?"

"Being a companion, I think."

"Is that what she said?"

"She didn't say anything to me. Her sister in San Francisco hired me. I haven't met Mrs. Omont yet. Lily kept saying she's dead. I think Mafi was going to tell me something, but then she disappeared."

Storey was looking altogether wild-eyed, so I poured him the last of the bottle. "I seem to have gotten my stories all wrong," he said.

"It comes of living on a yacht."

"You are telling the truth, aren't you?"

"I'm trying, since I have given up politics. I have lapses, however; Josephine was one."

"Whereas Lily Omont had a thousand and one stories."

There was another knock at the door, and Storey sighed. "Come in," he called. No one did. "I believe we may have to continue this conversation in a less public place," he said as he got up to open the door. No one was standing there with bananas or brooms. It was Pulu, the husband of Mafi, and he looked like he was about to pop his cork. I decided lunch was over.

"Well, goodbye," I said. "Thanks."

He nodded. "If you want to fly south with me tomorrow morning, meet me here at six."

In the hallway, I encountered Ever-Ready, who was clearly relieved to see me alive and who doubtless had been in charge of the cleaning crews. I asked what he had expected to happen to me. "He's not such a bad guy."

"No, of course," Ever-Ready said. "But perhaps, Lily went with him to his ship, the day she never came back."

I hiked up the half-mountain when I left the hotel, but I couldn't find a place that wasn't already occupied by spiders. The air was hazy, as if all the spinners in the world had wrapped it in webs. The distant green islands were disappearing into mists. I went on, down to the cove by Tarkington's station.

He wasn't there. A note tacked to his door said he had gone to Fiji and asked Pulu to check on his tanks till he returned. I went to see the tanks and, to be polite, said hello to the sand lump in the stone-fish tank. It moved. A head emerged. It looked grouchy, but I don't know if a stonefish has any other expression. I didn't see a second one and hoped this one hadn't eaten her proposed mate. "Under the circumstances, I wouldn't blame you," I said to it. I couldn't tell if it was staring at me or at nothing. A conversation with a stonefish is not so easy as an octopus. If they too hold ancient knowledge, we may never share it. "Do you want out too?" I asked. I couldn't find a net, however, and I wasn't sure how to pick it up without one. It was not the sort of thing you'd want to do wrong. "I will try to find a net," I promised.

I climbed the rocks and said hello to Dolores, somewhere at sea. "Here's the thing," I said. "Ever-Ready said Bette Omont is Lily's only known relative, but no one knows where she is. Joe Storey told the police he often takes care of business for Bette, so he arranged for Lily's body to be taken to Nuku'alofa. She'll be buried there.

"Ever-Ready also said Lily had arrived from Nuku'alofa on a private yacht. He thought she was staying on Bette's island, using her boat to go back and forth. But on that Saturday night of the dance, she couldn't find Bette's boat. She was making a ruckus at the harbor, so Joe sent one of his crew to take her to the Port of Refuge. She stayed Sunday night too. Ever-Ready said Joe came to the hotel on Monday morning and paid the bill, and Lily wanted him to take her to Bette's island, but he said no. Lily said, 'Then I will have to swim.' No one saw her again. The police think she must have tried to swim to Mrs. Omont's island, but Skip said she couldn't swim, and whatever else she was, Lily wasn't dumb. I think she stole Gravity's boat. But it came back. When did she drown?"

Like the stonefish, the sea withheld any answers. The sunset flamed over the sky, as if the heat of the day had ignited it, and I headed back to town. I came again into the gaudy cemetery with its beer-bottle decorations. The orange and red banners were drooping in the windless air. I had no wish to get lost in the graveyard this night, and so I went around it, but I saw a man standing in it, alone. It was Pulu. I wondered whether it would be better to be buried underground or lost in the sea.

"So long, Lily," I said, but I didn't really think she was gone.

30

Fresh Air was sitting in Foeata's garden beneath the vines of purple passion flowers.

"Malo e lelei, Seli," he said. Thank you for living.

"It is a fine night," he added as Foeata brought out tea. "I like it when the world makes you look at it, by being too hot or too cold or too wild. I am here, it says, do not forget me."

"It is too hot," Foeata said.

"It warms my old bones. Like the sight of a beautiful woman in her garden."

Foeata began energetically weaving a mat of pandana leaves. "Women," Fresh Air observed. "So full of mysteries. You had a good day, Seli?"

"I had lunch with Joe Storey. And about fifty other people," I added, so Foeata could stop clutching her head. "Why don't you like him?" I asked her.

"Of course I must love him," Foeata said dolefully, although it seemed that her Christian duty weighed heavily on her. "But he is a rich man. He could go anywhere. Why does he come here always?"

"Do you know how he got his money?"

Fresh Air sipped his tea. "It is said he was a poor man who married a rich woman."

"Oh, like—a lot of people. Where is she?"

"Dead," Foeata said, darkly.

"Of a long illness," Fresh Air added.

"Tarkington has gone away," I said. "But he left a captured stone-fish. I was thinking I should set it free, but I wasn't sure how to pick it up without a net. So I didn't."

"A wise decision," Fresh Air said. "It is not a good way to die."

"Does it happen often?"

"No, but it is the way my friend, Dr. Omont, died."

"The story of Lily is finished," Foeata said firmly.

"Is it?" he asked. "When is a story finished?"

"Who will care now?"

"Always there is someone who knows what is the truth."

She sniffed. "You? Maybe your friend Dr. Omont said to you, 'I will share a secret.'"

"He and I talked of many things."

"Yet I know more of the story of Lily. I know that one night a man came to hospital to ask Dr. Omont to go to a woman in the bush."

"No, the man came to his island," Fresh Air said. "And the woman was far away on an island in the Hai'pai group. Dr. Omont went to help her. One week he was gone. And he returned with the child."

"And it was said that perhaps the father was Dr. Omont," Foeata added.

"I did not know this."

"You do not know the talk of women. Why else would he die in a way so strange unless it was the angry father or brother come to kill him?"

"It was an accident." Fresh Air turned to me. "Often the fishermen brought him fish. He would wait on his dock, and they would throw a net filled with fish to him. One day, inside the net was a stonefish, and when he caught the net, it pierced his chest. The fishermen rushed him to Neiafu, but the injury was too close to his heart. Their remorse was great. No one knew how such a fish had come to be in their net."

Foeata sniffed. "This, I believe, for perhaps a man will not see his shoes on his feet, his food on a plate, unless he has a woman to ask, 'Where is it?'"

"So Mrs. Omont raised Lily?" I asked.

"There was no one else." Fresh Air shrugged. "She tried to be good to the child for the sake of her husband, but I do not think she loved Lily."

"Is that why she sent Lily to America?"

"It was for the best. After her husband's death, Mrs. Omont went away, but she returned. She brought Lily to the school where I was a teacher. Lily was very smart, but she was—what shall I say?—lost between worlds. Quick, quick, she could learn anything, but she was not happy as most children are. She did not have friends. She knew she was different. One day the minister from America came to school to talk to the children. He asked them what they wished to be when they grew up. Lily said, 'I want to be white.' The missionary said, 'Be a good girl, be a Christian, love Jesus, and when you die, God will make you white.' A week later, Lily said to me, 'Maybe I would rather be bad than white.'

"Bette sent her to a school in Nuku'alofa, but they sent her back. She took things. She made up stories. She was not nice to others. Mrs. Omont told me that Lily wished to go to America. I said, yes, this could be a good idea, for we all knew that in America, people can live as if the life given to them is a blank piece of paper. If they do not like the place of their birth, they move. If they are poor, they become rich. If they do not like the god of their parents, they find a new one. They change their names, their husbands, their wives, their noses, and the color of their hair. This is their freedom. So, Lily left, and no one heard of her for many years."

"Yet she came back."

"And now it is finished," Foeata said, "so we will speak of other things. Perhaps, Seli, you will learn to weave a mat." She gave me a machete to smooth the edges of pandana leaves. I tried to wield it without amputating anyone's arm, including mine.

"So small your hands are." Foeata held hers next to mine. It was like comparing a bunch of bananas to a bird's foot.

"Are big hands a sign of beauty too?"

"Palangi women do not grow so big," Foeata allowed. "Perhaps palangi men look for other bigness in their women."

This caused Fresh Air to chuckle and put him in momentary danger of being beheaded. "A big mind," he said. "A big spirit."

"Jackson's mother is big," I said.

"Fat?" Foeata asked hopefully.

"No, but she has big hands and feet. She calls them farmer's hands."

"A nice woman."

"Yes. She lives in Paris. She is a weaver, like you."

"And his father is also nice and lives in Paris?"

"No, his father—I don't know where he lives. He has houses in California and New York and San Francisco. Maybe Colorado."

"So many houses for one man. He is rich?"

"I guess so."

"And Jackison lives—where?"

"Nowhere really."

"And your father?"

"Was an artist who never sold a painting."

"But your mother—"

"I don't know what she was. There's a painting of her. She looks like a mermaid, that half-human, half-fish thing, or maybe a jellyfish, all blurry, green-gold, and fading."

"She was ill?" Foeata asked. "Of this she died?"

"No, one night she drove her car into the water and drowned. She had been drinking. She was sad because my father was dead, I guess." Both Fresh Air and Foeata looked appalled. "It doesn't matter now. It was a long time ago. Whatever she was is lost now, beyond reach."

"When my husband died," Foeata said, "many people said to me, 'What will you do? How will you live?' I thought, I have three babies; how will I not live? I have a house, a hot shower. I have lived in New Zealand. I know palangi ways. I can cook palangi food. Always, it is good to make jokes with palangis; they are so serious about life. I will make a guesthouse for them. So I have a good life.

"He was a good man. He built my house. He made my hot shower. But he liked the beer from New Zealand too much. I did not understand. When I taste it, it makes the world go away as if I cannot touch it, cannot feel it. But I know it is there. I know that if I stand under a tree in a storm and it falls, it is not good."

"Is that what happened to him?"

She nodded. "But I did not think it was so with women. Men— they cannot help it—they run so many ways. They want so many things. They must do something in this world, but maybe they do not know what this is. And if they have too much from which to choose, a man must look many places for this thing that he is. Is it here? Is it here?" She peered beneath her pandana leaves. "They must be strong, but many times they are only strong for lifting wood. Inside they are soft. But I did not think it was so with women, Seli, to be so—I do not know the word."

"Hungry."

"Yes. I have thought there is more peace in women. A woman

knows there is one thing she can give back to the world, and that is a child. When you have a child, Seli, you will know this." She paused to pour more tea. "Now you are quiet, Seli, and always you have something to say."

"I don't know anything about children," I said. "Foeata, tomorrow, I might go to Nuku'alofa with Joe Storey."

"Jackison would not like this."

"So what?"

With the air of a pope granting a dispensation, she said, "Tonight, you will take him his tea. Say to him, 'Tomorrow I will fly to Nuku'alofa with a rich old palangi who makes eyes at women like a shark.'"

"What do you think he'd do, forbid it?"

Fresh Air said, "This he would like to do, but he is palangi. He cannot."

"No," Foeata agreed. "But if you tell him this, tomorrow he will be well."

I took Jackison his tea, but he was asleep. I went to bed. The night was hot. I was lying on the dragons, wide awake, when I heard Fresh Air's voice: "Jackison, good evening. Ah, here is Sikipi too. There are many stars tonight, and it is fine here in this garden."

Fresh Air began telling them about ancient Tongan astronomy. In the older days, he said, Tongans believed the sky was made in layers, as many as a hundred; thus there was a connection between the sky and a great burial vault called *Mua*. The Tongan word for sky and vault was the same: *langi*. The stars were in the highest sky. Fresh Air recited the ancient names for them: *huma-utu; halia toloa; lua-a-tangata; moe-a-mahe*. His voice had a singing quality, and finally I fell asleep.

31

"Get in!" Gravity announced as he coasted into the Neiafu harbor. "Today, I am a taxi, and we will have an adventure!"

I didn't doubt this. In addition to Skip, Jackson, Lebeca, and me, at least a dozen Tongans were waiting to board his boat, whose carrying capacity I judged to be about half of the food Foeata had packed for a picnic lunch. The five of us were going to Mrs. Omont's island, and the others were catching a ride to different spots along the way.

I had not really intended to fly away with Joe Storey, although I did consider it when I got up in the morning and found Skip and Jackson were recovered enough to be amusing themselves with a conversation not worth repeating about Sherlock Holmes and Judy Bolton. I was heading for the door when Foeata produced the picnic baskets. She hauled Skip and Jackson to their feet, told them to be good or God would have something to say to them, and chucked them out the door. She gave me an encouraging shove to follow them. "They will be nice," she said.

I watched Gravity's boat sink lower as passengers climbed aboard. It was about half an inch above the water by the time it was my turn to get in. I hesitated. Jackson didn't exactly push me aboard. He just put his hand on my back and kept moving, so I got in.

Everyone applauded; this was for Skip and Jackson, Lebeca

explained, because of their happy recovery. One woman gave Jackson a bouquet of pink flowers, which he held awkwardly for half a second, then handed to me. The sun was hot, but I knew it was the attention, more than the heat, that was making him sweat. He pulled off his shirt and wiped his face with it. Three women began to giggle, and one fell overboard, causing a great ruckus of splashing and shrieking while she was retrieved.

Lebeca told Jackson not to worry; they knew he had been ill, so they should not mind if he was without his clothes. Jackson put his shirt back on, and we headed out to sea. There, the laughing and chattering of the Tongans turned into a chorus, which Lebeca translated as "Oh, God, we are going to die." Not to worry, Gravity said; it was tradition and no reflection on his ability as a sailor.

We glided past islands where flying foxes dangled like oversized dates in trees. Skip stared at the blue-green water; Jackson disassembled the flowers I was holding, petal by petal. When he ran out of flowers to tear up, he traced the pattern of hibiscus blossoms on my lava-lava.

"What is this?" he asked.

"You wear it over jeans so it doesn't look like you have legs. You are even supposed to swim in it. Tongan women know how to tuck them so they don't fall off, but Foeata put ties on mine, like training wheels."

"Shelley." His voice sank so low I could hardly hear it. "I'm sorry if I've been an ass."

"It's OK." I knew this was preferable to mentioning that he had been sick.

"No." He rubbed his head. "I don't know what's wrong with me."

"It's pretty flat here. It's no wonder your brain is sputtering."

He laughed and threw the beheaded bouquet overboard. "I love you," he said, and he kissed me. A ripple of applause rocked the boat. The passengers had all turned and were watching us; Gravity probably could have collected additional fees for entertainment. Jackson turned red, then white, then red again, and sank down into the bench. He didn't say anything else. He was beginning to remind me of me.

When Gravity had deposited the last of his other passengers, we sailed on toward the open sea. At a quiet spot, he turned off the engine and brought out a six-pack of beer. Lebeca popped the bottles open on her cheekbone, an impressive feat, although I don't know if it warranted all the fuss Skip and Jackson made. They persuaded her to open all six bottles.

"How about a swim?" Skip asked.

Gravity said of course. Jackson said why not. Lebeca said perhaps, and I said no, thanks. Skip and Jackson doffed their pants and dove in. Gravity also jumped in, but he kept his pants on. Lebeca laughed, put her feet in the water, and declared it was too cold, too deep, and too close to the coral reef for her to swim. I agreed with everything she said, but no one believed me, and it was only a small consolation that they were sorry later on. I didn't want to swim in the ocean. I couldn't see the bottom, and I can't swim if I can't touch bottom. It reminds me of infinity. Jackson used to know this, but he must have forgotten. He bobbed to the surface with Skip. "Aren't you coming in, Shelley? It's beautiful."

"It's fantastic," Skip said. "Wow, what fish! Shelley, come in." They both leaned about the side of the boat, and it tilted.

"No, thanks."

Skip said, "You can even take your lava-lava off. We'll never tell."

"Nope."

"Why not?"

"Giant squids. Giant clams. Unexploded torpedoes from World

War II. Scorpion fish. Nuclear waste. Sea wasps. Barracudas, Portuguese men-of-war—"

"I thought you grew up swimming in the ocean."

"No," Jackson said. "We lived on the north coast of California. The water was freezing, and there was undertow and sharks—but this water is warm, Shelley."

"Gravity," Skip asked, "have you ever seen a shark?"

"Oh, of course, many."

"No, no, you're supposed to say never."

"This is not true. But I see none today," Gravity added helpfully.

"Don't they stay outside the coral reef?" Jackson asked him.

"Oh yes, perhaps."

This did not qualify as a positive statement for me and did not make the water any less deep. "Come on, Shell, try it." Jackson smiled. "You'll love it."

"Yeah, you flaming coward," Skip said. "Jump."

The following really happened, and you should keep it in mind if two out of three people ever tell you that you won't see a shark in the South Pacific. I jumped in. Immediately I regretted it because my lava-lava floated up around my neck. I tried to untangle myself while holding on to the boat as Jackson and Skip swam toward an outcrop of rocks. Jackson turned to look back. I decided Skip could call me a coward until the end of time, but I wasn't going to let go of the boat. I wasn't going to swim where I couldn't touch the bottom without having hundreds of feet of water over my head and therefore being most likely drowned. As I thought all this, the surface of the water rippled. At first I thought it was Gravity, but it was a fin.

I retain a curious, slow-motion impression of the next few minutes. I was transfixed by the dark shape, glinting in the sun, gliding through the water. Detached from function or intent, it had a hypnotic beauty. I thought, is that a shark? No, of course not. Sharks are like monsters in the closet or bogeymen under the bed. You look for them to prove they aren't there. It couldn't really be a shark unless God, in his inimitable way, had granted me an excuse for not swimming, providing, as well, a brief editorial comment to those who would be too sure about anything in this world. Then I saw Jackson and Skip, and I thought how curious it was that, at this distance, their eyes looked larger than their heads.

With a shout, Gravity bounced back into the boat, and Lebeca whacked the water with an oar as I scrambled aboard. Something brushed against my leg. I don't know if it was the shark, although it was still there when I looked. At first, I thought it was larger than the boat by a factor of ten, but as it circled us, I had to admit it was not really more than forty feet long. It swam leisurely, sniffing the boat, as if to determine if it was in the mood for humans on wood, a traditional snack. It swam on. The fin vanished.

I heard noises in the water, but I only saw Skip clambering onto the rocks. A second later, Jackson joined him, but during the time in which I thought he'd been towed off by the shark, my entire insides collapsed as if I'd been dynamited.

Gravity started the engine and headed toward them. I examined my legs to see if by chance the shark had eaten one and my blood had drained away and this was why I felt faint. I counted two legs, but I knew this could be an illusion, and so I counted them again. I might now be in a padded room somewhere, counting my legs, if Jackson and Skip had not, just then, fallen back into the boat. Everyone was mute, even Skip. They all stared at me; I don't know why. I counted Jackson's legs until he put his arm around me. Then I very nearly strangled him.

"You're OK, aren't you?" he asked. His voice was strange, but possibly this was because he couldn't breathe. I let go of his neck and went back to counting legs.

"It was not so large as the shark that ate my mother's cousin and a horse," Lebeca observed.

"No," Gravity said, "and this was only the tiger shark who does not always eat something just because it is there."

Skip asked if there were any beers left. Lebeca said, regretfully, no.

"Ah," Gravity said, "here we are." The boat skidded up to a dock. This is the truth: I was the last one off the boat.

32

Mrs. Omont's island was a rocky, silent place, floating beneath a canopy of coconuts and twisted hardwood trees densely hung with vines and moss. Wild orchids bloomed randomly, like butterflies caught in the greenery. The house, perched on a high point, was reached by a winding path. Skip and Jackson, unnaturally humble, went looking for a door. Lebeca went with them. Gravity, with a frown, set off alone. I stayed outside on a deck overlooking a vista of endless blue undulating water, merging into the horizon.

I was feeling peculiar. Clouds were making the sun blink off and on, but even when the sun appeared, I couldn't feel its heat. This had little to do with the shark. All the shark had done was swim past us; Republicans could wreak far more havoc in fifteen minutes. The shark might have had perfectly honorable intentions or none at all. It was only its unfortunate public image that made the event loom larger than it was. I was wondering if I could write a story with a shark as the hero when Jackson came out of the house. He had taken off his shirt again, and I experienced a moment of empathy with the Tongan woman who had gone overboard. He does have a nice chest. Of course, I can remember when he didn't have hair on it.

"There's no sign of anyone here," he said. "You're right, Shelley, it is mysterious."

I knew this was a noble effort to appear to care one way or another; guilt is an amazing thing. "It's not your fault, Jackson, that there was a shark in the ocean."

"I know, but I wasn't sure you would see it that way."

Skip came out with a bottle of wine and glasses. He had decided Mrs. Omont wouldn't mind if he opened it. He gave me a glass. I drank it all, which was too bad because then I saw four Jacksons, flinching.

"She has a gas stove—there must be a tank—but no electricity," Skip said. "What a damned odd way to live." He sat down on a deck chair, and Jackson sat on the other one. I wobbled around, listening to their voices buzz like insect wings. I must have wandered close to Jackson because I felt his hand on the back of my knees.

"Do you want to sit down?" he asked.

I said, well, no, for I had retained my ability to count to two, the number of chairs.

"Oh, excuse me." Gravity reappeared. "Here is something I must tell you. I have found the boat of Mrs. Omont. But who has brought it here?"

"Oh," Jackson said. "That is, I don't know."

"Perhaps you would like to think about this another time?"

"Yes. I mean, yes, we'll think about it."

Skip stood up. "Tell you what, Gravity: let's go think about it now. Come on, Lebeca."

I would have gone too, but Jackson still had his hand on my leg. "You could sit down," he said. "You've sat on my lap before."

"No. You must have me confused with someone else. Probably Bird." Bird was Jackson's first girlfriend at Berkeley, a memorable disaster. She didn't go to Cal, but to a school for rich nitwits, and the relationship endured for nearly three months because they couldn't talk to each other enough to break up. She was always sitting on his lap. Jackson was tragically persuaded he was going to marry her when she dropped him for a guy she met in LA working on her tan.

"I wish you'd forget about Bird."

"I can't. I still don't know what attracted you to a woman who was so shark-like. Functional but limited to basics."

"You hadn't come to Berkeley yet." He ran his hand up the back of my leg, and I toppled over. My brain shut down, and I couldn't think of anything else to say, not even one snitty thing about Bird. "Do you want more wine?" he asked.

"No. It's gone to my head, somewhat."

"That's because you drank it all at once, goose. Why'd you do that?"

"I got nervous."

"Then we're even." His voice was hitting husky, unnerving notes. We had not veered this close to the edge in a long time; we had scared ourselves so thoroughly that even the few times we'd just been in the same room, one or the other of us would run. Now we were on an island and there wasn't far to run, if, in fact, one could actually get up and walk.

"The sad thing about sharks," I said, "is we used to look for them. We wished we could see one. Maybe it's physics. It takes all those light years for a wish to get to a star, and then, when you've forgotten it, it lands on the wishing star. 'Ah, kids on Planet Earth, western nether region of the universe, would like to see a shark. Request granted.' And twenty years later, we see a shark. I suppose there was nothing to worry about. All you'd have had to do is rub its head and talk to it; the shark would have rolled over or played dead or anything else you wanted."

"Is that right?"

"What are you doing?"

"Trying to figure out how many layers of clothes you're wearing. You're like a Tongan dessert. Ah, and here comes all of Tonga."

"Jackison," Lebeca called shyly. "Perhaps, could you help me open the box of Foeata's lunch? Kalavite and Sikipi have gone to look at the boat of Mrs. Omont. It is all very odd."

I reflected that it was odder that a woman who could open a beer bottle on her cheekbone could not open a box, and I was surprised to hear myself thinking such a catty thought. Jackson got up to help her open the box, and I fell asleep.

33

Raindrops falling on my head woke me up. The sun was sinking into waves of purple, gold, and scarlet in the sky, and the colors were mirrored in the sea. The rain was scattering broken bits of sunset like glitter on the hillside. Gravity's boat was gone from the dock.

They had left, and I was alone on the island that I'd agreed to come to when I was thousands of miles away. Was it a journey's end? I had not traveled much, yet I have a notion that you've reached it when you find something that reverberates in some lost part of yourself. Maybe, even in the most exotic landscape, it's the recognizable portion we're looking for. Maybe, rather than seeking out new, unknown worlds, we are really looking for the connection to one place we know. Or knew.

What was this island? It had ghosts, Lebeca said, but what are ghosts except lost things that return in dreams, real or imagined, light and dark? I didn't know who Bette Omont's ghosts were. There was no reason to think I'd find anyone, living or dead, inside her house; still, I felt that something was waiting for me. This is probably why I circled around it, until the rain began to pour like waterfalls off my head, before I went inside.

A curtain made of seashells opened to a spacious room, anchored by tree trunks at the four corners. Where the trunks ended, an artist had painted branches and leaves that framed a sky-blue ceiling with floating clouds. A teak wood swing hung from a beam, also painted to look like a tree. The swing was a dragon with its tail and head forming arm rests and its belly filled with silk pillows. Just beyond it hung the original of *Ile Perdue.*

A circular staircase, painted like a twisting vine with vivid bugs, yellow, red, and blue, led to upper and lower floors. Near it, a door opened to a world so fantastic it almost wasn't recognizable as a bathroom. The walls were translucent blue above a coral reef, a rainbow of towers and shapes, with schools of purple and yellow fish swimming through a seaweed forest, and a flower garden of anemones in gold sand scattered with starfish and sea urchins. A turtle glided on one wall, and a shark on another. There were three octopuses, one curled up under a rock, one shooting over the wall like a rocket, and one spread out like an umbrella about to descend on a crab. The sink was painted like a purple anemone, and the toilet a giant clam. A crowd of painted human faces peered up over the edge of a bathtub.

Another door led outside to a shower, unembellished except for a few frangipani plants, real ones, creeping over the corrugated metal walls. My clothes were stiff from the sea water and my skin patchy with salt. I decided to shower and rinsed out my clothes and hung them up to dry. I borrowed a purple-flowered lava-lava hanging on a hook and kept exploring.

I found a kitchen, identifiable as such because I could see a stove and a sink, but every inch of it had been painted into a fantastic jungle of flowers and vines, parrots, monkeys, snakes, and spiders. Our picnic box sat on a table, with a wine bottle, half full.

There was one more room on the ground floor, but it was an aberration, a bedroom with no disguise. The walls were covered with gold grass cloth, unadorned by so much as a single painted cockroach. A plain wood canopy bed had veils of mosquito netting tied to the bedposts with gold ribbons. On the windowsill were a beeswax candle in a seashell holder and a box of matches. The only other thing in the room, a lone chair, had snakes painted on it, curling up the legs and around the arms. The fantasy was unfinished here; the canvas was blank and waiting.

I went up the staircase to an open loft, a sort of lookout tower with an easel and a palette, made from a framed window, covered with dabs of colors. Canvases were everywhere, finished and unfinished. A narrow bed in a corner was surrounded by stacks of books. A few smocks and flowered dresses hung in an antique armoire. Shells, coral, mismatched earrings, stubs of pencils and charcoal, brushes, and driftwood were jumbled on a dresser top. It all gave me kind of an idea of what Bette Omont might be like, but not where she might be.

I went down to the lowest level of the house, which was backed into the hilltop, cellar-like. Bottles of water and wine and cases of tinned foods were stored on shelves. I opened one last door that led to a shadowy room. Its windows and outer door were overgrown with vines, real ones. I stepped on a skeleton.

When I recovered my wits, I realized this was most likely a professional skeleton, fallen off the hook near a massive wooden desk in what must have been the doctor's study. Shelves were lined with books and neatly labeled specimens of shells and dead sea creatures. An aquarium still had sand and water in it, although nothing else that I could see.

The incongruous element on the desk was a mirror, battery-powered, Hollywood-style, surrounded by light bulbs. I turned it on. It illuminated a clutter of makeup, hair rollers, brushes, and hair spray.

Two suitcases, matching, red with black trim, lay open on the floor. They were filled with flashy things, a purple satin night gown with gilt trim, a gauzy pink robe with tattered feathers, padded bras in black and leopard skin print, bikinis made of string and tatty lace.

I have never been much for shopping, but I'd gone along with Gabby Asher a few times. She hated cheap underwear. She said she'd rather wear nothing. She would have called all this stuff cheap, dime-store makeup and Frederick's of Hollywood lingerie, all props for a tawdry show; then I realized I was thinking picky thoughts about a woman who had drowned.

My mother had a mirror with light bulbs in her bedroom at the House of Lost Things, although she had never stayed there much. Her room was a shadowy place with heavy curtains, always closed. She had a lot of makeup, too, and bottles of perfume and a silver box with a pink powder puff. Jackson and I sometimes sneaked into her room to explore, and one time we made ourselves up; Jackson thought he would die when it wouldn't wash off.

I hardly ever thought about my mother, but lately I was doing it a lot, partly because of Foeata's curiosity, partly because of Lily. I had a strange notion that if I could understand one woman, I could understand the other, not that I should then understand myself. I am pretty sure that my mother would have cringed at the suggestion that she and I were alike, just as Lily had, and when I thought about the jellyfish painting, I was just as glad.

A gust of wind rattled the window, and outside, a white face materialized, pressed against the glass. Once more that day, I went into a state of suspended animation.

34

I had scared Jackson as much as he'd scared me, although I didn't know this until the door opened and I found myself in a stranglehold of mutual, mute hysteria. He recovered first, I believe because he noticed the underwear in the suitcases. He blinked at it, much struck. "Maybe we should go make tea," he said.

We went upstairs, and he prepared his British cure-all. "I was just looking around the island when a light went on in the lower level, and I saw the door," he said. "Who did you think I was?"

"I didn't know. The boat was gone; everyone was gone."

"You didn't think I'd go off and leave you, did you?"

"I thought you might come back."

He whacked me on the head with a potholder and gave me a cup of tea. "Lebeca had to go to work, and Skip had a Peace Corps meeting. You were asleep, so I told them to go on without us. Gravity said he'd come back later to get us, unless—unless you'd rather stay here." He spoke rapidly as the color rose in his face. "We have Foeata's lunch, eight hundred sandwiches, spaghetti, seaweed; it's no stranger than watercress, really."

The sun was setting in a blaze of light and color. Just before it vanishes over the horizon, you are supposed to be able to see a green flash, but I've never seen it, and I didn't then because Jackson, standing behind me, touched my bare shoulder. I could feel his warm breath against my neck. I put down my cup so I wouldn't pour hot tea on him.

"You look like a Gaugin painting, Shelley."

"You look like you're feeling better too."

"That's because there's the Pacific Ocean between us and the rest of the world."

"Do you like that?"

"Yes."

The rain had stopped, and mists were floating up from the water in patches that appeared and disappeared. As I watched, they grew thicker, stayed longer, and finally covered the view. The distant islands became shadows and finally vanished. He kissed my neck, and my heart fell to my feet and flopped about like a fish out of water gasping for breath. I knew all I had to do was turn around and face him. I wanted to, at least I think I did, but the same strange fogs were forming and reforming inside my head. Where his lips touched my neck, all the separate atoms ran amok and spun off, clutching their nuclei, groaning, "I'm melting, melting," but on the floor they reassembled into the floundering fish, and I just stood there.

There had been a time when, if Jackson had noticed this, he would not have been deterred, but now this wasn't the case. He let go of me and walked away. I made myself follow to where he stood, studying Mrs. Omont's painting of a lost island.

"It's called *Ile Perdue*," I said. He didn't reply. He can do this, retreat like a sea creature into a borrowed shell where no one can reach him. I stumbled on. "Jackson, if you want to make love to me and get it over with, it's OK. I panic and think about flopping fish, but still, it's OK."

A flock of birds rose from the trees and hooted as they flew away.

Even they knew I'd put it badly. I clutched my throat so I wouldn't say anything else, but Jackson went over to the dragon swing and sat down. He looked up at the ceiling; it was interesting, as ceilings go. Finally, he held out his hand. I came closer and sat down, and the dragon rocked as we leaned against the pillows. The sound of his heartbeat mingled with the patter of raindrops on the pandana leaves. Outside, veils of mist hid the sky, then revealed it. A soft wind carried in bursts of cool air. The blurry half-moon rose into view, and its light reached out with crooked fingers over the water. It was very nearly dark.

"It's not so bad, is it?" he asked.

"No."

"Shelley, I'd be lying if I said I came here just to be sure everything was all right between us. But I mean this: if you want me to lay off, I will."

"Really?"

"Really." He said it so sadly I knew he meant it. "I hate it that you're so afraid of me. You never were before."

"Yes, I was."

"No, you were just shy—and so innocent, like one genuine wild thing in Berkeley." He smiled, but it was more wistful than happy. "Do you remember when those hunters invited my father to their lodge for the start of deer season and they said bring David and me too?"

"When everyone hollered, 'Shoot! Shoot!' at you and instead you shouted, 'Run, deer!' and then they wanted to kill you instead of the deer?"

"It was the way it looked at me, like it was saying, 'I know you won't shoot me.'"

"David didn't shoot anything either; he just hid it better."

"Shelley, I know everything's different now. And it's just me—"

"No, it isn't."

His expression paused; I can't think how else to describe my impression of his brain, confounded, halting and backing up. "Do you mean you haven't—"

"Had sex with anyone? No."

"But it's been five years—I mean, I know you turned down Robinson, and that was a relief because I would have wanted to kill him and they need a surgeon here, but—but five years—"

"You were always a lot more normal about sex than I am, Jackson. I just didn't want anybody except you." For a terrible second, his eyes filled with tears, and Jackson would rather throw up than cry. "I don't know why."

He didn't say anything, but I am sure he would have recovered in a minute. There is no telling what would have happened next because the seashell curtain clattered, and Albert the missionary fell into the room.

35

Albert was spattered with mud and sand, and as he stared at us, a dull red color seeped through his white face in patches. "It's you!" he gasped.

"Were you expecting someone else?" I asked.

"No! No one! No one at all!" He closed up, as tight as a clam. I went into the kitchen to get him a glass of water. I figured if he opened his mouth to drink it, he would, at least, breathe. On second thought, I poured him a glass of wine and brought it to him. He took a gulp and froze, his eyes bulging. "What is this?"

"Oh damn. I forgot."

Albert took another cautious sip. "Oh my," he whispered, "it really is strong, isn't it?" He drained his glass and sank slowly to the floor as if he were melting from the feet up. "You look really beautiful tonight, Shelley."

Jackson got up. He went into the kitchen and came back with a plate of sandwiches and a tapa cloth blanket. "You might want to eat something," he told Albert. The blanket he dropped on me. Here's my theory about life: All people are Tongans at heart.

Albert's eyes flickered to him. "I know who you are. Shelley was in your room."

"Did you come here looking for her?" Jackson asked.

"It's not what you think! It isn't!"

"I'm not sure I think anything."

"I can't fall in love with every woman who is beautiful and kind, can I?"

"It would complicate your life."

"Do you love Shelley?"

Jackson's Brit accent surfaced. "Yes, actually."

"Would you jeopardize your immortal soul for her?"

"Sure."

"Would you expect something back?"

"No."

"No? Nothing?" Albert turned to me. "Shelley, how do you feel about Jackson?" He caught me with a mouthful of seaweed. Jackson began examining the inside of a sandwich. "Can I tell you how I felt about Lily? I saw her and I'd never seen anyone like her, but still, I felt like I knew her, like I always had. How could that be possible?"

Jackson said, "Some people believe that the fact that we're here at all means anything must be possible."

"Do you?" I asked.

"But is that love?" Albert asked.

"It sounds like you fell," Jackson said.

"I did? Yes. I did."

"Where did you meet her?" I had wondered where their paths could have crossed.

"At the hospital. I volunteer there. They need help with their filing and records. I was working there when she came in. The most beautiful woman in the world."

His voice had been changing like a channel with shaky reception. Now, it threatened to cut out altogether. I asked, "What did she want?"

"Nothing! Not much. To see a chart—a medical file. Well, two. For a project. I knew it was wrong, but I got them. She kissed me. I had never—I—" He disintegrated into speechless anguish. "She left. And she took them."

I asked, "Whose charts were they?"

"One was hers. So she had a right to see it, didn't she?"

"And the other?"

"I will get them back! I will!"

"Is that why you came here tonight?"

"God told me to come here."

"Are you sure?"

"What else can you trust, except the voice of God?"

"As long as you know it's the voice of God."

"What else could it be?"

"The Voice of America."

"No." His voice was nearly gone. "Lily is dead, and there is nothing we can do for her except to undo any wrongs that are connected to her."

"Come now," Jackson said, "none of this sounds so bad."

"You don't know it all."

"No," I agreed, "we don't."

"But I'm late!" Albert sprang to his feet. "Oh, what awful stuff wine is to make you think things you don't and shouldn't. If you lose God, then nothing is simple!"

He fled out the door.

36

Jackson and I followed a path from the house that twisted through gnarled trees dripping with vines. The mists were gone, swept away by winds that had shrouded the sky in clouds. Shadow-like birds unfurled and circled overhead. Flickering moonlight illuminated the landscape in bursts. I walked as close to Jackson as I could without stepping on him. Finally, he took hold of my hand.

"Faint-heart."

"I am, Jackson, I really am."

"Then why do you want to follow that nut case?"

"Why are you doing it?"

"Because otherwise you'd go alone."

"No, I doubt it."

Even in the dark, I saw him smile at me, and I thought, I love him. I had never thought this before, at least not in clear words, one, two, three, and I'd never said it, however easily the words had rolled off Jackson's tongue. I had thought it about other people, like Jesse Goldensohn, but I'd never said it to anyone. With Jackson, if the words had ever ventured near my brain, they would have fallen apart into frantic letters, all running around, crashing and splintering into fragments. But there it was, the words with all their pieces. I tried thinking it again, I love him; the words fell like a coconut on the brain, undeniable but debilitating.

Jackson stopped when I did. "What's wrong?"

"Nothing." I started to walk again, but in a pathetic, wobbling way. "Do you ever wonder, Jackson, why things are so much worse in the dark? Why that's when you think about, did I forget to pay a bill, or do I have a future, or what it's like to drown and be dead forever, or—"

Jackson gasped and collided with me. "Sorry," he stammered. "Sorry, Shell."

"I didn't mean to scare you that much."

"No, I just nearly walked into a spider web. Jesus, that is the biggest spider I've ever seen."

"I'm beginning to think that there might be a God. I might even like Him."

"Oh hush."

We climbed up a cluster of rocks that descended in a narrow promontory to the sea. The wind shivered the trees around us, but the night was silent. "Did you see that?" I asked.

"See what?"

"A light flashed at the end of those rocks. It's gone now."

"All I can see are your eyes."

"Did you hear that?"

"No, what? A bloodcurdling scream?"

"Footsteps."

We listened. "Do you know what it is?" he whispered. "It's the spider, working its way toward us, step by step, thinking of tender flesh. It will go for you, of course." He paused. Something grabbed my leg. I screamed. Jackson laughed.

"Jackson! You rat scumbag—"

"Jackson!" The voice echoed. "Jesus Christ, God dammit, take a hundred years off my life. Go ahead. What do I need it for? What are you two doing here?" Skip climbed out of the bushes.

I said, "We're looking for Albert."

"Where'd you see him?"

"He came to the house," Jackson said. "He was in something of a state."

"That's Brit for loopy," I translated.

"Ah," Skip said. "This is just fucking great. An hour ago, Gravity and I were trying to decide whether we really should go fetch you, on Foeata's orders, or not, when Albert turns up and asks if he can borrow Gravity's boat. Gravity says, 'Of course.' The kid runs off. I said, 'Does he know how to navigate?' 'Of course,' Gravity says, 'he is a palangi.' I drag him to his boat and there is the kid, tangled up in ropes, and it's clear he knows less than an elephant about boats. I urge Gravity to put his foot down. Gravity offers to taxi the kid. Where? Here. Why? Never mind. As soon as we hit land, Albert disappears. Christ Almighty, I am going to pack it all in and go be a dentist in Urbana." He was interrupted by a scream. "Oh, bloody hell."

Jackson said, "Shelley, will you stay here? Please?"

Here was the truth: I didn't want to chase shrieking people through dens of spiders in the dark. I said OK. Jackson looked more stunned than this really warranted. "Did I say it right?" he asked. I nodded. He kissed me.

"I guess I could go by myself," Skip mumbled. We heard shouts, not shrieks, now. Jackson kissed me once more, and they ran.

I sat still for a minute, double-checking with my brain. I thought, I love him, for the third time and the earth didn't stop spinning, the seas didn't part; the birds didn't even laugh at me; but at the end of the rocks, the light flickered again. The half-full moon appeared from behind clouds to reveal a boat moving silently, like a shark. As

I crept toward the edge of the cliff, I knocked some loose stones. A dark lump in the boat turned. I could see a skull and staring eyes. I made an unnatural trajectory traveling up and backward, the opposite of the one you would make if you were operating in accord with the laws of physics. I collided with something large and fell into a bush, and two heavy things landed on top of me.

37

By the dim light of a single bulb, the row of painted faces in the underwater bathroom watched as I put one arm, then the other under the faucet. Skip, in his boxer shorts, was sitting on the bidet cleaning the cuts on his legs. Jackson had a scratch on his arm, but I was by far the most banged up.

"It might be easier to take a shower," Jackson said.

"No," I said. "Have you ever taken a cold shower?"

"That's an unfair question to ask him, I'm sure." That was Skip.

Jackson dabbed iodine on my shoulder. "The trick is not to take a cold shower alone. Then it's not cold at all."

"How do you know this?"

"It's only a theory. I just thought of it. But I like it."

Skip said, "If you'll pass me the iodine, Jackson, I'll go to another room so you two can be alone."

I said, "You still haven't told me what happened."

"This is what happened," Skip said. "By the time we got to the beach, Gravity's boat had taken off. We looked around. We even jumped in the water, although I don't know why. We didn't find any screaming people. We were on our way back because Jackson was cherishing a wacky illusion that he would find you where he'd left you, when a thing that might have been a bat, but turned out to be you, came flying out of the dark."

"It's interesting that I could knock both of you down."

"What's more interesting is that Jackson thought you'd stay put, just because you said you would."

"This is really deep." Jackson was still poking about on my shoulder. "When did you last have a tetanus shot?"

"I don't know."

"What shots did you have before you came here?" Skip asked.

"None."

"You can't do that," they said together.

"I'm allergic."

"To what?"

"Shots. And doctors. Did you see any ghostly things out there?"

"Not aside from you," Skip said. "So here we are. I guess she won't care if we sleep here, not that we have any choice. You guys can have the bedroom. I'll take the dragon."

I could feel Jackson's eyes on me. The painted octopus was watching us, and all the fish and faces too. Maybe not the turtle.

Skip said, "I think I'll go look for my pants."

"How did you lose them?"

"I threw them somewhere before we jumped in the water. Then I couldn't find them."

We all stayed in the bathroom. Skip surveyed the night wherein his pants were lost. Jackson read the fine print on the iodine bottle. I wondered what would happen if I said, "Shall we go to bed?" but I was afraid Jackson would faint from shock and fall into the tub and crack his head open and suffer concussion and lose his memory, so I didn't say anything. I just stood up. I had every intention of going into the bedroom with him and seeing what happened next, but as I stepped out of the tub, a strange pain twisted through my insides as if someone had taken hold of them with a metal claw. It was odd, but it was real. I couldn't move. I couldn't even talk. I saw in Jackson's face the conviction that I'd just gone into a spasm because I had stood up to go to bed with him. I somewhat believed this myself.

"Something wrong?" Skip asked.

The pain vanished. "No. It's nothing. It's gone."

"What's gone?"

"Nothing. Maybe I cracked a rib. But it's all right now." The pain came back, like a wave smacking against a rock, and I couldn't say anything else.

"She won't tell you or me," Jackson told Skip. "Once, I nearly dragged her to the ER before she finally told me she had cramps. I thought she was dying."

I walked unevenly into the bedroom and fell on the bed. I could hear Skip hooting, and I knew Jackson had just told him I'd thought I was a boy until I was ten years old because I thought we got to choose.

I heard a spurt of a match as Jackson lit the candle. It filled the room with a honey-gold light. He was examining the ties of the mosquito net when, with a crash, Skip burst in from the deck. He was clutching a bottle of wine and looking bleached as a whale bone. He sat down on the bed; he was chanting in Latin.

"Is he praying?" I asked Jackson.

"No. It's parts of the body."

"Sorry," Skip said. "Excuse me. I just had the hell scared out of me." He took a long drink from the bottle. "Shelley, what did you see tonight?"

"A thing in a boat."

"A thing? I thought you thought it was a ghost."

"Well, yes."

"A sort of Halloween thing, with a hood and glowing eyes?"

"Yes. That's it."

"I saw it."

"In a boat?"

"No. I didn't get that far. I'd just thought I'd open another bottle of wine. Then I thought, maybe I'll go for a walk with it. But I'd only started back to the beach when I got the creepiest damned feeling and looked around, and there was this thing, staring out of the trees at me. It didn't make a sound, but it had eyes. Then it was gone. But I saw it. I apologize, Shelley, for thinking you were nuts."

I was gracious. He offered the bottle around. He was getting pretty looped, even worse than me that afternoon. Jackson took a swig and gave the bottle to me, but I gave it back to Skip.

"Shelley," Skip said, "that time you saw something strange in the graveyard, you thought it was Lily."

"Well, yes."

"What about tonight?"

"I wasn't going to mention it. I didn't want to upset you."

"I think it upset me more to see whatever it was I saw."

"A ghost," Jackson said. "Not little green men?"

"Why don't you go outside and tell us what you see?"

"I'm not drunk."

Skip handed him the bottle. Jackson said, "I'm still not going out looking for ghosts. I don't know what Lily looked like. She was dead when I saw her."

"She still would be," I pointed out.

"Skip," Jackson said, "this stuff scares Shelley. She really believes in it."

"This stuff really scares me," Skip said. "My mother believes in ghosts. She says the late Mr. Thornburg, who built our house, always turns up in the kitchen when she bakes pies."

Jackson rolled his eyes. "I can't believe they let you into med school."

"You used to see ghosts all the time in England," I reminded Jackson. "You wrote to me about them."

"But I only saw them to please you. You wanted me to find one so badly."

"I didn't see this to please Shelley."

"Yes, but she just might have planted the idea in your head."

"Yeah," I said, "like the spiders."

Jackson ignored this. Skip fell flat on his back and stared at the ceiling. "Lily." He wasn't quite drunk enough to disguise the feeling in his voice. "God dammit, if someone could be a ghost, she'd do it."

"Why?" I asked. "Because she liked life more than she let on?"

"No. Just to do it. It's more dramatic than just being dead."

"Was she an actress?"

"All of the time. Damn." He inspected the empty bottle. "I'll leave you guys. I'll just go lock the doors and hope I pass out."

"I don't think there are any locks," I said when he had gone. "There are hardly any doors."

"Maybe it'll keep him busy, looking for them," Jackson said. "I thought he was going to sleep with us."

He went back to fiddling with the knots in the mosquito net ties. He couldn't seem to get them undone, which was odd. He used to practice tying and untying knots in the shower with the lights out, which is only one of the nutty things rock climbers do.

The net came loose. He caught a cockroach crawling on it and tossed it out the door. He stood looking out at the dark. Finally, he took off his wet clothes and threw them onto the deck. He sat down on the bed, and there we were.

Before he climbs a mountain, he'll study it as if he's trying to see a route through the rocks. I've wondered if he is ever scared by the things he does, dangling by ropes over nothing but space. It scares me, but I know that doesn't signify much since it would take far less time to make a list of things that don't scare me than things that do. He is different, however, than most of the people he climbs with. They decide to climb something and go for it, whereas he, according to himself, sometimes falters halfway there. Sometimes, he told me, he wonders why he does it. Like when he's nailed to the face of Half Dome and it's raining and water is collecting in his hammock and he's trying to find a knife in the dark to cut a hole large enough to drain the water, but not so big he'll fall through it. Sometimes, when they've spent four days in a tent in a blizzard and have no supplies left but tea bags, he'll wonder if he really wants to freeze and starve and lose his fingers for the illusion that he's conquered a mountain that, in the next moment, could swallow him anyway. Still, when I asked him if he ever gets scared, he only looked as if he didn't know the word.

"Why?" he asked.

"Well," I said, "because you could die and then you would be dead forever in infinity."

"You don't think about that," he said.

Now, however, I wondered if he might be scared and if there was anything I could do about it, but I didn't do anything except wonder.

"What are you looking at?" I asked.

"You. With all your cuts and bruises. Shelley, let's go home."

"Home? Where?"

"I don't know. Where would you like to go?"

"But don't you worry about all this? Don't you wonder?"

"No."

"You won't worry about infinity, and it's there."

He didn't answer.

"Jackson, do you think Skip was talking about Lily like that because he was a little drunk?"

"I think he's drunk because he was in love with her."

"Really? How do you know?" I remembered how Lily had laughed when I'd said we were alike. We were hardly of the same species. Lily, in this candlelit room, on this hidden island, would have known what to do. She wouldn't have lain there, wondering if Jackson were cold or wishing he would come into the bed. She wouldn't have wasted time discussing me. "But I don't get the feeling he liked her very much. So when you say, 'in love,' what do you mean? She was beautiful. Is that what does it?"

"No."

"Then what is it?"

"It's just the feeling that hits you, like—like—"

"An avalanche?"

"Yeah, like an avalanche."

"Did you see any avalanches in the Himalayas?"

"No, but—" He gave me a wry, touchy look.

"Even if Lily hit Skip like an avalanche, I don't see why that matters."

"Shelley, you goose, it's the only thing that matters."

"Do you know, Jackson, I'm beginning to think that men care more about love than women. Well, it was their idea. They have to protect their invention, and it's worked for a thousand years. You can't count it a total failure if only now women are beginning to be skeptical. Gabby Asher doesn't believe in love anymore."

"Gabby will always believe in love."

"No. Gabby has made the amazing discovery that she can live without David Ilillouette, formerly the center of the universe. Now she's free to search for the Holy Grail. Maybe that's what Lily was looking for. Maybe Mafi went into the sea looking for it. Maybe Mrs. Omont went to Tahiti on a tip that it's there."

I was interrupted by a series of thumps on the deck. Jackson peered out the window over the bed. "Shell, loan me your skirt thing, will you?"

"Why?"

"Because my clothes are outside."

"Are you going out there?"

"It might be Albert."

"And it might be Lily. I doubt it's Skip; it's too quiet."

"It has a torch."

"I suppose if it's Lily, you ought to be wearing something." There was another thump and a face, thin, wild, and bloodless, appeared at the window. I might have removed half the hair on Jackson's leg, but he didn't notice.

"Good Lord." I had found my voice, cowering beneath my liver. "It's Mrs. Ogg."

When Jackson, wearing my lava-lava, opened the door, she staggered in, gray-white, bug-eyed, clutching a flashlight. Evidently, she'd had a shock, and although this might be expected if you are creeping about an island at night peering into windows, she did not seem prepared for it.

"You!" she said. "Whatever are you doing here, Miss Illywit?" Then she perceived Jackson in my lava-lava, and to her credit, she dropped the question.

"Are you all right?" Jackson asked, not knowing he was talking to the chief regulator of morals for God. "Can I get you anything, ma'am? A cup of tea?"

She nodded. Jackson left and I tried to sit up, but I had to do it slowly on account of my ribs, which were acting up again. Mrs. Ogg, enthroned in a chair with painted snakes on the legs, frowned at me. "Are you ill?" she asked.

"No, just a little sore."

"Miss Illywit!" Her fishlike expression became even more pop-eyed as Skip entered the room. He apologized for being clad only in his boxer shorts and explained how he had lost his pants. I don't know why we felt obliged to explain anything, but I suppose it was the way she looked from him to me as if she had found not just the scent of sin but the roasting of souls. Fortunately, Jackson returned with her tea. The fish look vanished. She smiled at him. If I'd been Jackson, I'd have run for the sea, no matter how many ghosts were outside, but he only said, "I don't believe we've met." His accent was distinctly Brit, which happens when he wants to impress a woman. I didn't know why he wanted to charm Mrs. Ogg, but it was possible she reminded him of his batty Aunt Marble, a Puritan from Massachusetts. Skip was bereft of words again, so I made introductions.

"What lovely tea," Mrs. Ogg fluted to Jackson. "It's just delicious. It must be an English secret. How did you do it?"

"With a tea bag."

"You must do something special." It was so interesting to see his effect on this spokeswoman for God I could almost have forgotten that we were having this tea party at midnight on an island that had been uninhabited until that afternoon and that Jackson was wearing my only article of clothing.

"It's his method for swishing," I said. "I wonder, Mrs. Ogg—"

She was busy fluttering at Jackson, however. "I've always admired Englishmen."

"Actually, I am Welsh."

"But whatever are you doing in Tonga?"

I said, "Missionary work civilizing Americans."

"I suppose," Mrs. Ogg continued, "you wonder why I am here."

"No," I said, "we've already figured out that no island is an island."

She frowned at me, and I decided that Jackson could have her. "I don't exactly know," she admitted, and I am sure this was a first. "We were nearby, heading toward Neiafu, when we heard a disturbance in the water. I told my husband to stop. We know Mrs. Omont lives here alone."

"That's kind of you," Jackson said.

To keep from gagging, I asked, "Where is the Rev, by the way?"

This caught her with a mouthful of the incomparable tea. "I don't know," she whispered. "I waited and waited. He—gets lost so easily."

"How long has he been gone?"

"Not that long." Her answer was prompt, if lacking conviction. I mentioned that it was a fairly straight path from the dock to the house. Even the Rev should have been able to manage it.

"Not a bad evening in all," Skip concluded. "We've lost Albert, Gravity, the boat, my pants, and now, the Rev."

"A sort of tropical black hole," I said.

"Did you by any chance see a ghost?" Skip asked. "I'm just doing a poll."

"A what?" You could tell she wasn't herself. She didn't say it was impossible.

"A shrouded thing creeping about looking ghostly," I said. Her reply was forestalled by the appearance of the Rev, who strolled up to the door. He was carrying binoculars, as if he were on a midnight bird-watching tour.

"Oh, here you are, Mother," he said. "Having tea with the natives, are you? I woke up and wondered where you'd got to. Saw lights, and then this young man docked alongside us. Showed me the way. Damn me if Tongans can't see in the dark like cats."

"Excuse me," Gravity peered around the bulk of the Rev. "I am sorry for leaving without you, Sikipi, but when I found Albert, he was not so fine. I took him fast to hospital, but I think it is best if the palangi doctors go to him."

"Was that Albert we heard?" I asked. Gravity nodded. "Did he step on a stonefish?"

"No, it was his heart."

38

It was Sunday morning again, and the Mormon chorus across the street was singing while chickens were clucking backup. I was lying in bed feeling an affinity for the hymns to the everlasting glory of God or to His mysteries anyway. Although I was replete with things to wonder about, such as why people were vanishing and reappearing like islands in the mist, I was only thinking about the night before.

"You two can stay here," Skip had said. "I'll go back with Gravity."

Before I could say anything, Jackson said no, we'd return too. He even wanted me to accept Mrs. Ogg's invitation to ride with them. Instead, I went with him into Gravity's boat, a bobbing cork in the sea. I huddled next to Jackson on the cold ride, but he didn't seem to notice I was there. He and Gravity were talking about navigating at night. "I will show you how to sail my boat, and you can teach me to climb your mountains," Gravity said.

When we reached Neiafu, Jackson went to the hospital with Skip, and so I did too, like a burr stuck on his socks. They looked more like a wandering troupe of belly dancers than one and three-quarters palangi doctors. Skip had tied my lava-lava over his boxers. Jackson had his pants but had not been able to find his shirt, so he had borrowed my T-shirt, which came about halfway down his chest. It made him legal, although I knew it still might cause some woman to fall off her shelf in the waiting room. I, having retrieved my damp cow shirt and jeans from the shower, was the most respectable by far.

I stayed in the waiting room while Jackson went with Skip to see Albert. I intended to think about what Albert and the Oggs had been up to, but instead my mind wandered off with a shadowy companion down a deserted road through a night all misty and warm with dawn faintly lighting the edges. We came into a richly scented garden and lingered there; we twined around each other as if we were vines amidst the lush growth.

I heard a voice say, "We'd better take this one home," and I opened my eyes to see Jackson bending down in front of me. Of course, I thought, a passionate interlude so spontaneous and free of nervous fits or extended conversations could only have been a dream. It was one thing to dream of Jackson dead and floating in the sea, but for my brain to conjure up an erotic scene all softness and sensuality—where could it have come from? It was distinctly different from our long-ago episodes in cars or dorm rooms or sleeping bags, initiated at Jackson's behest and serving his fiery urgency, not unpleasant, mind you, but I rarely caught up with him. As we returned to Foeata's, however, Jackson walked apart, and I had to wonder if maybe the shadow in my dream wasn't Jackson at all. At two in the morning, Foeata was sitting at her table, weaving a pandana mat. Solemnly she had escorted me to my room, and what became of Jackson and Skip I did not know.

Now, in the morning light as I lay in bed pondering everyone's odd behavior, most of all mine, another clear thought sprang into the light; this made two. I loved Jackson—I was getting better at thinking this—and perhaps I also wanted him or, at least, I wanted him more than I feared him. Even as I thought this, the voices of the Mormon choir rose so joyfully they drowned out the chickens. I got out of bed and forgot to look for spiders.

In the kitchen, Foeata was chiefly concerned that no one would be up in time to go to church, and, in her opinion, everyone could use an extra dose of God. The fact that Skip and Jackson had returned wearing my clothes had not been lost on her.

"Of course I cannot wake them," she said, woefully glancing at the doors behind which they were sleeping. "Perhaps they will not go to church." Perhaps the church would fall down if they did, her doleful expression added.

"It was a strange night," I ventured. I described it, most of it, anyway. Learning that Skip had lost his pants and Jackson his shirt in a good cause reassured Foeata, and she offered a theory that everyone had been adversely affected because it had not rained for several days, discounting a few drops here and there. She had heard that droughts caused a heaviness in the air that weighed on people's brains and caused them to go nutty. I told her often months passed in California with no trace of rain. She nodded as if she had suspected this. I'd never heard California explained so easily.

She had a letter for me. It was from Jesse Goldensohn, two pages of onionskin with his beautiful calligraphy. The first page was about the fog, which I gathered had been heavy for several weeks. There also might have been a small earthquake, but I couldn't tell if this reference was only metaphorical. Every word was absolutely *le mot juste*. He included a quote from someone named Montale: *"Non chiederci la parole che squadri da ogni lato."*—"Do not ask us for the word that can define everything." The unwritten scene, he wrote, was the one that determined the visible. I was wondering who Montale was when Jackson came out of his room.

Is love, after all, the worst kind of mental affliction? I had just been feeling encouraged because I'd had two clear thoughts about him, but seeing him, my brain collapsed at the possibility that he could read them. I don't know if we had been in love before as much as in physical fascination, and although he seemed inclined to resume this particular captivation, I had to admit that the prospect of my being in love with him, whatever that meant, could be enough to scare him halfway up any mountain. All this passed through my head in three seconds, as he walked by me, glanced at my letter from Jesse, and scowled.

"And here is Sikipi too," Foeata said happily. "Now we will all go to church."

Jackson's expression changed to a polite but strangled look of anxiety. He has always insisted I find Catholics harrowing only because I have no experience of Protestants. Skip said, "That's your department, Foeata. I want to go back to the hospital to see how Albert is doing. I'll take Jackson, if you don't mind. Shelley can pray for all of us," he added with a wink, "unless she'd rather come along."

"She wouldn't," Jackson said in a devastating way.

"Maybe I would."

"What do you know." Skip tossed a loaf of bread to Jackson. "I think she'd rather come with us."

"Would you?" Jackson sounded so doubtful I was reassured he'd been nowhere inside my head, and I went with them to the hospital.

They were both quite nice for the next half hour. The patients on the shelves greeted us like old friends. We went to Albert's room. He looked worse than I had ever seen him, which usually had been quite bad. When I said hello, his eyelids flickered. He mumbled, "Mrs. Ogg."

"No, it's only me, the heathen. Would you like me to get her?"

He began to flop his head from side to side as if to shake something out of it. "Shelley? Shelley? Did you find her?"

"Who?"

"She's there."

"Take it easy, kid," Skip said. "Tell us later."

"But I've lost it. Can you find it?"

"Sure," I said. "Find what?"

"The cave. But be careful. She's there."

"Who? Where?"

"It's so dark. It's gone. And I've lost it."

"Maybe it's only borrowed," I told him. "It will come back."

Jackson touched my arm. "Come on, love." My heart did an odd flip that in no way resembled a dying fish. "Let's let him rest."

As we left the room, I asked, "Is he dying?"

"No," Skip said. "He has a heart condition, but he won't die today. How about a cup of coffee, Shelley?"

I followed him into a small exam room. "What kind of heart condition?"

"Congenital cardiomyopathy. Thank you, Salote," he added to a nurse who brought in coffee. "Give us five minutes." She nodded and left.

Jackson offered me the jug of sweetened condensed huacow. I declined, but he and Skip poured it into their coffee. "Sit down, Shelley," Skip said. "I want to talk to you."

A thought leapt into my mind, and I looked around at Jackson, whose expression crumbled, so I knew I was right. "I'll just go," he mumbled.

"What a chicken," Skip chuckled as Jackson fled. "And this is the guy who climbs mountains where only goats belong. Shelley, you can't wander around here without immunizations. Well, you can, but it's dumb, so let's take care of it, shall we?"

On cue, Salote carried in a tray of needles, most of which looked large enough to tranquilize a Tongan spider. Sometimes you are caught in a way that the most effective escape—such as jumping out a window—lacks a critical dignity, like the time David's aide scheduled him to drop by a dinner that turned out to be a fundraiser for the opposition. Fortunately, the other guy was late, the food was getting cold, and the natives restless. David made a few jokes at the expense of himself and gained three converts before he left, but he didn't forget who had sent him there. With this in mind, I decided I could survive a tetanus shot.

Skip was examining the needles. "I thought we'd give you what the Peace Corps gets: tetanus, yellow fever—the gamma globulin can be painful, but Salote is good at this. I'll leave her to it." He coughed. "D'you want me to go get Jackson?"

"No. I do not want Jackson."

When I came out of the room, Jackson was leaning against the wall. He looked anxious and contrite, but this did not qualify as suffering to me just then.

"Shelley?" He caught up with me and took my arm. He did it gently, to be sure; what hurt was jerking it away from him. I wondered if I could knock him down, but the effort didn't seem worth it, as there were no spikes for him to fall on and pierce his liver.

"Shelley, slow down. I know you're mad. I'm sorry I left you there. I didn't mean to, but—I did. I didn't know how else to get you to have the shot. If I'd told you, you'd have talked me out of it. You know you would have, and I—are you going to talk to me?"

"No. Go away and leave me alone."

You can't say I didn't warn him. If he had listened to me and gone away, in fifteen minutes I wouldn't have been so mad, and when the parade of shots they'd given me all began to kick in, I might even have been glad to see him. But he is as stubborn as I am bad-tempered, and this is why we had the worst fight, not to mention the dumbest conversation of our lives, there, in the lobby of the Neiafu hospital, with all the patients lying on shelves looking on. I told him to go find someone else to call love, and his eyes flashed.

"Why are you mad?" I asked. "No one shanghaied you."

"I didn't shanghai you. I just didn't want you to be an idiot."

"If you think I'm an idiot, why do you bother with me?"

"I don't know."

"Then don't."

"Is that what you want?"

"Yes, if you're going to treat me like your idiot relative."

"You just don't seem to get the idea that some things are real. You and that ass Goldensohn."

"I know. That's not real. A rational relationship."

"You're only mad at me because I'm right."

"If you're right, then why are you so mad?"

"This is no use. This is just no use."

I know he didn't mean it the way I took it, but I took it that way anyway. "You're right. It's no use. Because you're still mad at me, Jackson. You've been mad at me for five years, and you always will be, and there's nothing I can do about it. So you might as well go away now because you always do anyway."

The look on his face almost knocked me out of my fit, but I spun around and walked away.

I went back to Albert's room. I just wanted to sit down, but as I came to the door, I realized something had happened. The shades were pulled, and the lights were out. Most of all, it was the stillness. I couldn't hear anyone breathing.

39

I decided I would steal Gravity's boat and go back to Mrs. Omont's island and live like a hermit in the cellar room with the skeleton. I only made it to the edge of town before my body began swelling up so greatly I perceived it would soon be unable to fit inside my skin and I would, therefore, explode. I sat down on the side of the road, and I doubted I'd ever move again. I was waiting for the fruit bats to begin circling when a truck passed me. It stopped, and a brusque voice asked, "Is something wrong?"

Pulu, the husband of Mafi, looked as fierce as an ancient warrior who would shortly make a salad of my brains. I explained that, in a quest to save me from getting sick, the palangi doctor had nearly killed me.

"You cannot sit there in the sun," he said. "I will take you back to Foeata's."

By then I'd been reduced to such a lotus eater I just got into Pulu's truck. As he drove, I focused my attention on a sticker on the dashboard, a red, white, and blue heart that said, "Missing you in Mississippi." At Foeata's, Pulu heaved me out like a sack of coconuts. "Don't let anyone else save your life," he said.

Foeata's house was deserted; her Sunday feast was over. I lay down in the garden and tried to make my brain work since my body was

attempting to decompose and become a hibiscus plant. The conversation I had with myself went like this: It could be worse. How?
You could be Lily. You could be Albert. Is that worse? Is this rigor
mortis setting in? No, you can't get rigor mortis on only one side
of your body. How do you know? Have you ever had rigor mortis
before? There must be something to think about besides rigor mortis.
Shakespeare? "This is as strange a maze as ever men trod."

Foeata rushed into the garden, followed by most of the Women's
Choir. Owing to the coconut wireless, all Neiafu knew Jackson and
I had quarreled, and they feared I had thrown myself in the sea. The
subsequent hoohah was relief in discovering me in the garden, not
dead. Foeata sent the crowd packing. Only she and Lebeca remained.

"For the record," I said, "I did not even think of throwing myself
in the sea."

Foeata spoke to Lebeca in Tongan, but I picked up *Sikipi* in the
stream of words.

"Please, do not go get Sikipi." I explained in morbid if meandering
detail the part he had played in reducing me to my present condition
on a mat.

"No, Seli," Foeata gasped. "No."

"Yes, so please don't let him do anything else for me. But, Lebeca,
could you find Gravity?"

"But he is not here. He is gone with Jackison. They went to sail and
climb rocks because"—Lebeca's voice wavered—"because tomorrow
Jackison will leave."

"What?"

Lebeca whispered, "He went to the Port of Refuge and Ever-Ready
called to the airport for him. Oh, we shall be so sorry if he leaves
because perhaps we shall never see him again."

I don't think all the shots had kicked in until then. I had been woozy and suffering great pain, as if I had been, say, pummeled with a shower of rocks. This last one was a boulder that landed directly on me, stomach, head, and heart.

They regarded me sorrowfully. "It could be worse," I said. "I could be Lily. I could be Albert." It did not seem to qualify as worse to Foeata. She told Lebeca to go find Gravity.

An hour later, Gravity bounded into the garden with Lebeca. "Ah," he announced, "we have had such a very most wonderful day! I must somewhere find a mountain for I have learned 'On belay!' and 'Belay on!' and it is wonderful to shout these things and climb! Ah, Jackison: When he goes up the rocks, it is like the dance of the Tongan warrior. And when he fell—"

"He fell?" I asked. "He never falls."

"Ah, but he did, a great and splendid crash. And he said this is an important lesson too, of what not to do. Not to think about, oh, women or something like this because flip, you crash. But, Seli, you wished for me?"

"Can you take me to Mrs. Omont's island? Tonight?"

"No!" Foeata exclaimed.

"Yes," Gravity said, "but do you not wish to go to the feast we will make for Jackison, for tomorrow—"

Foeata interrupted sternly in Tongan. I knew she was telling them not to mention Jackson was leaving because I would decline like an unwatered plant and croak in her garden. Lebeca chimed in that all the hearts in Tonga would break when he left, and Gravity agreed. I didn't know why they couldn't talk about how sad it was about Lily or Albert instead of Jackson.

The bushes rustled, and Skip ambled into view. He surveyed the funereal cluster around me and bent down beside me. "Something wrong? You having a reaction to the shots?"

"She suffers," Foeata said, so I didn't have to say anything.

"I'm sorry, Shelley. The gamma globulin hurts like hell; I know." He reached out toward my hip and must have gotten a bug-zapping look from Foeata; his hand bounced back into the air. "Trust me, honey, it's better than hepatitis; that's the real thing."

"Death might also be better than the real thing," I said. "When did Albert die?"

"Huh?"

"He's gone."

"I know. They took him."

"The tevolos?"

"No, his church folks. They want to send him home. Against my advice—there's a storm coming—but it's out of my hands."

"He's not dead?"

"Not the last that I heard."

"When I went to his room, he wasn't there. I thought he'd died."

"Why didn't you ask Jackson? Where is he, anyway? I expected to find him here, soothing your aching"—he cast a cautious glance at Foeata—"muscles."

"Packing." I felt sorry for Lily and for Albert, but even sorrier for myself on account of my own heart condition.

"Where's he going?"

"Home."

"He can't do that. If the storm is bad, I'm going to need him to help at the hospital."

"He's leaving."

"He won't fly off into a storm because you pissed him off. What did you say?"

"I didn't mean it. Not all of it."

"Hell, Shelley, you must have had fights with him before."

"No."

"Are you telling me he's never been mad at you?"

"Once."

"Once? Once? God preserve him for the saint that he is. And how long did it last? Five minutes?"

"Six months. No, a year." I was really beginning to fall apart; even Foeata was looking aghast. "Five years."

"Five years? What'd you do? Come on, he's not going to be mad at you for five years, no matter what you said. Christ, what is wrong with you two? Do you think he came here to climb the mountains of Tonga? Shelley, the guy is in love with you. You can make it up with him."

"No. There's nothing I can do."

"Now that's bullshit," Skip said. "Look, you take it easy. I'll go get you Tylenol. You need anything else?"

"*Hamlet.*"

"So that's what you call him? OK, we'll find him, and you give him one of your 'I'm at the Chicago stockyards and they're taking me to the slaughterhouse' looks, and you'll have a bowl of Jell-O on your hands."

"And perhaps," Lebeca added, "you must also give him a smile?"

"A kiss," Gravity said. "Oooh-la-la."

They departed. Foeata remained. She was silent. She most likely knew that however fine the ideas were, they were unlikely to work if I was the one who had to carry them out.

"There is nothing I can do," I repeated. "Is there? This is the problem, Foeata. I don't know what to do. I never do. I was somewhere else when everyone learned what to do. I always have such empty hands."

"Seli," she interrupted, "you must say to him, 'Don't go.'"

The chief obstacle to my doing this was standing up, but I accomplished this only after a few tries and two Tylenol. I dragged myself along the coral road to his fale. I stood outside the door and wondered how long it would be before he came out for one reason or another. The gods were not inclined to make things easy this evening. Jackson didn't open the door spontaneously. Finally I knocked lightly enough so that he might not hear, in case I wanted to decide he wasn't there. He opened the door. He was holding a book. He lifted his eyebrows. That was all.

"Hello," I said.

"Hello." He said it the same way he might have said, "Drop dead." I wouldn't have guessed it was possible to feel worse, but, all at once, I did. There is no more terrible way to spend your time than getting in and out of situations like these. Nothing justifies the misery, not proving you're not an island or continuing the species or showing constituents you have human connections. The worst of it is that, contrary to sense and inclination, you don't run away but stand there, struggling as if you've crashed into flypaper and are fatally stuck.

I said, "I wish you wouldn't leave." Then I burst into tears, and then I ran away. I knew it was not quite what Foeata had envisioned, but considering that twenty minutes earlier I could hardly walk, it was somewhat impressive.

I had just reached my room and buried myself under the dragon pillows when I heard Foeata say, in her most majestic voice, "Jackison. Good evening." She said nothing else. She didn't even offer him another dinner.

"Is Shelley here?"

"Ah." Foeata spoke mournfully, in a measure like a funeral march. "She sleeps. This is good. She has been so ill today."

"Ill? From a tetanus shot?"

"Perhaps not from that, but from the others."

"What others? He was only supposed to give her one."

"Who said this?"

"Well, I—"

"Perhaps she wanted many." She let this possibility fall, like a wooden spoon, on his head. "And there was Albert."

"What about Albert?"

"He is gone."

"What?"

"Yes, and this was so terrible for Seli because she was alone and weak and she went to his room and he was gone."

"Do you mean dead?"

"No. Gone from the hospital. But Seli, too, thought he was dead."

"Oh no. Oh damn."

"Yes, and she is not strong for these things. And it was such a blow to her heart that you will leave tomorrow."

"I—what? Why would she think that?"

"Everyone told her, of course."

"But—"

"It is not what you said?"

"I was just mad. I didn't think—"

"Ah." It is probably impossible to imagine the dark tragedy with which she imbued a solitary word; it hung in the air, draped in black crepe, delivered by the Grim Reaper himself. "Foeata"—he really sounded terrible—"is it all right if I go see her?"

A significant pause followed. "No. She looked so very bad. Now, she sleeps. I think you must not wake her."

I wished I could see his face. Not many people have ever said no to him, particularly not a woman who is as tall as he is and weighs more than he does, in a voice that brooks no nonsense.

Later, Foeata brought me a tray, which held a cup of tea, a jelly roll, and a vial of a German ointment. I knew it was from Jackson because it is the only medicine the mountaineer Reinhold Messner ever uses. One drop terrifies your body out of feeling anything wimpy, like pain.

"So, Seli, he does not leave," she said, and I hoped that Jackson wasn't somewhere tied to a coconut tree.

40

On Monday morning, Skip, Jackson, and Gravity were securing Foeata's roof, which is to say, Gravity was hammering while the other two argued about whether the coming storm was a hurricane, a typhoon, or a cyclone.

"We can ask Sleeping Beauty if she ever gets up," Skip said.

I didn't hear Jackson's reply, but Skip hooted. "You know, Jackson, if you finish med school, you might be able to find a girlfriend who isn't so much trouble."

"But, Sikipi," Gravity said, "perhaps he likes trouble."

"Yes, but if they don't talk to each other soon, Foeata will knock their heads together and I'll have to stitch up the pieces. Here I go again: Jackson, is it possible that Shelley Ilillouette, with hair like fire and eyes like lightning, has never been mad at you before?"

"Once," Jackson said. "She shoved me off a roof for telling her she had red hair. Well, twice, no, three, well, four—"

"And if she doesn't put a knife in you in the first three seconds, she's over it, right? Jackson, she's crazy about you."

Jackson's reply was drowned out by Gravity's chorus of "ooh-la-la." I made a mental note to drop by the Peace Corps office and recommend that they put Skip to better use as a communications system. They could just set him on a rooftop and let him bellow the news.

Nonetheless, I got out of bed with the intention of saying something civil like "Good morning." Just as I came into the dining room, however, Jackson turned away. I heard the kitchen door close as he left. My heart did one of its weird, falling-to-the-floor tricks again, but this time it just lay there.

"Have some coffee," Skip said. "I am glad to see that you survived."

Foeata cut up bread and papayas with a satisfied air. "You are looking so much better, my girl," she said, even though I didn't know where one pain ended and the next one began. "I have told Jackison he cannot stay in the fales by the sea when this storm comes unless he wishes to swim. So he will move his things to his room here, and all will be well. Now you can eat, Seli."

We were still at the table when the rain began to fall. The wind was rattling the screen wall as a battered truck screeched up to the door. The driver, wrapped in yellow rain gear, blew up to the door. It was Gabby Asher. "Shelley, Foeata," she gasped. "I need to find—I'm looking for—" She saw Skip. "Is it you?"

"I don't know." Skip stood up. "I hope so."

"Dr. Robinson?" Gabby swayed. "There is a woman in a hut out past Mafi's. She's having a baby, but something is wrong. Mrs. Ogg is with her, but please go to her." She fainted; both Skip and Foeata jumped to catch her.

"Go," Foeata said. "I will take care of her."

"Do you know where she means?" Skip asked me. I nodded.

"Shelley doesn't have to go. I will." Jackson had returned with his backpack. I heard myself insisting I would go—they didn't know the way—and the three of us bounced off into the bush to deliver a baby.

By the time we reached the solitary hut, the rain was pouring down in torrents, and the trees and bushes were swaying like a swarm of warplanes, about to take flight. We knew it was the right place because of the screams. Even the howling wind couldn't drown them out. Skip and Jackson rushed inside, but I stopped at the door.

Mrs. Ogg staggered out of the hut, looking a hundred years old. She sagged down onto a coconut tree stump. "Miss Illywit," she said, "you are here."

I sat down next to her. She mopped her face with a lace-edged hanky and found another in her handbag, which she offered to me. It was made of linen and embroidered with her monogram. We sat dabbing our faces as the rain whipped around us and thunder rumbled and lightning flashed. Skip ran out of the hut, his arms full of mats. Jackson followed, carrying the woman.

"All this fuss," Mrs. Ogg said.

"Have you ever had a baby?" Skip snapped.

Jackson handed me the keys. "Will you drive? Go as fast as you can, but try not to hit bumps."

"I'll drive," Mrs. Ogg said. "I know these roads."

She drove better than I would have. I tried not to stare at the woman in back, at her contorted face and swollen body. Jackson was shielding her, wiping her face and talking to her. I was glad for that.

"It is a dreadful business," Mrs. Ogg said. "Mercifully, one forgets, as one does most painful experiences." As if to make it clear she had never done anything as questionable as feel pain, she added, "I assume."

I wondered how it was possible to live a life like that. People like her present such impenetrable facades, you can forget that they, too, are made of the same mix of stardust as all mortals. "We seem to keep running into each other," I said.

"It is that way in these islands. You find yourself with people whom you would never know under normal circumstances."

"Like Peace Corps volunteers?"

"Miss Asher could have been a lovely missionary, except, of course—"

"Except she is a Cambodian Buddhist Greek Orthodox Jew."

"Goodness. I am sure I saw her at church services."

"Peace Corps has this odd notion of respecting local traditions. Why were you touring the bush with her?"

"I—I don't know. Miss Asher wished to come to Neiafu, and Joe Storey said he would bring her and they could deliver school supplies. My husband and I were going to leave for Fiji, but when Ronald heard Joe was sailing north, he decided we would come too. When we arrived this morning, they decided that I should go help Miss Asher make visits in the bush."

"The Old Boys' Club."

"Why, yes."

I was wondering what I would do if I discovered a bond of kinship with this woman when Skip shouted to stop. I heard screams. I covered my ears and closed my eyes until a burst of rain hit me as Jackson flung open the door. He was holding his shirt, squashed up in his hands; his white T-shirt was spattered with blood. Mrs. Ogg was out cold.

"Here." He gave me the bundle and sprinted around to the drivers' seat. He shoved Mrs. Ogg over. He drove as if he were racing a Ferrari instead of bashing through the bush in a battered truck with a fainting missionary falling into his lap and a suffering woman in the back. His shirt started to wiggle. I looked inside. It was a baby.

I had never held a baby before. This one was kind of a mess, and even if it was about the size of my cat, I didn't know what to do with it. I tried to imagine what it must be like to be bounced out of a shrieking person into a blooming cyclone.

"It's a nerve-racking way to arrive," I said to it. "Life is not always so wild, but this might be good preparation. I like a good storm, as long as my feet are on the ground. There are other good things about life too, such as Shakespeare and octopuses."

It seemed to be listening, and so I kept talking until we screeched up to the hospital. Jackson and Skip flew off with the woman. Mrs. Ogg sat up. "Goodness," she said reprovingly, as if she had caught herself dancing on a tabletop. "I must go. I'm late."

The baby started to holler, and I supposed I should go turn it in at the hospital. Then, I got a better idea, and zipping it inside my anorak the way I used to take my cat for walks when it was small, I took it to Foeata.

41

The baby looked more human after Foeata cleaned her up. News traveled swiftly over the coconut wireless, and soon the Women's Choir had filled the kitchen to coo over the baby, as Foeata held her, rocking and singing, pausing only to look at me and roar with laughter.

Gabby was drinking orangeade, but she sounded like she'd been hitting the gin again.

"Oh God," she mumbled, "do you remember when I used to terrify David by wanting five children? God, maybe he was right."

When the baby's grandmother and aunts arrived, Foeata reenacted my arrival for them by standing in the door, clutching the baby and bugging out her eyes. The women were all laughing and clapping when Jackson and Skip returned.

They were soaked with rain and smeared with blood. Skip went into the shower, but Jackson only stood in the doorway in a sick-looking daze. The grandmother brought the baby to show him and said something in soft Tongan. She carried the baby off, and the rest of the women left too, each pausing to praise and thank him. He only showed a sign of life when Gabby flew to him and kissed him. He smiled at her. I don't know how she does it.

Foeata made him sit down and drink tea, and Gabby drew him

into a conversation about the Himalayas—"How magnificent! You made it to the top, of course." When Skip came out of the shower, Jackson went in. Skip took Jackson's place by Gabby. As she poured him tea, she asked about the woman. How did she know to go straight to the point with Skip, whereas to avoid it entirely with Jackson?

"She bled to death," Skip said. "There wasn't a damned thing we could do."

"You saved her baby," Gabby said. "And the Tongans, who love their children so much, will love this little one even more because she doesn't have a mother. They will all care for her."

She went on, and in her graceful way, she picked up his spirits, wiped away the blood and pain, and gave them back to him. Jesse Goldensohn always insisted she could turn any man into a pudding, even him. Anyone, Gabby said, except the one who mattered.

By the time Jackson finished his shower, Skip was telling her about ruptured uteruses and retained placentas and other ghoulish things. Jackson sat down on Gabby's other side and began to argue about which was worse. Any minute, I expected them to go into a mating battle and start whacking each other with teacups. I was only stupid and useless, and no one noticed when I went back out into the rain.

I didn't know where I was going, but the rain was falling so heavily I couldn't see anyway. I just blew along with the wind. A bucket-like deluge opened up as I passed the Methodist church, and I considered stopping in, but I didn't want to drip on God's floor. I've never figured out why He would hang out in such places, anyway, when He could be outside. I walked until I came to the fales by the sea, and I watched the waves tumbling like acrobats. "I don't know where you go during storms," I said to Dolores, "but I hope you're OK. Just don't get knocked up, all right?" A rogue wave drenched me. I count this as one more conversation with an octopus.

I found the fale where Jackson had been staying. He had left a pair
of socks on the floor, and I put them on because my feet were cold.
He wouldn't mind.

"Seli!" Lebeca exclaimed from the doorway. "You are here!
Everyone said, 'Where is Seli?' I said perhaps you had gone up the
mountain to think. Now"—she looked worried—"perhaps Jackison
will climb the mountain alone."

"He'll be OK."

She was checking the fales for flooding, but now that the rain had
stopped, she was going to help unload the school supplies that Gabby
Asher had brought to Neiafu. I went with her. A throng was carrying boxes down a ramp to Joe Storey's yacht. He hailed us from the
deck. "Josephine, you look done in. Go on into the lounge, and I'll
tell Georges to bring you something warm. The work is nearly done."
He was dressed in a white dinner jacket, a polka-dot bow tie, and a
blue shirt printed with shooting stars and planets. He was dining
with the Oggs, he explained. "Connie likes to keep up appearances."

Lebeca gasped as we went into a spacious, wood-paneled room
and sank up to our ankles in a royal blue carpet. It was not the mag-
nificence but rather the school supplies that had enthralled her. "It is
all so wonderful," she said, examining the reams of paper, the books,
and the boxes of pencils, paints, and pens.

Georges, dressed in spotless whites, brought us cocoa and dainty
French biscuits. We sat down on plush blue window seats, and while
Lebeca turned the pages of a biology book, I looked out at the view.
The sky was growing dark, and the last of the light shimmered over
the water. The boat rocked lightly. I was born on a ship, by accident,
at sea. Sometimes I think it's why I've never belonged anywhere,
except my grandfather's house, which always quivered like a boat in
the wind every time it stormed.

"Do you think of love tonight, Seli?" Lebeca might have noticed, but was too courteous to mention, my socks.

"I am trying not to."

"Yes! I also!"

"Did you know that once a female octopus lays her eggs, that's it for her?"

"It?"

"She dies. I wonder if she knows. But she does it anyway."

"It is sad, but it is life."

"What love are you not thinking about?" I asked. Lebeca only sighed. I said, "It's better to think about mysteries, anyway."

"Ah, yes, mysteries: Judy Bolton!"

"Don't let those guys make you laugh at her. She was great." I told Lebeca about Judy Bolton. The first Judy Bolton books were written in the 1930s. Jackson's mother had read them, too, when she was young. In Judy's world, her father, the doctor, and her brother, the newspaper reporter, were the important big shots, and Judy's mother was a nice lady who was always cooking a roast. Judy wanted to be a police detective, but instead she got married. She did turn down the rich, fat-headed Arthur Farrington-Pett, and instead, she chose Peter Dobbs, a poor but upstanding FBI G-man. The books stopped abruptly in the 1960s, and no one ever knew if Judy got her wish.

"Wish," Lebeca echoed. "Do you have a wish?"

"Tonight, I wish I could sail away to somewhere I've never seen. How about you?"

"Me? Perhaps I wish not to wish for love."

"Gravity?"

"He is not so tall, so big as many Tongan men, but I loved him. He does not see me."

"Are you sure?"

She nodded. "If you do not wish for the love of a man, then what are you?"

"I don't know. The same, I hope."

We were interrupted here by a ruckus as two policemen came into the room. The police chief, a man no larger than a rhinoceros, was accompanied by Gravity's brother, Centimeter. Chief Taumalolo bowed to us and went to a corner where the last boxes were piled. "So it is true!" he exclaimed. He held up a red suitcase with black trim, with a tag that read Lily Omont. There were three of them, shoved in a corner behind a curtain.

"That doesn't make sense," I said, not that this is a deal-breaker for life.

Taumalolo turned to me. "This is what Joe Storey says." Solemnly, he explained: Someone had come to tell him of seeing Lily Omont's suitcases on the yacht. "Joe Storey said, search if we wish, but she was never onboard, and he does not know why her luggage should be here." His expression added, "And who can say that a rich palangi does not tell the truth?"

"I think it's the truth," I said. "We saw them—well, two of them— on Bette Omont's island last Saturday night." I described what we had seen in them. Centimeter opened one, and both policemen stared, confounded, at the collection of satin and feathers.

"I do not know the world," Lebeca whispered.

The third suitcase was a small, deep one, the kind to carry cosmetics and things like that. It smelled of seaweed, and the lining was damp and streaked with sand. It was empty except for two manila folders from the Neiafu hospital, the charts for Lily and Mafi Selisi.

The police carried off the suitcases, and Lebeca went home. I went to the Mormon church. In the office, I asked where I could find Albert. The secretary gave me a look that would have reminded God to say please and replied that Albert was not allowed visitors, but I could leave a message. She gave me a piece of paper. I wrote, "What is lost is found," and was about to elaborate when I noticed she was reading my note upside down.

"It is quite a thing to find God," I said, and she smiled, guardedly.

I watched the route she took to deliver the note, and after she returned, I retraced it to a solitary bungalow. Through a closed window, I saw Albert lying in bed. His face was bleached white, and his skin looked paper thin. When I knocked on the glass, he jumped and looked ghastly. He couldn't have done better for Banquo's ghost, but he got up and opened the door.

I told him about the charts. "The police are going to give them back to the hospital. So you don't have to worry anymore."

Albert said nothing. "Did you lose something else?" I asked.

"Faith." He went back to his bed and turned his face to the wall. I guess he knew it was nothing I could find for him.

42

As I neared Foeata's house, I heard voices and laughter in the kitchen. I stopped at the gate. A shadow was moving along the crushed coral road. Jackson stopped too, looking as wet and wind-blown as I felt. We stared at each other like strangers colliding at an airport.

"You're OK?" he asked.

"Yes. Are you?" He didn't reply. I had the same hollow, sick feeling I have when I try to imagine infinity. I said, "Thank you for Messner's ointment."

He opened the gate, but I think he was in no mood either for social gathering in the kitchen. He went to his room. I went into the parlor, where Fresh Air was sitting alone by a window, and I sat down on the floor beside his chair. He had been in town when the storm broke, he said, and Foeata had made him wait at her house until it subsided. "But I like storms," he added.

"I do too," I said. "We used to have wild storms at my grandfather's house. He would ask us, 'What is the wind saying? What is the sea saying?' And we would think up answers."

Fresh Air said, "I have been thinking tonight of my friend, Dr. Omont. He liked the old stories of Tonga, and one night when we had a storm so wild we thought the waves might cover our islands, he asked me, 'Do you have a story to explain such waves and wind?'

"I said some believe those who have died may ride to Earth again on such a wind, to ask forgiveness of those they have wronged or to finish something interrupted. So when it blows like this and you think of someone who is dead, it is good to forgive them before they visit you."

"Let's not talk about sad things tonight." Gabby carried a lighted oil lamp into the room. "Can you tell us a cheerful story?"

I felt a hand brush my shoulder, light as a bird's wing. Jackson had sat down behind me. Skip and Lebeca joined us, and Foeata served tea. Fresh Air told about the first woman who discovered a pineapple, and a man who set out to sail across the ocean and ended up on the other side of his island and lived there, happily persuaded he had found a new world. While Fresh Air talked, Gravity slipped into the shadowy room, and I wondered if he was really so blind as Lebeca believed.

"Do you know any love stories?" Gabby asked.

"He does not eat enough to think of love stories," Foeata said. "Dried fish. Pooh."

Fresh Air's eyes twinkled. "Perhaps I remember one love story. It is from long ago, when there were only two villages on this island. Between them, there had been a quarrel for so long that no one could remember how it had begun. But one day, by accident, a girl from one village met a boy from the other, and they fell in love. Because their love was forbidden, it was more sweet, and they decided to run away. The young man brought her to a cave that had been shown to him by an octopus, a creature who has knowledge of older worlds. In this cave, the girl stayed, hidden. Every day, the boy came to her and brought her food and water. Her village thought she was dead, but his village wondered about his new habits. Finally, several people followed him. When they learned his secret, they decided that this was love; he could marry her, and she could live in their village. Her own people, learning that she was not dead, were joyful and also agreed to the marriage. The quarrel was broken. So the legend says."

"It is not legend," Gravity objected. "It is the truth of what happened. I can show you the cave."

"Can you?" Gabby asked.

"Of course! Tomorrow. The storm, it will be gone."

Skip agreed, all enthusiasm. While they made plans, Fresh Air said good night. He would now return to his fale. Foeata told him he was a crazy man to walk in such a wind, and he only said, "A fine wind is what we need."

Gabby was sleeping at Lebeca's house, and Gravity escorted them home. Skip and Jackson went to their rooms. As I lay in my bed, I began to feel like I was back on Joe's ship, although it was no longer rocking gently but whirling about, and the room was sweltering. I got back up. The house was still; even Foeata must have been sleeping. The door to Jackson's room was slightly ajar, and I went in. He was asleep. I don't know how long I stood like an idiot outside his mosquito net before I went back to my room. I doused myself with Messner's ointment. You don't feel anything for a second, then flames overtake you. When they subside, you've forgotten what you might have been feeling in the first place. I only wished I could put some on my brain.

43

Huge puffy clouds were drifting over the vivid blue sky, catching the colors of the sunrise. The air was warm, and pigs were rooting through a new ground covering of flower petals, coconut fronds, and bits and pieces of houses. In the harbor, two yachts, side by side amidst the little boats, looked like elephants sitting in a flock of sea birds. I was wondering how to pay a visit on a yacht when Mrs. Ogg hailed me from one of the behemoths. "Miss Illywit! Good morning! You have recovered from our ordeal, I see."

I was doubtful on several points, least of all that it had been our ordeal. "Is that Joe Storey's boat?" I asked her. "Where do I knock?"

She beetled down the gangplank carrying a teacup. "I wouldn't do that."

"Knock?"

"Miss Illywit, I could tell you things—" As I started up a sort of gangplank to the other yacht, she went with me, tight-lipped but stoically chaperoning this ascent into Hades.

"Gabby Asher sailed here with him and lived to tell the tale."

"She is such a nice girl. I wonder how you know her."

"She was once engaged to my brother."

"Oh. I have also heard she was also once engaged to a man who is now a significant congressman."

"That couldn't be my brother. He will tell you he is only an insignificant congressman."

Her smile faded. The conversation, already on a downward spiral, was entirely terminated as we came onto the deck and saw Joe Storey stretched out on a table, stark naked. I whooped and stepped back into Mrs. Ogg. She whooped too and fanned herself with her teacup. We were, in that moment, a sisterhood of whoopers.

"Josephine," Joe Storey called. "You've caught me in my massage, but please, come aboard. Georges will get you coffee. Connie! Morning, darling! Why don't you run and get Ron to join us too; there's a good girl. Miss Ilillouette, you don't mind if I just finish up here? Hate to have only one side relaxed."

Georges led the way to a table on the deck. Mrs. Ogg, whose expression indicated she had no intention of being a good girl or running anywhere, sat down firmly on the chair facing naked Joe, leaving me with the seat looking at the harbor. I was getting to like the old bat.

Georges brought out coffee, croissants, and Champagne. Mrs. Ogg, who didn't drink, took a slug of her wine. I did too. The sun was already hot, and I thought I might melt and slither off the chair like a pound of butter. I wondered if it would be a sacrilege to pour Dom Perignon on my head. Abruptly, Mrs. Ogg's edgy mood dissipated, but it was not the Champagne that did it. Jackson was slouching up the gangplank with the *non compos mentis* air of one being prodded by a pitchfork. "Why, good morning!" she fluted. "Have you come to join us—why, I don't even know your name!"

"Jackson Owain Glyndŵr Llywelyn ap Gruffydd Wilder." I knew Jackson would want me to include Welsh.

"Oh my. Please do sit down, Mr.—er—"

Jackson managed a niggardly smile and sat down. George brought him coffee and Champagne. Joe continued, "I understand, Miss Ilillouette, that I am indebted to you."

"Well—"

Jackson interrupted. "What?"

"Someone found Lily's suitcases here, on Joe's boat," I said. "This suggested that Lily had, after all, sailed away with him. Except they are the same suitcases that we saw on the island on Saturday night, after she was dead. You probably remember them."

"How very odd," Mrs. Ogg murmured.

"Not really," I said. "The contents were memorable. But the police had thought she drowned. Now they have to ask, how did the suitcases get on Joe's boat? And why? And when? And even if Jackson and I hadn't seen the suitcases on a Saturday night before they turned up on Joe's boat on Monday, it would raise questions. If, for example, he'd thrown Lily overboard, wouldn't he have thrown the suitcases too? And wouldn't he have waited till he was further out to sea? He's not a nitwit."

Joe chimed in. "Thank you, Miss Ilillouette."

"It's not that my goal in life is to make life safe for millionaires, and I don't think you are entirely innocent, but what I am wondering is, why did Pulu come to see you?"

"We have to leave now." Jackson jumped up, taking my arm with him. As you may recall, I have a bad temper and never more so than when someone decides to haul me off a boat like a sack of beans, using his show-off, rock-climber grip. We were halfway down the gangplank before I could plant my feet. Joe Storey was hooting like a Bedlamite.

"Sorry," Jackson muttered. "No, I'm not."

"Jackson, this is real."

"I know! I know. Shelley, we have to talk."

Of course, that did it, and there we stood, mute as two mad fish as Gravity's boat chugged into the harbor, with Skip, Lebeca, and Gabby aboard.

"Here we are, Jackson!" Gabby called merrily. "Shelley, you didn't forget that Gravity is going to take us to see the cave of the lovers?"

"The cave of lovers? Now that sounds like a fine adventure!" The Reverend Ogg bounded down off his yacht, but Mrs. Ogg scurried to catch him before he hopped aboard the love boat.

I should explain why I decided to go. It was because I remembered that Albert had said to find a cave. Also, Jackson, having released my arm, had stalked away down the dock. I was already aboard when he swung around and got on too. Gravity started his engine, and we headed out to find the cave of the lovers.

We were not the jolliest group. Lebeca politely declined Gravity's invitation to sit near him, and, frowning, he invited Jackson to help him steer. Skip, turned quiet, studied the horizon. Gabby filled in the silence. "I had such an interesting dream last night. The government was being run by fundamentalist fanatics, and I was hiding with my two children. I knew I had to get away, but how? Then, in walked David. He said, 'We'll get away; we'll go over the mountains.' I said, 'What mountains? Where are we?' He said, 'The Himalayas. Dress the kids warmly.' While I was trying to figure out what to put on the children to take them over the Himalayas, there was a knock at the door. It was a soldier who knew I was getting away because I'd been caught putting coats on my kids. But we must have gotten away because next I was on a swing and David was pushing me, higher and higher. Then I woke up. I hadn't dreamt of David in years, but this was a nice dream, sort of. It all fits."

"What fits," I asked, "besides *The Sound of Music*?"

"Oh, everything! It's going to be a wonderful day."

Just when I was sure her brain would melt into ice cream, owing to dreaming about David, she said, "I've been thinking: Do you know there is a cave on Bette Omont's island? She likes to go paint in it. I wonder if she might be there. Although it would be odd to stay there for weeks."

"I can think of reasons to go live in a cave," I said. To tell the truth, I was feeling woozy and a bit seasick, even though the sea was calm, shimmering blue glass.

"We could look for it," Gabby said. "But first we have to visit the lovers' cave."

Skip turned away from the sea to smile at her, and they talked piffle as we skimmed over the water. We stopped in front of a rocky cliff carved by water until it resembled an ancient lace curtain, woven in gold. The water was the color of jewels, as if sapphires and emeralds covered the sea floor.

"So," Gravity announced, "for you, Seli, a legend."

"Where?"

He pointed. What Fresh Air had failed to mention was that the cave of the lovers had an underwater entrance, which is why the octopus had known about it first. To get inside, you had to dive and be washed in on a wave.

"Cool." Skip doffed his shirt and pants.

"If you're going to swim in your bathing suit, so am I." Gabby pulled off her Mother Hubbard. "I feel positively wicked, but it has been my fantasy to swim in my bathing suit without a dress over it."

"I'll never tell." Skip winked at her and followed her into the water. Lebeca leapt in too, and so did Gravity, although they both kept their clothes on. They all surfaced, waiting.

Jackson said, "I think I'll pass." Everyone stared at him the way they usually stare at me. Here is what I did: I jumped in. I thought, I don't care if I am wearing jeans, two shirts, shoes, and a lava-lava; I don't care if I can't see the bottom; I don't care if the sea is filled with sharks. I did take back this last thought, however.

I took a deep breath and followed Gravity under the water. Promptly, I realized I would run out of air before I reached the dim black hole that was the entrance to the cave. I tried to get back to the surface, but I was caught by a wave and swept forward. Sputtering and wheezing, I bounced to the surface.

I was in the cave. It was a dank, airless hole with slimy, mud-colored walls. It smelled of moldy seaweed and was filled with fog. It was just the sort of place where love could land you. A wave swept back out of the cave. The mist dispersed. I saw Skip, Gabby, Lebeca, and Gravity treading water, but in the murky light from the underground entrance, they looked like zombie shadows.

"Isn't this amazing?" Gabby asked.

"Unbelievable," Skip said.

"How do we get out?" I asked.

"The same way we got in."

"Yes, we ride the wave out," Gravity said. "Ready?"

A new wave surged in and with it, more mist. I could hear everyone laughing, and then the laughter faded. I was alone in the cave. In the churning water, I could see strange, swirling shapes. I could feel them entwining around my feet and legs. I found a narrow ledge and scrambled up onto it. The light dimmed as if the entrance were shrinking, and the din of pounding water increased as the next wave returned. I could see faces in the mist, greenish, twisted, and cadaverous. I covered my eyes and plugged my ears, but then I was trapped inside my own head, and every loopy thought in it was set free, like a thousand whirling dervishes. I wondered what Lily had thought about as she had drowned. Did she have time to think? I thought about Jack London drowning Martin Eden. I thought about Ophelia and Captain Ahab and Eustacia Vye. I thought about the passengers on the Titanic being sucked down in a whirlpool. I thought about Shelley the poet deciding to drown to find out whether there was a god or not. I knew I was going a little crazy, but you might too if you ever got stuck in such a cave. I couldn't undo what I had done, and so I'd never get out.

Something took hold of me, and I could hear a voice, soft and low. It might have been reciting the ABCs, for all I knew, but the sound filled my head until there was no room for anything else. After a while, I could hear the water thudding against the rocks again, but it wasn't so terrible.

"Better now?" Jackson asked.

"Maybe."

"Shall we leave then?"

"Well, no."

I felt his hand on my head. He rubbed it a little. "Shelley, I'm sorry—"

"About which thing?"

"Everything."

"Really? Even dragging me off Joe Storey's boat like Thor Bloodbeard the Ice Slayer?"

"Who?"

"I don't know. I just made that up."

"No. I'm not sorry about that. Well, a little bit. But, Shelley, you didn't see the way that crazy woman was looking at you."

"Do you think she is nuts?"

"Can we go someplace else to talk about this?"

"No."

"Why not?"

"Because I'm stuck." As soon as I said it, my brain came unglued again. "I can't get out, Jackson."

"Yes, you can."

"No. There's no way out of here. I'll have to stay here and eat seaweed forever."

"Everything OK in there?" Skip called.

"Yes," Jackson replied. "We'll be out in a minute."

I was sorry he sounded so sure about this. "I'm still stuck, Jackson."

"No, you're not."

"I can't get out. That's stuck."

"You got in here. You can get out the same way."

"No."

"It's the only way out, love."

"It's probably why that woman stayed here. They thought she was in love, but she was just stuck. I wonder what she had to say about love when she finally got out."

"Do you?"

I leaned against him and hoped I wouldn't knock him off the ledge. I didn't even mind his calling me names as long as he stayed in the cave, but I said, "You don't have to stay here. You can go."

"Don't be a goose. I'm not going to leave you in here."

"You might get bored."

"I doubt it."

"Sometimes you're nice, Jackson."

"You'd do the same for me."

"You'd never get yourself stuck somewhere." He gave me an odd look but said nothing. "I'm crazy," I added, so he wouldn't have to say it.

"No, you're not. You're just scared, but"—he added this hastily—"I don't think you're as scared as you think you are."

"Yes, I am."

The wave had returned and with it, the mist. He stared down at the water. I wondered if I might be contagious, and he was going to start seeing faces in the water and fall into a panic, and then Gravity would have to call the Tongan Coast Guard to get us out.

"Shelley, last night when you came into my room—no, no, wait—it's all right—I thought I was dreaming—but I didn't say anything, and then you were gone—"

I'm not sure what happened next, except that I felt like someone had plunged a knife in my ribs and I fell off the ledge. I was sinking but I couldn't make my legs kick. I panicked, even worse than before. I saw the light from the entrance and tried go toward it, but a new wave came in and knocked me back and tangled my lava-lava over my head. The pain grew worse, and I sank deeper. My lungs were just about to explode when something wrapped around me. I thought it must be an octopus; it had the grip of one. A light grew brighter until it filled the cave, and I thought how odd it was that I could see it when the lava-lava was wrapped around my eyes. I guessed that I had just taken a lungful of seawater or died or both.

44

I didn't drown, but quite soon I wondered if maybe I should have. This was when I had been dragged back into the boat, and twenty thousand eyes were all fixed on me while as many voices kept asking if I was all right. I felt like I'd been frozen into a block of ice and sent through a crusher to make a tropical drink. I felt like I'd been whirled in a cement mixer, sent through a shoot, and whopped several times with a trowel. I felt like I'd been left out in the rain for two hundred years and had lost my hair and eyes and most of my stuffing. I felt like I'd been sucked into a black hole and batted about with all the other things it had swallowed during eternity. But I said yes, I was all right.

The boat stopped. We were at Mrs. Omont's island. Everyone got off except Jackson and me. The others started up the hill, but Jackson and I just sat on it. "Everything's all right now, isn't it?" he asked. "You got out. You're OK. We can catch up with Lebeca and Gabby and look for Mrs. Omont's cave."

He stepped up onto the dock and held out his hand. I stood up, but all the seawater I'd swallowed sloshed around inside me and threatened to knock me down. I said, "I think I am going to throw up."

Considering the ways in which I had already gone cuckoo that day, this was fairly mild; still, Jackson's face turned a shade of greenish white, and I wished I were dead, but I took it back before God decided why not, since it would take very little effort on his part to make me dead altogether. The boat tilted. The world spun and went dark.

I had never fainted before, even though I'd often wished I could at certain opportune moments in my life. I am somewhat sorry I chose this moment to do it because it leaves me lacking details to describe what happened next, and Jackson insists he can't remember. His idea is I should just leave this part out, so I am left with my own account, which is that I thought I was flying but I wasn't; I crashed and landed on spikes, and a bag of knives fell on top of me.

"She's sick."

"Yes. She is. Just take it easy, Jackson."

"But she's really in pain."

"I know. And you can help her by calming down."

I wondered if, when I had fallen, I'd landed in the wrong body and was now bouncing along in the head of a woman in the back of a truck in a near-hurricane. Was I thinking my own thoughts or hers? Then I remembered that she had died.

"How bad is it?" Jackson asked. I said it was better if he talked to me, so he talked all the way back to Neiafu, although now he doesn't know what he talked about. When we reached the harbor, it took three people to hoist me out of the boat. The dock was filled with people all buzzing like mosquitoes, and if I could have moved, I'd have jumped into the water and hit my head on the nearest rock to knock myself out again. Amidst the blur of faces I recognized the Rev. Ogg. "Hullo there," he boomed. "Back already? Have a good trip? It looks like you had too much sun, Miss Illywit. Er—where's Miss Asher?"

"She and Lebeca stayed on Mrs. Omont's island," Gravity said. "I will go back for them, but first, excuse me very much. I must find Foeata."

"I'd not leave them on that island too long," Ogg said. "A new storm's coming. In fact—I think it would be a good idea—damn me, yes, I think—"

I thought I saw Albert, but I thought I saw Chaucer, Che Guevara, and the Beatles too."Hold on," Jackson said. "Just hold on."

The next thing I recall was the metallic click of a curtain sliding over a rod. I felt the cold metal of a gurney beneath me and got a whiff of antiseptic. I saw bare walls illuminated by a harsh electric light. I thought, holy mackerel, this is me, Shelley Ilillouette, and this is my body in some kind of revolt, and I am in a hospital and therefore likely to die. Jackson's face, as he twisted a green hospital gown into knots, confirmed my theory. He tried to help me untie my lava-lava, but he couldn't, and the nurse had to do it. He didn't even smile when I said he used to be better at such things. Skip came in, and Jackson sat down and wiped his face off with my shirt. It was some comfort to know I couldn't be feeling worse than he was.

Skip was holding a needle. "Shelley, we're going to take some blood. Jackson, why don't you take off for a few minutes? Unless Shelley wants you to stay." I nodded. "OK, then watch him, not me," he said. I didn't feel the needle, but Jackson looked as if Skip were draining blood directly out of his head. "You still want him?"

"Yes."

"OK. I'm going to get you something for the pain. Jackson, hold this and try not to pass out before I come back."

Jackson pressed a piece of cotton onto my arm, but I think he'd lost his voice. I watched his eyes. They are dark blue, like the night sky, or maybe like the ocean with shifting lights, when you are swimming in deep water, over your head.

"Will you tell me about the mountains, Jackson?"

"The mountains? OK. Well, they were big, bigger than—big. They were cold—" He found his voice, behind one locked door or another, and by the time Skip returned, I felt like I was up on some remote summit looking out at a faraway world.

"Well, Trouble," Skip said, "it looks like we're going to remove your appendix."

"You?"

"It's either me or Jesus. Shelley, I can't put you on a plane and send you to Samoa or Hawaii. There's a new storm, a big one, heading this way. Besides, I don't think there is time. I'd rather take it out here. It's pretty simple. You go to sleep, you wake up, it's gone. You'll be a little sore, but it'll be nothing to what you're feeling now. And you can have two weeks in bed with whatever character you choose. OK?"

"OK."

"Good. I have to ask you a few questions. Are you allergic to anything besides doctors?" As he started down a list of questions, his voice faded, in and out. Did I have caps on my teeth? A heart condition? "Have you ever had anesthesia?"

"Once."

"What was it for?"

The world was turning blurry around the edges, misty patches of light and color, not unlike a painting done in the style of *Ile Perdue*. I said, "Five years ago, I had an abortion."

Skip was fading. "Why'd she have anesthesia?"

"I don't know," Jackson said. "I wasn't there."

45

A light flared, and a blurry voice said, "Take it easy. She's just coughing."

Who was coughing, I wondered. I was drifting on a cloud through the mountains. I was surprised to find a bed in my path. I understood that this bed was for me, but I didn't know how to get into it because I didn't know where my body was. Someone lifted me, and I bounced up in the air like a cluster of helium balloons. I recognized Skip looking down at me and wondered how he could do that when I was bobbling on the ceiling.

"Well, here she is."

"Who?" I asked.

"You."

"Me? Where?"

"Cough again for me, will you?"

I thought about this but couldn't remember how to do it.

"Never mind. Well, Red, it looks like we did it."

"Did what?" I was goofy as all get out; my head was full of bubbles that were popping just short of a thought.

"And now that you've taken a hundred years off my life, I'm going to take a break," Skip said. "But Foeata is here, and Jesus is up to date on the situation. Shelley, we have you pumped so full of drugs you shouldn't feel anything for a while, but it will wear off. Don't let the pain get bad. If I'm not here, ask for something, OK?"

I nodded and said thanks. He kissed my cheek. "Ribs. When you're feeling better, get Jackson to give you a few anatomy lessons, will you? He's right here."

All I could see was a shadow that didn't move. "Jackson, she's going to sleep for a while, but she's doing fine," Skip said. "Come on, let's take a walk."

The shadow didn't move or speak. Skip left. I resisted the urge to drift away too. A soft, gold light was filling the room from the sun breaking through clouds. The wind was stirring. The shadow moved across the wall. It grew larger and more distorted as it came closer to the bed. It took hold of my hand. I tried to find more of Jackson inside this shadow. Like a blind person, I felt the bones of his wrist and the back of his hand.

"What are you doing?" The voice was splintery, but it was his.

"Trying to see if you are all here. I'm not sure I am." He pressed his head against my hand, and I found his face, the rough, damp stubble on his cheek. "Are you OK, Jackson?"

He shook his head no.

"But it's not so bad, whatever is happening. It's quite peaceful. Am I dying?" I just wanted to know.

"No. God, no."

"Then this is not so good a bedside manner."

He laughed, choked, and said, "Dammit."

"Shall I talk to you now?" He nodded. I told him about Dolores and about octopuses who, I had read, have three hearts. I remembered the stonefish in prison, and I asked if he would check on it. I said it was a sad thing to find there are mysteries, really, and there goes your appendix, all doolally. When I couldn't think of anything else, I said,

"My cat died of leukemia. I didn't know cats could get leukemia. Jesse said, 'He'll be waiting at the gate for you.' I wish I could believe it. Because maybe Gravity's dog would be waiting for him too."

"Maybe."

"Do you think so?"

"I don't know; I hope so."

"But if I died, I wouldn't wait for you. I'd haunt you."

"Promise?"

"Yes."

As we talked, the various parts of me drifted back, a toe here, an elbow there, but I couldn't feel anything as much as I felt his tears on my hand. When we were kids, I never thought about where Jackson ended and I began; it was only later that I realized we could be on two different icebergs, separated by a distance that might not be measurable, let alone bridgeable. Now one might be melting, or maybe both.

46

For a few hours nothing happened, but out at sea the cyclone was brewing. When I woke up, the room was dark. I had forgotten where I was, so when I tried to sit up, I got tangled in tubes and wires, which is why I thought I'd been trussed up by a spider. Fortunately, at this point I heard a greater ruckus of someone leaping up and upending a chair.

"Jackson?"

"Shelley?"

We collided in the middle of the bed. It was just as well that there were no lights, for the picture we presented couldn't have been any less goofy than the conversation we carried on.

"It's dark."

"Yes. The power must be out."

"Yes."

"Yes."

We have never agreed so much, before or after this. I knew I was in a hospital, but it didn't seem much like one, probably because Jackson had fallen, more or less, into the bed.

"Sorry." He untangled himself from my IV.

"It's all right, as long as I'm not dead."

He made a strangled noise.

"I did think I'd died, Jackson. It is a hospital, after all."

"Hush, darling."

"Why did you call me darling?"

"Because I wanted to."

"I'm dead."

"Shelley, cut it out."

"But I don't think I could call you darling. 'Why are you still here, darling?' No, I can't. But why are you here? Do you want to go to bed?"

"It's a hospital, love."

I had not meant did he want to sleep with me, but, as I considered it, I decided this was not so bad an idea. "There's room. Do you think anyone would mind?"

"Yes."

"But it's not like you would be castrated or anything."

"What?"

"Like poor Abelard. That would be too bad."

"You've never said anything like that to me before."

"It's probably the drugs. But we'll forget all this."

"No, we won't."

For various reasons, neither of us noticed the light that flickered into the room, but we did hear the gasp, followed by a burst of giggles. Jackson bounced up off the bed.

"Excuse me very much, doctor," the nurse said shyly.

"No! No, I'm not—"

"You have helped Dr. Sikipi?"

"Yes, but only when he made me—"

"Now he is gone."

"Gone? Skip?"

"You can help us?"

"Oh," Jackson stammered, "but you see I'm not—I haven't—"

"It is the generator."

"The what?"

"The machine for lights. It will not—march. We wish to ask if, perhaps, you can fix it."

Other than trying to put back together a worm that someone had stepped on when he was in fifth grade, I'd never seen Jackson try to fix anything, but I believe it was relief that he was not being asked to perform brain surgery that caused him to agree to try to fix the generator.

"I'll be right back," he said, but he didn't leave, probably because he was waiting for me to let go of his hand. "What is it, love?"

"I think the drugs are wearing off."

"Are you in pain? I'll tell them to get you something."

"No. But—I love you, Jackson."

I'd said it. Of course, I'd had to be knocked out, cut open, tied up, and drugged to the hilt first, not to mention softened by the preceding series of events. But I'd said it. I'd unnerved myself completely. I closed my eyes, not that I could see much anyway by the one candle's light. Jackson didn't say anything, but he kissed me and left with the nurse.

I lay in a strange but not unpleasant glow, irrespective of the darkness. Gradually, the iridescence dispersed and reformed itself into orange-headed monsters, the night companions of my youth. As I watched them, I had to admit that adult life had a quality that rendered orange-headed monsters comparatively lame. Their attempts to scare me witless were feeble and ineffective, gibber though they might.

"Go away," I said. "Begone. Vanish."

They obeyed except for one pair of eyes that remained near the door. Perhaps it was an inexperienced phantom that could not expertly poof. Instead, it came closer, to the edge of my bed. There they were, the yellow eyes. I recognized this ghost.

"Well, Lily, stay if you insist," I said. "Are you real or not? Do you have a purpose? Is it good or bad? If I weren't filled to the gills with drugs, I'd probably be skeptical, but under the circumstances I can only think this is a fairly exclusive interview. Here is a question: Are you here because I was thinking about you? Did I summon you? Or did the wind blow you in?"

Even in the dark, I could see an incredulity on the face of the ghost, and I hadn't even mentioned again that we were alike. "What's it like to be dead?" I asked. "Is it any different?" The eyes just kept staring at me. "Just for the record, can I ask you what happened? Everyone was set to believe it was an accident, that you decided to go swimming at night, even if you didn't know how to swim, because you were reckless and wild and took chances, because you were a palangi who didn't think there were rules. Then someone put your suitcases on Joe Storey's yacht. I don't believe it was you, mostly because you were dead by then, but now, everyone has to wonder—what happened? Did you jump, did you fall, or were you pushed?"

The phantom sputtered and raised its arms. I leapt, or rather, attempted to leap from the bed, but my knees had gone missing, and I plummeted to the floor. The IV apparatus crashed with me. The ghost ran. All I could see were its feet, which were much too small to qualify the owner for beauty.

47

A group effort returned me to my bed, and someone sent me off into Cloud Cuckoo Land, where I remained until the next day. Apparently, it had been decided that if I awoke and Jackson was not here, my heart would stop beating or do something equally calamitous. If anyone had asked me, I could have told them Jackson had gone to fix the generator and would be back, but every time I came out of my catatonia and tried to say something, I was pumped full of painkiller, and off I went again.

Only when the storm at sea developed into a humdoozy cyclone hurtling toward Neiafu was I forgotten. I woke up. My brain crawled out of its cloud cave and took inventory of who I was and where I was and noted that I was happy to be alive. But I was alone.

I recalled writers who were drug addicts and wondered if my present dopey state could make it easier to find a hero for a story and searched through my head, but I was reduced to studying the ceiling, which had a crack that looked like a map of China. I wondered if we should worry that China, not the Soviet Union, would take over the world one day. I wondered how, technically speaking, anyone took over the world. Wouldn't it be more trouble than it was worth?

Jackson's batty Aunt Marble is sure that one day, when no one is looking, the Russians will take over the world. We'd lose our freedom,

Marble says, although I've never figured out what she does with all her freedom except mind everyone else's business. She has declared Jackson is a Disappointment, but she also wrote to remind him to take long underwear to the Himalayas. She doesn't know why anyone let David into politics, but that doesn't stop her trying to tell him what to do too. She tried to give me advice once, but it was so delicately veiled in obscurity it was only by chance I figured out we were talking about the evils of sex, not Communism. At any rate, there I was thinking about goofy Marble, and the next thing I knew she was looking down at me with her long, horse-like face. I closed my eyes. You would too, if you were looking for a hero and got Marble. I opened them again to check reality.

"Mrs. Ogg!" Why had I thought it was Marble? Mrs. Ogg was no beauty, but compared to Marble, she was a knockout. It must have been the expression. Marble always looked the same way when David showed up at one of her events and made it clear that she knew a Democrat.

"I do not have much time," she said. "You must tell me. Why did you say that?"

"Say what? What did I say?"

"You are not stupid, girl!"

"No, so there must be a reason I said it. Ah! It was to clarify that you are not Marble. Therefore I said, 'Mrs. Ogg.' The drugs are wearing off."

"How do you know? Who told you?"

I was still stuck on why I'd said what I'd said; I wasn't ready to go on to what I knew. "Whom have you told?" she demanded.

"I doubt I've told anyone since I still do not know of what we are speaking."

Her eyes glinted, and the fog insulating my brain parted briefly. It was the eyes; in the dark, they would be yellow. I leaned over, as best I could, to look at her feet.

"Good lord, was it you last night?"

"Who did you think it was?"

"Lily Omont."

I had succeeded in rendering Mrs. Ogg speechless. My thoughts, which had been flitting about like so many little snowflakes, coalesced into one great lump that fell onto my head. I will not pretend that I understood everything; indeed, I still understood next to nothing, but for a moment, I understood something, I recognized something, although I couldn't name it. I remembered something, but I did not know what it was. It was a strange sensation of being suspended in time, trying to figure out what I knew. "Has it been you all along?" I asked. "In the graveyard—in that boat on Mrs. Omont's island—but why—"

"Be quiet!" Mrs. Ogg hissed. "These things that have happened, it is the hand of God. You must not question Him."

"Why not?" I asked. "What has He been up to?"

"I do not understand why He brought you here."

"And I could have sworn it was Continental Airlines. Mrs. Ogg, I will not distress you by telling you that you and I are not so different— the thought is as scary to me as to you—but I've spent seven-tenths of my time here in a panic and the rest of it bewildered, and I get the feeling it may be the same for you. Maybe if you and I pooled our respective confusion, we could figure something out. What are you afraid of? Is it Joe Storey? Is he so bad? Do you know who Lily's father is? Is it your husband? Does Joe know?" She gaped at me, horror-struck. "Mrs. Ogg, do you believe in the Devil?"

"He exists!"

"So I am beginning to believe. The hero of *Paradise Lost*, according

to Byron. The spiritual head of four-fifths of the human race for cen-
turies and political head of all of it. That's Mark Twain."

"Listen to me!" Her voice was low but rattling like a snake. "You
will not repeat your preposterous fantasies to anyone. No one will
ever hear them. Everyone is gone except you, and who would believe
you? You are all alone now, and God will take care of you too. He will
take care of everything. As He has always done—"

Just when she was humming along so well that little puffs of
sulfur were curling around her words, she shut down. From out in
the hall there came a crowing voice, and my brother David strolled
into the room.

48

The extraordinary thing was not that David had walked out of a blooming cyclone in immaculate form, from his Savile Row suit to his Italian shoes and matching socks; nor was it that his appearance caused Mrs. Ogg to shrivel like he'd doused her with a bucket of water. It was that he was accompanied by a woman who was out-talking him. She was a tiny fairy of a woman with wild white hair. She was wearing a yellow gown printed with poinsettias, dangling seashell earrings, and a profusion of necklaces made of beads and seeds.

"Goodness!" she said, "Connie Ogg! What a surprise!"

Mrs. Ogg made no reply but sank onto a chair, and once more I could have believed that she had just sat on a stonefish. David is used to provoking powerful reactions in women, good and bad, but mostly good. He merely smiled at her and turned to me. I felt all was right with the world, even though I knew this wasn't remotely true.

"Great accommodations you've found, kid."

"What are you doing here?"

"I was on my way to a trade conference in Japan—"

"And you got lost?"

"We'd just landed in Samoa when a storm hit. Dick caught the connection, but damned if I didn't miss it."

"And he didn't bail out and swim back with your schedule?"

He grinned and I laughed, but discovered it was less painful to fall out of bed.

"Here now," he said, "I understand you're held together with stitches. I've brought someone for you to meet."

I looked again at David's companion. "My dear," she said, "I had no idea you existed, much less that I had hired you."

So I met and shook hands with Bette Omont.

"A ramshackle way to proceed," David pointed out. "Thank God, Congress is ever available to protect citizens from themselves."

"I did ask my sister to ask you to help find someone to help me write my stories and keep Ile Perdue going," Bette replied, "but it never occurred to me that a congressman would do anything in less than five years."

"No," David said, "we are too busy flying around, checking to see if expatriates have lost their passports in Samoa."

"It was a lucky coincidence, meeting David in Pago Pago," Bette told me. "I should probably still be there filling out forms to prove I am who I am if David had not come to the hotel. Not that I knew who he was. I just wanted to draw him."

"It's my classical profile. It always prevents me from becoming bored when I am marooned on a tropical island."

"I only said you resembled a statue I once saw in Greece."

"A god, no doubt."

"A minor one! Shelley, I wasn't surprised to learn he was a congressman. There are so many of them and they are likely to be anywhere but Washington, but I was amazed at how quickly he got my passport for me. A congressman is a useful thing after all!"

"Egads," David said. "A mar on an otherwise perfect record. I shall be called to account for this. Being useful wreaks havoc on the lifestyle, raises expectations. I feel a bill coming on."

"He does talk a great deal, but I have to admit, Shelley, it is delightful to be rescued by a handsome young man."

I said, "We thought you were hiding in a cave."

"Oh, I was hiding, but Pago is more comfortable—" She stopped talking as if an invisible hand had clapped over her mouth. Joe Storey strode into the room. Holding out his arms, he advanced straight to her. She took one of his hands and shook it weakly.

"Samoa!" he exclaimed. "My dear, did I scare you that far away?" She turned a deep red, as fast as an octopus, and sat down next to Mrs. Ogg. I knew how her knees felt.

"Hello, Josephine!" Joe added. "Connie! Up to your good works?" He turned to David. "I understand I am in your debt, sir, as well as your sister's."

"Indeed?" David winked at me and turned to Mrs. Omont, who was as mute and motionless as Mrs. Ogg. "Speechless," he murmured.

"A feat," Joe agreed, but this nascent gathering of the Old Boys' Club was stymied as Foeata arrived with a tray of food. A goddess-like woman capable of tossing both club members out the window, she silenced them with her mere presence. She regarded them with an expression strikingly grave for Foeata.

"Foeata, this is my brother, David."

She looked from him to me, and her face said: "Ah, this is the lackwit you told me about?" I knew that nothing he had done, not ending a war that couldn't be won, removing a corrupt president, or saving the lizards of Sonoma County, could offset his having been so noodle-headed as to lose Gabby Asher. As daunting as her greeting might have been to nonpolitical mortals, it was routine for him.

"Foeata." He gave her his best dazzling smile. "I understand you have befriended my sister, as—er—Moses told us on the way here. I want to thank you for your kindness. I've been interested in your islands ever since I read Cook's accounts of them. He called them the Friendly Islands, didn't he?"

She nodded, still studying him for signs of intelligent life. "May I take this?" He gestured to her tray.

Her expression lightened by a degree. "You are hungry? You must eat!" She put him in a chair and gave him the tray. "Eat. I will bring more for Seli. Eat."

He ate, but although he praised her spaghetti on toast, this didn't raise her spirits. She studied the window, beyond which clouds were lining up, like soldiers for a battle.

"Have you seen Skip?" I asked her.

"I do not know where he is, Seli." Foeata glanced pointedly at Mrs. Ogg.

"Nor do I!" Mrs. Ogg sputtered.

It was clear from the way David was looking at Mrs. Ogg that he was trying to recall something without an aide to provide prompts. "Have we met?" he asked. I do not think he was implying they had met in hell or at a party fundraiser, but I believe it was Mrs. Ogg's unfortunate choice to snort that made Foeata decide to take her chance on the nitwit.

"David," she said urgently, "last night I am here for Seli. Jackison is with her, and all is well, but the lights go out, and Jackison leaves with a nurse. I sit by the door. And who comes in the dark but Mrs. Ogg—"

"Ogg!" All the bread David had eaten must have fired his brain cells.

Mrs. Ogg cut him off. "I only came to see how Miss Ililluouette was. My husband said she was ill. I wanted to invite her to tea on our yacht, when she is feeling better, of course."

Foeata gasped, "But this is not true!" She glanced upward as if looking for a lightning bolt to smite her, but none appeared. In the silence that followed, we heard a faint warble, like a birdling fallen from a nest. "Shelley?"

Albert peered around the door. When he saw Mrs. Ogg, his wits took a dive under the bed, but he clutched the doorknob so as not to follow them. "I promised," he stammered. "I promised—I promised Jackson to tell you: He will be back."

"Where is he?" David asked.

"Fixing the generator," I said.

"No!" Albert whispered. "He went to help the most beautiful woman in the world."

Mrs. Ogg stoppered him with a look. David said, "Who?"

Albert whispered. "Miss Asher and the Tongan woman were looking for a cave on Mrs. Omont's island."

"My cave?" Bette asked. "Why on earth?"

"Is that where Ron was going yesterday?" Joe said. "He took out of the harbor like a bat out of hell—"

"I hope they found the cave before he got there," I said.

Mrs. Ogg turned her gargoyle gaze on me. "My husband is a man of God."

David choked. "He is a what?"

"If he went to Mrs. Omont's island, it was only to be of help."

"Mrs. Ogg," David said, "I would not trust your husband alone with my grandmother, and she is dead."

Foeata looked heavenward, but God did nothing. Albert, as pale as if his nerves were gobbling up his blood supply, said. "No! They weren't alone. I went with him."

"Good show." David nodded at him.

Albert looked slightly dizzy, but he said, "I met Miss Asher when she needed people to help deliver school supplies. She is so kind, so good, so beautiful! I knew they had gone off in Gravity's boat, and I was on the dock when the boat returned, but Miss Asher wasn't on it. Gravity said they had hurried back because Shelley was ill, and Miss Asher and Lebeca had stayed on the island to find a cave. He was going to go back for them, but Reverend Ogg said he would go—and I went too because I knew—I know—about the cave. When we got there, Reverend Ogg said he would have a glass of wine while we waited for them, but I looked for them. Because I knew how to find the cave. We found the cliff, but the ropes, the only way to reach the cave, were gone. We knew that if anyone was in it, they would be trapped. We called, but the sound of the sea was so great—then we saw a light. Miss Asher said, get Jackson because he could climb down to it. They waited there while Reverend Ogg and I returned. I found Jackson, and he and Gravity went to the island. But he said, please tell Shelley. You were asleep. So I waited."

"Where is this island?" David asked. "How long does it take to get there?"

Joe said, "We could probably make it."

"Why wouldn't we?"

"Because a cyclone is coming," I said.

This is when Gabby flew into the room. Her Mother Hubbard was wet and ripped and spattered with mud, and her hair was in a wild tangle. "Foeata," she gasped. "We need—" She froze, and maybe time stopped too. I don't know how long she and David stared at each other. Gabby recovered first, although she sounded like she had been hollowed out by army ants. "Bette! You're here! Shelley, you look so much better! But where is Skip? I think Gravity broke his leg, and I don't know what Jackson broke, but I am sure he is conscious by now. A huge wave hit him—but they got her out. Albert, you were wonderful."

He blushed beet red. I asked, "Got who out?"

"Mafi."

"Mafi?" This was a chorus.

"It is where she has been, hiding." Gabby looked at the window, and when she had set her face in order, she turned to David. "Hello."

I doubt if any of David's strategy geniuses would have known what to do with him, but Foeata, standing next to him, might have nudged him. He stumbled toward Gabby, and in a voice that had no polish at all, he said, "Gabriella—hello." He offered her his hand as if he hadn't noticed she was holding out her own. Eventually, they managed to shake hands, and during what looked to be a handshake without end, I thought about how love is the great leveler that makes idiots of us all.

"How did you get here?" he asked.

"Gravity's boat," Gabby said. "I had to. Lebeca stayed with everyone. Mafi is all right but very weak. Oh, but, David, it wasn't like any ride we ever made. I've never felt like the ocean was so big and my boat was so small or whatever it was President Kennedy said. Joe, do you think you can get there? They need help and a bigger boat."

"We'll go right away," David said. "And you can rest."

Gabby gave him a curious glance. "You might want him, Joe. He's a good sailor. 'It's not the gales but the set of the sails' or something like that. But I need to go too. You don't know where you're going."

David gave her a rueful half of a smile. "There's nothing new in that, is there?"

Joe Storey cleared his throat, and he didn't even know that Gabby and David have a long history of forgetting the rest of the world exists.

The rescue party departed. "Well, Mrs. Ogg," I said, "what do you think? Is this the hand of God or not?"

There was no answer. Mrs. Ogg was gone, and there wasn't even a puff of smoke where she had vanished.

49

Albert was gone too, and Bette Omont left to get a room at the Port of Refuge. Foeata said, "I will bring you food, Seli."

"Tea and toast, Foeata. That's all she can have." Skip limped into the room. He was looking poorly. His clothes were rumpled, his head bandaged, and he had a black eye.

"Sikipi!" Foeata exclaimed. "I have waited for you all night! I have worried!"

"I was at the police station. Shelley, I need to check your stitches."

"Were you in jail?" I asked. "Did you get in a fight?"

"You're looking good, Shelley. Do you feel like getting up?"

"No."

He squinted at my chart. "How did you fall out of bed?"

"How did you end up in jail?"

"Come on, Trouble, let's take a walk."

I recalled wallowing like a blob of Jell-O on the floor the night before. "No, thanks."

"It helps get the intestines going again." He offered me his arm.

"Have you ever read *Oblomov*?"

"I can't say that I have."

"Oblomov is a great character who goes to bed when life gets to be too much for him, and he never gets up."

Skip sat down on the other bed in the room. Then he lay down. It struck me as odd, even as life goes. "How is it," he asked the ceiling, "that two weeks ago I arrived with a group of twenty-two people, and they are all learning Tongan, making baskets, and going snorkeling, while I am fleeing sharks, seeing ghosts, and landing myself in my own hospital?"

"You are special to God," Foeata told him.

"Great. That's just great."

"What happened last night?" I asked.

"Well, let's see," he said, "my nerves were somewhat frayed after removing the Queen of Sheba's appendix knowing her guard wolf was just outside the door. I decided to go for a walk. The police and the Peace Corps director were in the lobby. They wanted to talk to me about Lily." His voice trailed away. "They think someone might have murdered her."

Foeata gasped. I said, "Not you."

"Thanks," he said. "This time your doubt is heartening. I hope you'll visit me in prison."

Foeata interrupted, "No, Sikipi. They would not think a thing so terrible!"

"They questioned me for an hour. Hell, in Chicago, they'd never have been so polite."

I said, "What were they asking you?"

"They know I was supposed to meet Lily that night. They know I came to the hotel looking for her."

"Then they know she stood you up."

"How do you know I didn't find her?"

"Is that what they said?"

"No. They let me go. I don't know why. I tripped and fell down the stairs. Cracked my head open. Bled like a pig. They brought me here to get patched up."

"The Peace Corps won't send you home just because of this," I said.

"Not till the airport reopens."

"No." Foeata rose. "Sikipi, you must rest your head and do not trouble your heart. Seli, I will bring you food, but not now. I must go."

She exited majestically, like justice on the move. Skip lay motionless on the other bed.

"How did you know Lily couldn't swim?" I asked. He didn't answer. "Jackson thought you might have been, you know, in love with her."

"Jackson was being polite."

"Pussy-whipped?"

"Shelley, where did you—ah, I forgot about your brother, the politician. In love? I don't know. Pussy-whipped? Oh hell, yes."

He was talking slowly, like a person who had just cracked open his head and was looking for his words that had scattered on the ground. "It was near the end of my residency. I hadn't been anywhere except the hospital. I hadn't done anything except dream of sleeping. I applied to the Peace Corps and got an offer to go to Tonga. Where? A librarian found me a newspaper article about a new play opening, written by a Tongan woman. I called the theater. Lily called back. 'Come see the play,' she said, 'and we can talk.' I went. It was weird. People on the stage were standing in a circle around something wrapped in purple veils. They were jabbering away as they unwrapped it. When they'd finished, a naked woman was standing in the spotlight, while they were in the dark. It was Lily.

"We went out for a drink. It was snowing. It felt like it had been winter forever, and here was this woman telling me about islands full of sunshine and mangoes. I'd never have guessed she hadn't been there in twenty years. 'Why are you here?' I asked her. She gave me a mysterious smile, and all I could think about was how she had slid out of those purple veils. Yeah, I fell. It was a fucking plunge off the Sears Tower."

"How long did it last?"

"A week. Well, maybe longer. It took a while to figure out that she never really dropped the veils, longer to admit that mind-blowing sex isn't everything. I used to like to swim when I had a free hour. She said she didn't want me to give up anything just to be with her, which was sweet, even if it wasn't true. So, she went with me to the pool, jumped into the deep end, and damn nearly drowned. I said, 'Why didn't you tell me you can't swim?' She said, 'I could swim if I wanted to.' I said, 'Yeah, I'd take a few lessons first.' She said, 'I wanted to know how much you love me.' I said, 'You could have just asked.'

"She was so damned smart, so wickedly funny. So goddamned beautiful. But she could never just be happy. There had to be drama. Like—I wanted her to come home with me for my mom's fiftieth birthday. She said she couldn't because my parents would never accept a 'mixed-breed.' I said, 'My dad's from Nebraska and my mom's from California; you can't find a weirder mix than that.' She wouldn't go, but she got upset when I did.

"Then she wanted me to get her a prescription painkiller. 'Can't do it,' I said, but I could refer her to someone. Was she in pain? She was furious that I questioned her. Two days later, a detective from the Chicago police came to see me. Barry Johnson. He asked me how the hell was I mixed up with Lily Omont. Her play had been shut down for indecency or something, and when the cops found a stash of illegal drugs in the theater, Lily told them she'd gotten them from me. He said, 'I told her you'd taken three bullets out of me. I know how damned stingy that guy is with morphine.' He asked me, 'Do you know who she is?' I said I'd gathered she was a Polynesian princess in search of artistic freedom. He said, 'If I were you, I'd steer clear of the Queen of Moribunda.'

"I took the chicken-heart way out and didn't call her. She turned up at the hospital, all sweetness and concern. Didn't want me to worry if she'd been evicted from her apartment because she'd lost all of her money on the play. I told her about Barry. She was horrified. She'd never said anything like that. The cops were against her because of her past. What past? She was getting dramatic in the lobby, so we went to have coffee. She said, 'I know I have to tell you the truth.' She told me her mother had been wrongly convicted for murdering her father and had died in prison. She'd been sent to a foster home, ran away, landed in a brothel, but escaped. She had a baby. It was dead and she put it in a trashcan, but she got arrested. I believed it. Five years in a Chicago hospital, and you'll believe anything. I gave her the key to my place, but I said I was going to sleep at the hospital because we had a surgery scheduled next morning that would take at least twelve hours. I hadn't planned to sleep there, but it seemed like a good idea at the time. She said, 'You have earned my love.' I thought, damn.

"Here's irony: Our patient died half an hour into the procedure. I went home and there she was, having breakfast with some guy. At least they weren't in my bed. They left. And I remembered a poem we read in high school about a king who put a lion and a tiger in one arena. A lady threw in her glove as a challenge for a knight who was crazy about her. The knight jumped in and got her glove without losing any limbs. She said, 'You have shown you are worthy of my love,' and he said, 'Well, now that I think about it, no thanks.' That's how it ended.

"I had a beer with Barry before I left Chicago. I said I knew she was poison, but I was still sorry I couldn't help her. If she'd needed a new liver, I could have helped her. I knew I'd been damned lucky. I grew up on a farm with a brother, a sister, grandparents, a dog, and two parents who like each other. Not everyone has it so good. I told him her story. Turned out it was true; it had just happened to someone else, a fifteen-year-old girl. The story had run in *The Tribune* a few weeks earlier. 'You should read the damned newspapers,' Barry said.

"Barry had done some research. Lily had been a missing person. A Mrs. Omont was trying to find her. She'd adopted Lily, whose parents were unknown. She'd sent Lily to a posh school in Connecticut. Lily got into trouble, stealing, lying. Lily told the headmistress she couldn't help it because her adopted mother had made a slave of her. The woman told her to cut the crap; Lily had a trust fund. She ran away. The police found her eventually, but by then she was eighteen and wanted nothing to do with Mrs. Omont. She went to New York but didn't make it in theater. Went to Florida, then turned up in Chicago. She had a habit of spending a night with a guy and walking off with his wallet. Barry said, 'Although what she wanted with a poor schmuck like you beats me.'

"He told me he'd been raised by a single mom in the worst neighborhood in Chicago. She cleaned houses. She made him stay in school. Now, he'd bought her a little farm. She raised goats, which had always been her dream. He said, 'Some of the kids I grew up with, I've sent to jail, and others, I've sent to the morgue, but some have turned out fine. Life's a crapshoot, but what you do with what you get is one part luck and one part choice.' Anyway, I went home. I hadn't seen her in six months when she turned up at the club here, and all I could think was, get me out of here."

"You don't think she came here looking for you?"

"She didn't have to go so far to find a sap to drive nuts."

"You weren't afraid of falling off the Sears Tower again?"

"God, no. That night at Foeata's, Shelley, I was so damned glad when you came flying in with that palm tree I could have kissed you, but I was afraid you'd take it the wrong way."

"Why'd you ask her out to dinner?"

"I had to do something. I walked her back to the hotel, and she wanted me to come up to her room. I said, 'We're in Tonga, not Chicago,' and it went downhill from there. She said I hated her. I said I didn't. She said I didn't care. I didn't say anything. She said I wished she were dead. And I left. That's what all of Tonga heard. When I got back to Foeata's, I wrote her a note. I said I really liked Tonga and I thought I could do some good here, but I needed the respect of the Tongan people, so I was asking for her help. I didn't know what she wanted from me, but maybe we could have dinner and she would tell me. I wanted her to leave me the hell alone, but I was going to try to think of a better way to put it."

"What did you do with the note?"

"I took it to the hotel."

"But you didn't give it to her?"

"I gave it to someone to take it up to her room."

"Ever-Ready?"

"No. It was—who was it? Somebody."

"The police didn't find it?"

"They didn't know it existed till I told them about it."

He was studying the map of China on the ceiling. "She wasn't nice, Shelley. She wasn't good. But she was a person. I could tell you how she was made, bones, muscles, veins, but I know nothing about what made her the way she was. I did ask her why she never told the truth. She said, 'When you don't know what the truth is, it can be anything.' I said, 'No, it can't.'"

"It will all work out, Skip."

"Don't worry about it."

"But it will, and no one will think you're guilty of anything, not even you."

He said nothing. I asked, "Was she pregnant?"

He sat up, staring at me like I'd whopped him on the head with a bedpan. I had to fill in the terrible silence. "Skip," I asked, "do you think abortions are so bad?"

50

Skip got up off his bed and sat on the edge of mine. "I think there are as many circumstances as there are women who get pregnant," he said. "Do you think they are so bad?"

"No. But sometimes I don't know."

"Why?"

"I wouldn't tell Foeata."

He only nodded.

"My brother wasn't happy."

"Your brother will never wake up one morning and discover he's pregnant."

"Oh, he wouldn't pass laws—"

"Just pass judgment on his sister?"

"He was more upset with Jackson. Which wasn't really justice."

"Why? Where was Jackson?"

"Climbing Denali."

"Did you have anyone to talk to?"

"That didn't matter."

"It matters a lot."

"No, because no matter how many people are talking at you, it's really only you, alone, even if you don't know what to do."

"Five years ago? You could get an abortion in California, couldn't you? You didn't have to go to a backstreet butcher?"

"No. Jackson's father arranged it."

"His father?"

"I think he was afraid Jackson would have to marry me. His aunt was."

"What did she have to say about anything?"

"A lot, about anything. It was a mess, Skip."

"Do you want to tell me about it?"

"I'd probably need another shot of morphine first."

"Come on, I've just bent your ear about Lily for an hour."

I had never really looked at Skip before. At first glance, you might just think he had a nice, straightforward face, with everything fitting together, a nose, ears, eyes, and a friendly smile. But if you looked at his hands, you could see something fine about them that was also in his eyes. He had a high forehead, probably due to a big brain. His hair was short, but it wanted to curl.

"Tell you what," he said. "You're a writer. How about you write something down for me? I've got to go clean up and do some rounds. But I'll be back, and we'll take a walk. All right?"

He left, and a few minutes later, a nurse came in with a pen and paper. As she put them on the tray, I fell back into a cave, full of fear and pounding waves. What was outside such a place?

Octopuses? Dolores, so named by her captor, what was she doing? Dancing around, shooting through the water, changing colors, hiding under a rock, avoiding lovers?

I keep thinking about that plant with its blossoms of empty eggshells. It won't survive a storm, but it's replaceable, isn't it? It will only take a dozen eggs. Gardens are replaceable; so are roofs. It's other things

that are not, ones that have been battered by one too many hurricanes,
broken into far too many pieces, scattered too far and wide to collect
into anything recognizable.

I had written a page about octopuses and eggshell plants when the
wind gusted and banged on the window, like it wanted to have its say.

Have people grown too smart or too dumb? The faltering old
instincts draw you to a fire, but they don't tell you where to stop. Maybe
you don't believe the fire is real and not an illusion, until you touch it.
Then you bolt back to the dark and there you are.

Then this: not the wind.

Just like her mother, careless as a cat. What a disaster for David.
Worse for Jackson if he has to marry her. She'll have to give it away. She
certainly wouldn't know what to do with it.

Why was Jackson's Aunt Marble there, then or now? Who had let
her in? I hadn't told anyone. I didn't need anyone to tell me I didn't
know how to care for anything. All of a sudden everyone was talking,
but as I wrote down the things Marble had said—who had asked her
opinion?—the wind picked her up and carried her away. She was
gone. I wrote down other voices until my head was empty, except for
the one I could hear as clearly as if my grandfather had walked into
the room, in this faraway place, Tonga.

"*Well, you know, a hospital is a good thing for staying alive, but it*
is hard to live in one. Let's go home, you and I, to the House of Lost
Things. Let us talk of other things.

"*You ask me, what do I believe in? God? Maybe. Maybe not. Your*
grandmother, she believed in things. When we ran from Mexico, she
lost a child. I grieved to have caused her such pain. 'No,' she said, 'it is
only a mortal body that is gone. Maybe it was not the right time for us,
without a home, without a country, with only a strand of pearls from
another life. Whether this body had lived a day or a hundred years, it

is a blink of an eye in the face of time. The spirit flies on, perhaps to return, perhaps to find another home, to sit on a mountain, fly with a hawk, or see the world through the eyes of a spider.' There was another child, your father, but I lost her. I was alone, with this boy. Then I remembered what she had said."

It was the only time Antonio had ever talked about my grandmother, but I understood then why he had always talked to things that most people did not: roses, rocks, birds, bugs. I wondered if he ever talked to an octopus. He might have.

When I finished writing, I had filled five pages. I folded them and wrote Skip's name on the outside. Then I fell asleep.

51

It is too bad, I suppose, to sleep through great happenings, but that's what I did. While others were undertaking heroic deeds and untangling the past so that time, thus freed, could move forward, I slept. I didn't wake up until Lebeca and Gabby flew into my room, both talking at once. Mafi would spend the night in hospital under observation, and so would Gravity with his broken leg. They weren't sure yet what Jackson had broken.

"But his head is fine," Lebeca said. "When he woke up, he said only, 'How is Seli?'"

"Actually," Gabby said, "Jackson thought he'd hit the rock headfirst when he opened his eyes and there was David, making a splint with his tie. But I think he was awfully glad to see him, once he realized he wasn't hallucinating."

She was wearing David's jacket, but she glanced down at it, as if she were not sure if she'd dreamt him up herself, even as the real thing followed her into the room. I almost didn't recognize David. Even before he was a politician, he always dressed like one, careful and conservative, the only deviations being when Gabby crocheted him a hat or polished his toenails. Now, not only had he lost his tie, but he'd ripped his trousers and fallen in a lake of mud, and his hair was all in a hoohah. Joe, just behind him, was laughing. "That was a hell of a ride, Ilillouette. One hell of a ride."

"And such a procession from the boat," Gabby added. "Dogs, cats, goats, pigs, children."

Reverend Ogg bobbed in, the end of the parade. "Damned fine show," he bellowed. "Sorry I missed it, Joe! Congressman! Good to see you, sir. Damn me, I hardly believed it when Mother said you were in Tonga. She hardly believed it herself; she was so excited. 'Ilillouette,' I said, 'now that's a name I've not heard in the South Pacific!' Well, you must have dinner with us tonight. What do you say, Joe? Mother is already making plans."

He bounded away. Silence prevailed.

"You know him?" I asked David, although I could easily see Ogg peddling Paradise to Congress. They'd have bought it.

"He was a congressman from Mississippi," David said. "His family had been in politics for generations. I'd just arrived in DC when a woman died in a boating accident, and *The Post* reported that she was Ogg's mistress. He resigned, but only after Mrs. Ogg made the rounds on the Hill—she even visited me—to insist that newspaper got it all wrong."

"I doubt that," Joe said.

"Why did she talk to you?" I asked. "Of course, if it was Ogg, he might not have known which side of the aisle you were on, or which side he was on, for that matter." I stopped. David was raising his eyebrows. I felt an attack of weakness as yet another of my unshakable convictions bit the dust.

"I am sure Mrs. Ogg is a Republican," Gabby said, comfortingly. To David, she added, "I don't remember him."

"Well, there are so many amoral congressmen."

"I'd have remembered someone's wife coming to see you."

"That's probably why I didn't mention it. Remember, you disliked my secretary so much I didn't dare talk to her. I had to write her little notes—"

"You did not! She wouldn't have been able to read them, anyway."

He grinned.

"David! I was never such a shrew."

"No." His smile softened. "You never were." Then, I believe he was attacked by the genetic family disease, nervous fits. "I'll just go see how Jackson is doing."

Joe left too, David's new best friend.

Gabby said, "Joe told us—Shelley, remember I said that when I saw Bette in Nuku'alofa, she looked uneasy? Well, Joe had walked in on her just after she had met Lily at the hotel. Lily had said some awful things and Joe said, 'Forget about her. Marry me, and we'll sail away.' Isn't it romantic? He's loved her for years. I should have figured it out; he named his boat for her."

"*Eel*?"

"*Ile Perdue*. There it was, his heart on his yacht. So, it was Joe, not Lily, who had scared Bette to death. She caught the first flight to Pago, and he didn't know where she had gone. Which is why he's been wandering back and forth, looking for her."

"Why'd she run away? If she didn't want to marry him, she could have just said no."

"Not if she was afraid she might say yes."

"I shall go now to help Foeata," Lebeca announced.

"Yes, she is probably cooking enough food to feed China," Gabby said. "I'll go, Lebeca, if you want to sit with Gravity."

"No. He does not need me now. But Foeata does."

Gabby took off David's jacket, studied it, folded it, and put it on a chair. "Dammit," she said. "There we were, outrunning a storm, laughing with the wind at our backs. I'd better go now, hadn't I? Dammit."

David returned with Skip a few minutes later. He looked around the room, picked up his coat, and held it the same way Gabby had, before he put it on.

Skip had my five pages folded in the pocket of his white coat, and promptly all my morphine wore off. "Jackson's OK," he said. "He just looks like he's been in a brawl in a Texas bar. Cracked a few ribs, dislocated his shoulder, tore some ligaments, broke his ankle. But he'll be all right. He saved Mafi's life. So, how about getting up?"

"I've decided to stay in bed."

David looked down at me. "*Oblomov.*" He had read it before I did.

"What's the point of getting up?" I asked. "The world comes to me."

"Not all the world. You just might have to go to it." He tossed me the bathrobe Foeata had made from the fabric with the squids and octopuses. She had brought me the woven slippers with purple pompoms too. I got up.

Skip said, "I think I have to read this book."

We hobbled into the hallway. David cleared his throat. "Where's Gabby?"

"She went to Foeata's."

"Is that the woman who was going to brain me with the tray of pancakes?"

"Yes. Did you know Gabby was here?"

"Jesse told me. Did she say anything?"

"Dammit. She said 'dammit.'"

We came to a window. David stopped and stared out of it, as if he were debating whether to go out and face the forces that had blown him here or merely watch them. Skip and I walked on. "What you wrote, Shelley, I'd like to keep it," he said. "I'd like to give it to other women to read. But first, I think Jackson should read it."

"You do? You'd give it to him?"

"No, I think you should. But I'd like it back, OK?"

"OK." He handed the papers to me. I got just a little dizzy, and he put his arm around me. He felt different from Jackson, solid and sturdy. I wondered what it would be like to fall in love with someone like Skip, but I remembered Albert. You can't fall in love with everyone who is kind, can you?

David caught up with us and disentangled me from my doctor. I don't know why Skip thought this was funny. "David, I'm heading over to Foeata's," he said. "Do you want to come along? I should warn you, however, about a few things: first of all, kava parties."

52

I was alone, although I expected any minute to see Mrs. Ogg back for another visit. When she did not turn up, I decided to go see her. Fossilized old nut that she was, she mystified me. What was beneath the flint, and how had she grown it? Did she have a heart that beat? She had to, didn't she? This is the problem with life: You can't stop wondering, but as soon as you do, you're pulled back into everything. Questions are as bad as gravity, when you'd rather just fly away and find a pleasant, lonely cloud to float on.

I discovered it was true, as John Muir had said, that when you try to pull out one thing in the universe, you discover it's attached to everything else. One cut on my stomach had rendered the rest of me nearly useless. It took me fifteen minutes to roll out of bed and into my slippers and robe, and another hour or so to stagger to the door. I nearly fell over Albert, sitting on a chair in the hallway.

"Everyone left you," he stammered, "but I promised Jackson— where are you going?"

"To have tea with Mrs. Ogg."

"No!" He jumped up and followed me as I shuffled toward the stairs. "Why?"

"You said you know something. I think she knows something too. The thing is, in books when people know something but won't tell anyone, three pages later, they're in trouble. In Judy Bolton books, someone puts a bag on her head and locks her up in a shack; in Raymond Chandler, they're dead. In Shakespeare—"

"I don't care." His voice trembled with poor bravado.

"What about everyone else?"

"Who?"

"Skip, for one."

Albert scowled. "I don't like him."

"It's a good thing he didn't consider whether he liked you or not when you needed help. What about Lily?" I asked.

"She's dead."

"She's still entangled with people who are not."

"Why should I care?"

"Because—" We had come to the stairs. I told myself that if Dolores could get herself over sand to the water, I could navigate one flight of stairs, although I wished I had tentacles that could haul myself along the banister. When, at length, I shambled into the lobby, it was deserted and even the shelves were empty.

Albert parked himself in front of the doors. "You have to stay away from Mrs. Ogg."

"Albert, I am filled with pain-killing drugs, so I can say this: Mrs. Ogg is not so different from me or you, and you and I are not so different from anyone else. I think she needs to find some peace."

"You don't know what she did."

"No. Do you?"

"No!"

"Then we can ask her."

"No!"

"She won't kill us."

"She could!"

"I'm not crazy about her," I said, "but I don't think she's that bad. Cuckoo, yes, but wouldn't you be if you'd had to spend your life protecting that wackadoodle she married?"

"None of this matters now."

"Yes, it does."

"Why?"

"Because, oddly enough, the truth still matters."

"What truth?"

"That is the question. What do you think it is?"

Albert's demeanor had been progressively worsening, until now, when he resembled a long-dead, pop-eyed orange fish. "I don't know! I never had to think before! I just believed. It's terrible to lose your faith. It leaves a big hole in your head. There's nothing there."

"There's something."

"It's never happened to you, has it?" His voice was so forlorn he might have been announcing the end of the world, the last ship to nowhere.

"I've never had any faith to lose."

"I don't believe in anything now. And I don't care what happens to anyone, especially me."

"Then 'It is required you do awake your faith.'"

"Huh?"

"Shakespeare."

I could almost see a red heart pulsing in his paper-thin chest. "I will go see her, Shelley, but alone. I will come back and tell you everything. I promise." He pushed open the door, and the wind carried him off.

Clouds were spilling over the sky as if giants had overturned vats of liquid silver. The sky had turned ink black, and there was rain in the wind. I wanted to be in it. I went outside. I walked a ways; the wind held me up. I felt like I might be the only person in the world until I noticed a lone figure limping after me. He was wearing an anorak flung over a hospital gown. One arm was in a sling. One leg was in a cast to his knee. He had on one shoe. The grin on his face was slightly lopsided too.

"I looked out the window and saw one person out walking in a hurricane," Jackson said. "I knew it was you."

We lurched along together like an ant that had lost half its legs. "I wonder where we are going," he mused, and this cracked him up. He was on painkillers too. Probably the only reason we got anywhere was because the wind blew us to Foeata's. The house was dark and deserted; there were no people, no feast, and not even a loaf of bread anywhere.

"I wonder where everyone is," I said.

"I don't know. Jesse didn't turn up here too, did he?"

"No."

On the kitchen table was a white nightgown, trimmed with lace and blue ribbons, folded neatly. A note on it read: "For my daughter."

"Are you going to put it on?" Jackson asked.

"Do you think it's for me?"

"Yes, goose, I think it's for you."

Lightning flashed, thunder roared, and I said I would go brush my teeth. I peeled off my wet clothes and tried on the nightgown, but I took it off and put on my T-shirt. I brushed my hair, which had blown into a red mushroom. I was wondering what else I could do when I heard Jackson giggling. He was lying in my bed, except for his one foot in the shoe, which dangled out from beneath the covers.

"Do you need help?" I asked.

"Oh, no, but I just fell into the bed. Then I realized it's yours. Now it would take a crane to get me out. D'you mind?"

"No." I pulled his shoe off for him. He gave up and laughed about this too. So did I, although I had to lie down before I passed out from spasms in my stitches. It was a little bit nice, how warm the bed felt because he was in it.

"Are you OK, Shelley?"

"Yes, as long as I don't laugh. Are you?"

"As long as I don't move. It's funny how you do it anyway—laugh, I mean."

"Jackson, would you like to read something?"

"Hmmm?" He had closed his eyes.

"No, probably not. Probably, I'll carry it around for a few weeks. Then Albert can nick it and throw it in the sea. But Dolores will retrieve it and put it on Gravity's boat, where Lebeca will find it in a spider's web—"

He was asleep.

I stayed awake, however, listening to the storm as it arrived in its full, roaring force; it was a splendid ruckus of thunder and lightning, wind and rain. The wind howled, rain pounded down, and branches and tree trunks flew past the window. I loved it.

I've thought about that night, since then. It was one time when all the rest of the world was running amok, but we were not. Through it all, Jackson slept like one who'd staggered ashore from a shipwreck and collapsed on the sand. We were alone in the dark and the storm as if we had both stumbled onto an island, but it was, for once, the same one.

53

W hen I woke up, Jackson was gone, but a woman was sitting beside the window, bent over a notebook. The storm continued, and in its strange yellow light, she looked like a ghost, and not just because I thought all women, shadowed and half-seen, were ghosts; then I remembered that Jackson had found Mafi in the cave. She was even more bone-thin and frail than before, like the skeleton of a leaf. She showed me her drawing: a man flying on a thin rope over a wild sea. "I try to draw the things I might not see again," Mafi said. "This time, it would be a good thing."

She left and returned with Lebeca, who carried a tray of tea and toast. "We promised Sikipi," Lebeca explained. Skip had spent the night at the hospital, a good thing since the storm had blown out the windows in his and Jackson's rooms. He had come to the house early, and Jackson had gone back to the hospital with him to help. Mafi, after one night there, had insisted she need not take up a bed and so had come to Foeata's to sit by me.

"Sikipi was deranged, of course, to know you had left, but we understand," Lebeca said. "There are too many ghosts in a hospital. Once, my cousin saw three."

"Where is Foeata?"

"She—will return."

"How is Gravity?" I asked.

"He is fine too, I am sure. His mother, his sisters, his aunties will care for him."

But not Lebeca, I perceived. "Where is Gabby?"

Lebeca blushed a deep rose red. "It was like a movie from America, Seli."

"Oh, great."

"Yes! We came here, Gabby and I, but there was no Foeata, and here comes Sikipi with your brother. And no food! I said I would make tea, but Davy says, no worries, he will go to his hotel. He says to Gabby, 'Come with me?' She says no! Why, I wonder, when he is so beautiful?"

"Well, there are several reasons—"

"He walked away. Alone. We watched. Then, like the wind gave her its wings, she flew to him! Oh, how he kissed her! It was so romantic."

"Yep. I expect the heavenly angels were singing."

Mafi laughed; it transformed her face. "Why were you in that cave?" I asked.

"There is a word," she replied slowly. "Irony. I think this is the word for someone like me, who yearned to be free, but trapped myself in my flight. I was lucky. Unlike Lily."

As light and dark flickered around us, Mafi talked. "When Dr. Omont brought Lily home, I was fifteen. I had been living with the Omonts for five years. He had saved my life, first by taking me away from the fear my illness caused and then by introducing me to Bette, an artist. Now, he had saved this baby. So we had a bond, Lily and I, from the beginning.

"He said the mother could not keep this baby. Bette understood this, but she was not so happy to have a child. She had a secret place on the island, a cave carved in an ancient time before the mountain rose above the sea. 'Every woman needs her room,' she said. After Lily came, Bette went to this cave more often to paint. But I loved this baby, so beautiful and so alone. I named her Lily because she was like a flower."

And Mafi noticed a new fisherman had joined the men making deliveries to the Omonts' island. His name was Pulu. "When I saw him, so tall and strong, like an ancient warrior, I knew my life was linked to his." She learned he was from the south, but he wished to build a house on Vava'u. He had not spoken a word to Mafi when he asked Dr. Omont's permission to marry her. "I had been told no man would ever want me, and yet this man did, and he was so handsome I thought I could never grow tired of looking at him."

But Dr. Omont said no, she was too young. Then he died. Bette returned to America, taking Lily and Mafi with her to her family in Connecticut. A nanny took care of Lily, Mafi went to school, and Bette painted. "But we suffered from the cold. Finally, Bette said, 'Let's go home.' Pulu had built his house. He said it was waiting for me."

The marriage was strange from the beginning, but Mafi, having never been married before, did not figure this out right away. Pulu, full of dark moods, was quick to anger. His house was remote, apart from others. He refused to let Lily live with them. He did not want Mafi to visit Bette. He didn't want her to draw or paint, except on tapa cloth, which he said was proper women's work. When her running fits grew frequent again, he locked the doors to keep her inside. It wasn't long before Mafi grew tired of looking at him.

When the Ile Perdue shop opened, Mafi was astonished that tourists would buy her work, but she saved the money she earned and bought a boat of her own. Her husband said she was more like a man than a woman, but she went to Bette's island anyway. "Here is the question for a woman who wishes to be free," Mafi said. "Where do you go and how do you get there?"

Lily had been gone for many years by then. Mafi had written to her but never got a reply. "She wished to be free of us. We were surprised when a telegram arrived. Lily was coming home. Why? She did not say. She asked Bette to meet her in Nuku'alofa. Bette did not return, but you arrived, Seli, asking, 'Where is she?' I worried."

On that Saturday when I went on the hospital tour, Mafi had a different visitor: Lily. "She walked up to my house," Mafi said. "How beautiful she had become. The blood that was mixed in her had created someone so rare, so special. I was hopeful, until we talked. I asked, 'Did you and Bette come back together?' She said no; she didn't know where Bette was, nor did she care, because the rich, important Reverend Ogg had brought her to Neiafu on his yacht. She and Bette had quarreled. 'Why?' I asked. She said, 'Because I demanded the truth.' What truth? This is what she believed, Seli: that she was the daughter of Dr. Omont—and me! No, I tried to tell her, this was no truth at all.

"Then we saw that Pulu had returned to the house. He was standing in the door, listening. Lily left. So did Pulu. He returned in a mood I knew well, silent but angry. I asked, 'You do not believe Lily's story?' He struck me. He had never done this before. I thought he would kill me. I think the only thing that saved me was a truck that arrived, driving fast. He ran outside. He left in this truck. He forgot to lock the door. Many times, I had thought the only way to be free was to die and yet I was not ready; I was not finished. This night, it was not my illness but my life that said to me, 'Run.'"

Mafi set her boat adrift so people would think she had drowned and went to the harbor where Bette left her boat when she traveled. She took it to Bette's island. The next day, Sunday, she hid the boat, but was she safe? On Monday morning, as she nervously wondered what she should do next, Lily walked into the room.

"She said, 'I knew you had taken Bette's boat, but don't worry. Everyone thinks you are dead, and I won't tell.' 'But how did you get here?' I asked, but then I remembered when she was young, she used to take Bette's boat and sail into deep water. Now I was frightened again by the look on her face. 'Are you ill?' I asked. 'Yes,' she said, 'I am sick of life. It is the truth, and you know I have never liked the truth.'

"But then she said, 'Don't worry, Mafi. I have a plan for us. First, we had better find a better hiding place.' We carried food, blankets, water, and a lantern to Bette's cave. We were downstairs, where the supplies were, when we heard the sound of a boat. She said, 'Ah, something wicked this way comes. You had better run, Mafi.' 'But what about you?' I asked. 'Don't worry,' she said. 'I have a friend.' She showed me a something in Dr. Omont's old aquarium: a stonefish! 'Lily,' I said, 'It is dangerous—deadly!' She smiled. 'Just like me.' 'Lily,' I said, 'You are not as wicked as you pretend to be.' She only replied, 'What a difference it would have made, Mafi, if you had been my mother.'

"I said, 'Yes, because you would be plain and thin. It was some-one else who gave you beauty.' I saw a look on her face: It is when a dream has vanished into what is real, and you must let it go. A story you have created in your head is not true. Your Tongan warrior has neither love nor joy. The man of your dreams is, after all, only a man.

"Above us, we heard footsteps. 'Run,' she said. 'Come too,' I pleaded. She said, 'No, it is better this way. They will see I am alone. No one is looking for me. Mafi, let me do one good thing. I will come to the cave when it is safe.'

"So, I ran. I climbed down the ropes to the cave. I waited. Finally, I slept. When I awoke and thought to leave, I discovered the rope ladder was gone! There was no way to leave, except to leap into the sea. And Lily did not come."

Days passed. Mafi watched the sky and the sea. A storm blew rain into the cave. She knew from the wildness in the sea that another storm was coming. She watched the waves break higher and higher. They would carry her away. Then—was she mad or did she hear voices? Was it Lily? She tried to call but her voice was lost in the waves. She lit her lantern. No. Nothing. Night came, but then—lights! An angel appeared, flying through the night.

"I was glad to learn it was not an angel, but a man," Mafi said. "The rest, you know—or you know as much as I, for I do not know who came to the island or why Lily died in the sea."

I asked, "But why did you send me that tapa cloth?"

"You didn't recognize it? You had admired it. On the back, that was the map to my house, so you could visit."

"I didn't look at it. I was afraid. And then it disappeared."

"It was only a gift. I will make you another. I think, when you are afraid, you miss much."

54

We were interrupted by a knock on Foeata's front door. Lebeca opened it. A woman's voice said, "We are looking for Shelley Ilillouette."

"Me?" I got up out of bed. It was the woman from the Mormon church.

"We are looking for Albert," she said. "No one can find him. No one has seen him since yesterday. Someone thought he had gone to see you in hospital. We know he is your friend."

I felt a chill, like a hand of ice on my brain. "He was going to visit Mrs. Ogg."

"Mrs. Ogg?" she echoed. "Yesterday? But the Oggs are gone. They sailed yesterday."

"Into the storm?"

A swarm of questions buzzed around my brain as I fell back into bed. This is where I was when Skip arrived, bellowing, "Shelley! God dammit! You are more trouble than a bag of chickens." He put a thermometer in my mouth. "Don't talk."

Lebeca and Mafi had followed him; their eyes widened to saucers. Skip moderated his voice. "Miss Ilillouette, now that I have cut you open and sewed you up, you have become my patient. This means, among other things, that I, not you, get to say when you can leave the hospital. But since you have already waltzed off into a hurricane, I will only say that if you don't stay put, I will get Chief Taumalolo's handcuffs and chain you to the bed. It is better than strangling you, which would violate the Hippocratic oath." He removed the thermometer. "Now you can say something smart-assed."

"Who puts chickens in a bag?"

"What have you eaten? I figured no matter what I said, Foeata'd be dishing up curry and jellyrolls." He glanced around. "Where is she?"

"She has not returned," Lebeca said. "Also, Albert is missing."

"They're probably in a church somewhere."

"The Oggs are gone too," I said. "Their yacht is."

"You're kidding. They wouldn't have gone into this storm. Ogg's not an idiot. Well, he is, but Mrs. Ogg isn't."

Skip sat down wearily on the bed.

Lebeca asked, "You would like tea, Sikipi?"

"Thanks, I'm fine. People have been bringing food to the hospital all day. Your guy has got a nice way with patients, Shelley. Or maybe it's just that he is so banged up they take one look at him and decide they're OK. I told him to take off; he should be here soon. Maybe I'll take a cup of coffee—" Skip yawned, listed, and fell over onto my pillow.

I threw the dragon sheets on him and went to the kitchen. The storm had quieted but the power was out. Lebeca said she would walk with Mafi back to the hotel and then go check on her family. I wandered around the silent house. Foeata's door was open, but no one was there. In the rooms where Jackson and Skip had slept, the windows were broken and the beds drenched with rain. As I stood in Jackson's doorway, I remembered a Greek word I like, *eidolon*, spirit image. That's what filled the house that night.

"Here you are." I hadn't heard Jackson come in, and he was only a shadow in the dark. "I almost fell into bed with Skip. I'm glad I didn't kiss him." He put his hand on my shoulder; it felt warm, like one real thing, but still I couldn't move, so we just stood there in the wrecked room. "What's wrong, Shelley?"

"Everything. Maybe the truth is overrated, if you send other people to the bottom of the sea searching for it."

"What?"

I told him about the Oggs. "Albert went to see them. I made him. Maybe they hit him on the head and carried him away for asking questions. Maybe Foeata was already there." The wind blew a gust of rain into the room, and his hand was beginning to feel cold too. "Do you want to go to bed, Jackson?"

"Do you?"

"Maybe," I said. "Where?"

55

We slept crosswise in my bed that night, all three of us. Jackson was insisting that he should sleep in the middle when he conked out, leaving enough room for me to fit in between them. First, I found the pages I'd written for Skip. Everything else in the world kept vanishing, but they had not. I put them in the pocket of Jackson's anorak, next to the envelope he'd stuffed there; it was still unopened. He might find them; he might not. He might read them. It might finish everything. It probably would. I wiggled into the bed before I took them back.

It was cozy, like sleeping between two granite boulders. I left off worrying about the papers and wondered instead what happened if you sailed into a storm and changed your mind too late. I was getting close to thinking about infinity. I moved as close to Jackson as possible and put my feet on his, the one that wasn't in a cast.

"What are you doing?" he murmured.

"Sole to sole." That's Vonnegut, not Shakespeare.

"Don't make me laugh, Ilillouette."

"Jackson, why didn't we see the little suitcase? I think Lily stole Tarkington's stonefish and transported it in her cosmetic case, but why?"

"I love you, Shelley."

"Oh God, where am I?" Skip mumbled.

"In my bed. But Jackson is here too, so it won't offend Hippocrates."

"Shell, roll over me, will you, and I'll sleep in the middle."

"Jackson, watch it. She's got stitches."

"I can go sleep on the kitchen table, you ninnyhammers."

It was my first *menage à trois*, and my only one to date.

By the morning, the storm had blown on. Sunshine was coming through the window, along with Gravity's voice. Leaning on crutches, he was supervising a work crew in Foeata's garden.

"Hello," he sang. "We are preparing the oven for the feast!"

"Ah, great." Skip glanced at me. "We're going to be barbecued."

"No! It is for the brother of Seli."

"Congressman on a spit," I said. "A Tongan delicacy."

"No, Seli! For him we shall cook two pigs! Foeata will wish this!"

"Foeata? Is she back?"

"Soon! This morning, Davy—congressiman of America, so fine!— he drove into the bush to bring her and Fresh Air from the house of Pulu."

"He did?"

"It is a great thing."

"You've no idea—"

Jackson gasped, but this had nothing to do with the staggering news that David had driven himself somewhere. It was the spider bobbing on the mosquito net. I don't know how I'd missed it. It had to be the great primeval spider from which all wimpy tarantulas had descended.

"Holy Mary mother of God," Skip said. "What do you suppose it eats, horses?"

The spider lifted its front legs. It might have growled. Lebeca, carrying in a tea tray, noticed the spider too, and holding her tray with one hand, she gave the net a shake. Since she had first brought me a tray of food, people had been disappearing and reappearing like fireflies, and all kinds of catastrophes had filled the days. Still, she smiled the same cheerful smile and sent the spider flying through the air. Although a giant spider did not faze her, the discovery of two men in my bed did. She blushed and spilled the tea. Skip cleared his throat. "Jackson, can you lend me a hand again today in the house of ghosts?"

Lebeca recovered, once the naked masculine chests were out of sight. "How strong this storm was to blow everyone to their place, Seli."

"Is that what it did?"

"Is it nice to sleep with a man and wake up with him?"

"It's not too bad," I admitted, "although I'm not sure about two at once."

I got dressed and went into the garden. The sky was glowing blue, the road strewn with blossoms and palm fronds. People were hammering, sawing, sweeping, making stacks of fallen branches and broken doors. Some were singing. This is life, they seemed to be saying: A cyclone takes your roof off, so you get up and put it back on. And be glad you didn't fly away with it.

A mud-covered Jeep rumbled up to Foeata's door. David was driving, Gabby was next to him, and riding in the back seat like an immense yellow ball of sunshine was Foeata.

"Malo e lelei," I said. I really meant it.

"Malo e lelei, Seli." She burst into laughter. "What a story I have for you! But first I must make pancakes for Davy." He had been adopted too.

She descended regally, and only then did I realize she had dwarfed another passenger. I had never expected the sight of Albert to affect me with untrammeled joy.

"I must go—" he began.

"You must eat," Foeata said. Albert flashed her a shy smile, tinged with terror, and went into her kitchen. This was fortuitous because Foeata got busy making pancakes, and David and Gabby were as useful as two painted figures on a cuckoo clock, their feet glued on the same block of wood and spinning picturesquely but really having nothing to do with telling time. All of David's wits were consumed with stirring Gabby's tea while she put sugar in his. Albert was the only one capable of useful conversation.

I said, "I was afraid you had sailed away with the Oggs."

This momentarily distracted David from Gabby's teacup. "No. Not even Ogg would be such a damned fool."

"No," Albert whispered. "But she would—"

He explained: That day, when he went to the Ogg's yacht, he found only Pulu the fisherman, agitated and also looking for Mrs. Ogg. Pulu made a strange request. Would Albert go to his house, see if Mrs. Ogg was there, and tell her that Pulu was waiting for her at the ship?

"I didn't understand but I did this," Albert said. "At his house, I knocked at the door. No one answered. Then I saw something in a corner, a dark shape, eyes, hidden inside fisherman's rain gear. I thought it was Lily. But no, that was silly. I called, 'Mrs. Ogg?' I shouted Pulu's message. And something hit me. It must have been a tree branch." This was all he remembered until he opened his eyes to find Fresh Air and Foeata standing over him.

Here, Foeata paused in her pancake making to explain that she had gone to see Fresh Air, but when they realized the storm was moving in faster than she had expected, they were hurrying back to town when they saw Albert, lying in Pulu's yard. They carried him into the house. Pulu would not object. It was the Tongan way.

And the storm arrived. Throughout the night and following day, the

Tongans cooked and told stories, until with a thundering crash, the ceiling fell in, crushed by a falling tree. Foeata was buried in debris, and Fresh Air was stunned by a blow on the head. Albert moved enough wreckage to free Foeata, and they made a place for Fresh Air to rest. He crawled into the kitchen to get them food and water. At first light, Albert managed to wiggle out through a window. He ran to Neiafu to get help. As he passed the Port of Refuge, he saw David in the lobby.

"He was getting coffee," Albert said. "I told him what had happened. He said he would get transportation, but first he took the coffee to his room."

A few minutes later, David reappeared, and Albert was only a bit flumdoodled that Gabby came with him; he was getting more used to life. Ever-Ready procured a Jeep. They got Foeata and Fresh Air out of the wrecked house. They took Fresh Air to the hospital, although he insisted he was fine.

"And Albert is a fine, brave man," Foeata said. "When he eats more, he will be strong too."

Nervously, Albert ate seven pancakes, three eggs, and a banana; he reminded me of myself on that first day I had come to Foeata's. "If I eat any more, I might not fit through a window next time," he said finally, and he blushed the color of a salmon fillet when everyone laughed. He glanced at David. "I will go now to the police and tell them everything."

"Maybe not everything." David winked at him, and Albert, like a distant relative of an octopus, became tomato red.

"You must come back for the feast," Gabby told him.

"Oh," Albert stammered. "I've never gone to a feast, but they are sending me home."

"No," Gabby objected. "You can't leave Tonga without going to a feast."

"I invite you," Foeata said. "You will come."

"By the way, Shelley," David added, "I'll need a speech."

"*The Tempest*. No, *Moby Dick*. Or Tennyson—"

"Write it, will you? Shall we go, my—Gabby?"

David wanted to drive back into the bush to see if anyone else needed rescuing. They reminded me of two kids at Disneyland. David was the one who'd already been on every wild ride twice and was raring to do it again, whereas Gabby was the one who might have closed her eyes through a great deal of it. She seemed bewildered, but no more, I expect, than most Tongans would be to find a US congressman at their door, or what was left of it, inquiring if he might be of any use. But she went with David to the Jeep. First, she kissed Albert's cheek, and David shook his hand. Albert's face suffused with light and blood. He may not have known what he believed anymore, but I think he still knew there was a Heaven.

"I still don't know what you knew," I said to him.

"It's what I promised David I would tell the police," he replied. "He is so wonderful, Shelley. I understand if Miss Asher prefers him to anyone else. And he believes in God, but so do you. Even if it is Shakespeare."

I wondered if David had noticed that Albert was falling in love, and this might be the real thing, but he had probably been too busy buttering toast for Gabby, with all our disaster-prone, trouble-seeking ancestors egging him on.

"Do you mind," I asked Albert, "if I go with you to the police?"

56

I knew the part where Lily Omont had come to the hospital and dazzled him into giving her the medical charts. In love, he followed her everywhere, so he knew that a problem had occurred with the Oggs, on whose yacht she had been staying. When Mrs. Ogg threw Lily's suitcases off the ship, he carried them to Bette's boat, watched Lily leave, and waited for her to return. She reappeared, finally, on the night of the dance at the Port of Refuge. He was reassured when she left the dance alone, although her mood was not so good, especially when she discovered that Bette's boat was gone. Mrs. Ogg wouldn't let her on their ship, even when Lily shouted that she had nowhere to sleep. Joe Storey, hearing the ruckus, sent someone to escort Lily to the hotel. Albert went, too, and asked Lily to marry him. "David said I might have gone too fast," he said.

On Sunday, he followed Lily to the church, to Foeata's, back to the hotel. That's where he was when Skip brought his note for her. Albert offered to take it up to her room, but he didn't give it to her. "I meant to, but she was different. She was nice—and sad. She said she was all alone, but she had to get to Mrs. Omont's island. I told her about Gravity's boat. 'You are good,' she said. 'Can you show me how to be good? No, it is easier for me to teach you to be bad.' And—I can't tell you this part."

"That's OK. I can imagine."

"No, you can't. Because you're innocent. I came here to save sinners, Shelley, and instead I became one."

"If it was a sin."

"It was. And God sees—" Albert hadn't entirely lost his faith in God, at least not in His ability to be a nosey parker.

"If God happened to look anywhere else just then, like, Washington, DC, whatever you were doing would be mild on the celestial offense scale."

"No, Shelley, not David! He is the most wonderful man—"

I steered him back to the topic at hand and learned that when he heard, on Monday morning, that Gravity's boat was gone, he knew Lily had taken it.

"That night, were you waiting at the cove for her?"

He nodded. "I saw a light as a boat came in. But it went to the other side of the cliff. I had to climb over to see—I am sorry if I knocked a coconut on your head."

"What did you see?"

"Mrs. Ogg."

"In the boat?"

"She was on the beach. There was no one in the boat."

We had come to the church. Briskly, he told the secretary that he was back and well. He had been caught by the storm; that was all. Now, he had one thing to do. From his room, he fetched a battered manila envelope, and we walked to the police station.

Police Chief Taumalolo, the size of seven Alberts, listened thoughtfully to his story, abbreviated because David had said that was OK. From his envelope, Albert took a crumpled piece of paper. It was the note Skip had written to Lily. "I was going to throw it away," he said, looking as if he expected to be locked up. Chief Taumalolo only nodded.

The second thing Albert took from the envelope was a piece of tapa, a painting of a long-haired woman in a cave above the sea; swimming below her was an octopus that could have been her sister. "Lily took it from your room, Shelley," Albert said. "She hid it in her dress. It fell out when—" Again, he cast a terrified look at the policeman, who remained unfazed. "She said it should have been hers. It told her that Mafi wasn't dead. She told me about a hidden cave that you had to find with ropes."

"She gave this tapa to you?" Taumalolo asked.

"No."

"How is it that you have it?"

"Because someone left it in this envelope at the church office. My name was on it."

Taumalolo turned the tapa over. On the back was a map to Mafi's house, carefully drawn in black ink. A note in delicate calligraphy read, "Dear Shelley, please come to see me any time." Beneath this, scribbled in red ink, was a rough drawing of Bette's island and a trail to a cave. A different, hurried hand had scrawled, "Pray, love, remember. L."

"Ophelia," I said.

"No, it was Lily's writing," Albert said. "When I saw it, I didn't know why I'd been so frightened. I realized that Lily must have stayed on the island and the Oggs had stopped there, and Mrs. Ogg had brought back Gravity's boat, because, of course, she wouldn't think it was right to steal boats. And Lily had sent back the tapa cloth for me to return to Shelley, and Mrs. Ogg had delivered it." His voice faded.

"Then Lily turned up in the sea," I said. "What did you think?"

"I don't know! I mean, I knew I had to think but I didn't know how to. But I knew I had to go to the island. So I asked Gravity for his boat. And that guy showed up with him."

"Skip?"

"I hated him. And there he was saying, 'You look like you could use help.' And you were there, Shelley, with Jackson. You were kind, but I didn't know who to trust, so I ran away. I tried to follow the map, but it ended at a cliff. And below, in the sea, I saw a lifeboat." Albert's voice sank to a whisper. "It was Mrs. Ogg."

That was when his heart, never strong, had given up. "And that's all."

Chief Taumalolo thanked him. Albert and I went back outside, and he leaned against a coconut tree to recover. "When do you think Lily wrote that note to you?" I asked.

"To me?"

"She wouldn't have called me 'love.' Was it before or after she took the ropes away from the cave to be sure Mafi was safe, before or after she got in the boat with Mrs. Ogg—"

"She meant remember the ropes?"

"She meant remember the night. And you might remember the ropes."

"I will remember. But it is all over."

"Not quite," I said. "You had better come to Foeata's feast. Or she will come to get you." He started, for there she was, walking with Fresh Air. She had sprung him from the hospital but forbade him to talk until they were home, and he had eaten a few meals to restore his strength.

"Tea and toast," she exclaimed. "Fa!"

57

Foeata was creating a dessert: cake, pudding, Jell-O, more cake. I was trying to get her to tell me why she had gone to visit Fresh Air. He, drinking coffee, had said little.

"Seli, what is 'Tennyson'?"

"A poet. He wrote, 'Come, my friends, 'tis not too late to seek a newer world.' David likes that almost as much as he likes 'La Vie en Rose.'"

"And what is this?"

"A French love song. He used to sing it for Gabby because they like France."

She cast a broody look at the door through which they had gone.

"Palangis don't do so well when they actually land in Paradise, Foeata."

"They are smart about many things, but not the heart," Foeata conceded. "Yet, he is a good man. I said to him, 'I am not so important for you to take all this trouble,' and he said, 'But I am hungry for more pancakes.' Perhaps he has not eaten enough for many years. Perhaps if he eats more, his brain will work better.'"

"And his heart?"

"Oh, it works, Seli. But it is a problem what to do with his wife."

I envisioned David packing the pristine Pamela off to Tonga and getting her back fat and jolly, or better yet, baked in a Tongan dessert.

"But I do not judge," she added, "for I have spent two nights alone with two men, and God has said nothing to me!" She laughed one of her great roaring laughs, and I could almost hear God's echoing chuckle. "Now, Seli, I must tell the women what to prepare for our feast—a grand feast!—you will go to write down for Davy what he will say and also for me."

"For you?"

"Yes. You will write down the story that I shall tell tomorrow."

"The story of what?"

"Of everything. Of love."

"But I don't know everything."

"Ha! Now you are like Fresh Air. 'I don't know,' he said to me. 'Ha!' I said. 'You have said always someone knows the truth. Now is time for you to tell what you know, for Sikipi, for everyone.' Then, a storm, a hit on the head, and—poof!—he remembered."

"It was not my story, Foeata," Fresh Air interjected. "I only knew the pieces that my friend Armand Omont had told me. I had no names."

"Now we have names."

"We do?" I asked.

"Love is a story that has many faces, Seli," Fresh Air said. "This time it is Pulu; it is Mrs. Ogg."

The sun was setting when I went to my room. I sat at the dressing table with the flowered skirt. I had my notebook and three pens. I lit the ruby glass light. But this is as far as I got because when I opened my notebook, it wasn't empty. Another hand had written: *We know what we are, but not what we may be. Ha. Tell the truth. Lily.*

In the rose glow of the room, I could see her, standing there, as she must have when she slipped into my room and nicked the tapa cloth. Of course, she would open a notebook to see what someone had written. I'd have done the same thing if I had found a notebook of hers."You might have written more, Lily Omont," I said to the shadows. "You might have written the story that would explain everything. Instead, you left it to an idiot and risked that she will get it wrong."

To the stories I had heard from Skip, Mafi, and Albert, I now had the strangest one of all, the one Fresh Air had learned from a long-dead doctor.

It began on the night when a panic-stricken Tongan boy came to his island, pleading for help with a girl about to give birth. Omont went with him to an uninhabited island where he discovered not a Tongan, as he had expected, but a white girl. She was livid with Pulu for summoning a doctor. She told Omont to go away; she wished to die. When it looked like she might, Omont understood that the boy was not her servant, but her lover. The girl was the daughter of a missionary so important even the irreligious Omont knew his name. This missionary, so high above the people he would serve, had not allowed his daughter to go to school or in any way mingle with Tongans. A widower, he would not allow a woman servant in his house to tempt him. His daughter was his servant, and her only friend was the houseboy, who had left his poor family eager to learn Western ways. Pulu.

"What happened next was nature," Fresh Air said.

When the missionary discovered his daughter was pregnant, he beat her, but she refused to name her lover. Believing she had been seduced by visiting soldiers, he ordered his houseboy to take her to a remote island and leave her to God's judgment. Pulu took her away, but he didn't leave her. The girl survived the birth but refused to look at the baby. She told Pulu to throw it into the sea. Pulu pleaded with Omont to take the baby away.

Dr. Omont left with the infant and was surprised when, several months later, Pulu turned up in Vava'u. He said he had taken the girl back to her father. There was nowhere else for her to go. The missionary could not kill her, so he had sent her to relatives in America, and he paid Pulu to go away and never tell the story. Pulu wished to give the money to the doctor. Omont told Pulu to keep it. He asked if the girl knew what had become of her child. "No," Pulu said. "That story is over."

When I had finished writing this down, I began a list of questions. They filled five pages in my notebook. Finally, I gave up and wrote a speech for David. When word came that the two palangi doctors would sleep that night at the hospital—the shelves were still full of people waiting for help—I was just as glad to sleep alone, with all my questions.

58

The sky was wild with colors: crimson, gold, violet, and peach. All day, as the others had prepared the two-pig feast, while the women cooked and the men rolled out mats and erected a canopy over a dais, I had been writing in my notebook. Now, the torches were lit, and the women were carrying out dish after dish. From my window, I watched the men arrive. Albert looked wary but dazzled when he was summoned up to sit on the dais with the big shots.

David and Gabby came to my room. He looked every inch the cannibal king in his purple wraparound skirt, shirt and tie, straw mat, and flip-flops. Gabby's dress was scarlet, printed with frangipani blossoms and birds of paradise. She wore white blossoms in her hair. She glowed like the sunset. David didn't stop watching her. I gave him the notes I'd made. He wandered off to read them, but Gabby lingered. She threw her arms around my neck. "What am I going to do?" she said. "I am going to love him all my life."

She went to join the women, but I decided to watch from my bed. I didn't really belong with the men or the women, and I had a ringside seat.

The feast began. Fresh Air read a message from the king, and David gave his speech, to much applause. Then Foeata rose. She wore red flowers in her hair, woven jewelry on her arms, and around her waist, the short grass skirt, the ta'ovala, sign of respect. Her long brown dress was patterned like tapa cloth, with black stick figures that, in the flickering torchlight, seemed to be moving in a dance.

"A story is made like a tapa cloth," she said. "A piece from here, a piece from there, and much pounding. I have for you a story, and you will say if it is true or legend or both. It is a story that will be told again and again before the world goes into darkness. It is, of course, of love."

As she was talking, Skip and Jackson showed up, but they declined a seat on the dais. They sat in the back. Skip didn't eat much. He just listened, his head leaning on his hands.

The Methodist Ladies Choir sang three hymns, followed by "Wichita Lineman," "Some Enchanted Evening," and "Love Me Tender." When David asked if they would sing a Tongan song, they turned to Gabby, who summoned Skip to sing "Ise Isa," the song the Peace Corps had been practicing on the plane. It's about farewells and partings and hearts breaking. The choir joined in. Then everyone did.

Next, Foeata announced, David would sing "Lavy in Rose." He looked surprised, but, since they'd all been drinking kava and beer, he sang it. I was sorry Dick the campaign genius wasn't there to see David dressed in a skirt and singing French love songs for Gabby Asher. He'd have pulled his own head off, but it was such a hit with the Tongans I believe David could have given up Congress and run for assistant king.

Drumbeats began. Tongan women danced sitting down, moving their arms like flowing seaweed, and men leapt into action, flashing swords and painted shields in an ancient warrior's dance. When the drums were at their loudest, Gabby Asher slipped away. She went to the gate, paused, and glanced back before she went through it. A few minutes later, David looked away from the dancers to where she had been sitting, but she was gone, dancing down the coral road.

"A story? You wish to hear a story?" Fresh Air asked. The torches were nearly burned out. "I will tell the story of how men met women, for there was a time when the men lived in one group, and over the mountain, women lived in another. The men were hunters and fisher-men, but they did not know how to make fires to cook the things they caught. They ate their meat raw, and their hands were often covered with blood. Except when, by accident, they fell into a lake, they did not bathe. The women only ate what they could grow. But they knew the secret of making bread on a fire. From their plants they made clothes and shelters. From the earth they made bowls and beads.

"It happened one day that a hunter, returning to his camp, lost his way and came to the village of the women. He watched them, and he thought, maybe this looks good. These creatures were so clean and decorated. Their food smelled good. Their shelters would keep off rain. He was interested; he came closer. A woman working in her garden saw him, smeared with blood and mud and carrying dead things. She screamed and threw rocks at him, and he ran away.

"Then this woman began to think, what did he do with those dead things? Might they be tasty? She decided to find him. She had to cross the mountain to reach the settlement of the men, and by the time she reached it, she was cold and dirty, scratched by bushes and wild-looking herself. The men, when they saw her, threw rocks at her and shouted, and she ran away.

"But the man who had seen the village of the women decided to find the woman. First, he bathed in the river and wrapped himself in animal skins. 'Where are you going?' the others asked, and when he told them, they decided to bathe and follow him.

"The woman also told her villagers what she had seen, and they set out to find the camp of the men. Somewhere on the top of the mountain the men and the women met. And they all thought, hmm, there could be something good here."

Fresh Air paused. David asked if the legend was Polynesian or specifically Tongan. "No," Fresh Air said. "It is a story I heard many years ago of your own people. Cherokee, or perhaps Cheyenne. Those are nice words to say. I also like the word 'Iroquois.'"

I saw lights blinking in the sky. The flashing red made a trail through the stars. A plane had taken off from the Neiafu airport.

"Shelley?" It was Jackson, outside my window. "Are you in there?"

"Yes."

"Why didn't you come to the feast?"

"I am writing it all down."

"Shell, tomorrow Joe Storey is sailing to Nuku'alofa. David is going with him to have lunch with the king, and Skip is going to visit the hospital. Would you mind if I go?"

"Me?"

"Do you want to go too?"

A new story: *The Old Boys Club Sets Sail.* "No, not really."

He leaned against the screen. "Can you unlatch this? The women are in the kitchen, and I can't, you know, just walk into your room."

I unhooked the screen and he climbed in; it took quite a while for someone who has scaled the face of Half Dome. The table went over with a crash, but I caught the lamp. Jackson landed on his knees. The door flew open.

"Seli?" Foeata asked. "Oh! Jackison!"

He scrambled back up—insofar as he could scramble—but whatever he said was drowned out by Foeata's joyful roar. She threw her arms around him, and he fainted dead away.

He and Skip slept at the hospital again that night.

59

Everyone was coming to say goodbye. Albert brought me the tapa cloth, but I told him to keep it, take it to DC. David had offered him a job. "And watch out for your heart," I said.

He smiled. "I know you and I don't believe in the same things, Shelley. When I came to this island, I thought I knew what was good and evil. Now, I don't know, except that I know you are a good person."

"Well," I said, "all along, I knew that the hero of something I might write has red hair."

Joe Storey brought me a bottle of Dom Perignon. "I hope you will come aboard the *Ile* again," he said. "With your hothead, of course. You'd be welcome to sail with me for a while. I guess by now you have an answer to your question of why Pulu came to see me. He wanted to pay me for doing what he could not do for his daughter."

"Do you think Pulu sailed off with the Oggs?" I asked. No one had seen him since the storm. Joe had been checking; there were no sightings of one lone yacht in the sea.

Joe said, "If he did, there's just a chance they might have made it somewhere besides the bottom of the ocean."

He didn't say anything about Bette; she and Mafi were going to her island. Bette said I was welcome to join them, but I thought she had enough companions. I offered to pay her back for the ticket and advance, but she waved it away.

"You did something for me, Shelley. I had heard the stories about Armand and Lily too. I understood why he had to save that baby, but why did he want to keep her? Poor Lily—it was a silly fantasy about Mafi, but with men, you never know. Maybe that's why I ran so fast and far from Joe. Here I was, nudging fate on Gabby's behalf—to see what happened if I asked my sister to give David a call—and Fate turned on me. How ridiculous it is to be my age and still be in a muddle about love. But do I want another husband? It's hard to leave your island when you have painted it just the way you want it."

I said it was encouraging that she was still thinking about love. "Maybe by the time David and Gabby are as old as you are, they will have figured things out. They can potter around together, watching birds and growing petunias."

"We are not that old! Shelley, I've decided to get rid of *Ile Perdue*. I painted it when Armand died and I thought I'd lost him forever. Now, I have him back. Would you like it?"

"I would, but maybe you should give it to David. He has a wall to hang it on."

Mafi gave me a roll of tapa cloth. I looked at this one. It was a painting of a man dangling over the sea by a thin rope; there was an octopus in the water below him.

David brought a gift for Foeata. He had asked Gabby what he might give her; food and flowers were superfluous, and a six-pack of New Zealand beer wasn't quite his style. When Gabby asked Foeata if there was anything she would especially like, Foeata, struck with inspiration, replied she had long coveted the bolt of white satin at Burns Phillips. Now, she danced around the kitchen with it. "Such a wedding dress I will make."

"A good joke you can't resist?" I asked.

"Oh no, Seli. A man on his knees, it is no joke."

Since David was leaving, she had to weep as well. She made him promise he would send her his photograph to hang next to John and Robert Kennedy. When he said he would bring it in person, she cheered up and asked, then would he bring her some Tupperware too?

David and I went for a walk. "Where's Jackson?" he asked.

"At the hospital."

"Are you going to marry him?"

"Why would you ask that?"

"Because he asked my permission."

"He is a ninnyhammer."

David only laughed. "It was when we were carrying him off the island. He was probably delirious with pain. Knocked on the head. Didn't know what he was saying."

"Would you do it?"

"No." He said this so promptly it gave me a bit of a pang. "I don't think he and I would suit."

"You're not mad at him anymore?"

"I wasn't—well, yes, I was. But don't marry him because you think it's the only thing you can do. If you're going to do that, you might as well marry the guy who has already finished med school. Of course, he is a Republican."

"Who? Skip? No."

"Imagine that. And he stood over you, knife in hand." David thought this was hilarious.

"I don't have to marry anyone."

"No. You could come and write for me." The king had asked him to give his speech again, and he was probably going to have to sing

"La Vie en Rose" too. I might not have looked enthusiastic because he only said, "Do you need money? You'd better take some while I have it."

"Really?" I didn't mean, really, would he give me money. I meant, really, was he planning on being poor again. He hadn't said a word about Gabby, but I knew if I asked him directly, he'd start talking about Plato or Franco or who might run for president of Zimbabwe next year. So I told him about Jesse's letter. "It's funny that it was Jesse who got us both to Tonga while he stayed in his flat in San Francisco."

"That's what poets are for."

I asked what he thought could be the word that defined everything. He said "miracle." At least, that was what it would be if he got what he wanted. "You have to live as if nothing is a miracle or everything is," he added.

"Who said that?"

"Einstein."

"You're reading Einstein?"

"No. Do you remember the kid who worked in my first election? Smart as hell and a nice guy too. Rory McIntyre. He came to DC to intern. He stayed with Pam and me, and I think he suffered almost as much as you did, except he was more polite about it."

"What happened to him?"

"He gave up politics to study physics."

"Oh."

"But he's a good writer. He writes for me from time to time. He throws in Einstein, and I sound intelligent."

"David, why did you marry the Lamprey?"

"Who?"

"Sorry. Was it because you thought it was the only thing you could do?"

"No."

"Were you in love?"

"That's not what it was about, not for Pam or me."

"What was it about? Love didn't matter? Is that what you think now?"

"No."

"Do you think she might divorce you?"

"I don't know. Not if—"

Not if she discovered he'd been chasing Gabby around Tonga. Not the Lamprey who had a tiger skin rug and two deer heads on her wall. I said, "I don't like her much."

"I know this."

"Well, she doesn't like me."

He was laughing again. "She can't get rid of you."

"Maybe the dark ages are ending, David, and you don't have to be a politician anymore." He didn't agree or disagree; he just asked me if I knew what the hell Tupperware was.

I walked with him to the harbor, but I didn't see Skip or Jackson before Joe's yacht disappeared into the clouds at the horizon. Leave it to David to have a feast without having to go to church.

60

"If you turned it into a story, would they get a happy ending, a ménage à trois in a new world? Or would the ocean close over one small ship?"

It was the following day, and Lebeca had wanted to climb the half-mountain to think. She was mulling over my list of questions while I talked to spiders. "But only one thing did happen, Seli."

"And no one might ever know what that is."

"I wonder," Lebeca began and she burst into laughter. "Now, I am like you! I wonder!"

"Wonder what?"

"The palangi who sells seashells—"

"The weird fish guy? But he went to Fiji."

"Ever-Ready said he has returned but not for long."

"Lebeca, you're going to be the Tongan Judy Bolton."

She chuckled. "No, not Judy Bolton, but I will tell you a secret. While we waited on the island, I told Gabby Asher my wish to be a teacher, like her. She said it was a good idea. Now, if my family agrees, I will go to Nuku'alofa to work at her school and to study—at university! This is a big idea, perhaps too big for me."

"No, it isn't. But what about Gravity?"

"That was a dream of love when I was young, Seli. This is a dream of me."

We descended from the mountain, and past the wreckage of Pulu's house we found Tarkington. His hut was still standing, although the aquarium tanks were smashed. He was rummaging through the debris on the shore.

"Palangis can't resist collecting things," I said.

He jumped and turned. "I'm just looking for my stonefish. Lost her."

"I thought you had two."

"No—"

"Did you give one to Lily Omont?"

"Who?"

"You mentioned her the day I was looking for Gravity's boat."

"Oh, yeah. Her."

"That night, when Gravity's boat came back, did you see anything?"

"What are you, a journalist?"

"She drowned, you know."

"I heard. Damned shame. She was beautiful. Of course, I only saw her once."

Some people can lie just as easily as opening their mouths. Maybe the more powerful you think you are, the more easily you think you can decide what is true or real. Until, of course, truth whops you on the head. Tarkington, however, was not so good at lying.

The next morning, as I sat down to work, my long-absent, weak-kneed character showed up. He did have red hair. Did he have a weak heart also? I wasn't crazy about the names, however, and I was trying to think of new ones. I hadn't gotten further than Notalbert and the Princess from Nowhere when Foeata summoned me to tea. The Methodist Women's Choir was in the kitchen, and sitting in the middle of them was Jackson. Despite his cup of tea, he was looking discomposed. He stood up.

"Did you fall off the ship?" I asked.

"I flew back—on a plane." He glanced at the choir. "Shelley, will you walk with me?"

There was applause, but Foeata refrained from hugging him again. She chucked me out the door. When I glanced back, she was dancing with her bolt of white satin. Jackson picked up a duffel bag. "How far are we going?" I asked.

"Gravity said there's an uninhabited island, not too far away. He said we could use his boat. If you would like to find it."

"Just us?"

"I've got a map. And life jackets."

61

Gravity's map was a dot with a ragged arrow pointing to it. He'd been distracted by the news that Lebeca was leaving, Jackson said, but he had a plan to impress her by being the first Tongan to climb Mount Everest. First, he had to go see snow and ice and also a mountain. After Jackson explained this, he became absorbed in starting the boat's engine and maneuvering it into deep water. The sea witch must have taken his voice in exchange for a calm sea. To fill in the silence, I told him everything I'd been writing down.

"What I wonder is, why, with all the world to choose from, would Mrs. Ogg come back here?" I said. "Had she forgotten Pulu? Did she think Pulu had thrown her baby in the sea? Pulu must have known who Lily was, but did Mrs. Ogg? When did she find out? Pulu went to see her; he disturbed Ogg in his bath. The church has a truck. Did Mrs. Ogg drive it back to go see Pulu? Did she run over Gravity's dog? You can forgive a lot but not the dog. And why did she stay here, acting cuckoo, running around in the dark? She must have been the one who put the suitcases on Joe's yacht. Why? I think she was afraid that someone would tell her story, but who? Why didn't she just sail away?

"Lily must have taken Gravity's boat to get to the island. And brought it back. Why was Mrs. Ogg at Gravity's cove? Was she waiting for Lily? Did Lily know Mrs. Ogg was her mother? Did she see Mrs. Ogg and say, by the way, would you deliver this envelope to Albert because if you are my mother, I am going to go jump off a cliff? Don't you wish this boat could talk?"

Jackson said, "I think that's the island ahead. At least, I think it's an island."

It looked like a green bush in the middle of the sea. I wondered if, by chance, it might be the island that kept sinking out of sight.

"Are you planning to live here?" I asked as he unloaded his duffel bag.

"Maybe." He waded ashore and spread out a blanket beneath coconut trees. Sitting down, he unpacked bananas, bread, a jar of peanut butter. He always takes peanut butter when he travels because he had to go seven years without it when he was at school in England. "Will you sit down?" he asked. "Why are you kicking the sand?"

"I am just checking. It's not really an uninhabited island. There are lizards and birds. Spiders, no doubt. Probably mosquitoes. There might be a stonefish."

He took off his shirt and used it to dry off his cast. I sat down. "What?" he asked.

"Nothing." I sat down and touched his side, purple and gold with bruises. "Does it hurt?"

"Not much. How are your stitches?"

"They're fine. But do you remember that movie where the people were carried away by passion and rolling around a beach? I bet they didn't realize they might roll onto a stonefish. It's not funny," I added because he was smiling.

"Do you remember, Shelley, when you asked me if I ever wondered how Adam and Eve figured out what to do?"

"I did?"

"Yes, and I realized you were thinking about sex. I thought I might drop dead, but I hoped I wouldn't." He cleared his throat. "Maybe we should walk a bit. Because we should, you know, talk."

We got back up. We walked along where the sand met dense green bushes. The sun was warm and the sky cloudless. New blossoms were opening on vines. A bird darted by.

"Well, go on, curdle my blood," he said. "At least, we're not on the high seas, so I won't swoon and fall overboard."

"I'm going to give up wondering."

"No, you aren't."

"Yes. I'm going to give up trying to figure out what's true and write stories about the invasion of frog people and five-hundred-year-old women giving birth to five-headed babies that bark like dogs, and Jesus appearing at the Republican conventions to sell pardons—"

"Shelley, you were wondering who Mrs. Ogg was afraid of? I think it was you."

"Me?"

"Yes. You are a terrifying person. Do you want to talk about Lily?"

"Yes, but I don't think you really care."

"I don't; that is, I didn't, but you do, and—that's how it works, I think."

"What? Mysteries?"

"Love."

"Oh."

We had come to what might be a path into the interior of the island, and we began to climb. We came to a lookout point where a tree had fallen. We sat down. He studied the view, which was not too bad, as endless sea goes.

"Did I tell you about the sinking island, Jackson?"

"Why? Do you think we've found it?"

"You never know."

"Shelley, what do you want?"

"Want? Me?"

"I've never asked you. I realized this on Joe's ship. We ate dinner that night on the deck. It was just us and water and stars. The moon rose and we saw dolphins, swimming along with us. It was beauty, everywhere. David said, 'Here we are, the Lonely Hearts Club.' Joe said, 'Hell, we're the damned ship of fools.' Skip didn't say anything, but I knew he was thinking about Lily. I knew when I got back you'd want to talk about it. So I asked Joe what he thought."

"You did? What did he say?"

"He said he didn't like Lily because she reminded him of himself when he was young and thought the world was his to do with whatever he could get away with. He changed his mind when he came up against something greater." Jackson hesitated. "Skip said you knew that Lily was pregnant."

"Did he find out for sure?"

"He asked at the Nuku'alofa hospital about her autopsy. A doctor came to talk to us. He said there hadn't been one because she drowned, but he had seen Lily when she was alive. She'd come to the hospital just after she'd arrived. She told him she'd started feeling sick in Chicago. A man gave her money to see a doctor. She didn't, but she told the guy she was dying and wanted to go home to Tonga. She thought he might cough up more money, but instead he bought her a one-way plane ticket, nonrefundable. She decided, why not? By the time she got to Nuku'alofa, she was afraid she really might be dying. When the doctor told her she was pregnant, she laughed. She said, 'So my problem is not death, but life.' The doctor didn't see her again, but he remembered her. Skip said, 'Of course, he would.'" Jackson paused. "I read what you wrote."

And there went my nerves, on the wings of a mosquito, out to sea and over the rainbow.

"When?"

"On the ship. I wanted to draw the dolphins. I found some paper in my pocket. It was your letter." He stopped talking. He was waiting, I guess, for me to say something. Finally he gave up.

"Shelley, I was never mad at you. I didn't want a baby. I just wanted you. I was mad at anyone who tried to tell me—anything. My father— God, I hated him—he said, 'Marry her now and in a year, you'll hate each other. Is that what you want?' I said, 'Yeah, and you're the one who knows about love.' I didn't understand anyone, except David. 'Come near my sister again and I'll break your neck.' That I understood."

"But you ignored him."

"He couldn't run for Congress if he killed me."

Abruptly, Jackson stood up. He paced about, stopped at a tree, looked in his pockets, rubbed his head, came back, and sank down on his knees in the mud in front of me.

"Are you all right?" I asked.

"No." He shook his head. "Shelley, you said I never get scared, but it's not true. I've never been so scared as—all the time I've been here. The day I got here. That night. When we saw the dead body in the water. The shark. When that woman bled to death, and I thought I'd give up sex forever until you came into my room that night, and I thought, do something, idiot, but then you were gone. When you dove into that cave. In the hospital, when I watched you go to sleep and thought, what if she never wakes up?"

"And when you were dangling on the rope at night over the crazy waves?"

"No, that wasn't anything. But I've decided: I'm not going to ask you to marry me."

"Were you?"

"Yes."

"Today?"

"Every day since I got here. Well, almost every day. I thought about it all through the mountains, especially when I was cold. I decided this time I'd do it right, make time begin again, even if that isn't possible. In Katmandu, I found a ring. I was going to give it to you that night, but—the pig ate it. It's why I went to Nuku'alofa, to find another ring."

"And you changed your mind?"

"Yes. I decided I'm going to wait until you ask me."

"Me? Ask you?"

"I'll say yes, just so you know."

"You want me to propose to you?"

"I think you trust me a little, Shelley. Well, you got into the boat."

"Shall we have sex, Jackson?"

"What, now?"

"No, just—sometime."

"I have a duffel bag full of condoms."

"I asked Skip if he knew how to get birth control pills in Tonga."

"You asked Skip?" This cracked him up. "Shelley! I think we just talked."

He got up out of the mud and sat back down beside me. "There's something you should know. I'm not going back to med school. So my father cut me off. It's his right, of course. But I won't have anything. Least of all a future."

"You never seemed to like med school much."

"I hated it. And I was terrible at it. I had just thought—everyone was always asking, 'What will you be?' I remembered when my mom was sick and then you were sick—the two people I loved most in the world—I just wanted you both to—to live. But I hated being inside, cutting up dead people, hearing really sad stories. Everyone else was so interested in brain tumors and blood clots, and all I could think was, we're all going to die."

"Skip doesn't think you're terrible."

"I'm not like him. He's smart and kind, and if he worries that life is too short, he doesn't let on. His heart's in it."

"And yours is somewhere wild."

He leaned his head against mine. "I love you, Shelley."

The sky was taking on new colors, lavender, rose, and pale gold, one of those moments when the world says, "Look at me. I am here, this gift, this beauty, this truth." I might even have proposed to Jackson, except below us on the sand, something moved. A hairy thing had found the duffel bag on the blanket. By the time we got down to the beach, it was sitting on the blanket eating peanut butter and bread. It looked up.

"Damn me," the Reverend Ogg said, "if I might not believe in God after all."

62

"The hand of God." This was all Ogg said on the boat ride back as he sat clutching the peanut butter. Jackson thought he might be in shock. After we had hauled Ogg ashore, Jackson went over the rocks to Tarkington's. He returned with more blankets and a bottle of Jack Daniel's. He said Tarkington would bring a truck around to drive Ogg to town.

After he'd drunk half the bottle, Ogg started down the tortuous route of explaining how he had come to be marooned on an uninhabited island. "That day—went to see a lady. Connie's idea. Having doubts about her faith, this lady. Husband was there. I—went back to the ship. Strange. Empty." He had to open his own bottle of Chateau Margaux. "Just poured a glass—realized: we were moving! Found Connie with that fellow Pulu—leaving! He'd sent the crew ashore! I said it might not be the best idea—storm coming—wild sea—no cook—"

Mrs. Ogg wouldn't turn back, but Pulu got Ogg a lifeboat, threw in food, water, and wine, and pointed him to shore. The wind thought otherwise and blew him to this island. He was only taking a short wine break when the storm arrived and carried off the lifeboat.

"Where were they going?" I asked.

"Away." Ogg shrugged. "They had—history. Well, I never thought it was natural to be as good as Connie was. Married her because my father said I had to—had to settle down or—no more money. Never really wanted to marry anyone, but we got along."

Until he met Lily Omont in the bar at the International Dateline Hotel. "Pretty little thing. All alone. No money. Needed to get up north. Wanted to find her family. I said I was happy to help, give her a ride. Connie wasn't pleased, but I said, 'Now isn't that what missionaries are for?' It was when Lily told us the story of the doctor, it rattled Connie something powerful. She threw Lily off the ship when we got to Neiafu. I said it wasn't any fault of Lily's what her parents had done. Didn't know till—I was in my bath when Pulu came to see Connie. Couldn't help but hear. I never liked Connie so well as when I knew she was a sinner too. Told her that. Not much good at judging others, she always said. I never made much of a missionary on that account. I expect you heard I had some trouble back in DC. It was Connie's idea, to come out here. Hell, who doesn't want to escape life at one time or another?"

I asked, "That morning, when you and Joe were going to race to Nuku'alofa—"

"One good thing about coming here, meeting Joe again," Ogg said wistfully. "Salt of the earth, Joe. The war—"

"That day—"

He took a swig of whiskey. "Lily needed a ride to that Mrs. Omont's island. Said she had to find her friend, Mafi; said she wasn't dead. Joe wouldn't take her. I said I would. Felt like a father to her. I told her I practically was. Someone had to tell her the truth. Didn't mean to upset her. Or Connie."

"You, all three, sailed to Bette's island?"

"Well, no. Left Lily there. Knew I'd lost the race, went on anyway." It wasn't until he got to Nuku'alofa that he noticed that his wife wasn't onboard. "Hadn't looked for her. Sooner run into a cottonmouth than Connie. Knew I'd annoyed her. She turned up in Nuku'alofa soon enough. Didn't say much. Worried me. This hand of God, always taking care of things for her. When I heard Lily had drowned, I said to Connie, 'Maybe you had better tell me what that hand of God has been up to now.'"

He took another drink. "She told me. She took a boat, got herself out to that island. Always a good sailor, Connie. Lily was there but she said it was all a mistake about Mafi. She wasn't on the island. Asked Connie for a ride back. I don't know what happened. Didn't want to think of little Lily, left in the dark in the sea."

"There was a stonefish," I said.

"Well, Pulu took her away," Ogg said. "He loved her, bless his heart."

As we were talking, Tarkington had arrived. He'd stood back, listening. He was holding a burlap bag. He showed us what was in it. Jackson took a drink of whiskey. I knew that the next time he considered rolling around on a beach, he'd check for stonefish first.

Tarkington said, "I lied to you, Shelley. I just didn't want to think I'd seen a ghost. I did have two stonefish. I did give one to Lily. She wanted it. I didn't know why. She offered me a fair exchange, a study of the mating habits of humans. What a woman. What a night. Next morning she carried off the stonefish in her little suitcase.

"And I did see Gravity's boat return that night. I thought I saw Lily in it, but when I went closer, it wasn't her; it was like Lily, grown old and shriveled. It scared the liver out of me. Next morning, the boat was there, bobbing in the sea. I went to anchor it for Gravity. I found Lily's suitcase, opened, empty. Sometimes you don't want to think about what it all means. I was going to Fiji. Lily had told me she'd been staying with some rich church folks on their yacht. I took the suitcase to the church. They said that was you." Tarkington turned to Ogg. "They'd give it to you when you got back."

Ogg was silent. I asked, "Was there anything else in the boat?"

"Just an envelope, dropped on the bottom, covered with footprints. It was addressed to some guy at the Mormon church. I dropped it off there for him. That was that." He stopped talking as he—carefully and with gloves on—picked up the stonefish. "I've always thought the truth lies at the bottom of the sea. Shelley, I understand you wanted to set this lady free. As you did my octopus."

Even a stonefish should get to go home, but I let him do the honors. At the water's edge, Tarkington sent the stonefish flying through the air.

"Good night, ladies, good night, sweet ladies, good night, good night." Shakespeare always has something to say.

63

I was a bit tired, and when Foeata gave me the new nightgown, I put it on and went to bed. I opened my notebook. The blank page stared back at me. I couldn't find words, only pieces that added up to an image: two women, mother and daughter, in a small boat on a huge ocean, in the dark. Alone, except for one stonefish. What had happened? Did it matter? In the end, they had killed each other, hadn't they? Was the hand of God a skulking fish with bulbous eyes and poisoned spines? I was pretty well terrifying myself when I heard a faint knock on the door. Jackson came in, like the wind, the rain, and the wave that sweeps away everything, at least for a time.

"I just walked past Foeata." His voice was somewhat dazed. "All she said was 'Goodnight.'" He glanced at the door. I moved over so he could get into bed. He took off his shoes, but he kept his clothes on, I suppose in case he got hauled away. He sat down and touched the lace on the sleeve of the nightgown. "I feel like I am sleeping with Jane Austen," he said. "Or Mrs. Radcliffe. Are we going to talk about dead people?"

"No."

He took a parcel from his shirt pocket. "I meant to give this to you today, but I got nervous and left it in the duffel bag. I'm glad

Ogg didn't eat it." He held out a squashed, lumpy brown envelope. I smoothed it out. On one side was a sketch of three dolphins.

"Did you draw them?"

"Oh—I was just doodling. I found it at that shop, Ile Perdue. I didn't want them to put it in a box and scare you. It's a ring—but just a ring."

I waited for the sky to fall into pieces, for a giant spider to drop down from the sky, or a shark to knock at the window. Nothing happened, so I opened the envelope. Inside was a pearl, white like moonlight, in a setting of eight gold threads: an octopus.

He said, "It's from the ocean between us, Shelley."

I nodded.

"Will you put it on?"

"I should propose first."

He smiled. "OK."

"But, Jackson, I am wondering why—"

He leaned back against the dragons and closed his eyes. "Because, Shelley, I am starting to worry about infinity."

64

Joe Storey was sailing to New Zealand, and Foeata was going with him to visit her son. "This ship, I do not think I shall sink," she said. "Ha!"

Gravity signed on so he could see a mountain, and Jackson and I decided we'd go too and see where the wind took us next. I worried that Ogg might join the party, but he said no, he was going home by plane. If humans make themselves extinct, probably Ogg and stone-fish will survive. I hope octopuses do too.

Fresh Air said he would stay in Tonga and wait until everyone returned.

Before we left, Skip and I went to John's Takeaway and ate ice cream with forks. I gave him back the five pages.

"Are you a Republican?" I asked.

"A what?"

"David said—"

"I think David was pulling your leg."

"I'm relieved that you're ignorant."

"Shelley! I know what a Republican is. I voted in the last election; at least, I think I did. By the way," he added, "thanks for everything."

"I figured cranking the truth out of people was more useful than falling in love with you."

"I don't know about that." He touched his glass of ici kelemi against mine. "Malo e lelei, Red. I hope our paths cross again someday, but if not, we'll always have Tonga."

Acknowledgments

I wrote the first chapter of this novel in 1984 when I needed a writing sample to apply to Berkeley's journalism school. After long years of rejections and revisions, I was elated in 2020 to find She Writes Press and honored to join their sisterhood of writers to publish this story of the Kingdom of Tonga.

Even though you must lock yourself away to write a story, you need others to make it into a book. I was extremely lucky that Catharine Way, a friend since first grade at Browns Valley Elementary School in Napa, had, in the intervening years, become a superb international editor. Tim Yagle, much missed in the newspaper world but a great copyeditor nonetheless, took on a novel instead of news stories, and Kathleen Iudice added her polish with painstaking proofreading. The incomparable Georgeanne Brennan and Jessel Miller, inspiration by example to artists, shared generous and welcome encouragement.

I am grateful to my two children, Sam and Ariel, who not only provided enduring support but have turned out all right, despite growing up with my cast of characters as peculiar distant cousins. Not to be overlooked were Pippi and Puck, who took charge of organizing walks to explore the world, when I had been sitting in front of a computer for too long.

Most of all, I want to thank the people I met on a long-ago visit to Tonga. Their kindness has stayed with me all of my life. Especially one remarkable, joyful woman named Foeata.

About the Author

© Chuck O'Rear

S asha Paulsen lives in Napa Valley, California, where she has written about food, wine, art, and travel for two decades. A graduate of the UC Berkeley School of Journalism, she published her first novel, *Dancing on the Spider's Web*, in 2019. Her love of travel has taken her across through Europe, across Russia, Mongolia and China, into the mountains of Tibet and Nepal, and to the Kingdom of Tonga in the South Pacific.

SELECTED TITLES FROM SHE WRITES PRESS

She Writes Press is an independent publishing company founded to serve women writers everywhere. Visit us at www.shewritespress.com.

Water On the Moon by Jean P. Moore. $16.95, 978-1-938314-61-2
When her home is destroyed in a freak accident, Lidia Raven, a divorced mother of two, is plunged into a mystery that involves her entire family.

Last Seen by J. L. Doucette. $16.95, 978-1-63152-202-4
When a traumatized reporter goes missing in the Wyoming wilderness, the therapist who knows her secrets is drawn into the investigation—and she comes face-to-face with terrifying answers regarding her own difficult past.

Keep Her by Leora Krygier. $16.95, 978-1-63152-143-0
When a water main bursts in rain-starved Los Angeles, seventeen-year-old artist Maddie and filmmaker Aiden's worlds collide in a whirlpool of love and loss. Is it meant to be?

A Drop In The Ocean: A Novel by Jenni Ogden. $16.95, 978-1-63152-026-6
When middle-aged Anna Fergusson's research lab is abruptly closed, she flees Boston to an island on Australia's Great Barrier Reef—where, amongst the seabirds, nesting turtles, and eccentric islanders, she finds a family and learns some bittersweet lessons about love.

Peregrine Island by Diane B. Saxton. $16.95, 978-1-63152-151-5
The Peregrine family's lives are turned upside-down one summer when so-called "art experts" appear on the doorstep of their Connecticut island home to appraise a favorite heirloom painting—and incriminating papers are discovered behind the painting in question.

The Island of Worthy Boys by Connie Hertzberg Mayo
$16.95, 978-1-63152-001-3
In early-19th-century Boston, two adolescent boys escape arrest after accidentally killing a man by conning their way into an island school for boys—a perfect place to hide, as long as they can keep their web of lies from unraveling.